TEARS *of the* JAGUAR

Text copyright © 2012 by A.J. Hartley
All rights reserved.

Printed in the United States of America.

Published by Thomas & Mercer
P.O. Box 400818
Las Vegas, NV 89140

ISBN-13: 9781612183800
ISBN-10: 1612183808

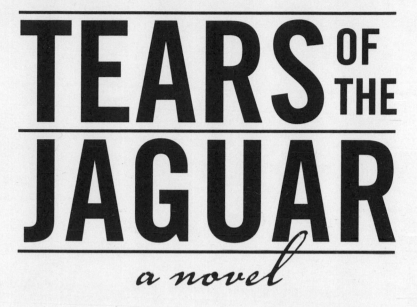

TEARS OF THE JAGUAR

a novel

A.J. HARTLEY

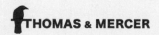

THOMAS & MERCER

Dedication

For my family, and for all those friends and readers without whose support this book would never have been finished. Thank you.

AJH

PART 1

Chapter One

Deborah Miller lay under the mosquito netting listening to the distant thunder.

Please God, she thought, *don't let it rain.*

It was June eighteenth, and like every other day in the Yucatan jungle village, it had started with a frenzy of birdcalls the moment the sky lightened. Roosters crowed and grackles shrieked, and Deborah had lain there, watching the flicker of lightning, dreading the sound of rain. There had been too much rain already; more and the site would become unstable.

With the window still dark, she rose, splashed lukewarm water on her face at the stone basin by her bed, brushed and tied her hair back, then pulled on a khaki shirt covered in pockets and voluminous shorts. They were the longest she had been able to find but still didn't reach her knees, and they flapped wide of her skinny legs like flags. She pulled them up, then pushed them down onto her hips, then sighed at her reflection in the mirror.

Well, it didn't matter. At least her outfit was practical for the Ek Balam site, where the work was hot and muddy. It wasn't like she was going to meet a tall, handsome stranger out here in the jungle. She smiled wryly to herself. *Most guys aren't taller than I am, anyway*, she thought.

Deborah smoothed her shorts reflexively as she walked under the coconut palms and bougainvillea to the breakfast buffet, served under the palm-thatched patio. She glanced back toward her cabana through the tropical foliage. Dark clouds had moved in fast and now looked threatening. There was an eerie calm, no sounds of traffic noise or people talking. She heard nothing beyond the clatter of Adelita in the kitchen. Even the birds had gone quiet.

Adelita Lucia del Carmen Lacantun lived down the street with her parents. She was eleven and the granddaughter of Eustachio, the Ek Balam site foreman, who had been on every dig in the area for the last thirty years. They were Mayan through and through: short, stocky as they aged, their skin brown as teak, their noses strong and hawkish. Adelita was rail thin, like all the girls round here, though she would probably turn more or less square in middle age. She had big, black, intelligent eyes that made her look birdlike, and she worked constantly, moving with speed and purpose from one adult task to the next.

Adelita came into the seating area with a vast urn of coffee, dressed in a worn turquoise T-shirt, tie-dyed skirt, and flip-flops. Her feet were tough and scarred, her hands calloused with work, but when she smiled—peering at Deborah over the top of the urn—her face radiated her true age.

"There's a storm coming," said the girl, eyeing the sky, shrewd as a farmer. "Again."

Deborah registered the wind that was coming in stiff across the garden and agreed in her ponderous Spanish.

"One of the dogs got out," Adelita said, rolling her eyes. "The gray one. The boy. He ran after Mrs. Uk's pig and I had to chase it all the way to the church."

"How did he get out?"

"Someone left the gate open," said Adelita significantly, glancing toward the wrought-iron arch that separated the stucco walls of the house from the roughly paved street beyond.

"One of the tourists?"

The girl shrugged, her head on one side, then checked there were none around.

"Probably," she whispered. "I'll get the eggs and *chaya*. There are fresh tortillas on the counter."

Deborah had eaten *chaya*—a traditional Mayan vegetable like spinach—every day since coming to Ek Balam. Raw it was poisonous, but cooked, they said, it was a miracle plant, loaded with healthy properties.

Adelita turned and took a step, then froze as a thunderclap split the air, loud as an artillery shell. Deborah ducked instinctively, and before she was back up, the rain had started.

It had rained every other day since Deborah had arrived, sometimes for a couple of hours, but always a steady pattering shower. This was no shower. The rain came down in sudden shafts, great wet bullets that turned the garden gray and hazy. In seconds the gravel was swimming in water and the trees were leaning perilously. Deborah stood up, moving farther under the sheltering roof, but the wind still drove the rain at her. It was getting heavier by the second and she could no longer see the swimming pool through the trees. Deborah turned to Adelita and the child's black eyes were wide, her grown-up manner gone. She looked scared.

Deborah, accustomed to what they called popcorn thunderstorms in Atlanta, offered her hand and took a step back toward the wall that bordered the street. In the same instant, a lightning flash tore through the air like a flare in front of her face, so that for a second after it had gone, she couldn't see. The thunder followed right on top of it, like a great mace beating the earth, and Adelita slapped her hands to her ears. The wind tore paper napkins from the table and shot them across the lobby. A glass shimmied to the edge of the table, fell, and shattered—almost soundless under the drumming of the rain—and then the table itself began to move.

This was no popcorn storm. It was big and it wasn't going to just blow through. Another flare of lightning lit the sky like a bomb and Deborah ducked. The rain was spraying them like surf, even though they had backed up to the wall. Looking up, Deborah could see the thatch flapping with the wind, filaments of palm tearing out and hurtling like shrapnel. The garden was already submerged, and through the gate Deborah could see a fast, brown river where the street had been. It got deeper and swifter as she watched, and bore part of a log fence away like a raft. She looked up, considering the sheltering roof, and wondered just how bad things could get out at the site.

If the water washes away the ground beneath the structures? Pretty bad.

She couldn't see out to the garden, but heard something heavy fall and burst in that direction. She looked up again in time to see the lightning flash through a hole in the thatch, wincing at the bark of the thunder, and when she straightened up again, still holding Adelita's tiny, hard hand, she could smell burning.

Deborah looked wildly around to see where the fire was, and then—as if the physical laws of the universe had temporarily been suspended—the ground buckled and dropped. Adelita screamed. Deborah grabbed the girl's hand and threw herself backward, scrambling to firm ground as the hole spread in all directions like a mouth opening in the earth. The table where they had been sitting plummeted with a clatter of crockery and silverware, and then the boiling gash in the ground spread wide and, with a great, tearing crash, the perimeter wall sagged. Adelita pulled at Deborah's hand dragging her out into the rain and, in the same instant, the masonry exploded as the wall collapsed into the sinkhole, and the thatched roof came thundering down.

Even as it did, a single despairing thought screamed through Deborah's head:

Oh God, the site. The site!

Chapter Two

■ ■ ■ ■ ■

Eustachio Lacantun, the Ek Balam dig's sixty-seven-year-old site foreman, was lying in his blue nylon hammock in the cabana he had built with his own hands from local *ya* wood when the storm hit. He recognized it for what it was right away and rolled out easily—his left leg dragging slightly on the dirt floor—stepping out into the rain to look at the sky. He knew that Adelita had already gone to work at Oasis, but he checked her bedroll anyway, then limped over to the cinderblock house, calling to his son.

Across the street he heard a creak and a splintering crash. One of the cabanas had collapsed. Eustachio turned, half crouching, one hand raised protectively over his head, but he couldn't see what had happened, and by then Juan was appearing in the doorway, his pregnant wife behind him.

Eustachio moved into the dim, square concrete room, lit by the greenish light of a flickering TV set—some braying game show with that woman who was all teeth and tits—sidestepping

6

a pile of laundry. Ten years ago, no one in the village had a TV. Now they all did, and the infernal machines seemed to be on constantly. The game-show host laughed and the audience applauded and then there was a little pop and the TV died.

The three of them stood in the darkness, and Eustachio watched the roof critically. The cinderblock houses had been the government's gift after the hurricane of 2005, built by high-altitude Mexico City bureaucrats who never paused to think what a structure like that would be like in the hundred-degree summer of a place only a few meters above sea level where no one had air-conditioning. He called them *los hornos*: the ovens.

Juan sat Consuela down. She had her hands on her belly, shielding, and her eyes were alert but composed.

"Get over there," said Eustachio to his son, nodding over the street. "Something fell. Make sure the Uks are OK."

The Uks were in their sixties and the only elderly couple in the village without grown-up children living close by.

Juan's eyes flashed to his wife, who shaded her eyes with one floury hand as she looked at him and nodded.

"She's fine," said Eustachio. "I'll stay with her."

Juan nodded and took a breath, as if about to dive underwater, then ran out into the storm. Eustachio watched him pick his way across the road, avoiding the deepest potholes and stepping around a frightened turkey and it was only then—amazingly—that Eustachio thought of the site.

The site. It was normally the first thing he thought of the moment he opened his eyes, a constant lurking anxiety at the back of his mind as it had been for his father and his father's father.

He was struck by an impulse to run, to get his bicycle and ride over. He had to make sure. But he had said he would stay with Consuela. His eyes flashed back to her, sitting in the corner, her eyes on the street. The thunder roared and the rain drummed on the roof, but she looked serene as ever. Maybe he should have sent her to check on the Uks. She was the level head in the household, the strong one, pregnant or not. Juan watched too much TV.

Well, he wouldn't be doing that for a while.

Who knew how long they would be without electricity? It wouldn't make any difference to Eustachio, who had no fridge, TV, or air conditioner. He looked out through the door, as if imagining he could see the pyramid through the rain that sheeted the pueblo, and his neck prickled with unease. He needed to be there, to make sure it was secure. That was his charge, his purpose in life, a trust handed down through generations.

"You should go," said Consuela.

He gave her a questioning look, trying to look confused and innocent.

"To the site," she said. "You should go. Everything here will be all right."

He thought for a second, then nodded, grateful.

"I'll come back as soon as..."

His voice trailed off and she held his eyes. He nodded once, then ducked outside.

Shuffling through the mud and pooling water where the hard earth had been only moments before, he hobbled back to his cabana where the old black Mercurio had been propped unlocked against the wall. It had blown over, but he got it upright and maneuvered himself onto the seat.

He pushed off without looking at Consuela, who he knew was watching him from the door of the concrete house, and as he turned onto the road he thought he heard her call. He raised a hand in acknowledgement but didn't look back, bending low against the wind and the rain as he began to pedal through the village.

Sixteen years before, Eustachio had been working on a peripheral site near Chitchen-Itza, when a barrow full of tooled stone had overturned, crushing his left ankle. He had been taken to hospital in Valladolid, and they had saved his foot—and his life, he supposed, given the amount of blood he had lost—but he had never regained full use of it. Nerve damage, they said. On his bicycle, he did almost all the work with his strong right leg, pushing hard so the heavy machine surged forward, coasting as his feeble left took over, then pressing on with his right. It wasn't easy, and if he didn't time it right he could lose momentum and stall, but it worked pretty well most of the time.

When it wasn't raining like Chaak himself had set a new task for Noah.

Eustachio always thought like that, the threads of his Catholicism interweaving with the ancient Mayan beliefs that the Spanish had tried vainly to eradicate, like different colors in a complex hammock. Tales of trickster rabbits coexisted with the crucified Christ and the shiny televisions, though the influence of both the ancient Mayan and the Christian were, he suspected, fading.

He could see faces in the doorways as he cycled down past the cabanas—their roofs flapping alarmingly in the wind—past the school and the church, and then he left the village behind. He pressed on, dodging by memory the submerged potholes, and pedaled through the flat jungle scrub that lined the road and concealed patches of crop fields: some agave, mostly the corn that kept the village alive. They had built the fancy new blacktop road to connect the ancient site to the 180, but hadn't bothered to resurface the road to the village itself. The dead of Ek Balam got asphalt and road markings; the living got dust and potholes deep enough to drown a pig.

Well, that was just the way it was.

The past was their future, it seemed, and not just for Eustachio, whose interest was particular and secret. The villagers needed to keep that past alive or they may as well sell off the land to be planted with sugar cane or the stuff they made into diesel, and move to the city. No one wanted that. The kids went to school in the village, and church in the village. They worked at home, and most would do so forever. Eustachio wondered about Adelita. She was bright, did well in school. But her family needed close to two hundred of the handmade, fist-sized tortillas a day, and the necessary grinding, shaping, and cooking took most of Adelita's time. Consuela knew it. He caught her watching the girl as she worked and he felt the division in her heart. She didn't know what she wanted most, to keep the child with her till she married and moved to a cabana down the street, or to push her away. Eustachio hated to see children leave the village, but Adelita was special. She could work in Valladolid or even Merida and be close enough to visit. She might even go to college…

The rain ran in his eyes, but he blinked it away and pushed forward, the bike a foot deep in brown, fast water. It wasn't like riding, he thought. More like sailing, the front wheel the prow of a boat. He felt it push at him, threatening to turn him off, but he adjusted and rode on.

The road to the ruins showed no sign of damage, but that meant nothing. It was what he would find inside that worried him, and worse, what others might find if he did not get there first. He surged across the parking lot, propped the bike against a wind-bent Mop, peering through the rain for signs of anything out of place or damaged. His heart was beating fast as he began to limp down the ancient *sacbe* and into the site.

Chapter Three

■ ■ ■ ■ ■

Deborah drove carefully over to the site from the Oasis Retreat the moment everyone had been pronounced safe, twenty minutes after the rain stopped. The sky was now an almost implausible blue, the air fresh and cool, but it didn't fill her with optimism. She knew carnage might await her at the site. If the rain could collapse walls in the village, it could do untold damage to her dig.

It was hard to believe that just six months earlier, working at the Druid Hills museum in Atlanta where she was curator, she'd never heard of Ek Balam. Now, she'd seen every inch of it, personally. It was a large site of about fifteen square kilometers of continuous urban settlement that had flourished for roughly three centuries until falling into decline approximately a thousand years ago. It had a core of pale step pyramids, ritual centers, and civic structures. It was mysterious, beautiful, desolate, and—for a little while—hers.

TEARS OF THE JAGUAR

When she'd agreed to join the consortium she had done so to keep the museum alive in a culture that viewed the past as something best forgotten. With the economy not so much faltering as entering free fall, what private money was available had been diverted from the air-conditioned halls of galleries, theatres, and museums toward environmental and humanitarian debacles. She could hardly blame the struggling people of Georgia for not wanting to spend their time and money on Creek Indian artifacts and Mycenean gold, but "fiscally speaking"—a phrase constantly on her lips in board meetings—the situation was getting bleak. Worse, she had only been running the museum since her mentor had died, and the prospect of it failing completely on her watch felt like an insult to his memory. In such a mood, the consortium had looked like a godsend. The organization connected museums and galleries from all over the Southeast, anchored by a Chicago-based nonprofit called Cornerstone.

The official offer to sign on with Cornerstone had come in September, two days before Rosh Hashanah. She'd flown to Chicago and nearly broken her wrist snatching the proffered pen from Steve Powel—Cornerstone's slightly eccentric president—getting her name down before he could change his mind. The Druid Hills museum was still being overhauled, and the money on offer would allow them to open their new galleries a year ahead of schedule. It was worth what she hoped would be a few student interns following her around and asking what they should catalogue. Even at the time, she had known the help wouldn't come *that* cheap, but she had opted not to scrutinize this particular gift horse too closely.

So she had sat in Powel's old-fashioned wood-paneled office in Chicago trying not to grin like a kid accidentally locked in the ice cream parlor. The situation had been surreal, and that was without taking into account the number of bizarre and frankly creepy artifacts on display—including a necklace of skulls. Then again, given that he was in the museum world, these things were perhaps more normal than the huge number of shiny women's figure-skating trophies that crowded his bookshelves.

"My daughter," he explained, catching Deborah's curious gaze, and rotated a picture of a lithe teenager in sparkly pale-blue skating costume, her cheeks pink with cold and her blue eyes bright with childish joy. "Angela."

"My sister used to skate," said Deborah. "Still does, a little."

She said it casually, trying not to show that she had always been a little jealous of Rachel's talent for all things graceful and pleasing to their parents. Deborah, by comparison, was the troublesome one, the antisocial one, the one whose teachers sent notes about her stubbornness and quickness to argue. The one called to the principal's office because she had punched Tommy Werstein on the nose for muttering "*freak*" as she loped by.

Deborah focused on one picture of the girl, a teenager here, but still compact and elegant, whereas Deborah at about the same age had been gawky, stalking about the ice like a heron as her sister swept past, all wings. Powel's daughter had her blonde hair tied back and a supremely confident smile. Around her neck, she wore a glittering gold necklace with a single garnet-colored pendant. This, Deborah thought to herself, is a child of privilege. Then, even though the girl looked nothing like Rachel, Deborah found her old resentment stirring. It rose suddenly, like an animal that had been curled up in a patch of sunlight suddenly obscured by cloud.

After all this time, she thought. *You should be ashamed of yourself.*

So the contract was signed, and the first check changed hands. It was weeks before it became clear that she wouldn't just be hosting student interns, and by that time she had already started using the money. Still, her first response to her "assignment" had been incredulity. She was cleaning out a Creek Indian display in the museum in Atlanta when the phone rang. If she was honest, she had forgotten that she had to actually *do* something to fulfill her side of the deal.

"You want me to go *where* and do *what*?"

"We want you to coordinate the Ek Balam dig," said Powel over the phone, as if he were handing her the keys to the city. "Lead the dig then develop a mobile exhibition based on the site."

Ek Balam? Where the hell was Ek Balam? It sounded Arabic. If he thought she was going to sit in a tent in some desert with shells whistling overhead...

"In the Yucatan," Powel prompted, as if this were obvious.

They must have discussed it at their Chicago meeting, when she had nodded and sat there like Oliver Twist proffering his gruel bowl: *"Please, sir, may I have large amounts of money."* She remembered little about Ek Balam, but she knew that Cornerstone had interests in Mayan sites dotted throughout Mexico, Belize, and Honduras.

"Right," she had said, half remembering and scouring her shelves for a book on Mayan ruins. "Ek Balam. Fantastic. And what exactly will I be doing?"

What she would be doing, said Powel, was recruiting and vetting college student applicants to the program and then escorting them to the sites for a crash course in Mayan archaeology for a week. There would then be a week's surveying of the site, after which she would serve as field director for the subsequent dig.

On its completion she would develop a dramatic, educational, and portable museum display that could be trucked around the country and set up according to blueprints she devised.

"Hello? Deborah, are you still there?" he had said.

Field director?

"Sure," she covered. "Fantastic. When do we start?"

She was still scanning the bookshelves for something on Mayan archaeology, but her eyes were moving faster now, sweeping in great, jittery arcs that saw nothing. She was totally unqualified for the position.

Her solution, predictably, had taken the form of labor. Deborah had always met challenge with work.

"You don't even know how to relax," her mother had once said, and Deborah had stored the barb away as a compliment.

In the six-month gap between that phone call from Steve Powel and her touching down in Cancun, Deborah had devoured every book she could find on Mayan archaeology. She was a museum curator, not a field-worker, and she had spent a good deal more time figuring out how best to display artifacts than she had digging them up. She loved being on the ground, brush and trowel in hand, but she hadn't done much of it, and the idea of pretending to be an expert—and on the Maya in particular—for a bunch of smart-ass college kids had terrified her.

At least all her reading had solidly grounded her in the history of the place and the myth about the jaguars that protected it. That was even how it translated: *Ek Balam. The City of the Dark Jaguar.*

The name of the place made her job here sound exciting and mysterious, but that wasn't entirely accurate. Her duties at this stage, in fact, were fairly simple. Each day, she drove eleven miles south to Valladolid, the town where the students stayed, and the home of the archaeological institute, which housed the real experts and their lab. Deborah was glad to be staying instead in the tiny village closer to the site, where she didn't have to socialize too much. It gave her time for her other duties, like assigning student reading.

She escorted the kids on tours of the surrounding area and its major sites—which meant footnoting some of the more florid accounts of the ruins coming from the local guides—and chaperoned them as they watched the Ek Balam site survey. The core of the ancient city had been excavated twenty years ago, but in preparation for the dig, the site was being carefully mapped and its features fully recorded.

Those tasks fell to other people. Her job, she had decided, was to introduce a future generation of archaeologists to fieldwork and make sure they didn't break anything crucial in the process. Her real work would kick in when the dig was closed and she could turn her experience into building the mobile exhibit. For now her title was field director, but in real terms she was a cross between a public relations exercise and a shepherd. Hold the kiddies' hands, get their parents and their schools excited enough to open their pocket books in the interests of history and anthropology, and Steve Powel and the board at Cornerstone would be more than happy. Find some aesthetically pleasing and preferably valuable artifacts that would look good on the museum banners, and they'd be ecstatic.

Powel's version of archaeology smacked of an *Indiana Jones* movie. Last time she saw him in Chicago, she said as much, and he just shrugged.

"You know how much money those movies make?" he said.

He had a point. Nobody wanted to shell out for the fiddling details on which archaeologists built new theories about ancient Mayan diet and social structure, but come back with a stone sarcophagus engraved with skulls and the Druid Hills museum might actually turn a profit.

"How about I build a coffin out of plywood and egg cartons?" she said. "Spray it gold and throw in some beef ribs and say we found Tutankhamun."

"If you find any real tombs, grave goods and such," he said, ignoring her joke, "I'll come down myself."

"Why?"

"Just…" He paused and shrugged, smiling quickly as if embarrassed. "An interest of mine. To tell you the truth, I'm a little jealous. You are going to enjoy Ek Balam, Deborah."

And he had looked so odd—wistful, like he was dreaming of exotic locales that dripped with magic and treasure—that she had agreed with him.

Now, Deborah and her dozen students had two more days of pre-excavation work, and then they got a week off, a week in which most would return to the States, to burgers and air-conditioning, traffic and hot, high-pressure showers, before coming back, pick axes and sifters at the ready. By then, Martin Bowerdale's survey team would be done and Porfiro Aguilar, the artifact analyst, would have finished setting up the lab in Valladolid, and they would be ready to begin digging. Whether they would find anything that would excite the likes of Steve Powel, she had no idea, but her anxiety sometimes gave way to a thrill of excitement at the possibility.

Chapter Four

■ ■ ■ ■ ■

As Deborah got out of the car and caught her first glimpse of the storm-tossed dig site, she realized that her students could not be allowed back because of fallen masonry and other structural damage. She would have to call Valladolid and send them to their break early. It had been one hell of a storm.

Cell phone signals were weak in the region, and impossible to get from ground level. The first thing she had authorized on accepting the details of the dig was the construction of the cell phone tower on top of Structure 2. Ordinarily, a tower like this would be set in holes blasted out of the bedrock, but since this one was built on an archaeologically significant structure, its four posts were packed into concrete that had been poured into blocks around them. A zigzagging series of ladders secured to the structure led up to a thatched platform. It was sturdy, but since it rose up from a structure that was already sixty feet high, it was unnervingly tall. At the top, her phone got three bars and she could have as good a conversation as if she were sitting in her living room at home.

She hurried around the structure to make sure it seemed stable, then started to climb. At the top, she paused to catch her breath, looking out over the wet jungle and the pale, ancient stone structures that rose out of it. Closest was Structure 3, shaped like a pyramid—probably some kind of governor's palace—which was to be the primary focus of their dig. She sighed with relief. The scaffolding around it looked OK.

It was quiet. Deborah had thought of jungle as being impenetrably dense and towering, alive with screaming monkeys swinging from tree to tree. But Ek Balam was in the northern lowland reaches of the Maya homeland, and the jungle here was dry tropical forest, low growing and patchy. It was nothing like as lush and dark as she had expected, and, a little disappointingly, she hadn't seen or heard a single monkey since her arrival. As to the jaguar that gave the ancient city its name and which had been the supreme Mayan symbol of royalty, there hadn't been regular sightings for almost a decade.

She called Porfiro Aguilar, the deputy field director and artifact analyst in Valladolid. He sounded sleepy and harassed, so after she had ordered the dismissal of the students, she told him that she would be in touch again in an hour after she had inspected the site. She was standing there, looking out over the sodden landscape of silent ruins and trying to decide whether to call Powel in Chicago, when her phone rang again.

She gave it a quizzical look, didn't recognize the number, but answered it anyway.

"Hello?"

"Debs? That you?"

It took her a moment.

"Rachel?" she said.

It had been at least six months since she'd spoken to her sister.

"You got a minute?"

"Actually, I'm kind of swamped," said Deborah, making the pun just for herself. She wished she could joke away the uneasiness. Her sister so rarely called. "What's up?"

The kids, she thought, trying to picture the children but unable to see their faces. She wasn't even sure how old they were now.

"Ma got married."

Deborah felt her spine stiffen. One hand gripped the rail of the cell phone tower. There was a fractional pause.

"What?"

"It's that Steve guy. Do you remember him?"

Deborah stared at the jungle below and the rain-ravaged site, and her sense of the absurdity of the situation turned to anger.

"Steve Greenfield?" said Deborah, trying to picture the face. "The guy who used to run the deli at Coolidge Corner? The guy who used to play tennis with Dad?"

"They've been living together—or as near as makes no difference—for six months, Debs. Last week, they took a trip to Vegas and came back with wedding rings. I thought you'd at least want to know. I thought maybe you'd want to call her and say congratulations. I think it's a good thing. He's a decent guy."

Deborah snorted. "Please. I haven't spoken to Mom in three years. Not since she started dating that guy Marty a month after Dad died."

"Dad's gone, Debs," said Rachel, sounding suddenly quite tired.

There was a long silence.

"I've really got to go," Deborah said. "There's things I have to do."

"One more thing, Debs."

Deborah looked around her and took a breath.

"The house is for sale."

"What?" Deborah felt tears spring into her eyes. She pictured her father's favorite rocking chair, the dollhouse he built for her, all his paintings. Her father, who had always encouraged her, who had provided the only bright spot against her mother's judgment and disapproval...

"She's getting rid of all of it, Debs," said Rachel, cautious now. "She's going to move in with Steve, and his place is small."

Deborah steadied herself and took a breath.

"Debs, you still there? I know how you feel about Dad's stuff. I thought you might want to come and pick through his things."

Deborah stared hard at the ancient pyramid, pushing down tears. "Rachel, I've got to go. But listen to me. If you and Mom throw everything of his away, I'll never forgive either of you."

Rachel sighed. "Duly noted," she said. "Maybe you could call me when you've had time to calm down. Talk soon, OK?"

"Sure," said Deborah, in a voice barely above a whisper. "Bye."

She climbed down the slick wooden tower slowly, forcing her mind back to the tasks the storm had brought her and away from her infuriating mother.

There's too much to do, she reminded herself, *and you're in charge.*

She spotted a few fallen tree limbs and an unsettled stone or two, but the central square flanked by the pyramids and ball court looked stable enough. Her big concern—though it wouldn't be a part of the new dig—was the main pyramid, the acropolis, because it was there that Ek Balam set itself apart from other Mayan ruins. Damage there would be devastating.

Sell the house. Dad's house. Come and pick through his things...

Deborah took a long, steadying breath, then spotted a tall figure emerging from behind a high stone wall, trailed by two others. Bowerdale, the leader of the survey team, was coming toward her, leading his graduate student assistants. She stifled a smile at the sight of him picking his way through the mud. With his trim six-foot-three frame, closely cut black hair, and precisely tailored clothes, he usually looked immaculate, but at the moment he was soaking wet. His fancy suit was wrinkled and plastered to his skin like tissue. "Everyone OK?" he said, considering his fingernails as if he thought he needed a manicure.

Deborah wasn't sure who he meant by "everyone" and doubted he cared one way or the other.

"In the village, yes," she said. "I spoke to Porfiro. All the students were inside eating breakfast when the storm came in, so they're fine."

Bowerdale nodded noncommittally and looked away. Deborah, irritated, turned and found herself looking at his students. She didn't particularly like either of them. The girl, Alice, was pale and tattooed with small, hard, dark eyes and a perpetual sneer on her lips. The boy was named James. He wore Clark Kent glasses, and his spindly arm was thrown protectively around Alice's narrow shoulders.

"You guys all right?" she said.

Alice looked defiantly fine. "It rained," she said, unwinding herself from the boy's half embrace. "No big."

The boy looked disappointed, but rallied.

"Hell of a storm," he said, and grinned nervously. He looked sweaty and a little nauseated, like he'd just got off a mean roller coaster.

They were standing in the center of the site. Deborah's eyes roamed across the view before them, searching for anything that needed repair. She could see Structure 2, the one with the phone tower she had just descended. And there was "Las Gemelas"— the Twins—which earned its name from its unusual parallel chambers. The ball court looked intact too. To her eye, none of the structures seemed obviously damaged.

Bowerdale spoke like a general whose authority was beyond question.

"Leave the gear here," he said. "Spread out and do a quick walk through the site. The ground was already saturated; the storm could have caused some serious erosion. Don't assume anything is stable. Back here in twenty minutes," he said, checking his watch. "And note anything that looks different. Anything at all, no matter how small. Our job just changed."

He strode off. The kids glanced at each other, surly but resigned, and loped after him. Deborah stood there feeling redundant and outranked, knowing there was nothing for her to do except watch, maybe take notes. Assessing structural damage was way out of her wheelhouse, while Bowerdale's expertise in such things was so well known that he'd occasionally been hired into the far-better-paying realm of government contract work. A topographical survey of the White Sands missile range in New Mexico was at the top of his résumé—in the place where someone like her might put membership on an editorial board. She had to respect his qualifications. Still, Bowerdale's self-assurance rankled. He was just too slick. It seemed like he was always hearing a commentary in his head: *What would Bowerdale do in a situation like this? How would a suave, rugged, confident archaeologist handle this precise moment?* Then, when he had found the answer, she thought, he acted. She wondered how far he would go to bolster his image as the big man on campus.

And you certainly aren't bitter because he knows what he's doing while you're standing around waiting for instructions.

OK. That too.

Deborah squatted and touched the grass. There were muddy pools here and there, but it was amazing how quickly the rain had been absorbed. The Yucatan was a limestone shelf, and therefore porous. It was also flat, and there were no significant bodies of water aboveground. The rain soaked through the rock and collected in underground lakes and rives that honeycombed the area. In places the erosion opened the rock above, revealing the underground water in sinkholes or wells called *cenotes*. These had been the ancient Mayans' water sources, and when they flowed deep and cool, the people had prospered. When the rains stopped and the subterranean rivers dried up, they had moved away or died. It was hardly surprising that so many of the Mayan ruins were adorned with the grotesquely ornate face of the rain god, Chaak, which featured an elephant nose, staring, bulbous eyes, and fearsome teeth.

Bowerdale was climbing the acropolis—Structure 1—the biggest, most imposing monument on the site. It housed Ek Balam's most famous find, the tomb known as Zac Na, resting place of a famous king who died in 840 AD: Ukit Kan Le'k Tok'. The door to the tomb lay at the center of a facade shaped like a great, monstrous, tooth-lined mouth. The carved stucco was adorned with elaborate sculpted winged figures, geometric patterns with glyphs and masks of threatening gods. Zac Na, or White House, as it was also called, had no equal anywhere in the world.

When it was uncovered in the 1990s, the tomb had been there for twelve hundred years, and it was a good part of what made Ek Balam special. Its riches, which included offerings of pearls, seashells, alabaster, and jade, were considerable. What made it truly unique, however, was the way it had been meticulously buried: the great pyramid's fragile stucco relief had been carefully packed with dirt and rubble so it was perfectly preserved. When the archaeological team found it, they had had to do little more than carefully remove the surrounding fill. The stucco itself had needed no restoration.

Recent work had erected a thatched lean-to around the Zac Na entrance to protect it from the elements, but the thatch would certainly need to be replaced. Deborah hoped to God there was no damage to the structure itself. She felt annoyed that Bowerdale had gotten up there first. She didn't want to hear bad news from him. After all, that magical "no restoration" tag was Ek Balam's claim to tourist fame. It would be tragic if the stucco relief had survived over a thousand years underground only to be damaged after its discovery. She watched Bowerdale as he continued to climb the steep, narrow steps of the acropolis, her eyes shaded. Then she marched to the foot of the structure and yelled in his direction.

"Is it OK?"

He shouted back something she couldn't hear, so she started to climb the stairs of the acropolis. They quickly narrowed to a single vertical flight, about twenty-five feet wide, and rising up almost a hundred feet. As with the steps of most Mayan pyramids, they were high and narrow, sloping slightly downward so that the water ran off them. Deborah's instinct was to use her hands like she was on a ladder, but she caught Bowerdale watching her from above and decided to walk—carefully—instead. He descended the stairs and met her halfway.

"I have this covered, Miss Miller," he said. "There's no need for both of us."

She had introduced herself as "Deborah" but he always called her "Miss Miller," a politeness that somehow made her less professional and certainly not his equal. He was, after all, *Doctor* Bowerdale. Deborah had a Master's degree. She had risen from within the world of practical museum curating, not from the upper echelons of academia.

"I am ultimately responsible for the dig," she said, gazing up the stairs to the thatched lean-to of the Zac Na and the great stucco mouth of the tomb door.

"And I am responsible for surveying the site," he returned. "This falls under my job description, not yours, and given the crisis precipitated by the weather, I think you should rely on my expertise."

Deborah didn't like his use of the word "crisis." It might become a justification for a complete usurpation of her authority. She opted not to press the issue and managed a smile, as if she hadn't noticed his challenge.

"I'll leave you to it, then," she said. "I thought I saw something down there that needed closer inspection anyway."

"What?" he said. "Where?"

But she had already turned and was starting to make her cautious descent.

"I'll let you know if you need to come and look," she called back, feeling better.

It was a lie, of course, but she relished his hesitation before he turned back up the stairs toward the Zac Na. She knew he would be watching her when she reached the bottom. Going down the pyramid was actually worse than going up, the vast openness of the site swimming before her, and she turned sideways to take the wet steps, her left hand finding the edge to stabilize her as she descended. There were no handrails, no handicapped-accessible ramps, none of the warnings without which such a site would be a legal impossibility in the States. If she fell, she'd fall hard and long. She picked her way down, trying to decide where she would go when she reached the bottom.

In the end she went along the base of the acropolis, heading to its north side where no reconstruction had taken place: while meticulous steps had been built on the south side, from this angle the acropolis was just a mound of rubble. The path hung with the dense undergrowth of the jungle scrub that always threatened to reclaim the site.

Her miniscule triumph over Bowerdale faded, and Deborah found herself feeling lost and depressed as the old anxieties returned: Bowerdale was right. He had the real authority here. Hers was based on nothing more than a letter from Cornerstone and would have no weight if it hadn't come with a check attached. Even the students suspected it, and she guessed Bowerdale had said as much to those he most wanted to impress. The girl, probably. Alice. Bowerdale had a reputation where his female students were concerned.

She stopped, trying to process what it was she was seeing. The jungle on the north side of the acropolis looked different. It looked wrong. She tried to remember what had been there, and it came back to her slowly: a deep depression in the earth, what the locals called a *rejollada*; a sinkhole, not unlike the one that had opened up under Oasis. It had looked like some giant had taken a great ice-cream scoop to the earth, though in time the area had become a tangle of matted vegetation and brush right up to the path at the base of the acropolis. The ground didn't look like that now. In fact, Deborah realized, staring wildly, that the ground wasn't there at all.

Chapter Five
■ ■ ■ ▪ ▫

Eustachio had spotted Bowerdale and the *norteamericano* students as soon as he entered the site. He had hoped that they would have chosen to come later, but they were here and this made things difficult. There was only the one van in the parking lot, so the rest of the students were probably still in Valladolid, and there was no sign of Deborah Miller's rental car. Yet. He knew her well enough already to know she couldn't stay away, and then he would quickly run out of choices.

Fidelia would have told him he worried too much. "First, see that there is a problem, then worry about solving it," she would have said. He missed her, suddenly. She would have known what to do. And maybe she was right. It had rained, hard, but it had rained many times before, and life went on unchanged, or almost unchanged. But he had to look. He had to be sure. It was his duty.

But how did you search for something you had never seen?

He doubled back, hobbling west toward the second *sacbe* and the perimeter wall. It would take him longer to walk around the edge of the site but it would help him stay out of the *gabachos'* way. He was pretty sure he would see them before they saw him. No one knew this place better than Eustachio. Yes, the gringos had the fancy contoured maps, but he knew the stones themselves, and the trees. He knew the *motmot* in the branches and the skink that watched from the grass.

He reached to touch the sticky bark of a *chakaj* tree and crossed himself, then began his swift, limping walk. Hopefully, there would be nothing to find. A few minutes in, he spotted one of Bowerdale's students coming through the brush. She turned but didn't see him. He watched her balefully. If he'd ever learned his grandmother's spells, maybe he could have slowed her. She was getting too close. If his misgivings about the state of the site were correct, if what he had guarded for so long might at last be visible, she would have to be stopped.

Chapter Six

■ ■ ■ ■ ■

Alice wasn't sure what she had signed up for, but it sure as shit wasn't trekking around to see if a few rocks had shifted in the rain. She scowled to herself. Archaeology had seemed a hell of a lot more interesting before she'd actually started doing it. She remembered the lectures in her intro courses at Brandeis, all those beguiling photographs of statues and mummies. That had been cool, and she'd doodled little sketches of ancient coins and jewels in her notebook margins. Her first actual fieldwork had revealed that archeology was anything but exciting. Her team's only "discovery" had been a few stones from an old foundation and a handful of potsherds that the dig leader had positively wet himself over. Three weeks of back-breaking digging and cataloguing for that: a footnote to some academic paper no one would ever read.

So she'd looked into doing site surveys. That seemed better. Less actual shouldering of pickaxes and more walking around taking pictures and sketching. She had a good eye and a better hand, and had even considered being an art major once. She thought she'd hit the jackpot when she was selected by Bowerdale. He was, after all, pretty much the god of the field, even if his tales of past adventurers and the bags of money paid to him by the military got old fast. It had taken him exactly two days—right after some pompous speech about how the old ways were the most reliable, and that there was no substitute for staring through a transit lens with a pencil behind your ear—to suggest he wouldn't mind getting into her shorts.

She had considered it, even been flattered by his interest, and for a few days had sort of flirted with him in a noncommittal kind of way. At first he had seemed to enjoy it, and she thought she'd found an easy way to stay on his good side, but it soon became clear that he expected something more tangible. She might have done it too. It was, after all, no big deal. But then he tried to stick his tongue in her mouth without asking, and Alice—who liked to make the first move herself—had told him where he could shove it. That had been the end of that. Now he barely looked at her except to complain about the way she was doing something. She had a nagging feeling that the glowing reference letter she had hoped to get from him at the end of all this was dead in the water.

She scowled up at Structure 2.

"Looks like a pile of old rocks," she muttered aloud. "Which is what it looked like yesterday, and the day before."

She rubbed a sunburned shoulder where she had a tattoo of a rose twined with barbed wire, two fat drops of blood dripping from the thorns. They'd have been done if Bowerdale had let them use laser measures instead of all the antiquated crap he insisted was "field tested." You could pick one up at Home Depot for like a hundred bucks but no, she had to use the leveling rod, as archaeologists have since time immemorial. As used by Morley, Thompson, John Lloyd Stephens, and all those other nineteenth-century geezers. She rolled her eyes and thought, *As used by the fucking ancient Maya themselves.*

Deborah Miller wasn't much better than Bowerdale. True, she hadn't shown up at Alice's bedroom door with a bottle of tequila and an I'm-not-as-old-as-you-think speech, but she had his knack for ignoring her. The woman was clearly out of her depth. Even James said so, and he barely said anything negative about anybody. She was nice enough, Alice supposed, and she had a toughness that deserved some respect, but Miller didn't like being questioned and that was what Alice did best. In other circumstances, Alice conceded, she might think Deborah Miller was OK, maybe even interesting if some of the stories were true. Like the one about working as an informant for the FBI during a case involving neo-Nazis and ancient Greek gold. But as her *boss*? Forget it.

She frowned and rubbed her arms, which were prickling as the morning's relative coolness gave way to the ruthless heat of the sun. With her pale skin that never tanned, she had to wear long sleeves in spite of the soaring temperatures. Just as well, she thought. If she bared any more skin, poor James might lose his mind and Bowerdale might try his advances again. Alice snorted. She wasn't a classic beauty queen, but with her slim figure, light blue eyes, and dark hair, most of the red-blooded men in her orbit seemed to think she was their best option. Lucky her.

"Goddamn Bowerdale," she said, even though nobody was around to hear. "I wouldn't mind taking him and throwing him right off the top of that—"

She heard something in the underbrush off to her left and stopped, peering, startled. She could see nothing but vine-strangled trees and an uncanny speckling of crimson flowers, but she was suddenly sure there was someone there.

"James?" she called. "That better not be you, asshole."

There was no sound in response. She stood there, feeling the heat reflecting onto her from all sides and—behind it somehow—eyes.

She was on the west side of Structure 2, completely cut off from the central court and the others. She was alone. Doubling back would take longer than going forward, so she began to walk quickly, trying to deny her own fear. She glanced involuntarily off into the jungle to her left, stumbling as she did so.

It could have been an animal, she thought, a little desperately, a wild boar maybe. Maybe even a jaguar, which would be scary but kind of cool, so long as it didn't fucking *eat* her.

For the first time she felt completely alone in the site, as if James and the others were hundreds of miles away, not yards. It was as if she had wandered into this ancient place by herself, a place in which she did not belong, a place that did not want her. She quickened her pace till she was jogging. Somehow, over the noise of her footfalls and increasingly labored breathing, she sensed movement back there in the trees. She began to run flat-out.

Alice was not athletic. Exercise bored her, and though she had cut down, she still smoked half a pack a day. But now she sprinted ahead under the shadow of the great ruined structure as if she were a marathoner. Fear made her legs churn. She felt as if she was trespassing, as if she was the first person to step on this path in a thousand years. All around her in the changeless forest, she felt eyes in the leaves. Then, breathless, she rounded a corner and saw someone. A woman, tall and lanky...

Deborah Miller.

Alice called out, a joyous and unguarded shout of relief.

Chapter Seven

■ ■ ■ ■ ■

Deborah barely saw Alice come running around the corner because she was staring too intently at the space where the sink-hole had been. The girl looked rattled and seemed to have been running, but Deborah didn't wait to hear explanations.

"Come here," she called, and started pushing her way through the vegetation.

The girl was saying something in a panicky voice, glancing behind her, but she stopped as soon as she got close enough to see.

"Whoa," she said. "What the hell is that?"

"That," said Deborah, "was a *rejollada.*"

"A what?"

"A sinkhole caused by erosion from collecting water. The water drains through the limestone but the sinkhole itself does not connect to the water table below. That's what it was."

"What is it now?"

"Now," said Deborah, "it's a *cenote.*"

The storm had caused a torrent in the underground rivers, and that torrent had caused massive subsidence under the sinkhole. Now the hole went all the way down to dark, rubble-strewn water.

"The water runs right under the site?" said Alice, who had forgotten her former panic.

"Yep," said Deborah. She climbed to the edge of what had been the fifty-foot-wide *rejollada* but now had a yawning hole in its center about half that width. She peered down but could only see the contours of a dark cavern below.

"So everything, the pyramids and...everything, is sitting right on top of an underground river," Alice said.

"At least one pyramid is," said Deborah, noticing that for once the girl's sneer had been replaced with a look of wonder. "There are several sinkholes around the site where the ancient Maya punched through the rock to reach the water below. There's a well they made like that on the east side of the site."

"We'll have to cancel everything," said Alice. "Nothing will be stable."

"No," said Deborah. "We won't. But we will have to change our plans."

Deborah crawled to the edge and looked down. The first few meters were a straight drop, but below that the hollow opened up into a cavern. The sunlight flashed on the water perhaps seventy-five or a hundred feet below, and it was bright enough to see ropelike tendrils reaching all the way down to the bottom: roots. Her eye followed them down and then back up. Along the way, a shape caught her gaze like a barb snagging in fabric, and she stopped to stare.

What the hell is that?

There was a square opening in the upper northern quadrant of the bowl perhaps twenty feet below her feet. As her eyes adjusted to the light, she realized what she was seeing.

"Steps," she whispered.

And now that she recognized them she could see that the square opening was not simply a natural feature of the rock. It had hard, man-made angles, the sides marked with the telltale lines of regular stone blocks.

It couldn't be, she thought. *It just isn't possible.*

Alice, sensing her intensity, came to her side and stared down into the hole.

"What?" she said. "What are you looking at?"

"There's a passage," said Deborah. "The entrance must have been back here somewhere, hidden underground."

"Where does it go?" said Alice.

Deborah looked north into the tangled scrub, but she could see nothing on the surface. She peered back into the hole.

She turned to look at the opposite side of the cavern, the side closest to the acropolis, and though the light was lower on this side she saw it immediately: a matching square hole, this one with fractured masonry where some of the blocks had been torn out by the collapsing rubble. The passage had extended right across the *rejollada.*

"Where does it go?" Alice repeated.

Deborah hauled herself to her knees and looked at the girl standing in front of the great pyramid.

"Right under your feet," she said.

Alice flinched and looked at the ground below her.

"It goes under the acropolis," said Deborah, the full scale of the thing finally hitting her. "It leads inside the pyramid."

"Inside," Alice echoed. "Seriously?"

"You'd better get Bowerdale," said Deborah, trying to keep the tremor from her voice. "And some rope. And the cameras. All of them."

Chapter Eight

■ ■ ■ ■ ■

Alice still had that dazed look when she left, and she seemed to hesitate before going around the acropolis via the east end—the long way, but Deborah was too stunned by the find to wonder why. Deborah's dig had just become Deborah's find, and she would have to handle it with only a couple of students for assistance. And Bowerdale, of course.

Her heart sank. He mustn't be allowed to take over. Deborah considered the newly created *cenote*, thinking hard. She had read all there was to read about Ek Balam, and this sure as hell wasn't on any map she had seen. A passage inside the acropolis meant an underground chamber—rare in Mayan pyramids, but not unheard of. It would probably be old. Older than the building on top of it: Early Classic, perhaps. Maybe even pre-Classic. Her heart was racing.

This is huge.

Beyond huge. It would make headlines, which would delight Steve Powel and Cornerstone, even if they found nothing significant inside. But unless the chamber had been robbed, there *would* be things to find.

She laughed with delight, but the sound died on her lips. She turned around quickly, sure that there was someone in the underbrush behind her. She had heard something. A snapping twig, perhaps. A stealthy, cautious sound.

Deborah stared at the foliage, but there was no movement. She realized she was holding her breath, and exhaled slowly.

Still nothing, but she felt a chill, and the hair on her arms prickled.

You're imagining it, she told her herself. *There's nothing...*

A leaf, one of those huge elephant ear things, shifted fractionally despite the lack of wind, and for a moment she saw—or thought she saw—eyes watching her.

"Where is it?"

Deborah started and looked up. It was Bowerdale, looking flushed and expectant, Alice jogging to keep up.

"It's a tunnel?" he called, scrambling down to where she stood. "You're sure?"

"A passage," said Deborah. "Built with stone blocks and roofed with slabs. Yes, I'm sure."

He staggered over the uneven ground and thrust his face over the edge.

"We should reinforce this area," said Deborah. "We've no idea how solid this lip is."

"If it was going to collapse, it would have done so already," muttered Bowerdale, gazing into the cave below. "But we're going to need to build a brace across the top, and get the winch so I can get down there."

"You?"

"I'm the surveyor."

"Of known monuments," said Deborah. "This is not one of them and falls under my jurisdiction. I'll be the first one down there."

Alice was watching Deborah carefully.

"With all due respect, Miss Miller, this is a potentially hazardous situation and I think a man might be a better choice to..."

Deborah just laughed and peered down toward the water.

"There's a ledge over there," she said, pointing. "Lower me in, and I can swing over to the passage. Do we have the lamps?"

"They're in the van," said Bowerdale, taken aback. "But I still think I should be the person to investigate. My credentials as a surveyor have been recognized by the highest authorities, and not only in archaeology. I worked as..."

"Surveyor at White Sands," said Deborah. "Yes, you said."

"Well then," he replied, as if that settled it.

"Where's James?" she said, ignoring him and shooting a glance at Alice.

"He was over on the east side," said the girl.

"Go get him," said Deborah, "and bring whatever flashlights are in the van."

Alice looked apprehensive, but she nodded once, her pale face blank, and then she was gone. Bowerdale watched her leave then turned to Deborah, his voice low.

"Now look here," he said, "I am the senior archaeologist on site."

Deborah rose, took a step away, and drew her cell phone from her hip pocket.

"What are you doing?" said Bowerdale.

"I'm going to go up that damned phone tower and call the lab at Valladolid," she said. "They can bring more gear."

Bowerdale reached over and closed one large, tanned hand over the phone. He didn't take it from her, but he held it firmly, his fingers clamped over the number pad.

"Now hold on," he said, and there was something different in his voice now, something quiet and a little dangerous. "Let's just think this through."

"What?"

"We've just stumbled upon what may turn out to be one of the great Mayan finds in recent decades," he said. His face was close to hers now, his voice low and urgent. "We have no idea what we're going to find in there. It could be special. Very special. We might be better restricting the number of people who know about it till we see what's inside."

"I'm talking about telling *our* people," said Deborah.

"And I'm saying, let's just hold on. If you and I go in alone, we get to tell the world exactly what we found. No one could contradict us. We take the pictures, shoot the video. We get the scoop. The *National Geographic* exclusive. The *Discovery Channel* documentary. This is how careers are made, Miss Miller."

"Why would anyone contradict us?" she said, genuinely confused. "Surely the more people we take in, the more secure our story."

"Too many cooks," he said. "And besides"—and now Bowerdale's voice dropped to a whisper—"there might be things inside that could have more value going through less *authorized* channels."

TEARS OF THE JAGUAR

"What are you saying?"

"Just that some items that would otherwise gather dust on the shelves of your museum might be of great interest to private collectors. Even minor artifacts could fetch the kind of money that would keep your museum running for some time."

"You're suggesting that we smuggle pieces out to raise money on the black market," she said. She felt so completely thrown that she had to piece together the implication of what he was saying.

He seemed to watch her for a second, studying her face. Then, quite suddenly, he laughed, a throaty chuckle that filled his chest.

"I think I had you going there for a second, Miss Miller," he said. "Kidding, or as my tiresome students like to say, *psych!* Cheer up. This is a day you'll remember for the rest of your life."

Deborah stared at him, but he had already moved to the edge of the depression and was signaling to James and Alice, who had rounded the eastern end of the acropolis at a run. Deborah watched him, unable to shake the uneasy feeling his manner had left with her. Bowerdale certainly knew how to get a rise out her, so perhaps he really was just teasing, but there was something about the way he'd reached for her phone. He'd been humorless. He'd been—what was it? *Threatening.* The word jumped into her mind and she found she could not push it away.

Chapter Nine

■ ■ ■ ■ ■

Eustachio watched from behind a huge *k'u'che'* tree a few yards from the northernmost edge of the place where the ground had collapsed, and he knew that it had happened at last. Strange that it should be now, after he and everyone else had spent years digging only a few feet away. Strange too that it should be rain that did it. After all the barrows of dirt, the spades, picks, and mattocks, it was the rain that had uncovered the secret his forefathers had vowed to protect. There had been times over the years when he had doubted their secret had been based in anything real, but now he knew for sure, and his life had changed. If only it hadn't rained.

But then, Chaak had always ruled the Maya. When he bestowed his rain there was plenty and when he turned his face away there was death. Perhaps this too was his will.

Eustachio listened to the *gabachos* talking about ropes and winches, and he blamed himself. He should have seen the danger of the sinkhole, should have guessed years before what lay beneath it. But then, the sinkhole had existed for many decades and neither his father nor his grandfather had imagined it obscured the secret place. What would happen next, he could not say. But he felt a ripple of fear course through his chest.

Terrible things would come. He sensed them in the pit of his stomach, looked into them like the *gabachos* peering down into the dark water that ran beneath the tomb of Ukit Kan Le'k Tok'. Terrible things.

He prayed to Chaak in the hybrid way he had learned from his father.

"I call to the bringer of rain in the name of the father, and of the son, and of the holy ghost..."

Chapter Ten

■ ■ ■ ■ ■

They lowered Deborah down and swung her over the brownish water of the new *cenote* until she could reach the trailing roots and pull herself into the mouth of the passage. The tunnel itself was lined with stones, though some of it had collapsed into the sinkhole, with a corbelled vault ceiling—an inverted V-shaped roof that in the center was almost high enough even for Deborah to walk without stooping. She unslung the flashlight and snapped it on, dimly aware of Bowerdale's voice, scolding the students for taking too long to get him roped in.

Deborah didn't wait.

She moved a few yards down the tunnel to where a stone slab had been set as a door, permanently closed, except that the shifting of the ground had split it into three pieces. Deborah studied it, holding the flashlight beam on the fragments, carved with what resembled a stela, a royal figure seated in profile, along with ornamental birds, jaguars, and snakes. It was a tomb.

The carving represented the man who had been buried inside. Deborah's heart beat fast and she could hear the rush of blood in her ears.

A tomb! she thought, deliriously. *Powel will be on the next plane.*

Deborah squeezed through the shattered doorway and down two steps, the flashlight beam turned to the paving stones. The ceiling was lower here and the tunnel felt cramped. She raised one hand to the roof so that she could feel how far it was from her head as she walked. It was her hand rather than her eyes that registered the sudden rise in the ceiling, though she sensed the space around her and shone the flashlight up.

The passage had opened into a large chamber hollowed out of the rock, but it wasn't empty. A stone structure shaped roughly like a step pyramid had been built inside. It stood about twenty feet high, rising right up to the cavern ceiling. It was coated with stucco that, though faded, was red as blood. When she trained the bright beam of her flashlight on the pyramid, she could make out forbidding masks flanked with bird wings in green and yellow, and dour, hawk-nosed faces. It reminded her of the Rosalia in the Mayan city of Copan, Honduras, but this was different. For one thing there was a doorway framed as an open maw lined with teeth, and terrible eyes: a hell mouth like the Zac Na set in the pyramid above it.

"Oh my God," she whispered.

"What?" The voice came from behind her.

Bowerdale.

"What is it? What can you see?"

And then he was inside and he stopped talking.

"The plaster is intact," said Deborah.

"Yes," Bowerdale managed.

"Are you getting all this?"

She took her eyes off the monumental structure to look at him and saw that he had the video camera at shoulder height, its video screen unfolded so he didn't have to look through the eyepiece.

"Shall we?" she said, nodding toward the great jaws of the building.

She moved into the hollow, stepping carefully over the fang-like teeth that lined its lower lip and then stood to the side so that Bowerdale and his camera could see in.

Inside the gateway was a recess ten feet deep. At the back, lolling in a stone construction that was half box and half throne, was a skeleton, now fragmented, but still wearing a green stone mask with white eyes made of shell. The remains of the rib cage were dotted with fragments of bone and jade that had once been necklaces and other adornments. Around it, arranged on the ground and on shelflike alcoves built into the larger hollow, were grave goods: Ceramics. Amphora-style jugs. An inverted red bowl with a parrot effigy. Flaring side bowls paired lip to lip. A trichrome open bowl and other polychromatic vessels. Deborah moved the beam of light and caught the flash of obsidian blades. The chosen weapon of human sacrifice for the Maya.

"Shine the light there," hissed Bowerdale, whose voice was low and hoarse. "What is that, chert?"

Deborah shone the light on what looked like flint tools and nodded, before her attention moved to a dark greenstone axe head. And there was more. There were carved bone tubes that might have been feather fan holders or bloodletting instruments. There was jade jewelry, some of it a rare blue color. There were two metates, the stone mortars used for grinding corn. Then there were stingray spines and red ocher sticks. There were bones, some of them parts of deer heads, and when she looked back to the collapsed skeleton she saw that it was wearing a large round pendant carved from bone into the shape of a human skull, the eyes set with jade. The skeleton was flanked by clay statuary not unlike the figures on the Zac Na, and in its fallen lap were bundles of what looked like bones.

Human bones.

The skulls, which looked too small to be adult, were set apart from the bundles, staring sightless toward them.

Sacrificed, then, she thought. The fact of it still registered, despite her excitement, lodging like something cold and dark in her stomach.

"Congratulations, Miss Miller," said Bowerdale from behind the camera. "We just made history."

"What's that?" she said, gesturing to a small bundle beside the throne. It was wrapped with fabric that was—incredibly—intact.

Bowerdale peered at it, then handed her the camera.

"Here," he said. "Hold this."

He produced a pencil and began to tease the wrapping open gently.

"We should wait till we can do this properly," said Deborah, but he had already got the first of the fold open, and the rest unrolled with it.

Inside were bones, mostly small, though two were about a foot long. Inside the bundle something dislodged, giving off a metallic flash as it fell onto the stone floor.

"What the hell?" breathed Bowerdale.

Deborah shone the light onto the floor, and Bowerdale got down on his knees and carefully picked it up.

It was a fragment of dull yellow metal, about three quarters of an inch long, inlaid with a remarkable pale crimson stone, translucent as crystal. Bowerdale held it up, his face quizzical in the flashlight beam, then turned back to the bundle he had unfurled.

"There are more fragments here," he said, pointing with the pencil. "And there's something else."

But he didn't need to say that because Deborah was already staring at it dumbstruck. It was a rod of yellow metal, perhaps eighteen inches long, and on one end there was something that looked like a dove, white and glossy as enamel. There was also a polished wooden log inlaid with jade and, encircling one of the many small bones, what looked like a ring engraved with an unusual design.

"What the hell is that?" Bowerdale whispered, his voice carrying the same baffled awe that Deborah felt breaking out all over her like sweat.

"If I didn't know better," she said, "I'd say most of this stuff was…"

"Gold," he finished for her.

It can't be, she thought. *It's not possible.*

There was no gold in the Yucatan. That's part of the reason why the Spanish paid it so little attention. And the tomb was too old for there to be imported gold from other parts of Mexico.

And yet, she thought, dazzled by the way it sparkled in the beam of her flashlight, *there it is*.

Chapter Eleven

■ ■ ■ ■ ■

Porfiro Aguilar looked at the chaos of half-unpacked lab equipment and wondered, not for the first time, what the hell he had been thinking. It was one thing to sign on as assistant field director to the woman from the States, but handling artifact analysis and conservation for an entirely new find was nuts. He would be stuck in Valladolid for weeks. He hadn't even seen the tomb yet and didn't know when he'd be able to go.

Sweating, he put a box of sample containers on his desk. The air-conditioning in the lab whirred like a stalling biplane, cooling the room by ten degrees, maybe less. Outside, the usual hundred-degree midmorning heat blazed. Sometimes he really hated the Yucatan.

Porfiro Aguilar was from the hip Colonia Condesa neighborhood of Mexico City, which, with its museums, clubs, and café culture, was another country entirely. He had been raised in Santo Domingo but had been a bit of an urban sophisticate even before he had the money to live that way, and he felt almost as out of place in a provincial town like Valladolid as the damned *gringos*. Almost as out of place as Miller herself, who—he imagined—was out of place everywhere. She could have been pretty if she wasn't quite so angular and awkward in her movements. She had to be a couple of inches over six feet tall, which meant she loomed over almost everybody but Bowerdale. Her thick, unruly brown hair was always pulled back, but he had a feeling if she took it down and put some makeup on her dark almond-shaped eyes, she'd turn a head or two. Still. Her workaholic personality made it impossible for him to see her as anything besides yet another boss.

He had seen the village where Miller was staying, the way the people lived there. Naked kids on dirt floors. Pigs and turkeys everywhere you looked, all waiting to be Christmas or Easter dinner. Those Goddamned palm-thatched roofs. Everyone still living off corn three hundred and sixty-two days a year as they had before the Spanish—his true ancestors—arrived. It was the fucking third world. Aguilar had made the Maya his professional life, and was proud of their history and achievements, but when he had to deal with their living descendents, he felt something like contempt. He didn't like the feeling—hated it, in fact—but there it was. In the end he had more in common with *norte-americanos* than he did with the Maya. He even looked more like them, and until he spoke, he could pass for one of them on their streets. In Ek Balam, everyone but Miller and Bowerdale was a head shorter and two shades darker.

He liked Miller well enough. She knew her own mind and wasn't too proud to let him know when she needed help. Bowerdale, however, was a smug son of a bitch. He was good at his job, sure, but he'd take advantage of anyone if there was fame or skirt to be had and never feel bad about it. Aguilar bore his prejudices against the Maya with the humility of failure and sin. He felt no such failure for hating Bowerdale.

Aguilar rolled his eyes at the sight of Miller and Bowerdale walking into the lab together, looking earnest, excited. Bowerdale handed him the only sample taken from the tomb: a fragment of gold-colored metal mounting a pale, red, uncut crystal the size of a bottle cap.

"What am I looking at?" said Aguilar, adjusting the setting on his microscope.

"We were kind of hoping you could tell us," said Miller.

Aguilar peered at the red stone again and, sensing Bowerdale watching him critically, felt a sudden flash of anger.

"I'll need to do some serious analysis before I can tell you anything concrete," he said, as calmly as he could manage, "but I can give you some preliminaries."

"Shoot," said Bowerdale.

"Well," said Aguilar, pushing back from the microscope, "I think it's fair to say that I'm not nearly as stupid as you think I am, and that the next time you want to see if I know my job you can look at my damned resume."

He stared them down, his face flushed with anger. Miller looked at Bowerdale, and then back to Aguilar.

"I don't understand," she said.

"You didn't get this stone from the site," said Aguilar. "I am as good at my job as anyone you might have brought from the States."

For a moment Miller looked genuinely taken aback.

"No one doubts your credentials, Aguilar," she said.

"So what's this about," he shot back, with a curt nod at the red stone. "Where did it come from?"

"I was there when she went in," said Bowerdale, as if his word was worth more then Miller's. "She got it from the chamber under the acropolis."

"Where did you find it?" said Aguilar, his eyes still on Miller.

"In the tomb," said Miller. She said it carefully, emphatically, and held his eyes. He held them for a long moment and then shrugged.

"I don't understand how that could be possible," he said, his voice carefully neutral.

"And yet," said Bowerdale, with a smug smile.

There was a long silence. Aguilar shrugged.

"OK," he said, "I need to do some tests but I am as sure as I can be that the stone isn't Mayan. My guess is that it's from Europe. I'd need better equipment than I have here to estimate its age, but I'd say it was mined a long time ago. It's clearer than any natural stone I've ever seen. Then there's the metal, yellow and malleable."

He gave them a pointed look and they glanced at each other, but he still saw confusion rather than amusement. He decided that maybe this wasn't a practical joke after all.

"This isn't Mayan," he said, becoming more serious. "It's gold."

"It's not the only piece," Miller said. "The stone—what is it?"

"Corundum, probably," he answered. "The red kind, which makes it..."

"Ruby," said Bowerdale.

"Of a sort," said Aguilar. "Paler than usual."

"What's it worth?" said Bowerdale. "The stone."

"As jewelry? Less than you'd think. The color is too watery. So," he said, and paused, "you want to explain how an early medieval European crystal shows up in a Mayan tomb?"

"Someone must have gotten inside fairly recently," said Bowerdale.

"And put artifacts *in* the tomb?" Miller replied, studying the crystal. "That would make a change. And besides, I'd swear that entrance has been covered up for a long time."

"That's your opinion as an archaeologist, is it?" said Bowerdale.

"I've seen packed earth before," she said. "It takes time to settle as densely as the dirt over that passage. At least a hundred years, maybe five times that."

Aguilar watched her closely, trying to see how sure she was.

"You said you've never seen anything like it before," she said, turning to him.

"Natural crystals are almost always flawed at the microscopic level," he answered. "This is clean."

"You think you could search for these same properties and see if anything comparable has been turned up elsewhere?"

"I can try, but I can't do much more than look at it and do some rudimentary chemical tests here. I'll need to send it to a more advanced local lab, then to the US for further tests, which means clearing it with the government first."

Mexico owned everything that came out of the tomb regardless of who found it.

"Do it," she said.

"You're going to have to lock the site down, you know," he added.

"What do you mean?"

"I don't know what this is," he said, nodding at the gem, "but it complicates what was already a remarkable find."

"There'll be a feeding frenzy," Bowerdale said, cutting in. "We need to manage publicity."

"Probably so," she said.

"So we talk to no one," Bowerdale pressed. "Strictly *need to know.*"

Miller took a breath as if to steel herself. "I'll make that call, thanks, Martin."

Bowerdale's eyes hardened and his smile quivered, as if threatening to turn into something nastier, but then he recovered his composure and snapped his smile back into place.

"Sure," he said, shrugging. "What*ever* you say."

He strode out. Miller watched him go, then turned to Aguilar, who met her eyes, held them for a moment, and then nodded fractionally in approval.

Chapter Twelve
■ ■ ■ ■ ■

Deborah spent half the day on the phone, which meant standing on top of the cell phone tower instead of being in the tomb. Adelita ran updates from Bowerdale, who was documenting the find. The slight girl could scale the tower in half the time Deborah could, swinging up and down with fearless childish grace on her long, brown limbs.

"Careful, Adelita," said Deborah periodically. "It's a long way down."

"I saw the jewels," said the girl in Spanish, unable to stifle a secret smile. "Beautiful. Red, but not dark. Like—" She searched for words. "*Sangre y lagrimas.*"

Blood and tears.

The girl flashed her brilliant grin, pleased with the phrase, and scurried down the ladder.

Deborah called Powel, she called Valladolid, and she called various labs in Mexico and the US talking timetable and resources, experts, equipment, and, of course, money. The find changed everything, not least who would be coming down for the dig proper. If she didn't have the right team on site, the university affiliates would start weaning her off the project, and if there was the faintest hint of incompetence, the Mexican government would shut them down.

So she forced herself to leave the site, and spent the rest of the morning instead in front of a laptop screen at the Valladolid lab, scanning CVs for specialists who might be prepared to drop what they were doing and get down here within the next forty-eight hours. Steve Powel was doing what he could to funnel names to her, but it wasn't easy, given their decision to keep the contents of the find quiet. She caught herself having phone conversations that began, "I have to ask you to keep what I'm going to say confidential, and if you don't think you can do that, I'm going to hang up." It made her feel absurd, like a secret agent in a sixties spy movie.

The weakest link in their team was in Maya osteology—bones—and she didn't know where to start. Eventually she gave up and sidled over to Aguilar, who was laying dustless paper on three long tables ready for the first of the tomb artifacts. He looked harried. They all did. They hadn't intended to start analytical work for another ten days, and had expected no more than soil samples, maybe a few seeds or potsherds.

"You need to tell Bowerdale to wait," said Aguilar. "I need more people. The artifacts are best left on site."

"The heat might affect them," said Deborah. "The tomb has been cool for centuries. Now it's open and heating up fast, and after the flooding, there's a lot of humidity. I'd rather get everything crated up and brought down here to a climate-controlled environment, even if we can't start the analysis yet."

"We're rushing," he said. "This is how mistakes get made. I should be on site documenting and cataloging there. You let those kids move stuff and things are going to get missed or damaged."

"The *kids*, if you mean the undergraduates, are on their way to the airport," she said. "The big storm meant they got an early start to their week off."

"So we have no labor?"

"Other than the two graduate students and whoever Eustachio hires from the village, no," said Deborah.

Aguilar swore.

"The upside is that the undergrads never even saw the tomb," said Deborah. "There are rumors, of course, but they don't really know anything so they won't be able to tell anyone what we have till we're ready to talk."

"I need to be up there, at the site," he insisted.

"Give me a half hour and we'll go up together," she said.

He frowned and laid down a set of calipers.

"What else needs doing here?" he said.

"I have to hire an osteologist. Today. Can you give me some names?"

"Not really my field," he began, but Deborah cut him off.

"It's nobody's field except theirs. Who do you know who's good?"

"There's Rylands at Texas A&M," said Aguilar. "Pain in the ass, but good at his job. Penn State has a good program. I think Keri Havers is there. She published a piece in *American*

Archaeology on dentition and diet that got a lot of attention. She's cute too."

"Thanks," she said. "I've got to call Powel. Again."

"I guess I should stay here, anyway," he said, regretfully. "There's too much to do. Just make sure they're careful, and photograph everything *in situ*. Everything. And get some experts down here soon or we're going to be in serious trouble."

Deborah smiled, pleased by his earnestness.

"Doing my best," she said.

He glanced at his computer. "Wait," he said, looking up. "Just got a preliminary chemical composition report on that crystal I sent to the lab."

"Go on."

"OK," he said. "Let me see. This isn't really my field..." He caught her glance. "It's corundum, specifically ruby. The usual aluminum is replaced with chromium once every fifty thousand atoms or so, which is what gives it its red color and changes the way the stone interacts with light. That's not that uncommon, but this is."

"What?" said Deborah.

"See there," said Aguilar, pointing to the data breakdown on the screen. "In addition to the chromium plus three, we've got Fe plus three: ferric iron."

"That's unusual?"

"A combination of chrome and iron?" said Aguilar, frowning. "Very rare indeed."

"And what does that tell us?"

"Other than the fact that our lab isn't equipped to handle whatever is in that tomb?" said Aguilar. "I have no idea."

Chapter Thirteen
■ ■ ■ ■ ■

Bowerdale hadn't left the dim, silent tomb in over three hours. He denied that he was guarding the find, but he was and even Miller knew he was right. He didn't think anyone would deliberately break in to plunder the tomb, but he didn't want curious tourists messing things up or helping themselves to a few shiny souvenirs. The locals knew better than to mess with their cultural legacy, but they were dirt poor and you could only expect so much loyalty to abstractions like heritage. This sort of find needed a watchful eye at all times to keep it secure.

Bowerdale scowled to himself. It was taking far too long for Eustachio and the Mayan laborers to get the access stairs finished, and it was likely to be at least another day before they could even begin moving stuff out of the tomb, probably more. They had built a framing scaffold over the hole and had been able to anchor a ladder down to the passage opening, which made getting in and out easier than swinging on ropes like a bunch of apes, but

they wouldn't be able to move artifacts until they had a real staircase or ramp system in place. They didn't have enough lumber
with them and had already wasted half a day trying to recover
a piece of tube steel scaffolding that had been dropped into the
cenote. When Miller got here, he'd have some choice words for
her in regards to her choice of workers, and if she chose to fire
him, so be it.

Except, of course, that this wasn't a find he could afford to let
slip through his fingers. There were going to be articles and photographs and TV shows, and he had to make sure he was front and
center in all of them. His tenured faculty performance review at
Princeton had not gone well, and his chair had quoted the com-
mittee as suggesting that he was "sitting on his laurels": a polite way
of saying he hadn't done anything in the last three years. And there
had been that messy business with one of his undergraduates when
she'd recast their little dalliance as something predatory, something
less than entirely consensual. It was a lie or, more accurately, a trick
to pay him back for moving on so quickly to another student he
found more enticing, but the chair had read him the riot act.

If they could just process the site properly, examine what they
had, and get their findings published quickly. If, in the process,
they could solve the riddle of those odd crystals that Aguilar had
told him had a rare combination of iron and chrome, so much
the better.

He heard someone inching down the ladder and turned to
face them as they entered the tomb. It was James, the thin and
bespectacled graduate student who read comic books like an
eight-year-old. Bowerdale sighed.

"Eustachio wants to know what we're going to do tonight,"
said James. "We've only got a couple more hours of daylight

left and there's no way we'll have moved anything off site by then. We can't just leave all this stuff here. I'd ask Dr. Miller, but..."

"*Miss* Miller is not here," Bowerdale concluded.

And she wouldn't know what to do anyway, he added in his head.

"We'll have to cover the hole," he said.

"The entire *cenote*?" said James. "We'll never do it. We don't have the materials."

"Then we had better get them, hadn't we?" said Bowerdale.

"OK," the kid said with a shrug, his tone suggesting that it wasn't OK at all. "I'll tell Eustachio."

"And tell him he can come down here himself next time," said Bowerdale. "I don't like dealing with errand boys."

James bridled.

"He can't manage the ladder safely," he said. "His leg..."

"Then maybe he should find a new line of work."

James took a breath and said, "You want me to pass that along too?"

"Just get them to cover the hole," said Bowerdale.

The student didn't speak or nod. He just turned and made his way back down the passage. In seconds, Bowerdale could hear the ladder creaking as he climbed up to the surface.

James was right, of course. There was no way they would be able to cover the *cenote* in any way that would really keep people out, and he wouldn't have insisted on it if he hadn't started to feel so crossed. He adjusted the light he had brought down with him so he could look at the jewels and the rest of the bundle with the carved piece of tree trunk, the ring, and the gold rod with the dove. It annoyed him to admit it, but Miller was right. They just didn't belong. He needed to find out what they were and quickly. In the right hands, he was sure they would be worth something. Possibly a great deal.

He heard the noise of the ladder but didn't bother turning until he realized it was her, bent almost double in the low passage.

"You told them to cover the entire hole?" she said, without preamble.

"We have to protect the tomb."

"Not like that, we don't. That could take days, even if we had the materials, which we don't."

"So what's your solution?"

"We set up fence posts and ropes to cordon off the *cenote*, for safety as much as anything else…"

"That won't keep people out if they want to get in."

"That was why I was about to propose that we stay here overnight. We can work shifts, some preparing the lab, the others watching the tomb."

"For how long?"

"Until we can safely move everything out," she said.

"That could be weeks."

"It won't be that long. It can't be. We'll get work lights out here so we can start shifting stuff out as soon as they have the storage space ready."

"Days, then," said Bowerdale.

"I put in a request to get the official archivist down here as soon as we made the discovery yesterday. I'm hoping we can get him tomorrow or the day after. When he gets here, we can start the cataloging process. In the meantime, we ready transit crates and we prepare the lab to receive the artifacts. OK?"

He wanted to argue, doubly so now that he realized that James was behind her, shadowed by her great stork-like frame, listening.

"You're the boss," he said.

Chapter Fourteen

■ ■ ■ ■ ■

James had volunteered to take the first watch because he knew
Alice didn't want to do it and because he thought she would
be impressed by how casually he agreed to sit in a tomb in the
jungle in the dark. Alice was sexy, in a grungy kind of way. She
wore no makeup except black eyeliner and had a tough-looking
tattoo on one shoulder. Her skin was so pale it was almost translucent, like she'd been living underground for most of her life.
She had strong, sinewy arms, and her legs were made for hiking
boots, but her chest and belly were soft. She had great boobs.
Not real big, but shapely. Sometimes she went without a bra and
you could see her wide, pink nipples through her shirt. Nice.

He walked around the rope that circled the *cenote*, looking at
the sky. He'd never seen so many stars in his life. James, who had
been raised in Hackensack, had barely spent a day in the country
in his life. His folks had taken him camping in Pennsylvania
once but they had come back early when he reacted badly to

a bee sting. He'd been a city kid ever since, which was perfect really, since he was the kind of out-and-proud geek most at home in front of his MacBook or PlayStation, venturing out only to go to classes, the library, or the movies. Being here in the dark, with no one around, and just the chirping of crickets and frogs, was like being on another planet.

Alice.

He hadn't fancied her that much when he first met her. But he'd gotten used to her scowl and the way she looked you right in the eye when she talked. And she didn't have the same smug look as a lot of cute girls he'd seen, the look that said, *Forget it, loser.* Sometimes the two of them sat up late and drank tequila together, talking about the clueless undergrads and Blowhard Bowerdale. Soon, he hoped, she might sleep with him. She wouldn't think it was a big deal. It was to him, but she didn't need to know that. His best chance with Alice was if she thought they were just fooling around, and that it didn't mean anything. That was partly why he liked her. She was immune to other people. He envied her that, wished he cared less about things, including her.

He checked his watch. He had already been there an hour, sitting under the deeper shade of the ancient acropolis. He spent ten minutes at the mouth of the tunnel flicking stones into the *cenote*, listening for their distant splash, and then decided to check out the tomb. He could sit down there in the dark and listen to Bauhaus on his iPod: crank the whole eleven minutes of "Bella Lugosi's Dead" down there among the bones.

Cool.

He got a flashlight, stepped over the rope, and eased his way off the platform and onto the aluminum ladder. They had lashed it at the top with nylon rope and pinned it into the earth below with steel pegs, but the metal had a natural spring in it, and it felt precarious. He hadn't admitted it to anyone, but he didn't like heights, and the prospect of falling into the *cenote* with its underground river and who knew what swimming in it scared the crap out of him.

The birds had discovered the new water source before the sun had gone down, and he'd watched what he thought were swallows diving down and skimming the surface with their beaks. He thought it was one of them that whistled past his head as he began his descent, but he realized as it whirred and fluttered away that it was actually a bat. He wasn't crazy about bats either. They had vampire bats down here too, he thought.

Just focus on the ladder.

With each footstep, the metal bounced and shifted under his weight, and he was glad to get a foot on the remains of the passage floor. He turned carefully, because the roof was low. Deborah had to virtually crawl just to get in. James wasn't so sure about Deborah. He liked her OK, he guessed, but she seemed kind of hard, not with Alice's *whatever* apathy, but with something else, something deep and focused. Determination, maybe. She was kind of cute, for an older chick, but she was a good four inches taller than him, and that wasn't cool.

Deborah had said they probably wouldn't have work lights and a generator for at least another day. He snapped on the flashlight and the beam fell on the carved faces flanking the fanged hell mouth with the measuring rods they had set up for the pictures. He moved the beam into the opening and found the skeleton with the green death mask, its eyes and teeth made of unnaturally bright alabaster shells, and he shuddered. The place had been weird even in daylight. Now, in the dark—the kind of dark a city boy like James had never seen before—with only the yellowish circle of his flashlight, it was beyond creepy, like being miles under the earth. Every sound reverberated oddly, and he could hear the soft lapping of the water in the *cenote* funneled up to him like it was being amplified through some old-timey ear trumpet.

Still, weird or not, it was also kind of cool, he told himself. He imagined what kind of mileage he'd get out of it back in the States. Any time anyone mentioned Bauhaus he'd have the best story about this one time in Mexico when he listened to Peter Murphy chanting about the virginal brides filing past Bela Lugosi's tomb, while he was sitting in an *actual* tomb with this ancient Mayan king lying exactly where he had lain for fifteen hundred years or more, with *real* vampire bats wheeling and swooping in the night just outside the tomb's entrance.

Ting.

James looked up. It was the sound of the ladder. The sound of *weight* on the ladder. He listened, motionless.

Ting.

And something else, a shuffling, scratching sound. Someone was coming down. Someone who was moving slowly, as if they did not want to be heard.

For a second he sat immobile, staring at the black hollow of the door, and when the sound came again, he felt his heart rising in his throat. He remembered the flashlight and spun it toward the entrance. It showed nothing but the tunnel itself and, if he bent and squinted a little, the very bottom of the ladder. Whoever was on the ladder wasn't down yet. Perhaps the light would warn them off. He played it around the tunnel walls and then, on impulse, began to talk, naturally as he could. Not shouting, just chatting, as if there was someone in here with him.

"Just down Essex Street from the medical center," he said. "You know it?"

He hesitated and then, without really deciding to, added a kind of grunt in a lower register, something that might sound like another voice.

"Lived there all my life until college."

He added another grunt, and behind it, out in the passage, there was silence. His eyes were wide, fixed on the entrance to the tomb, his mouth shaping words that hadn't gone through his mind, all his attention focused on what he might hear outside.

"Anyway, I figured I'd just..."

Ting.

The sound stopped him. He tried to find the thread of his imaginary conversation and it came again.

Ting.

Whoever was on the ladder was moving quickly now, less cautiously.

The only question was whether they were going up or down.

Chapter Fifteen

■ ■ ■ ■ ■

Martin Bowerdale moved silently down the hall from the dormitory and tried the key to the lab door. He eased it open gently, slowly. He could see no light, but Aguilar had a habit of working unpredictable hours.

He breathed a sigh of relief. The lab was empty, the computers powered down. He closed the door behind him and locked it. He turned on Aguilar's PC and entered his own name and password so that the system logged him on. He then accessed the ball-shaped webcam Aguilar never used, which sat on top of the monitor, angled down toward the keyboard. Bowerdale was an old-fashioned archaeologist in the field, but he had long ago conceded the value of computers and learned how to use them. When they had returned from the site that evening he had turned this machine on, set the webcam to record, and then asked Aguilar to access his data on a pot from the tomb. He now replayed the stored video, rewinding to the point where the Mexican's hands tapped out his password on the keyboard: *Nieves*. His dog's name, if Bowerdale remembered rightly.

Isn't that sweet.

Bowerdale turned the camera feed off and deleted it, then hit the "switch user" button. He typed in Aguilar's login name and the password and pulled up the folders he had created from the Ek Balam artifacts. He opened his own e-mail, addressed a message, and attached everything he could find on the red crystal in Aguilar's files before sending it. He got an acknowledgement ninety seconds later. While he waited for his cell phone to ring, he shut the computer down.

Bowerdale set the phone on the desk and watched it for half an hour. Then another. He checked his watch. When ten more minutes had passed with no call, he got up and began to walk around. He listened at the door, and the hallway outside was quiet, but he had begun to sweat.

What was taking so long?

Ten more minutes and he'd call preemptively, protocol or no protocol. He stared at the phone where it sat, mute, beside the computer.

Finally, it buzzed, wobbling like a big black roach on the desk. He snatched it up and answered it in a thick whisper.

"What the hell took you so long?" he demanded.

"You need to not call me again, OK, Bowerdale?" said the Texan. "We're done."

"What are you talking about?" asked the archaeologist, baffled. "Clements, you called me, remember?"

"I mean, I don't want to talk to you anymore," said Clements. "You got me? No calls, no e-mails, no schemes."

"What about the stone?" Bowerdale demanded.

"You aren't listening. I said, I want out. I don't want to see anything about those stones again. Ever. You understand me?"

"Excuse me?" said Bowerdale. He was trying to sound cheery, upbeat, as if this was just bargaining, but he had never heard the dealer sound so scared.

"Goodbye, Martin. Have a nice life."

"Wait," he spluttered. "What's the problem? I'll give you good terms, just tell me what you think it's worth."

"To me? Nothing," said Clements.

"But you said I was right," Bowerdale hissed. "You said it was valuable."

"Not to me, Martin. And believe me when I say that the people who will want it are not guys you want to deal with."

"This is nuts," said Bowerdale.

"People are coming for this find, Martin. Bad people. For all I know, they may already be there. If I were you, I'd forget you ever saw that tomb and I'd get out of Mexico. Now."

And before Bowerdale could think of a response, the line went dead.

Chapter Sixteen
■ ■ ■ ■ ■

The experts Deborah had hired to investigate the new find drove in from Cancun and Merida airports first thing in the morning. She waited for them at the lab in Valladolid feeling nervous, not just because there would suddenly be several new faces on site looking to Deborah for direction, but because their arrival reminded her of just how big the find under the pyramid was. It went without saying that any one of them was better qualified to lead the dig than she was. While she waited for their van to arrive, she called Steve Powel in Chicago and told him as much, but he didn't want to hear it.

"This is a Cornerstone project," he said, "and you are our man on site."

She wasn't certain if that "man" was a joke or some weird term of authority that she was to take as gender neutral. Maybe it was supposed to be a compliment, she thought, her heart sinking.

"You know who is coming?" she said, refusing to be diverted. "Krista Rayburn, the environmental archaeologist from Florida U. Marissa Stroud, the epigrapher from Minnesota who wrote the closest thing to a dictionary of Mayan glyphs we have, as well as that history of world royal regalia. Not to mention Chad Rylands, from Texas A&M, who wrote the world's most important study of Mayan bones *before* he was tenured."

"I know," said Powel. "I suggested two of them, remember?"

Deborah hadn't believed they could get Stroud, but Powel had pushed her to inquire. Stroud, it was rumored, had been so obsessed by her research that she had divorced a husband years ago and given him custody of their child without so much as a fight.

"Yes, they are top people," said Powel. "But so are you. Orchestrating this dig is not a matter for specialists, Deborah. They lean toward the things they find most interesting. They divert resources toward their pet projects and ideas. Running the dig is about coordinating experts, getting them to work together for the good of the whole, and that—Deborah—is a job for a generalist. If you don't think you can do it, tell me now, and I'll replace you, but don't mistake their expertise with bones and seeds and glyphs for the ability to run a dig."

"OK," she said.

"You have a photographer on site?" he asked.

"One was supposed to arrive today," she said. "A Brit. But he pulled out, and his university is sending someone else. It may take another day or two to get him here. In the meantime, Bowerdale will take charge of the pictures and video."

It was all good, she thought. Except, of course, that it wasn't. There was something *off* about the tomb. The gold, those weird gems. She suddenly wished she wasn't there at all, that she was back at the museum where she could simply orchestrate exhibits and manage advertising and personnel—the stuff she was good at. She envied Steve Powel in his office with his family pictures and trophies.

"How's your daughter doing?" she asked, thinking of the blonde girl with the sparkling red pendant necklace whose image saturated his office.

"I'm sorry?"

"The skating. Any major contests lately? I know how passionate families get about that stuff."

"Oh right, yes," he said. "No, nothing major on the calendar right now. Just the usual."

Memories floated up, distracting Deborah for a moment. *Having to sit for hours at the rink before and after school, trying to read while Ma told her instead to help stitch those loose sequins back on. Trying to shut out the blaring music as Rachel worked through routine after routine, while her coach modeled each spin, each impossible jump, until there'd been that one double axel when Rachel had twisted and fallen like a marionette with its strings cut—*

"It must be a lot of work for you," Deborah said, snapping back into the moment. "All that driving to training and competitions."

"It's what any good father would do," he said.

Just then, the van pulled up in front of the lab, and Deborah hurriedly finished the call. Moments later, all three of the people she'd just been discussing so reverently with Powel were coming toward her, dragging luggage and squinting at the sun. She'd suggested they stop at the hotel in Valladolid first, but all three had wanted to come directly to the lab.

Deborah introduced herself and immediately started talking too fast. She worried that if she stopped, one of them would ask her something she couldn't answer. Aguilar and Bowerdale emerged from the lab to shake hands. Aguilar knew Rylands, though their greeting was professional, almost brusque. Predictably, Bowerdale knew them all.

Within a few minutes, everyone except Aguilar had piled into the van and Deborah got on the road to Ek Balam. She didn't mind driving. It gave her the chance to fully check out each one of them in the rearview mirror.

Chad Rylands, the wunderkind osteologist—tenured at thirty and a full professor just a few years later—was businesslike to the point of rudeness. He wasn't interested in Deborah or anyone else for that matter. He just wanted to get to the site to "see how badly you've screwed things up." Deborah bristled and he added, "No offense," in a voice that said he didn't care one way or the other.

He looked out of the van window and said, "Someone always screws things up where bones are concerned. I spend half my life doing damage control."

He had bright blue eyes, a blue that was deep and hypnotic, like the water in the *cenote* now that the rubble and dirt had drifted to the bottom. But they were hard, unsmiling. He should have been a handsome man, Deborah thought, with his chiseled features and strong, rangy body, but there was something cold about the man that immediately put her off. He was a store window mannequin with the brain of a computer and the personality of a kitchen appliance.

The women couldn't have been more different from each other. Krista Rayburn was young and brimming with energy and enthusiasm. She had a tanned round face—pretty in an ordinary sort of way—and dirty-blonde hair that she wore in a ponytail that made her look younger still. She couldn't have been more than two or three years Deborah's junior, but she could have passed for a student, maybe even an undergraduate. She smiled a lot. When Deborah had introduced herself, Krista had flashed that sunny smile and said, "My! Aren't you tall?" Deborah said that yes, she supposed she was, and Krista said, "Awesome," patting her arm as if congratulating her on a job well done. Then she'd thanked Deborah repeatedly for the "opportunity" as if she had won the lottery, rather than being the author of the closest thing to a definitive book on Mayan environmental archaeology.

Marissa Stroud was the strangest of the lot. She was in her midfifties, Deborah guessed, and wore her graying, wavy hair long. It constantly fell in her face, but the woman would just stare through it, like it was a veil, and it was all Deborah could do not to reach forward and part it for her. Stroud was big, not fat so much as solid and powerful. She wore a long brown skirt and faded floral blouse with a tie at the throat, and clutched a stained and battered rucksack. Between her awful outfit and her brownish, uneven teeth, it was clear that here was a woman who paid absolutely no attention to her appearance or what people thought of her. Deborah wanted to like her for that, but she wasn't what you would call warm, and she had a way of staring at people that unnerved them. After meeting her, Deborah found it easy to believe the rumor of her leaving her husband and child so that she could spend more time in the field, but harder to imagine how she had gotten married in the first place. Maybe there was someone for everyone after all.

Ha! laughed her mother's voice in her head.

If Stroud looked ill-kept, her résumé was anything but. A few decades ago, experts had been able to read little of Mayan glyphs beyond proper nouns and calendars, but things had changed drastically of late, and a whole new picture of the Mayan world had begun to emerge. Stroud had been part of that revolution, and her name was all over every monograph on the subject. She was also an authority on royal regalia, European as well as Mayan, and her popular history of royal jewelry had received that rarest of accolades for academic work, a review in the *New York Times*.

She smelled odd, though Deborah couldn't place the aroma. Some herb extract, perhaps, dry and dusty with a little musk. It took over the van as soon as she got in, and though it wasn't exactly unpleasant, it made the air feel heavy, even with the AC on full blast. Rylands pulled a sour face and opened his window, but if Stroud noticed, she didn't let on.

Deborah grinned with relief as she swung the van into the site's parking lot. In person, this group of experts intimidated her less than she had expected, their strangeness somehow making them manageable. Perfect people—or people who seemed to think they were perfect, like Bowerdale—bothered her. Misfits, she could deal with. Misfits (*freak!*) she knew all about.

She stepped out into heat. It took her a second to realize that the person running toward them from the site entrance was calling her name, and another to realize it was Bowerdale's graduate student, Alice. She looked frantic.

"What is it?" said Deborah. "What's the matter?"

"Someone got into the tomb overnight," said the girl. "We just found out. They stole everything. It's all gone."

PART 2

Chapter Seventeen

Chad Rylands reminded himself that he shouldn't be surprised by their amateurism. Still, this was incompetence on a new and appalling level. He blamed the Miller woman, who had no business running a find of this scale. At least the situation wasn't as bad as he had feared. The thief had stolen the knickknacks, the jeweled trinkets on which so many archaeologists assumed everything depended. The good stuff, by which he meant the bones, was still there, apparently undisturbed.

As an osteologist, an expert on bones, Rylands did not practice what the old-school establishment considered "real" archaeology. Or as he thought of it, dirt archaeology: squatting in mud and poking about till you found something that you then misinterpreted, publishing your arbitrary speculations in some big-shot journal to the applause of all. He, by contrast, was a scientist and could get more real, hard information out of a handful of skull fragments than they could out of a square mile of digging. It was hardly surprising the dirt diggers felt threatened. They ought to. They were the dinosaurs of archaeology, lumbering about with their pickaxes, while the osteologists scurried between their feet, out-evolving them.

"Why don't you go look for your precious *artifacts*," he said to Miller, spitting out the last word like it left a nasty taste in his mouth, "and leave me to do some actual work."

They had climbed down the ladder and were standing in the tomb, everyone from the van ride squeezed in together. For a moment he had stood there, breathless, not daring to speak in case he gave away just how astounding the place was. He gazed almost hungrily at the masked skeleton seated in place and the sacrificial bones bundled into its lap, the adolescent heads set on the ground around it. It was magnificent. They should have stationed armed guards outside the moment they found the place.

Morons.

The story as he understood it was that the site staff had taken turns watching the tomb because the lab in Valladolid wasn't ready for the contents to be moved for cataloging. It was an idiot move. If there was half the gold and precious stones in there that they had bragged about in the e-mails they had sent to lure him here, they should have known that the half-starved natives would try to grab what they could. Leaving a couple of dopey graduate students armed only with a cell phone that couldn't get a signal till they climbed a hundred-foot tower at the other end of the site was beyond bush league, and he planned to let their organizers in Chicago know it.

Anyway, some idiot kid—James, his name was—had been in the tomb by himself in the middle of the night and had heard someone coming down the ladder. He had waited them out and then, when he thought the coast was clear, went back up top to make sure they didn't come back. Except, of course, that they hadn't gone. They were waiting for him when he got to the top, hit him from behind with a log, and then ransacked the tomb. The kid had seen nothing and was now sitting in the shade of a tree under the acropolis with a bandage round his head and a pathetic look. While the rest of them were down here in the tomb, James was waiting for the police, though Rylands knew what that would yield.

Miller and Bowerdale were screaming at each other while Marissa Stroud stood unnervingly still, staring fixedly at the skeleton in the throne like she was trying to talk to it. The environmentalist girl looked like her puppy had been run over, but she wasn't saying much. He wished they would all get out and let him do his job.

"You have more pictures than the ones you e-mailed me?" he said.

"What?" said Miller, who had been yelling at Bowerdale for trying to blame her for the whole fiasco.

"Pictures of the tomb," he said, frosty. "And video. I want to see exactly how everything was before you people fucked it up."

Miller took a breath.

"Yes," she said. "We tried to document everything as thoroughly as possible, though the official site photographer hasn't arrived yet."

He considered the lights inside the tomb and the power cords running up to the generator.

"Get me a video monitor and whatever you stored the data on," he said.

"Here?" she said, incredulous. "You can't just watch them at the lab?"

"No," he said simply, moving into the recessed alcove where the skeleton sat and pulling a pocket lens from his shirt. "I need it here."

She opened her mouth as if to protest, thought better of it, and nodded.

"I'll do what I can," she said.

"And I need the rest of these people out of here," he added.

"Now look here, Rylands," Bowerdale began. "You aren't any more important than the rest of us."

"You've had plenty of time to look at what was here, Bowerdale," Rylands countered evenly. Bowerdale was always a pompous ass but he was acting more defensive than usual. "Since most of what these people came to see isn't here anymore, I see no reason for them to get in the way of my work. I came to look at bones. You have lost everything else, but we still have them."

"He's right," said Miller. "But I want another detailed video shot of the tomb as it is now before anyone starts working in here."

"A good idea," Rylands acknowledged with a cool smile.

It took ten minutes to get the cameras back in and to shoot their sad little documentary. They all stood silently out of shot while Bowerdale shot the video and Miller added commentary in a pathetic voice: "This is where the fabric bundle was. This was the location of the gold rod and the red crystals."

Idiots. The only thing they'd saved was the one stone that the Mexican deputy—Aguilar—was analyzing back at the lab. Still, he had his bones, and that was what mattered. And now that he came to think about it, as they stood around like mourners at a funeral—mourners who had been cut out of the will at the last second—it was kind of funny. Actually, it was the perfect image of what had happened in archaeology, people like him moving into the light while the dirt guys, baffled, resentful but knowing they were beaten, gave ground.

They need you now, Chad, he thought. *Ain't that something?*

No trinkets to play with. No jewels. Just bones. Bones only he could read.

Chapter Eighteen

■ ■ ■ ■ ▪

It was Bowerdale who first noticed that Eustachio was missing. The elderly Mayan was invariably on site by sunup and he had never been this late. Bowerdale decided to drive over to the village himself without discussing it with anyone. He had to get away from Rylands and the tomb anyway, just to clear his head. By the time he got back, everyone would have realized the same thing, but in the intervening half hour or so, he'd get the jump on finding the guy. Maybe he knew something.

He told Miller he was going back to Valladolid, which was a mistake, because Stroud woke up and said she wanted to go back too. She had nothing to do so long as "that bone man" was in there, and she wanted to get out of the heat. She could search the pictures they had already taken for glyphs that might help identify the body in the tomb.

Once they'd climbed back up the ladder and started for the van, James—the idiot who had let all this happen—said he wanted a ride back as well so he could lie down.

"You'll still be stupid when you wake up, you know," Bowerdale snarled, but the kid came along anyway.

So what should have been a half-hour trip tripled. He dropped James off at the dorm beside the lab, gave Stroud a cursory tour and set her up with a computer stuffed with images from the new site. When he had spent enough time sauntering leisurely around the lab that Aguilar told him to get out from under his feet, he bolted back to the van and hit the road.

Bowerdale's Spanish was so-so and he had only a few words of Yucatekan, but he could tell the village was already buzzing with the news. He asked for Eustachio, but his son—a fat, lazy-looking guy called Juan—kept dodging. Didn't know where he was. Hadn't seen him leave. Assumed he was at the site. In fact, said Juan, not quite looking at him, he probably was. It was a big place.

"Isn't that his bicycle?" said Bowerdale.

Juan stared stupidly at it like he'd never seen it before, and shrugged. He guessed so.

"So an old man with a limp walked over to the site?" said Bowerdale.

"Guess so," said Juan, his eyes flashing over to his wife. She was too old to be pretty exactly, but she had a stillness and thoughtfulness Bowerdale liked. Maybe later he could find a local girl to bring back to his hotel.

"You seen him?" he asked her, in English.

"*No hablo ingles,*" she lied, her eyes returning to the pot she was stirring.

"Where's your motorbike, Juan?" he said, splaying his arm and miming revving the throttle with his right fist. "Your *moto-cicleta*. That big black thing you have."

Juan lied fluently, but too fast. Among the stream of Spanish, Bowerdale caught "*taller de reparación*."

"Oh, it's in the shop," he said, smiling. "And where's that?"

Another half glance flicked toward his wife, then Juan told him it was in Valladolid. They couldn't fix it in the village. It needed parts.

"Yeah?" said Bowerdale. "What's up with it? Clutch? Carburetor? Cam cover gasket?"

Juan smiled and shrugged. He just rode it, he said. He didn't know how it worked.

"I guess you can explain all this to the police," said Bowerdale. "*La policia*, yeah?"

Juan's smile flickered, then held.

Bowerdale gestured to a cabana across the street. "That where he sleeps?"

Juan nodded.

Bowerdale walked over to the dirt-floored structure and peered inside. The old man's son seemed happy to let him look, so Bowerdale didn't bother. He took a couple of steps back toward Juan and his wife, giving them one last look. He thought she smiled slightly, before going back inside. Now Bowerdale had Juan to himself. He met the man's eyes and raised a crooked finger, beckoning. The Mayan hesitated, glancing behind him, then crossed the street to where Bowerdale stood.

"You find out where your father went," said Bowerdale. "Then you let me know, OK?"

As he spoke, he plucked out his wallet and unfolded several hundred-dollar bills. Juan glanced around nervously, but his eyes were hungry, and he took the money, pocketing it quickly.

"Good man," said Bowerdale.

He got back in the van and drove down to Valladolid, but before he reached the lab his cell phone rang. It was Miller.

"Where the hell are you?" she demanded. "I've been calling for an hour."

"Couldn't get a signal," he said.

"I thought you were in Valladolid?"

"I had to take the van in," he said. "The brakes needed adjusting. Maybe new pads."

"They seemed fine to me."

"I only noticed on the road back."

"It doesn't matter," she said, steamrolling him—luckily. "You need to get back here. Rylands has found something."

She hung up, and Bowerdale threw the phone onto the passenger seat feeling caught out and no further forward.

Chapter Nineteen
■ ■ ■ ■ ■

"It's a stingray spine," said Krista Rayburn. "Where did you find it?"

"On the floor by the door," said Rylands, his eyes on the video monitor.

Krista didn't much like Rylands yet, which bothered her. She was, she thought, usually so accepting of other people, liking them for the idiosyncrasies others found off-putting, but the man was more than just rude. He was hostile, and Krista, who was unused to not being liked, felt disoriented.

Everyone assumed that being attractive made life easy. Not, Krista thought, in academia. She had realized some time ago that compliments on her appearance and youth were slightly backhanded, that they implied that she wasn't serious or smart enough. Perhaps, she sometimes thought, if she was meaner, harder, quicker to rub her achievements in people's faces, life would be easier. But then she would be a different person, one she didn't wish to become.

"It's not unusual to find stingray spines at a royal burial site even a long way from the sea," she said. "The Maya imported the spines from the coastal regions and they had great ritual significance because they were used in bloodletting rites."

She grimaced playfully, guessing that they would know how the spines were used. They were passed through parts of the body, the blood being caught on fabric or paper or in some kind of vessel, and offered to the gods. Sometimes thorns were used, fastened to string or rope and threaded through the tongue of the self-sacrificer, but stingray spines were particularly special.

"The barbs mean that you can't go back once you start," she said. "They have to go all the way through. Men usually put them through their penises. I imagine it must have been very painful."

Martin Bowerdale raised his eyebrows at what he clearly took to be an understatement, but Rylands just gave her a withering stare.

"You done with the lecture?" he snapped. "We know what they were used for. We also know that they are usually found in the groin area of the body because they were carried in some kind of pouch there. And there is one like that on the body, see?"

He trained the beam of his flashlight inside the coffin with one hand and used the pencil in his other hand to indicate a slender spine down there among the bones and dust.

"But the one I found over there," he said, nodding toward the door, "is different."

He gently raised the second spine for their inspection. It was much more polished, and the difference between the two was instantly visible.

Krista, who had flushed at his rebuke, went quiet and stared at the spine, her eyes prickling.

"But the site has been tainted," said Deborah Miller. It clearly pained her to say it, so Krista managed an encouraging smile to the project leader. "Maybe whoever stole the other artifacts dropped it."

"Fished it out of the groin of the skeleton," said Rylands, "but didn't bother to get the other one that is still there or disturb the bone bundle that was on top of them, and then dropped it on the way out? No."

"Was it on the video we shot when we first opened the tomb?"

"Not on the floor, no," said Rylands. "But it was...*here*."

He pointed at the video monitor to a bundle, the one that had disappeared. It had contained, they said, a handful of strange red stones, a carved and polished length of wood, a ring, and a gold rod with a dove on the end, though in the video the bundle was still rolled up, about eighteen inches long and tied with bright thread. The fabric had moldered, though not as badly as Krista would have expected given the tomb's age, and you could see a dozen or so small ivory-colored objects showing through the bundle: bones. Lying with them, poking out through the decayed fabric was a black, needlelike spine.

"So the thief took the bundle and the spine fell out," said Bowerdale. "The fabric was shot and it fell apart when he picked it up. So?"

Rylands had fast-forwarded to footage of Bowerdale unwrapping the bundle. One of the red stones fell out and the light fluctuated as they searched for it.

"Have you found any of those small bones as well?" said Deborah Miller.

Krista watched Deborah Miller wince at the video, the appearance of amateurism as Bowerdale fumbled for the dropped gemstone. She understood why Miller had made the decision to lock the site down till the lab was ready to bring everything in. The thought that it had, in fact, been the wrong decision—a *disastrous* decision—pained her for the other woman.

"Two," said Rylands. "Also close to the door. There may be others that fell into the *cenote* as the thief went up the ladder."

"And?" said Bowerdale, who was getting impatient.

"And that's odd," said Rylands. "A thief breaks in and steals gold and gems. That makes sense. But why take a bundle of bones, particularly if you aren't going to take the main skeleton?"

"Are you sure the two bones you found aren't from the main skeleton?" said Krista, pushing back into the conversation.

"Of course I'm sure," said Rylands, dismissive.

"Why?" said Krista.

"Look at them," he said, nodding to where he had set them beside the monitor. "Look at the pictures. They are totally different."

She had to admit he was right. The small bones from the bundle were paler than the royal skeleton.

"Could they have been better preserved by the wrapping?" she ventured.

He shook his head.

"Fabric isn't my area," he said, "but I'd say that the bundle shouldn't be there at all."

"What do you mean?" asked Bowerdale. They were all staring at the video monitor as the pictures scrolled across the screen.

"I mean that the bones look different from the main skeleton for the same reason that the fabric is still there: we're looking at two internments maybe a thousand years apart."

"They reopened the tomb for another burial," said Deborah to herself. "But there's only one corpse. Did they remove the older one?"

"I'll have to do some tests," said Rylands, "but I'm almost sure they didn't. The skeleton we have is probably late pre-Classic, contemporary with the construction of the structure. They left it there when the tomb was reopened, which was long after the present acropolis was built on top of it."

"So where's the second body?" said Krista. "Or are those animal bones? Something small, like a monkey or..."

"Oh no," said Rylands, and he was smiling now. "The bones are human. It's premature to guess, but I'd say that the tomb was reopened—which would have been a huge undertaking—relatively recently. No second skeleton was buried. Only this bundle."

"Containing?" Krista pressed the point, but she didn't like how much Rylands was enjoying this. Something was coming.

"Containing a stingray spine, which—as we all know," he replied with a pointed look at her, "is one of the supreme Mayan symbols of self-sacrifice; and a gold ring that you can just see there, which looks like it has a design on it. Intricate. Maybe heraldic."

"Heraldic?" said Krista. "Like a class ring or something?"

"Maybe," said Rylands. "Not my field. Looks like a coat of arms."

"Not Mayan," said Deborah Miller.

"Not ancient Mayan," said Rylands. "If it's postconquest, though, who knows? It could be Spanish. But the ring isn't the interesting part. The bones are the interesting part. They always are. The ring is on a finger."

"And?" said Krista, pressing the point. She was tense, and a part of her didn't want to hear the answer.

"You can't really get a sense of scale from the video," said Rylands, "but it's clear from the bone piece that was left behind. The ring finger is very small. Someone opened this tomb long after it was first sealed up, and among the things they put inside it was the hand of a child."

Chapter Twenty
■ ■ ■ ■ ■

"How recently was the hand put in the tomb?" asked Deborah.

Rylands had spent the rest of the afternoon carefully dismantling the skeleton while the rest of them had packed up their equipment and returned to Valladolid for the night. Deborah had been itching to ask the question and cornered him in the lab the moment he got in.

"I can't say without further tests, some of which are going to have to be done elsewhere," he answered, eying Bowerdale, who had just appeared in the doorway. "We don't have the equipment. We might want to consider DNA, even carbon dating. That will take time and money."

"All this may be a bit moot, wouldn't you say?" said Bowerdale, his voice booming.

"What do you mean?" Deborah asked.

"I mean what you think I mean," said Bowerdale. He used his bulk to shield them from anyone else who might be listening, and his voice dropped. "This may well be a police matter."

"No chance," whispered Rylands.

"The decay is too extreme for this to be a recent crime," said Deborah.

"Define *recent*," said Bowerdale. "This didn't happen a few days or weeks ago, but I'm used to seeing bones that are a thousand years old, and all I can tell you for sure is that these ain't them. Right, Rylands?"

Rylands looked away, not liking the option, then nodded.

"They may be a few hundred years old," he said, "or a few months. Until we know what sort of shape they were in when they were placed there and have a better sense of the conditions for preservation inside the tomb, we can't say more than that. The tomb is late pre-Classic, maybe 200 CE. One set of bones are contemporary with that date, the others are a lot later."

"Thus spake the bone man," said Bowerdale. "So until we have a clearer idea of just *how much* later that hand is," he went on, "I don't know if we are looking at an archaeological site or a crime scene."

"I have to contact the local police," said Deborah, thinking aloud.

"That's not what I'm saying," said Bowerdale. "Talk to the police and the site is going to be shut down for weeks, maybe longer. They will screw everything up. All these people will have to go home, and I wouldn't bet on you being able to get them back. In the meantime, the trail of whoever took the artifacts from the tomb will go as cold as anything in this godforsaken country ever gets, and you'll never see the contents of that tomb again. Ever."

"So what would you have me do?" said Deborah. She hated asking for his advice but in this case felt like she needed it.

"Sit on it," said Bowerdale. "Tell nobody anything. And I mean, *anything*. Don't let Aguilar e-mail his buddies with fun facts about bundles of hand bones. Don't talk to the press or the cops. Alert them to a theft at the site, by all means, get them looking for the artifacts, but say nothing about those bones."

"I don't have a choice," said Deborah.

"You're the field director," said Rylands, fixing her with his deep-blue eyes. "You always have a choice."

He got up suddenly and left the room, and after a long, watchful silence, Bowerdale did the same. Deborah stood at the window and watched the traffic in the street below, wishing she knew what to do next.

Child sacrifice was well known among the ancient Maya, perhaps because they were considered purer than adults, perhaps because they were considered expendable—particularly if they were orphans or slaves taken after battles. Dismemberment was also well known, but it was usually heads that were cut off, the skulls flayed and buried together under important buildings, like those placed beside the royal skeleton they had found. Deborah could think of no instance in which a hand had been found in circumstances like these. And even without Rylands's professional hunches, she had known there was something wrong about that tomb from the first moment they went in. It was and was not a pre-Classic burial.

Deborah sighed, but she really did not have a choice: choose not to pursue the possible murder of a child for fear of disrupting the already disrupted dig?

Please.

She had been more than disappointed about the theft, overwhelmed by a sense of colossal failure, but this was different, was, in fact, almost like reaching clear air after a storm. It lifted her above her misery and humiliation and gave her a sudden clarity.

The hand of a child.

It had been placed there, it seemed, long after human sacrifice had vanished from the Mayan way of life. She thanked God she had no choice. What kind of person would have? Deborah didn't know if she would ever have children, didn't feel especially comfortable with even her sister's kids. Yet she remembered what it was to be one, remembered the vulnerability, the powerlessness (*freak!*), the sense of being at war with even her own mother, and she felt an unexpected but powerful surge of pity for the child whose hand had been placed in the tomb. She pulled out her phone, looked at it for a moment, and dialed 065. When the switchboard operator answered, she asked for the police.

Chapter Twenty-One

Alice was surprised to find that she wished the new people had never come. She had been looking forward to seeing some fresh faces, but now that they were here she wished she had the jungle ruins to herself again, even if they freaked her out from time to time. Stroud was a sideshow freak, Rylands was a card-carrying asshole, and Krista Rayburn acted like she was doing cereal adds on TV.

The theft had changed everything, of course. A few hours ago, they looked like they were en route to the cover of *Newsweek*. Now? Who the hell knew. They'd brought in these experts who—apart from Rylands—now had nothing to do, and Miller had called the cops about the missing kid bones, so the site was locked down. There was nothing to do but sit around in the blazing heat, waiting for the cops to tell them they could go back to the dorm. And tomorrow? More of the same. Maybe she should just leave, go to the beach or something.

James was more pathetic than ever. He clearly felt stupid for being the one who had got himself thumped, and was moping about. She had sat with him for a while, but he didn't want to talk, and at one point she thought he was actually crying. Well, if he thought she was going to play mommy until he felt all better, he had another thing coming.

She had climbed the rounded terraces of the oval palace, which was the southernmost major structure on the site, and sat at the top, watching the iguanas in the grass and smoking. Once in a while she saw some of the cops wandering about, but otherwise the place was deserted.

The police were a weird mixture, a couple of young, beefy guys in blue fatigue pants and white shirts toting honest-to-God machine guns, a couple in rumpled military dress uniforms with peaked caps, and one guy in a suit. He did all the talking, though there wasn't much of that. Alice had given her statement, not that there was much to say, and they had waved her away but told her not to leave. So here she was, getting sunburned and watching lizards. Quality time.

She saw the new guy come walking in past the great four-way triangular arch cut from blocks of honey-colored stone. He was wearing khaki pants and a white Oxford shirt and carrying a duffel bag over his shoulder. Even at this distance you could tell he was buff. He had dark, wavy hair and a slight tan. He paused at the arch, climbing the wide steps at its base to get a better look around, then he was walking again. He was halfway across the central court area when he saw her. He hesitated and then raised a hand.

"Hello," he called. "Are you with the dig?"

He had an accent. A Brit, perhaps, or an Aussie. Alice liked Aussies. She had known a few exchange students from Melbourne back in school: serious party guys. She raised a nonchalant hand and nodded. She sure as hell wasn't going to shout. He seemed to think about it for a second and then started climbing up. It was a hard climb, like all these damned pyramids, but he managed them with athletic ease.

"Hold it," she called as he reached the halfway point. "I'll come down."

She stubbed out her cigarette and navigated the stairs carefully, trying not to look too cautious. The guy was cute, and it wasn't like she had anything better to do than try to make a good impression.

"Looks like I'm going to have to work on my mountain goat skills," he said, as she got down. "Hi. I'm the cameraman. Nick Reese."

"Alice," she said simply, taking his hand and shaking it once. "I'm a graduate student working with Dr. Bowerdale, the surveyor. You probably know him."

"Bowerdale," said the man. "Right. Yeah."

He had brown eyes and a bit of stubbly shadow around his mouth and jawline, kind of like David Beckham wearing his "scruffy" look. Handsome but not clean-cut. She liked that.

"You'll be wanting to talk to Deborah," she said, adding, "Miss Miller," when he looked uncertain. "I'll take you to her."

"Brilliant," he said. "Thanks. Is it always this hot?"

"Always," she said. "I'd say you get used to it, but you don't. It sucks, pretty much."

"Indeed."

"You might want to get yourself some shorts," she said.

"I don't really do shorts," he replied, smiling.

"You're a Brit?"

"Guilty as charged. What gave it away, the accent or the aversion to shorts?"

She laughed. The day was looking up.

They walked past the ball court and she watched him scanning the site.

"Impressive," he said.

"Yeah," she agreed, as if realizing it for the first time. "It's pretty cool, I guess."

"Old news to you, no doubt," he said. "But this new find sounds extraordinary. Is it all Miss Miller says it is?"

Alice snorted disparagingly.

"Well, it *was*," she said.

"What do you mean?"

He was still smiling, but he looked suddenly different, careful somehow. Wary.

"Oh you won't have heard yet," said Alice, enjoying the knowledge. "Yeah, we found this new tomb. Pre-Classic. Super old. Full of all kinds of cool stuff."

"And?"

There it was again, an urgency the smile couldn't quite hide.

"It got robbed," she said, smirking.

"*What?*"

He had stopped on the grass and was now quite still, staring at her. Suddenly, he seemed not just well-built, but physically intimidating. His eyes were so cold that it seemed ridiculous that they'd been bantering just moments before. Alice took a step back.

"Robbed," she repeated, her tone less jokey now. "Someone got in and lifted a bunch of stuff last night."

"Everything?"

"Not the bones or the grave goods," she said, "but they took the jewels. And there was this bundle of bones that they say is a kid's hand, and that was taken too, so the cops are here, but…"

She stopped talking and watched open-mouthed with surprise as he turned his back on her and walked away fast and with purpose, as if he knew exactly where he was going. He was heading for the acropolis.

So much for a hot new boy toy, she thought. She'd never seen anyone change in manner quite as fast as the photographer had the minute he sloughed off that friendly smile.

She started trotting after him, feeling her interest mount. Alice's first real boyfriend had been capable of transformations like that—though they usually happened right before he started hitting her. She didn't want to end up in another relationship like that one. But there was no denying the guy was hot.

Chapter Twenty-Two

■ ■ ■ ■ ■

Deborah watched the plainclothes cop from Merida. He let the captain with his braided cap strut about, ordering the other uniforms around, but he was in charge of the actual investigation, and he moved with a careful, professional slowness. He spent an hour in the tomb, another in front of the video monitor studying the footage of what had been there before the break-in, and two more listening to their statements. Meanwhile, he had one officer take measurements of the tomb entrance: they were going to put up a lockable steel door.

"For how long?" Deborah had asked in Spanish.

The detective tipped his head on one side and frowned, but he wasn't really considering the question.

"Until we know what we are investigating," he replied in English. He was about her age, more Latino than Mayan, and crisply professional, though he wore some kind of fragrant oil in his curly black hair. "If it's a murder, the tomb will stay closed for some time. Weeks, perhaps. I cannot say yet. Our resources are limited. We may need your help."

"How?"

"You have a laboratory in Valladolid. I may want to send one of my people there. Is that convenient?"

"Sure," said Deborah. "What about the dig?"

"You can excavate in other parts of the site," he said, shaping a slightly apologetic smile but offering no room for negotiation.

"And the stolen grave goods," she said. "You'll look for them?"

"Of course," he answered, "but the homicide—if it is one— will be the priority. We can talk to—what do you call the people who sell stolen goods?"

"A fence?"

"A fence, *si*," he said, smiling. "But…" He shrugged.

"You can't just start a search?" she asked, knowing she sounded desperate and stupid.

"Where?" he replied, smiling not unkindly. "Look around you, Miss Miller. The Yucatan is isolated villages and small towns separated by miles of jungle. There are paths that only the local people know, and many ancient Mayan structures so remote that no one but the snakes and vultures know them. You know the city of Uxmal?"

"Of course," said Deborah. Uxmal was the great Mayan site of the Puuc region south of Merida, a vast complex of imposing buildings, carved stonework, and colossal pyramids. According to legend, one of them, the Pyramid of the Magician, had been built overnight by the dwarf son of a witch from nearby Kabah. Deborah had hoped to see it before she left, but now, who knew what the next day would bring.

"It has been there for a thousand years," he said. "But it was ignored by the Spanish after the conquest and forgotten by all but the locals until archaeologists 'rediscovered' the site a hundred and seventy years ago. It is easy to lose things here. And when they are lost, they stay lost for hundreds of years."

"But our things haven't been lost," said Deborah. "They have been stolen."

"True," said the policeman, smiling, "but that difference may be...unhelpful. I do not know how well you know the local people, Miss Miller, but I can assure you that they know how to keep secrets to themselves, sometimes for centuries. After all, Uxmal was not truly lost either," he said, looking down to the notebook in which he had been writing. "The Maya always knew where it was."

The conversation over, Deborah walked up toward the acropolis figuring she could find a quiet spot somewhere in the central compound where she could think and get away from the questions and accusatory looks. She replayed the events in her head. If they'd just moved the artifacts to the lab to get them into safekeeping, none of this would have happened.

Deborah sighed. Figuring she may as well use the time, she rewatched the recording of the grave goods on her laptop. When she got to the close-up of the bundle that had turned out to be the child's bones, she found the moment that gave her the best look at the ring and paused the playback.

She opened her editing software and transferred the image to a new window. It was digital video, so the image degeneration was minimal even when she enlarged it to fill the screen. The ring was quite clear: yellow metal and slim, like a signet ring with what looked like a seal or crest on the boss. It was diamond shaped and intricately molded into four quadrants, the upper right and lower left marked with tiny circles, while the other two sections were scored with what looked like a checkerboard. Beneath the diamond was an elliptical shape like an eye. It didn't look like any Mayan symbol she had ever seen. It looked, as Rylands had said, like a European coat of arms, albeit an unusual one.

An idea struck her. She ran quickly over to the structure with the cell phone tower and climbed up to the top without stopping. She activated her web browser and started looking for anything on heraldry. Commercial sites devoted to tracking family crests and selling versions of them in badges, posters, and rings came up first. There was a function to search alphabetically by family name, but she could find no provision to search by the elements of the coat of arms itself.

She tried other search terms: "coats of arms," "family crest," "shields," "escutcheons." Most of the sites that came up were similarly searchable by name only, but then she found one that showed thumbnails of the coats of arms and the names associated with them. It was divided by country. She chose Spain: perhaps the ring had belonged to someone who had come with the colonists. She suspected Rylands was right, and that the hand buried with the ring had not belonged to a Mayan child interred a thousand years ago.

There were pages of Spanish crests: beautifully ornate shields adorned with castles and lions, crowns, birds, and all manner of weapons and symbols like fleurs-de-lis, pages and pages of them. Her eyes flickered as she processed the thumbnails, eight to a line, twenty lines to a page. Patiently, she scrolled through the whole website.

It was actually quick work, because nothing looked close to the design on the ring. In fifteen minutes she had seen all the Spanish emblems the site had to offer, and come up empty. She knew that the search was far from exhaustive, that there would be shields not recorded there, but it felt like progress. She began on the German coats of arms.

The German shields didn't look—to her untrained eye—significantly different from the Spanish, and there were at least as many. She waded through them, page by page, no longer dazzled by their drama and whimsy, now seeing only that they were not what she was looking for.

"Hey!" called a voice from below.

She looked down and saw a man she didn't recognize and Alice trailing behind him. He was well built, even athletic, and looked furious.

Deborah frowned and began the slow climb down the tower without answering. He started shouting before she reached the bottom.

"You want to tell me what the bloody hell is going on here?" he yelled.

Deborah said nothing till she reached the ground, steeling herself to remain calm.

"I'm sorry," she said politely. "You are?"

"He's the photographer," Alice said. "Nick. From England."

"OK, Nick from England," said Deborah. "What's your problem?"

"My problem," he said, "is that I just flew across the Atlantic to photograph something that isn't here, and I'd like to know what you are going to do about it."

"Look," she said. "I'm sorry you've had a wasted journey, but I've got a lot on my mind right now. I suggest you go get settled in at the hotel in Valladolid. We're all going to be leaving soon anyway."

He seemed to see her exhaustion and something of his anger drained.

"Can you just tell me what happened?" he said.

Deborah sighed, blowing out the air like a diver steeling herself on a high board.

"Walk with me," she said.

He nodded, and Alice piped up. "I'll come too."

"No," said Deborah. She caught the edge in her voice and tried to soften it, but it was too late. "They could use a hand loading the gear," she said.

Alice pouted and shrugged in that way she had that was something between *like I care* and *up yours*. Then she snapped her playful grin on. "Bye, Nick," she said.

"Oh. Right," said the Brit. "Bye."

Deborah began walking back toward the Twins.

"Seems like you've made a friend," she said.

He nodded dismissively. "So," he said. "This theft. The girl said something about a child's hand?"

Deborah told him the story as they walked, staring straight ahead, recounting it all like it was something she had read. She never looked at him, and when she got to the end, she just kept walking in silence, as if he wasn't there.

"Sounds like you've had a rough couple of days," he said.

She wasn't sure why he was suddenly trying to be nice, but she thought she'd take it. The last friendly word she'd gotten lately was from Adelita.

"You could say that," she said.

"Hence my saying it," he said. His smile was at least three parts apology. She noticed that the Brit was handsome, tall, and powerful-looking in ways archaeologists and photographers generally weren't. She wasn't in the least interested—her problems were just too big—but she could see why Alice had been tailing him.

She blew the air out of her lungs again, throwing her head back and shutting her eyes again. When she looked at him again, he was turned slightly away and staring into the trees, as if on alert for something.

"Sorry," she said. "I really don't know what happens next. It doesn't help that this is the first real dig I've been in charge of, and Bowerdale—Martin Bowerdale—clearly thinks I've screwed everything up royally."

"How could someone breaking in and stealing stuff be your fault?" he said.

"That's what I said, but...I don't know. I feel—"

She stopped herself. She didn't know this guy. She wasn't about to tell him what she felt.

He nodded, as if he already knew.

"I could use a drink," he said. "I'm guessing you could too. What do you say, after we get back, you point me in the direction of some sleazy neighborhood watering hole and...?"

"I don't think so," said Deborah. "Thanks, but I don't really feel like a drink tonight."

"Then you can watch me have one," he said, undaunted. "Come on."

"I actually have a room in the village so I'm not even staying in town. And the others will be better company. Alice, for one..."

"Ah yes," he said. "Miss Alice. I can tell her all about the nineteen eighties. As an archaeologist, she'll love that."

Deborah laughed in spite of herself.

"She probably will at that," she said. "If she's interested in conversation."

"I'm sure she's a vestal virgin," said the Englishman, straight-faced. "So what do you say? A wee dram to welcome me to the team?"

"No, I'm sorry," she said. "I have too much to do."

He pulled a pained face.

"Another time, perhaps," he said.

"Perhaps," she replied, turning and walking quickly away before she could change her mind.

Chapter Twenty-Three
■ ■ ■ ■ ■

The dream was always the same. He was riding up front in a captured military truck abandoned by the Dutch UN peacekeepers outside Srebenica. Dimitri—so he now called himself—remembered the day, knew what had happened that day in Bosnia, but the dream was different, loaded with dread and a sense of impending disaster that he had not felt at the time. He had been smoking, and one of the guys had been recounting what Mladic had said to him that morning before they had gone to the school in Konjevič Polje. They had been joking and sharing a flask of vodka that one of the regular army soldiers had given him. Dimitri and his men were Scorpion paramilitaries, locals called Chetniks.

By the time the truck had reached the school, the separation of the men from the women and children had already happened, so Dimitri didn't see much of it. Not there, anyway. He had seen it before, particularly in Potocari, and he had grown immune to the pleading and crying. But in the dream the women and children were still there, following the truck somehow, visible in the side-view mirrors when he looked back, a column of them, somehow keeping pace with the truck no matter how fast they drove.

When they got out into the fields, they pulled over, and it was Dimitri's job to open up the back of the truck and get the men out. Some of them were blindfolded and had to be helped down, others had their hands lashed behind their backs. Few of them had any shoes or anything else they could use as a weapon. It was weirdly quiet, and, for the most part, they all did what they were told. Mostly the men ranged from their late teens to their sixties, though there were a few old men and boys among them too. Dimitri didn't know why and didn't ask. Clearly they'd pissed someone off.

They had stayed quiet as they walked single file to the ditch between the field and the woods, and the air was damp and full of the scent of the wet grass and trees, and that scent filled the dream too. A hundred yards or so away were the women and children, all silent and watching, always maintaining the exact same distance and never blinking. In reality, of course, they hadn't been there. That, like the raw and dragging horror, was just in the dream.

Then the shooting started and the men began dropping. It had been almost comically undramatic. Dimitri was a good shot and had rarely needed more than one round per person. When the truck was empty, others had come, and Dimitri had helped out with the lining up of the prisoners and the shooting. He lost track of how many times he changed the magazine in his assault rifle. And that was how it had been: methodical, businesslike.

There had been some laughter and some hysterics, but for the most part it was just a job, like carrying the crates of bottles that had been his first wage back in the crappy little Belgrade bar his uncle had owned before the war.

In the dream, he went about the shooting itself with the same focused composure he'd managed on the actual day, but there was that nagging sense of darkness and fear underneath, though he couldn't stop what he was doing and didn't see why he should. It came from the presence of the women and children who had no business being in the dream at all. They had started getting closer once the shooting started, and as they inched across the field to the road where the trucks were parked, he became surer that his gun wouldn't work on them. He didn't know why, but he was certain, so they had to finish up and get out before the women and children reached them. If they didn't, they'd be as defenseless as the men they were routinely executing. It made no sense, but he felt a power in them that he would not be able to stand against if they reached him. He had to finish up the shooting and move on quickly.

But the job wouldn't end. Just as they finished dealing with the contents of one truck, another would arrive, and the colonel would start handing out fresh ammunition and telling them to get on with it. Dimitri warned them about the women in the field, but it was like no one else could see them, and after a while he had tried shooting at them to drive them back. For a moment it looked like it was working, but they came on anyway, unaffected by his bullets as he had known they would be.

It was then, always then, as the children and their mothers started to hedge him about so that he could no longer aim his weapon, their eyes locked on him as he tried to find a way back to the truck, that he woke up, sweating, his heart racing.

This time his phone was ringing too.

He took the call and made some notes, then hung up. It had been a mistake not to get a room with air-conditioning. He had never experienced heat like it, not at night anyhow, and with the memory of the dream still only just under the surface, he doubted he would get back to sleep. He sat on the edge of the bed and looked through his phone messages and the notes he had made from previous calls.

People were queuing up now, and that made him smile, even if some of them were probably terrorists. To Dimitri, who had never been a religious or nationalist zealot, it was all about money. If the goods were anything like he was told, he was about to make a fortune. Even if they weren't quite as billed, or if he sold only information rather than the items themselves, he was looking at a shitload of money by any standards. Where it came from, he didn't care. Hell, he'd sell to the Americans if they'd pay him enough, and they might, if only to keep the goods from falling into unwanted hands.

Dimitri smirked at the thought of so many eager buyers and flipped open a folder full of data printouts: phonon and photon transmission, particle vibration measured in terms of frequency and amplitude tied to temperature increase, and, most importantly, scattering rates estimated from phonon-phonon interactions and lattice imperfections. The science meant little to him, but he knew the implications for power and cooling cycles, and it wasn't surprising that they had piqued a lot of curiosity. Sure they might be duds, useless for the purpose he was selling, but there was enough in those sheets of paper to have the price doubling by the moment, and there was something marvelous about their recurring question: *How do we know you haven't faked the data?* Because he could no more fake this shit than go to the fucking moon. All he had to do now was get hold of the goods before anyone else got wind of where they were, and he would get spectacularly rich. It seemed like the best way to do that was to eliminate the middleman and just help himself; no more dealing with that weasel Clements and his archaeologist pal. The archaeologist—Bowerdale, his name was—might still prove useful, but why pay someone to get what he could take for himself?

He lay back on the cheap pillow, grinning to himself, and popped out a cigarette from the pack on the nightstand. He considered trying to go back to sleep, but even imagining his massive success wouldn't keep the dreams at bay. He opted to smoke instead, and thought about the cherry-red Enzo Ferrari that would be the first thing he'd buy when the deal went down. Then he cleaned and oiled his guns and shuffled through the TV stations till he found Bugs Bunny cartoons dubbed into Spanish. He didn't speak much, but they were still pretty good. The voices were funny, and you could get the gist.

At dawn he would make for Ek Balam. It would be a good day.

Chapter Twenty-Four
■ ■ ■ ▪ ▫

The motorbike had done well. Better than Eustachio had expected. It was noisy and slow, but in the black Yucatan night, slow was good. There were too many potholes and the headlamp was set high so the road right in front of him was dark. One bad bump and the bike would throw him. Still, he was nearly there.

Eustachio knew he would have been missed, knew also that he would probably be arrested as soon as he returned to the village. He had known as much before he left, and that was OK. He would tell them nothing, would deny having touched the contents of the tomb, would say he couldn't imagine where they were now and—eventually—they would have to let him go. Anyone could have taken the grave offerings. He even had a cousin near Uxmal who would swear he had spent the night with him, that he had been visiting family because there was nothing for him to do on site till the new find had been dealt with. He would say that over and over until the authorities had to produce real evidence or release him. It might take a while, and Eustachio knew what kind of treatment he might get from the police, but that didn't matter.

The motorbike reached the turnoff to the village; he kept going toward the site. The moon was down, which was all to the good. Eustachio got off the bike a couple of hundred yards short of the parking lot and pushed it into the underbrush, watching his feet for snakes. He had ridden barefoot all the way with no difficulties, except when he had stopped for gas outside Valladolid and stepped on a shard of glass from a beer bottle. It had bled a little, and though he had wrapped it in leaves from the *chakaj* tree, it stung when he put weight on it, and it made his gait even more shambling and tortuous than usual.

With the bike stowed, he unsheathed the machete that was strapped to the pannier, checked the stars to get his bearings, and pushed cautiously into the site. There would be no one around at this time. The police didn't have the manpower to guard the dig, particularly if there was nothing worth guarding anymore. But he wasn't listening for people. He wouldn't hear a snake until it was close enough to strike, but he might hear other animals. There were peccaries in these woods—what his ancestors called *kitam*—and he didn't like the idea of stumbling on a big one without his rifle.

Years ago he had seen a neighbor gored by one as it ran past him. Well, not so much gored as nicked with its tusks. They had cornered the animal in a tangle of *k'u'che'* trees, and it had rushed them, spotting an opening between Eustachio and Fresco. Eustachio had been a young man then, with two good legs. He had dived clear of the boar, but Fresco was slower. He had stepped aside, but the boar had turned her head as she charged past and bitten Fresco's thigh, opening a terrible wound. The blood sprayed far enough to splash Eustachio across his face, though he was ten feet away. Fresco had screamed, more in fear than in pain. With the boar vanished into the jungle, Eustachio had used his shirt to stop the bleeding. He had tried dragging Fresco back to the village, but it took too long, and he'd had to leave him while he ran back for help. By the time they had gotten back to him, Fresco was unconscious and had lost a lot of blood. They built a fire, heated a roasting spit in the center, and cauterized the wound, but even the searing of his flesh did not bring him round. He died an hour later.

Without a doctor or medical supplies, with the hospital miles away and only one truck in the village, there was nothing he could have done. But Eustachio still remembered the look in Fresco's eyes after the peccary had gone, when he saw his blood on Eustachio's face, and it still knotted his guts with a sense of failure. He remembered, and sometimes that was all you could do. The past was past, but he had learned early that it was important to remember.

He kept the machete held in front of him as he walked. Something large moved off to his left, but it was light and careful, probably a *keh* deer. Some said jaguar still lived in the jungle scrub, but Eustachio hadn't heard or seen sign of them for almost a decade. They had been hunted into the true jungle of the highlands, which was probably just as well. The peccaries and deer were almost gone from the woods now, so there was nothing for the hunter to prey upon. It saddened Eustachio. Ek Balam was named for the jaguar, but now those creatures were gone, lost like the people who had lived here.

One more thing to enshrine in memory, he thought. *Did the beasts of the forest feel loss? Did the jaguar weep for its lot, its shrinking world, its steady displacement from the center of things?* He couldn't say.

He moved easily through the brush despite his limp, emerging beside the sheds where they kept the wheelbarrows and inexpensive hand tools, and from there he was on a well-worn trail that traced its way into the central court. He passed behind Structure 2, where he had supervised the building of the cell phone tower, and around the acropolis. Even in the darkness he could see the great hell-mouth doorway of the Zac Na, and he felt sure his forefathers approved of what he was doing. He bowed in acknowledgement and moved round the back to where the new *cenote* had opened up, and the new tomb.

Eustachio took the small, inadequate flashlight from his pocket. In its small patch of light, he could see that the ground around the edge of the *cenote* had been beaten smooth with foot traffic and the ladder had been replaced by a two-stage ramp, anchored on joists driven into the earthen walls. He considered the work with a critical eye. There was a heavy metal door at the mouth of the tomb, but—and this sounded the first note of unease he had felt since the last time he had been here—it was open.

Eustachio stood there looking down at the deep shadow of the doorway for a long minute, listening to the night. The birds and bats had discovered the *cenote* and had already colonized it. By day it would be filled with their calls. Now there was only the shifting and rustling of feathers, strangely amplified by the sinkhole. He shone the flashlight on the door and the yellowish glow sparkled on the hasp where, he thought, a padlock should have been. He moved the light down, but if someone had cut the lock off, it was as likely to have fallen into the water below. He waited one more minute, then pushed the machete through his belt and began picking his slow, ungainly passage down the ramp, glad at least that he did not have to negotiate the ladder again.

It seemed solid enough. Juan's work, perhaps. One of the few things his son did well. Eustachio hadn't wanted to tell him where he had hidden the grave goods, but he had no choice. Protecting the contents of the site had been passed on to Eustachio by his father, and he had given the same information to Juan. That was how it should be, even if it made him uneasy. Juan had let so many of the old ways slip. But someone had to know in case something happened to Eustachio, and such things were best kept to family.

He was taking a risk coming back here at night, even if the place was no longer guarded. His hand went to the note in his pocket. He'd found it tucked into the pocket of his work shirt, which had been hanging in the wheelbarrow shed most of the previous day until he'd grabbed it just before leaving. He hadn't noticed it when he was going home, probably because he was irritated after being told by the student that Bowerdale wanted enough construction materials to cover the entire *cenote*. But that morning, before he'd set off on the motorbike for Coba, he'd discovered it.

Now he pulled out the note and read it again by the beam of the flashlight: "The contents of the new tomb need not go to a museum. Meet me there tomorrow night to discuss how your heritage might be honored."

It was written in careful Spanish, but whether it was a man's or woman's hand, Eustachio could not tell. He planned to give nothing away tonight, but he figured it would be useful to discover what others knew or suspected. As to talk of somehow honoring his heritage, he took that with a grain of salt, though maybe—just maybe—there was a way to honor the past while serving the needs of the village today.

The first stage of the descent into the *cenote* took Eustachio away from the tomb, and he found himself uneasy with the thing at his back. He moved quickly along and down, too quickly in fact. He stumbled slightly and had to take a breath. He held on to the rail—a *chakaj* log with the bark polished off—and turned awkwardly as the ramp doglegged back toward the tomb.

The second stage of the ramp was longer and his flashlight beam barely reached the doorway, but as Eustachio looked ahead, he was sure it looked different from down here. From above the door had looked wide open. Now it seemed half closed. He paused as it occurred to him for the first time that whoever had written the note might have bad intentions. He felt his unease turning into something else, something he hadn't felt in a very long time: fear.

He moved the flashlight around, but it caught only the roots that draped the sides of the *cenote* like vines, reaching for the water below. He stared at the not-quite-open door and wondered if he had the courage to go any further.

But he needed to find out more. What did it mean, *to see how your heritage can be honored*?

He took a step, releasing the handrail and then grasping it hard again. Then another. Slowly, he descended into the sinkhole, his eyes and the thin light fixed on the doorway ahead. Reluctantly he released the handrail and drew out the machete. Two more steps and he was off the ramp. He led with the flashlight, the machete raised so he could feel the cool flat blade against his right ear. He shoved at the door with his elbow to open it completely, no longer sure if it had looked any different from above, and raised the flashlight to eye level so he could peer down its poor beam into the stone hollow beneath the acropolis.

He saw nothing. Nobody. Just the tomb structure with its hell mouth, echoing the threshold of Xibalba, the Mayan underworld, the contents gone, save for the stone box that had served as a coffin. No grave goods. No bones. He turned the light into the corners of the tomb but the darkness swallowed it up. He was standing still, looking for a figure in the darkness, when he heard the breathing behind him. He felt suddenly cold, as if plunged into the *cenote* water itself, and for a moment he did not move, but listened in spite of himself, as the breath rose and fell, strange and unearthly, somehow muffled and amplified at the same time by the chamber. Suddenly, he felt an overwhelming dread of the thing in the shadows behind him, the thing with the strange breathing that was so clearly waiting for him to turn, enjoying the terror that had gripped him. So he did not turn, not even when it spoke his name in a voice he was sure he'd heard before. Not even when he felt its terrible hands on his shoulders. Only then, when it twisted him round, when he saw the dreadful mask and the stray wisp of hair he was sure he recognized, did he begin to scream.

Chapter Twenty-Five

■ ■ ■ ■ ■

Deborah angled the car carefully, swerving between potholes and peering into the night until she reached the junction and took a left on the good road—the tourist road—to the site. She had been in bed, had actually slept for about an hour and a half, but then she had woken and it had quickly become clear she wouldn't drop off again. This wasn't unusual. She slept little—rarely more than five hours a night, often less—and once she got that restless feeling and her brain started working, sleep was out of the question.

She had woken thinking about that gold ring with the heraldic symbols on it, the one wrapped with the child's finger. She may even have been dreaming about it. The ring symbolized everything wrong with the site, everything that had made the dig feel somehow off-kilter long before the theft. She was missing something, and until she found it, nothing was going to make any sense.

She needed to call Steve Powel and see what resources he could dedicate to tracking the symbols on the ring, which she was pretty sure they could get from the photographs and video. He wouldn't thank her for calling him at this hour, but she had to do it now or it would drive her crazy. She hadn't been able to get a cell phone signal at the Oasis Retreat, so that meant going to the site and scaling the tower in the dark.

She parked in the lot by the entrance and checked her flashlight. She had brought the good one, the big Maglite that made her feel like Scully on the *X-Files*. The darkness out here was almost absolute. There was no moon, and the only light came from the stars themselves. The jungle was alive with sound, insects and frogs, she thought, and the occasional high, rising call she took to be a bird, though she had no idea what type. It was a rich, primal sound that made her feel like the only human for a thousand miles. She slipped on her backpack and started to walk.

She didn't mind the darkness, but she kept the flashlight down in case there were snakes. She had no great fear of snakes, but she had done a little research into what she called "the local nasties"—spiders, scorpions, and snakes—and seen some none-too-pleasant pictures of the extensive necrosis some bites produced. Of course, if there were jaguars in the woods, as some of the locals still claimed, she might have an altogether different problem that cautious footwork wouldn't solve. Still, she thought, to see a jaguar in the wild would be something. Preferably not something that wound up killing her, of course, but getting a glimpse would be a treat. No, not a treat. Not these days. An honor.

As she thought this through she traced the old *sacbe* into the site proper past the four-way triangular "arch" with the oval palace behind it and round the back of the Twins. Though being surrounded by the jungle had not bothered her at all, being here in the familiar confines of the site in the unfamiliar darkness of the night was more unsettling, like she was trespassing on hallowed ground. The high stone walls loomed. She moved the white-bright beam of her flashlight over the stone, and the shadows leapt and flickered with each fractional shift. To her left, nestled at shoulder height, a great green iguana—almost four feet from head to tail—scuttled suddenly back into the darkness. She jumped, then took a long breath and blew it slowly out.

The footing was as treacherous as ever on the way up to the cell tower. Climbing it took both hands, so she reluctantly stowed the flashlight in her backpack and began feeling her way up the ladder. Almost immediately she caught sight of something in the corner of her eye: a flash like distant lightning to the north. She paused, listening for thunder, but none came. Holding the rungs of the ladder tighter, she turned toward the acropolis and scanned the sky. For a moment there was nothing but the stars and the distant looming blackness of the pyramid, but then the light returned, not in the sky but lower, bouncing off the pale stone of the structure itself: a flashlight. Someone was there.

She came down the ladder but resisted the urge to turn on her flashlight. She frowned and then turned cautiously and began retracing her steps in the darkness, feeling for the stone lip of the platform edge with the soles of her boots. She descended slowly, turned half into the structure so she could feel the stone with her left hand as she inched her way down to the grass of the central court. All the while, she watched the acropolis pyramid for another flash of light. None came.

Perhaps he—or she—is doing the same as you, she thought.

But then another possibility occurred to her. Maybe the light had shown her not where the other person was so much as where his flashlight beam had happened to fall, in which case he could be almost anywhere. She paused and looked around. No movement, no light, nothing out of place. Nothing, indeed, to suggest there was anything here except her, the lizards, and the ancient stones.

So either he is out of sight, or he has turned off his light.

She didn't like the implications of the latter. The only reason someone would do that was to stay hidden, which meant he had seen her.

So go. Run back to the car and drive straight to Valladolid. Wake the others and call the cops.

It made sense. But this was her site, Goddamn it, and someone had already ruined it once. Someone had plundered her career when they emptied out that tomb, and she was not about to run from them when they came back. Beneath her anxiety, she felt a spark of anger. She had to know who it was and what they were doing.

She decided. She would keep her light off, move closer to the acropolis, and take a cautious look around. If she didn't see the light again or if she felt even a whiff of danger, she would go straight to the car and get out.

She began to walk toward the acropolis. Her stride was longer now, a little less cautious. She had the flashlight ready, though she hadn't turned it on. There was no point announcing her presence till she had seen something she could use, something that might turn this whole nightmare situation around. Recover the stolen artifacts, and she might yet make *National*

Geographic and the kind of publicity that would put the Druid Hills museum firmly in the black.

Deborah picked up the pace, veering left again, moving north around the side of the acropolis. Here the jungle seemed to encroach into the site, and she felt the humidity coming off the vegetation like it was something she could touch. At the corner, she paused, then she was out, moving silently toward the sinkhole.

She saw nothing, but there was almost immediately a sound: someone was in the tomb below her. She stared hard at the ground, trying to pick out the rim of the *cenote* and edge along it. If she could get around the other side, she might be able to see down into the passage. She knew that descending into the tomb with no sense of who was down there was absurd.

I'll just look, she thought.

She moved gingerly around the edge of the *cenote* until she got to an angle where she could see the bright, shifting light that played at the entrance of the tomb passage.

Found you.

She squatted, staring toward the passage, but couldn't see enough down the tunnel. She had to get lower.

The only way into the tunnel itself was via the gangplank ramp, but that made too much noise and took her too close. She peered down into the *cenote* itself. The walls were steep, but perhaps there was a place she could climb down part of the way, just far enough to see straight down the passage. She crawled to the edge and looked down, but it was just too dark. Perhaps if she just flicked the light on for a moment it would go unnoticed and she could see how to navigate a way down.

She positioned the light as precisely as she could, snapped it on, did one quick sweep of the *cenote* walls below her, and turned it off. The whole movement had taken less than two seconds. Then she waited, her eyes on the passage mouth. The light from inside still seeped out, flickering as the person inside moved around. There was no sign that they had seen anything.

Deborah processed what she had seen, then thrust the flashlight into her backpack. She turned her back on the tomb and cautiously dropped her legs over the stone lip of the *cenote*. She felt for the first ledge with her feet, couldn't find it, and eased herself down another six inches. When she found it, she put her weight on it cautiously. It held, and she lowered her whole body down into the great stone basin. She was effectively blind now, her face pressed up against the cool rock, brushed by the long fibrous roots that snaked down to the water like rat tails. She took hold of one and tested her weight against it.

Slowly she stepped back into the dark air, lowering herself with both hands gripping the stiff root, feeling with her feet for the outcrop she had seen in the momentary flash of the lamp. For a moment she was hanging there, just suspended over nothing, then she let her hands slip another foot or so down, and the root tore a little. She dropped another half yard and felt the scattering of earth and stone fragments against her face, but it gave no more, and with a long reach of her right leg, she found the stone outcrop. She let herself down another few inches and took her weight off the root with relief, though she held onto it for balance. Then—wondering how on earth she would get back up—she sank to her haunches and turned slowly.

She was on the same level as the tunnel now, directly across from it, and she could see clean through to the tomb. The passage narrowed her view, but she could see enough, though for a moment, she could make no sense of it. There was the light, still turned away from her, but bright as lightning in the darkness, and there was the movement of a person in a strange, shapeless robe. The figure turned, and she gasped as the face revolved into view, because it wasn't a real face at all, but a horror of wild, staring eyes and a gaping mouth full of daggerlike teeth: a mask, over-sized and garish like that worn by some ancient Mayan priest. And then the figure moved and the light illumined the chamber proper, and Deborah felt a new rising sense of dread. The tomb was there as they had left it, but the color was all wrong. She could see right through to the back wall of the tomb and it was a red far brighter than the colored stucco she remembered. It was a deep, glistening crimson like new paint.

But it wasn't paint. Even from here, without being able to touch or smell it, she knew it wasn't paint.

Chapter Twenty-Six
■ ■ ■ ■ ■

She had to get out, get back to the tower and call the police. This went far beyond old bones, theft, and a blow to her career.

How do you paint a room with blood? Why would you?

She pushed the thoughts away and concentrated on climbing back up. To do so meant turning her back on the tomb, and though a part of her was glad to do so, the act itself filled her with terror. She was blind again in the darkness with whatever was going on in that tomb behind her.

She focused on the climb. There was a notch in the rock that would take one foot, but there was little to hold on to above it but roots. She reached, grabbed, and tugged tentatively. When the roots held, she launched herself up, hauling as she tried to find purchase with her other foot. For a second she hung, reaching with one leg for something that might not be there, then she found something hard in the *cenote* wall—a jutting root perhaps—and set her weight on it.

She heard movement, surprisingly, not from the passageway behind her but from above. It wasn't the masked figure in the tomb. Someone else was there standing out near the rim of the *cenote*. Was it possible she was surrounded? She scrabbled for the vines, trying to move upward quickly.

Too quickly.

Her newly positioned foot lost its hold and she dropped two feet, twisting on the vine-like roots and snapping hard when there was no more slack. The impact seemed to tear the plant above her. There was another scattering of dirt and debris from above, and then the roots were fastened to nothing at all, and she was falling.

She turned in the air but it was too dark to see if she would hit rock or water, and she knew nothing till the cold splash, which sent roosting birds soaring out overhead. The shock of the fall had barely allowed her to close her mouth in time, but she hit nothing but water, and surfaced feeling lucky.

A flashlight from above the edge of the *cenote* found her almost immediately, but she could see nothing beyond the glare of the lamp and the deep-blue water where the black catfish swam. She almost cried out for help. But when the first gunshot rang out, she dove.

Chapter Twenty-Seven

■ ■ ■ ■ ■

The volleyball coach back at Brookline High School had begged Deborah to try out, but, suspecting that height alone wouldn't compensate for her physical awkwardness or aversion to team activities, Deborah—then fourteen—had declined. For the perceived sleight she had been packed off to the Tappan Street pool and told to complete her PE requirements there, plowing up and down the lanes two mornings a week. She had been a good swimmer, long and powerful, maybe even competition material, but though she had enjoyed the silent focus of the thing, the isolation of it, she had never seen the value in devoting all her time to shaving half a second off her hundred-meter freestyle. When old Joe Winters, the swim coach, had told her that she could be great if she'd put in the work, she had said, genuinely confused, "Define great."

"All-state," he said. "Maybe more. Who knows, with work, you might get an Olympic tryout."

Deborah, who already spent her free time immersed in books, just shook her head. All that work just to be a little faster than other people in the pool, working every hour like her sister did on the ice? Never. She didn't get it.

She remembered all that in the moment that the second bullet hit the water. She tucked her stomach, pivoted at the waist and slid down through the black water headfirst, pulling with her arms till she felt her feet follow her under. The bright, chlorinated lanes of Tappan Street couldn't be further from this deep darkness, the water scented with leaves and decay, teeming with fish and who knew what else. She kicked and pulled her way farther down, knowing she hadn't taken enough air to stay under much longer.

She turned and opened her eyes, looking up to the surface, where she saw first nothing, then the swift pass of a flashlight. Someone was looking for her, ready to shoot as she broke the surface. For a second she felt only horror at the strange escalation from theft through the blood-stained tomb to this. She was being hunted, and all—presumably—because there was a case of mistaken identity.

Who did the shooter think she was? Who was that shooter and who was currently standing in the blood-spattered tomb robed from head to foot like a Mayan priest?

Her air was almost gone and her body was instinctively starting to surface. She tried to get her bearings so she could swim for the *cenote* wall. Perhaps she could find a crevice where she could breathe unseen. She pushed away from where she had entered the pool, making for the rock wall, and when she felt the long, trailing roots in her fingers, she tried to slide in among them. With excruciating slowness, she allowed herself to drift up, feeling the air on her face as she broke the surface. As quietly as she could, she released the breath and drew in another, looking up through the root strands to the passageway.

The gunman was there still, though she couldn't even see enough to be sure it was a man. She saw only the merest shadow and the brightness of the flashlight held out away from his—or her—body. It was moving over the surface of the water, slowly, meticulously, and she knew that the other hand had a weapon trained wherever the light went. The light in the tomb had gone out and there was no sign of movement there at all. She waited, breathing hard. How long did she have? Eventually, surely, she would be noticed.

The light was inching toward her. She took another breath, then, trying to brace her hands against the rock, she pushed herself under the water as carefully as possible. She held the position, her face only a couple of feet below the surface, and looked up, waiting for the light to move over her. It crept up from the left and immediately seemed to stall.

I'm not deep enough, she thought. *He can see...something.*

Suddenly, uncannily, it was like she could see herself from his position, floating mermaid-like amongst the weeds, the paleness of her face under the water. The light held another second and she knew the shot would come. She surged sideways, kicking off against the rock as the gun roared, loud even though she was deep underwater, and she felt the tremor in the water where the bullet passed her. She swam hard, desperate to keep moving, toward the center of the pool, snatched the longest breath she dared, then dived once more.

He fired again.

Deborah thrust herself down as far as she could, pulling hard with her arms, frog-kicking her legs. She had no idea how deep the pool was, and there was no strategy to her actions now, just a desperate desire to go so deep he couldn't possibly get her. What she would do when she ran out of air, she couldn't think.

And then, quite suddenly, the water went cold and she felt it pushing against her body: a current. It was moving back to the wall she had come from and she arced into it, letting it move her. She swam two strokes before she realized that she had gathered speed. More alarmingly, she was sure the *cenote* wasn't big enough to have let her go so far in one direction. She should have hit rock.

It came to her like a hand around her throat. *Cenote*s weren't simply pools. They were cave-ins above underground rivers. She had gone too deep and was no longer in the *cenote* at all. She was in a channel that might wind miles before it opened to the air again. Deborah spread her arms, trying to find something against which to brace herself, to stop her momentum, but there was nothing. She tried to turn and swim back against the current—better face a gunman than drown in this airless rock passage—but it was too swift. It swept her on, and her head banged hard against stone so that she gasped, losing what little air she still had, and swallowing the tangy water. She opened her eyes wide. Frantic now, panicking. There was no way out and she knew the closest *cenote* was a kilometer or more away.

She was almost out of air. Her stomach contracted and she felt the nausea rise up in her throat. She swallowed it back, but it wouldn't be long now. She reached up, vainly hoping to find a recess above her, a pocket where air might be trapped, perhaps a cavern, but the water went all the way to the smooth rock above her. The river suddenly tightened into a narrow tube, and she was picking up speed, bumping her elbows and knees against the limestone as she hurtled through. She felt the disorientation of the twists and bends, but knew also that she was blacking out. The nausea surged back, and this time—fight it though she did—she opened her mouth and felt the cold water flooding in. It was almost a relief, that coolness, that stifling, black end. She could feel her eyelids fluttering and the muscles of her neck beginning to spasm. Then nothing.

Chapter Twenty-Eight

■ ■ ■ ■ ■

Aguilar hung up the phone and cursed. There was no sign of Miller, and people were starting to freak out. One of the local Maya had speculated that she had been the one who had ransacked the tomb and had now made a run for it. The story was being circulated as something with real weight till the kid who brought the food and water for the laborers, Eustachio's granddaughter, Adelita, got wind of it. Aguilar had never seen anything quite like that skinny twelve-year-old reading the riot act to village men two and three times her age. It was, he remarked to Krista Rayburn, something to behold, the men skulking like whipped dogs, some drifting away, others suddenly finding the sun-scorched grass just about the most fascinating thing they'd ever seen.

But the girl's anger also showed concern. Miller had become a kind of mentor for the kid in the last week or so, showing her around the dig, talking to her like a grown-up. The child, for her part, had obviously taken to her and Aguilar had caught the quiet, watchful look on Eustachio's face when he saw them together, chatting. The old Mayan had been happy and sad at the same time, and you could guess why: Adelita saw in Deborah Miller something of what she might be if she ever escaped the village with its dirt roads, its wandering turkeys, and—more importantly—its punishing regimen of manual labor. The kid was smart, and underneath the bashfulness that was expected of girls her age in a place like this, she was a live wire, as the scolded men who had disparaged Miller had discovered. Aguilar felt a stab of disdain for the old Mayan. If Eustachio wasn't so damned in love with the backward life he called his culture, he'd put the kid on the first bus out.

Aguilar wasn't good with kids, particularly Mayan kids, but he had given her an encouraging smile and said Miller would turn up any moment. She responded not in the Yucatekan she used with her family but in careful and polite Spanish, which served to remind him that he was—to her and her people—almost as foreign as Miller. In her formal tone he heard how much she saw through his show of concern, maybe even glimpsed something of his contempt for her family and the village in general, and he felt as humbled as the villagers accusing Deborah Miller of plundering the site.

He excused himself and walked through the ball court and round to the acropolis, keeping his eyes open for Miller and for Krista Rayburn, the former somewhat reluctantly, the latter with a sense of anticipation he hadn't felt since his wife left him. He trekked round to the new *cenote* and the gantry access they had built, wondering if the environmental archaeologist smiled that way for everyone or if there was something happening between them. He had to play it carefully. He would be working in close quarters with Krista if this dig ever really got going, and any tension or awkwardness would quickly become excruciating.

The door to the tomb was open.

Miller, he thought, his heart sinking a little.

There was something odd about the light this morning. It seemed to reach into the tomb and show more than he would have thought possible, and where the plastered structure inside had been painted that pinkish red, it seemed darker but more vivid now, the color closer to a rusting crimson.

He descended the creaking ramp but stopped before he actually got inside, though he wasn't sure why. Something was wrong. It took him a moment to realize that he was reacting to a smell: sweet, but also somehow metallic, a familiar and dreadful scent...

Blood.

And then he was stepping carefully inside, looking for Miller's body, and when he saw the scarlet-daubed limbs hanging lifeless over the edge of the coffin-throne, it took another moment for him to realize that under the spattering of blood the skin was too brown. Too old.

Aguilar was clutching his stomach and running back out into the air before the remains of the face registered in his mind.

Eustachio.

He clutched the wooden rail the old man had built and vomited into the *cenote*. And beyond the nausea, beyond the horror of what had been done to the old Mayan, beyond even the sense that being close to any death was somehow a brush with your own, Aguilar felt Adelita's childlike and accusatory stare.

You thought him less than a complete person, said the eyes. *A machine that would lift and carry for you, or a mule...*

"No," he whispered to himself, defiant but fearing the child was partly right.

He ran to the cell phone tower, climbed to the top, and called the police. Then he stayed there, technically still on site, but as far from the tomb, psychologically, as he could get, up there above the trees, looking down on the highest of the Ek Balam structures.

Ten minutes later, he saw Bowerdale, picking his way across from the parking lot in a cream linen suit. Aguilar watched him, wondering what he was doing there alone. He seemed to loiter as he passed the Twins, then peeled off toward Structure 3, finally doubling back toward the Oval Palace. What was he doing? Why didn't he go to the tomb? That was surely why he was there. He wanted to look again at what was inside.

Unless...

He hadn't completed the thought when Bowerdale seemed to look up and see him at last. The surveyor raised a hand in salute, which Aguilar returned, then Bowerdale was walking toward Structure 2 and the base of the tower, recovering his customary swagger. Aguilar, glad he had already spoken to the police, began the long climb down the ladders.

Chapter Twenty-Nine
■ ■ ■ ■ ■

Deborah felt the cold slap of water hit her face, and her eyelids fluttered. In the same instant she felt her belly convulse and her neck twist as she voided the cold, tangy water from her stomach out of her mouth. For a second there was no air, and she thought she would black out again, but then she spewed more and her lungs filled with oxygen again. She continued to spit and retch, but she was breathing. Only then could she reconnect with her body, its contorted position, and the fact that her face was in air and mottled light, while her body from the chest down was submerged in dark, cold water.

She was lodged against a small, hard outcropping of rock, but she felt the subterranean river moving steadily around her waist and legs and it felt that if she pushed back under the ground she might float away into the darkness. She opened her eyes briefly and found herself looking skyward up a stone-rimmed tube about a yard across.

A well.

It was one of the old Mayan water sources, drilled down to the underground river but not used for centuries. That she had surfaced unconscious here, her head and shoulders above the water while her body still hung in the slow, pulling current below, was the kind of luck Deborah generally didn't believe in. She must have been out for hours, lodged in this spot as the horrors of the night before had played out. If the gunman or the figure in the Mayan mask had found her before she came to... well, they hadn't. More luck.

She remembered the splash to her face that had woken her and looked up toward the blue sky again, perhaps twenty feet, to where the small brown face of Adelita Lucia del Carmen Lacantun peered down at her, a bottle of spring water poised to dump down the well if the first didn't get enough show of life.

Deborah called the girl's name, then coughed.

"Stay there," said Adelita in Spanish. "I'll bring people."

She was gone no more than ten minutes, though it felt longer, and Deborah had time both to recover her breathing properly and to feel the dread of being pulled back into the darkness. She could understand why the ancient Maya had considered *cenotes* gateways to the underworld. After the bright, arid conditions of the surface, the world beneath felt like another planet, an opposite realm full of strangeness and danger.

"Blessed are You, Lord, our God, King of the Universe," she thought, surprised how easily the words of the *Birkhat Ha-Gomel* blessing for those surviving danger came back to her, "who bestows good things on the unworthy, and has bestowed on me every goodness."

She thought also of Adelita, who seemed more than usually earnest, and uncharacteristically unsmiling. As the events of the night before came back to her, a dreadful sense of anticipation began to swell inside her, chilling her like the water of the underground river. She had interrupted someone, but not in time. Someone had tried to kill her, but someone else had already died—been murdered, which was different—and thinking of Adelita's gaunt face, a part of Deborah feared she knew who it was.

God, not Eustachio.

They dropped a rope down to her and she lashed it round her waist with an expert bowline, then used her hands and feet to help push at the walls of the forgotten well as they pulled her up. Aguilar did most of the organizing, but the muscle came from Eustachio's son, Juan, and another Mayan whose name she didn't know. She thanked them, then started asking questions even as someone draped an extra cloth tarp from the wheelbarrow shed over her wet shoulders. It was only when she looked up from squeezing water from her lightweight khaki shorts that she saw the policeman hovering at the edge of the anxious circle, waiting to speak to her. She started to move to him but doubled up with a sudden cramping nausea that left her spewing water in the grass.

The women gathered around her but she waved them away, closing her eyes against the indignity of their watching, and spat till her stomach felt clear. She had a lump on her head, but if it had bled, it had already stopped, and though it was a little tender she thought there was no concussion. She stayed where she was, crouched on the ground, feeling the sun burning her neck, until she thought she was ready. Then she stood, coughed once, and started talking as if nothing had happened, demanding to know everything. They watched her a little warily, but once it was clear she was not interested in further assistance or concern, they led her to the tomb to see what they all knew was there. She saw, then she talked to the police about what she had and had not seen the night before.

When they were done Deborah broke from the circle of policemen, walked quickly away from the loitering huddle of archaeologists and their students, and got as far from the tomb as she could. In a few minutes she would have to climb the cell phone tower and make a series of difficult calls, but for now she had to breathe and—if she could—shut out the things she had seen.

It was Aguilar who had reported that the tomb was no longer sealed, and he had warned her that what was inside was "very unpleasant." That was an understatement. It had taken a moment for her to realize what she was seeing, because the tomb looked so different. She had fled without looking closely but the impression of the shining red room and the twisted, broken body at its core was burned into her mind like a bright light you still see after you close your eyes and turn away.

The police had talked her through what they thought had happened, had mentioned a blow to the foreman's head that had immobilized him, signs of rope burns on his arms and legs, the thirty terrible holes they had found in his flesh, the corresponding urchin spines, and the flaked obsidian knife blade. Eustachio, they said, had been tortured to death, but the technique was modeled on ancient Mayan bloodletting rituals. A rope studded with thorns had been passed through his arms, his stomach, and his genitals. Of the usual body parts targeted in

Mayan sacrifice, only the tongue was untouched: presumably so he could still talk. The process, they thought, had taken as long as two hours.

They didn't say—and didn't need to—that someone had assumed that Eustachio had emptied the tomb of its treasures and had tried to extract their current location from him, someone invested in the site and with knowledge of Mayan ritual practice. They didn't say—and didn't need to—that the archaeological team was at the top of their list of suspects. Whether the killer had gotten the information he or she wanted out of the old foreman, no one knew.

She found Adelita sitting on Structure 2 and joined her in silence.

"Thank you for finding me," she said.

"I was looking for somewhere private," said the girl, plucking at the grass and studying it. "I heard the water moving so I looked in."

She said it simply, stoically, like it was of no great consequence, a duty like feeding the chickens or grinding the corn.

"I'm sorry about your grandfather," said Deborah. "He was a good man."

Adelita said nothing, but after a moment, she leaned into Deborah, who put an arm around her shoulders.

"He was," she said in Spanish, "the only one who knew me. Until you came. He told me to work hard in school so that I could go away, maybe to university. My father thinks I should stay home and do chores."

"What about your mother?"

"She thinks I should go, but..." She hesitated. "It's hard for her to imagine, and she needs help. Soon there will be another baby and then maybe I will never leave. I'll be like the other girls, except that I'm not, so I'll be unhappy."

Deborah felt a wash of emotions, confused and powerful as the sweep of the underground river: empathy, sadness, a paradoxical joy, and a concurrent sense of panic.

She already has a mother, she thought. *One who belongs here. You don't.*

But then neither did the girl, and as the bright and pugnacious Adelita started to weep, Deborah sensed she knew it.

Chapter Thirty

■ ■ ■ ■ ■

Deborah climbed the cell phone tower to call Steve Powel and the American embassy, but also because she knew she could be alone at the top. Although the tower had felt rickety and precarious, she felt safer up there in the light where everyone could see her than she would in some private corner of the site. Because Deborah was thinking what she imagined they were all thinking. If Eustachio had not revealed—or not known—what the killer wanted to hear, they might all be targets of similar torture and murder.

Was it possible that someone she knew could have done this?

She tried to shrug the thought off, but she knew the police were right. Eustachio could have been killed by a neighbor or family member for some unknown personal grudge, he might even have been the victim of some psychopath who stumbled on him here, but it was considerably more likely that he had been killed for the tomb treasures, and that pointed squarely at the archaeologists.

So now what?

They had been due to begin the excavation work proper in a week, once the interns returned from their break back in the States. But now everything was up in the air. The new find had derailed the schedule—albeit gloriously—and they were behind on the surveying. With a full-blown murder inquiry in addition to the less intense inquiry into the child's bones, on top of the investigations into the theft of the grave goods, the site would surely be shut down. She should just tell Powel that they had to cut their losses and close the dig indefinitely. Then she realized that even if it closed, the authorities might not let the team out of the country. Might not let *her* out of the country.

God, what a mess, she thought. *My mess.*

She leaned on the rail and gazed out over the site, the stone structures rising up out of the trees beautiful and awe-inspiring still, but tainted now by the pall of her failure. Her hair was tangled and thick with silt, her clothes still slightly damp. She squeezed her eyes shut, biting back the urge to shout or weep or *something.*

Bowerdale would have to stay to finish the surveying—assuming the police gave him access to the site. Aguilar could return home without difficulty. Rayburn, Rylands, and Stroud could all stay, she supposed, and get some productive work done on what they had already unearthed. There were, after all, bones to be analyzed, glyphs to be read, vegetable matter traces to be processed. Even the Brit could make himself useful with his camera. It was only Deborah, it seemed, who had no clear purpose if they weren't actually digging. But as site director, she couldn't leave if anyone was doing anything, even if the police let her go.

What a goddamned mess, she thought again. Then another thought, even more familiar: *You don't belong here.*

That might have been the usual anxiety about her professional competence, but it went deeper than that. Up here on the tower, surrounded by jungle and by the structural remains of a civilization she barely understood, she wondered what she was doing here. This was not her world.

But then what was?

Below her a motmot lurched out of a tree and glided in a flash of turquoise and green onto a branch fifty yards away. As her eyes followed it she saw Nick, the British photographer looking up at her, watching. When he saw she was looking at him, he motioned her to come down. She shook her head and brandished her cell phone.

"I have to make a call," she called down.

"What?"

"I have to call Cornerstone," she shouted.

"Come down as soon as you're done," he yelled back. "The police want to talk to you again."

She closed her eyes and nodded, suddenly exhausted. When she opened them she was annoyed to see he was standing there still, waiting to escort her back. She dialed the Cornerstone number, stabbing each key in turn, then taking a long, steadying breath as it rang.

"Steve Powel," said the voice on the other end.

"Hi, Steve, it's Deborah. Listen, I'm afraid something very bad has happened."

She talked for two and a half minutes, and he listened. When she was done, he said, "OK. I'm going to have to make some calls. Can I reach you on this number?"

"I only get a signal when I climb the tower," she said. "I'll be up here as much as I can today, but the police want to talk to me so I can't stay forever. We could set up a video conference for later if I can get to the lab at Valladolid?"

"Sounds good," said Powel. "I'll get in touch with the embassy. Anyone here you need me to call?"

Deborah thought of her mother at home in Boston, heard her sister's voice saying, *Come pick through Dad's things...*

"Not yet," she said. "Let me see where this is going."

"OK. I'll call back. And Deborah?"

"Yes?"

"Hang in there, OK?"

"Sure," she said, and hung up.

Out of the corner of her eye, she could see the English photographer starting to pace below. She turned to make it harder for him to see and dialed another number.

"Come on," she muttered, as it rang. Almost immediately the phone was picked up.

"Federal Bureau of Investigations, how can I direct your call?"

"I'm trying to reach Agent Chris Cerniga," she said.

She was about to add that she was an old friend of his, but decided that that wouldn't help and wasn't strictly true anyway. Their past interactions had been entirely professional, and in one of them she had briefly been a suspect in her mentor's murder. There was a long, staticky silence, and then Cerniga's voice came on the line.

"Hi, Chris," she said, taking a chance at familiarity. "It's Deborah Miller."

"Let me guess," he said, barely missing a beat. "International art smuggling."

She didn't attempt to prevaricate. "I wish it were that simple," she said. "I need your advice."

There was a long pause, perhaps while he closed an office door or sat down, then he said simply, "Go on," and she told him everything: the find, the theft, the murder, the swarming police and their suspicions. When she was done, he blew out a long sigh, but when he spoke his voice was urgent and uncompromising.

"You need to get out," he said.

"Out of town?"

"Out of the country," he said.

"I can't do that."

"Deborah, listen," said Chris. "The laws in Mexico are changing, but a good deal of it still depends on the old Napoleonic code, which for a lot of people still means guilty until proven innocent. They can arrest and hold merely on suspicion, and it could be months before you get out even if they can't build a case against you. There are a lot of good cops in Mexico, but there's also a lot of corruption, and a lot of police testimony is extracted from arrestees under severe duress."

"You mean…"

"You know what I mean, Deborah. It's not supposed to happen, but it does, and the courts often turn a blind eye if the confession can get a conviction. US citizens are subject to Mexican law while in Mexico, but they are also targets of extortion while in police custody, either as 'protection money' to other inmates, or in the form of bribes and fines to the authorities themselves.

US citizens have been beaten, raped, and killed in Mexican police custody. If you are arrested, it could be months before the State Department can put enough pressure on the Mexican government to get you out, and by that time who knows what you will have been through. So let me say it again, Deborah, and it's what the embassy would tell you if they could: you need to get out of the country. Now."

Chapter Thirty-One

Krista Rayburn couldn't believe what she was hearing. She had told the policeman—a small man in a sweat-stained synthetic uniform who kept eyeing her breasts—all she knew, which wasn't much. She folded her arms discreetly across her chest, but she had been polite and as open as she could be, which meant freely offering that she had no alibi for the hours in question because she was alone in bed in Valladolid. The policeman had smiled at that, but he didn't seem unduly concerned, and when she got up to leave had simply said that he would like to speak to her again later. But now she was back with the other archaeologists and there was a brewing hysteria that caught her completely off guard.

"You're suggesting we should run from the police?" she said, unable to suppress a smile. "Isn't that a little melodramatic?"

"I'm just passing along what I've been told," said Deborah Miller. "I suggest you take what action you think appropriate."

"You think you can flee the country and the government will invite you back in to complete the dig?" said Rylands. The sneer he always seemed to wear had grown harder since the news of the murder. "If you leave now, you're never coming back."

"I can't leave," said Bowerdale. "I have to complete the survey in preparation for the dig for whenever things start up again. And for whoever leads it."

Deborah Miller gave him a thoughtful look but didn't rise to the bait.

"This is crazy," said Krista. "If we hightail it out of here now, it just makes us look guilty as hell."

"They already think we're guilty, Krista," said Miller. "A man—a local man at that—has been killed, a man who probably knew the whereabouts of archaeological treasures we unearthed, things *we* value more than anyone else would. And he died after suffering through the kind of ancient Mayan bloodletting rituals that aren't exactly common knowledge, and on *our* site. Who knows more about those practices than us? The police would be crazy *not* to consider us suspects."

Krista opened her mouth but could think of nothing to say. She looked to Aguilar, whom she'd quickly come to trust, but his face was unreadable. Stroud was exactly the same as usual, saying little, seeming hardly to listen and staring fixedly at nothing.

"I am not leaving till my work is done," said Bowerdale again.

"Martin," said Miller, quiet but urgent. "They could throw you in jail for months."

"I can't leave," he said. "I won't. We've made one of the most important discoveries in Mayan archaeology and haven't even begun the work on Structure Three that we originally came for! If I leave now, someone else will take over."

"This is no time to worry about who gets credit for—" Miller began, but Bowerdale cut her off.

"It's not about getting credit," he spat. "It's about being there at the moment of discovery, like Howard Carter at the tomb of Tutankamun, Leonard Woolley at the royal cemetery of Ur, Schliemann at Troy, or Arthur Evans at the palace of Minos in Crete. I could be Hiram Bingham, overlooking Machu Picchu. I will not give up my place in history because of a few bullying cops."

Krista stared at him. What had begun as a little pompous but impressive had strayed over into something that looked—for the briefest of moments—like obsession. Miller seemed to recognize it too, because she raised her hands in surrender.

"You do what you think is best, Martin," she said. "At least call the embassy and talk to them, and do it quickly. The police will act soon, I think. They don't need much of a case to arrest us."

"You're going to leave?" said Bowerdale to Miller. "Isn't the captain supposed to go down with the ship?"

Miller seemed to hesitate.

"Maybe," she said at last, and she seemed defeated, shrunken. "But I didn't sign on for this. If there was a principle at stake, that would be one thing, but to go to jail and deal with Mexico's judicial system? No. I won't go down with the ship, Martin. I also won't stick around to get shot at again, and I'd advise you not to either."

"What if we get caught?" said Krista suddenly. "Even if we jump in our cars and go, they can catch up with us or flag our passports so that we can't get a flight."

"You may have some time," said Aguilar. It was the first time he had spoken up, and everyone looked at him, expectant. "There will be several branches of law enforcement involved in this and they will not be well coordinated out here. The *Federales* will be involved because you are foreigners and because of the theft, but they haven't even gotten here yet. When they do, things will tighten up. But you may have a window. The dead man is a Mayan, not some Mexico City politician. The police will take longer to get seriously involved." He said this last with his eyes cast down, though Krista wasn't sure if this was embarrassment or something else. Guilt, perhaps. It lasted only a moment and when he looked up, he seemed determined. "If I were you," he said, "I'd go now."

Bowerdale turned away, staring at Structure 3.

"Thanks, Porfiro," said Miller. "So. If you leave and they catch up with you, just tell them the dig had been closed and you were due for a trip home before coming back. No one told you not leave. I don't see how leaving can be worse than being arrested on suspicion of murder. Once out of the country, I'll talk to Cornerstone and our sponsors in the Mexican government offices to try and clear things up and—hopefully—prepare for our return. With luck, all this will blow over quickly, they'll solve the murder, and we'll be able to get back to work. And if anyone does stay and is arrested," she said, looking pointedly at Bowerdale, "I will do everything in my power to see that they are released."

Krista felt a rising sense of panic and something darker beneath it. She assumed it was fear of her predicament, but it was only later, after the group had dispersed to make their decisions and plans, that it occurred to her what it really was. Everyone was acting as if arrest was an inconvenience, an injustice. But what if it wasn't? What if the police were right, and one of them was a killer?

Chapter Thirty-Two
■ ■ ■ ■ ■

Deborah spent an hour with Eustachio's family at their square cinderblock house in the village. She was anxious to be gone, but she had to at least acknowledge the man she had known in the presence of his family, and she needed to see Adelita again. As she approached the house, she put her hands behind her back, trying to fight the impulse to check her watch. She hadn't known what to expect and was braced for both expansive grief and accusations of responsibility. It was, after all, her dig. What she found in the little spartan house was, however, something quieter, sadder. Juan fiddled with the heavy knot at the end of the hammock he was making, and Consuela washed clothes in the sink, from time to time arching her back to balance the weight of her pregnant belly. Adelita made tortillas in the cabana behind the tiny house, patting out the cornmeal, squeezing it into shape with her fingertips, and dropping each one onto the flat pan over the fire. She didn't speak and didn't cry, but she looked older than ever, weary somehow, as if a little of her childhood had been siphoned off overnight.

Deborah offered to help each of them in their tasks, but though they were polite they didn't want her help. Adelita's parents spoke little English and Deborah's Spanish wasn't up to serious conversations about death, so she sat with the child, watching her turning the tortillas with an almost mechanized precision, plunging them briefly into the fire itself till they puffed, then stacking them and moving on to the next.

There was a math textbook by the fireplace, dog-eared and grimy from use. Deborah had seen the girl engrossed in it, smiling delightedly to herself as she worked out the answers to her homework. And what would she do with math? Use it to count knots on a hammock, or measure out cups of corn flour?

So what if she does? There are more versions of success than yours.

But looking at the girl, she wanted to envision a bigger future for her.

After a while she heard the TV go on in the house, heard the crack of an opening beer can, and decided she could wait no longer. She hugged the child, feeling the girl's thinness against her chest, told her that she would see her again, and left.

"I'll come back to see you," she said. "Soon."

A promise.

On the way out she tried to speak to Juan, but his eyes wouldn't leave the television, and, feeling suddenly uncomfortable, she left. She was already in the street before Consuela called her back.

"You think it was one of the archaeologists?" she said.

Deborah had never heard her speak so much English so the question caught her doubly off guard.

"The police seem to think..." she began, but the Mexican woman stopped her.

"What do *you* think?"

Deborah had no idea. She thought for a long moment, and the weight of the question settled on her for the first time since the possibility had been raised.

"I don't know," she said. "I hope not. I hope..."

But she couldn't think of a way to end the sentence that wouldn't be insulting.

I hope it had nothing to do with me, that it wasn't my fault.

She thought of the gemstones that Adelita had described as the color of blood and tears mixed, then shook her head and smiled sadly.

"I am sorry for your loss," she said, hearing the hollowness of the phrase as it came out. "Eustachio was a good man. I will do what I can to help find the person who did this."

Consuela's frank, appraising eyes held hers for a long moment, and then she nodded in acknowledgement and turned back inside, where the TV seemed to have gotten louder.

Chapter Thirty-Three

■ ■ ■ ■ ■

The two graduate students opted to stay in Mexico. They told Deborah that their plan was to lose themselves on the beaches south of Cancun. That way, they could get back easily enough if the situation improved.

"At least there we'll be able to get a cell phone signal without having to build a siege tower," James quipped.

Bowerdale had insisted on staying, and Aguilar said he would stay on for a while before returning to Mexico City, where Krista also planned to spend some time. Rylands wouldn't say what he was doing, but when it was time to head out to the airport he made no move to go with them, so Deborah drove to Cancun with only Nick Reese and Marissa Stroud for company. Before leaving, she ran inside the lab in Vallidodad and took the external hard drive that stored the video, pictures, charts, and documents they had built after discovering the new tomb. There was still so much to figure out.

Deborah avoided the toll roads with their checkpoints and groups of heavily armed police, and checked her mirrors constantly. The road took her through towns and villages where they had to crawl through traffic, often reduced to ten miles an hour because of the numerous, oversized speed bumps that Reese, sitting next to her and navigating, called Sleeping Policemen. Normally this would have struck her as funny, but today she was not in the mood.

She had left most of her things at the Oasis cabana. Deborah gripped the steering wheel and tried not to think of Eustachio's gaunt, smiling face. She couldn't suppress the thought. She had to wonder if she was aiding his killer's escape, and suspected the same question was in the minds of the others. After the murder, everyone on the team had simply stopped talking to each other. Professional rapport didn't amount to trust or to the certainty of innocence in a case like this. She reminded herself of the two promises she'd made to Eustachio's family: that she would return, and that she would help find the person who had tortured the old man to death. She kept those promises at the front of her mind as she stared at the road ahead. She *would* keep them. She had to.

Reese talked as they drove, describing his boyhood in Lancashire and how out of place he felt when he first moved to London, where everyone sounded so different. He said he wished they'd had time to find some really spicy Mexican food and wash it down with a couple of cold beers. He asked her about her work for the museum and even managed to get her to admit that there was no one special in her life. He raised it casually like it was just another professional detail, but his eyes flicked to hers and his shrug didn't completely hide what looked like genuine interest.

Another day, she might have been flattered, and even with all the other stuff in her head she found herself smiling briefly as she turned and looked out of the side window. Throughout, Stroud sat in the back saying nothing, apparently unaware that the conversation was taking place.

In the airport, she took leave of Reese and Stroud, ducking into the bathroom to let them get ahead. When she emerged, she looked around the airport for signs of anyone watching her closely—particularly police—then checked her watch. She had no idea how long it would take for some kind of flag to be placed on her passport. It may have already happened. She wouldn't know until she tried to get a ticket, and maybe wouldn't be alerted to the fact until she actually tried to board the plane.

Deborah's smart phone chimed: a new e-mail message. It was from Aguilar and contained two links, a table of numbered data, and a single sentence. The first link took her to an obscure local history and archaeology journal coming out of Lancaster University in Northwest England. The article entitled "Pendle's Malkin Tower Found?" was attributed to Professor Francis Hargreaves.

Deborah was confused. What did this have to do with anything? Her eyes flashed over the account of stone remains found in a farmer's field during plowing. In a box buried in the centre of the structure was a "pale-red gemstone."

Deborah stared at the words. How could a Mayan tomb be connected to an English farm?

The second link took her to a page of mineralogical data apparently breaking down the unusual properties of the Lancashire gem. Aguilar had highlighted the crucial information: chrome and ferric iron, with virtually the same numerical values for the sample stone recovered in the Mayan tomb.

Deborah wondered how much longer she would be able to go on thinking of the tomb's most compelling properties as Mayan. Everything was starting to point elsewhere. Lancashire?

"Next, please," said a voice.

She had reached the front of the line without even realizing it. She looked up from the computer and moved quickly to the desk, proffering her passport.

"One-way ticket to Atlanta via Chicago, please," she said.

"Heading home, Miss Miller?" said a slightly brittle-looking strawberry-blonde woman.

"What?" said Deborah, a realization coming to her like she was just waking up. "No, actually. I'm going to England. Can I? Well, I guess I can. How much will it cost? Either way, I guess I need to buy a ticket. Yes, one ticket to London, please."

The woman gave her a stern look and her lips tightened.

"You're in the wrong line," she said, as if this was to be expected given the people she had to deal with every day. "You need to be over there."

Deborah followed the woman's eyes, but she hesitated, struck by what she was planning to do. This was nuts.

The woman looked suddenly concerned.

"You OK, hon?" she said.

"Yeah, thanks," said Deborah, still not moving.

"And you're sure you want to go to England?"

Deborah blinked, then nodded.

"Yes," she said, stepping into the other line and returning her eyes to her phone. "Thanks."

Lancashire? What on earth was she doing?

"Could I see your passport, please?"

She looked up. An officious-looking woman in a uniform was staring at her.

"I'm sorry...?" Deborah began.

"Your passport," said the woman. "You are from the United States, yes? You speak English, yes?"

"Yes. Hold on. I have it here."

She fumbled in her bag and her hand was trembling slightly. She didn't know if the woman worked for an airline, for airport security, or for some larger branch of law enforcement. She couldn't ask. Her mouth was dry. She continued to poke in her bag as if she couldn't find it, but that clearly wasn't going to help. In the end she plucked it out and stood up. She was a foot taller than the other woman, who had iron-grey hair and broad shoulders. If the police were looking for her and had sent a description, that was it. She stood out like...well, like she always did.

She opened her mouth to speak, but nothing came out, and she could think of nothing to say. The woman snatched the passport from her and flipped it open. Deborah just stared, unable to even look around to see if their exchange was being monitored by anyone else.

The woman punched some numbers into a handheld computer of some kind, then slapped the passport back into her hand.

"Thank you," she said robotically, moving to the next person in line. "Enjoy your flight and thanks for visiting Cancun."

Deborah heaved a sigh of relief and turned her attention back to her phone, but now her eyes slid past the details about the red gemstone from Lancashire. She saw the only actual words that Aguilar had written in his e-mail: *Bowerdale arrested for murder.*

PART 3

Chapter Thirty-Four
■ ■ ■ ■ ■

Deborah flew Delta via Atlanta, where she had an hour and a half layover—not time enough to go by her apartment or the museum—and arrived in London at seven the following morning after fifteen hours of traveling. She had slept for perhaps three hours and felt fresher than she would have expected, but Gatwick was gray and daunting, a maze of long walkways and caustic officials who moved the crowds through passport control and customs like they were herding sheep. From there, she took the rail link into London Victoria, a packed underground train to Euston, then a Virgin train to Lancaster.

She arrived a little after lunchtime feeling drained and completely overwhelmed.

It was more than tiredness, of course. This wasn't the first time she had made an impulsive journey to get to the heart of something she didn't understand, but she felt curiously out of place, even more than she had in Mexico. Those places had announced their foreignness in ways that made her oddly comfortable, separate—certainly—even alien, but unproblematically so. Here she just felt wrong. Everyone spoke English, but not her English. Their clothes were different, but not in ways you could pinpoint. The streets, the cars, the countryside: they all felt *off* somehow, as if the plane had brought her into a mirror universe where reality was tweaked out of the familiar. The one constant was that she still seemed to loom over every woman she met.

Maybe you should get a job in Sweden, she thought. *Or Norway. Somewhere all the women make the volleyball team...*

She munched on an egg salad sandwich and sighed as she peered at the bleak rain lashing the windows of the café she had chosen at random. At least her cell phone worked here without having to scale a log tower. After she finished her lunch, she called the Lancaster University local history journal, but this Hargreaves who had written the article on the gemstone wouldn't be around for weeks.

"Summer break," said the secretary, as if this should be obvious. "It's when the faculty do their primary research. Since Professor Hargreaves is a local historian, of course, he might be in the area, but I don't know. He sometimes volunteers at Lancaster Castle."

"Volunteers as..."

"A guide," she said. This time her tone spoke less of how self-evident this should be and more of her own bewildered disdain: walking tourists through castles was apparently beneath the dignity of a university professor.

Deborah shivered as she stepped out into the street. The English climate, even in summer, was about as far from Mexico as possible. She was going to have to buy not just a raincoat and an umbrella, but a sweater or two and some jeans. It was surprisingly cold for late summer, it felt more like November. She was dressed—absurdly, she felt—in shorts and a safari shirt, like she'd stepped out of a Tarzan movie. It was hard enough to find pants that fit her in Atlanta. She had a feeling she'd never find a new pair in Lancaster. The town was bustling but seemed ancient and provincial, its streets winding and narrow. She pushed aside her worries about her odd outfit and hurried up what seemed to be the main road to the castle, wishing she had picked up an umbrella as the rain ran down her neck.

The flat cobbled approach bent up to a massive dark stone gatehouse, where two huge black doors reinforced with heavy bolted grid work loomed over her. They were firmly shut. Her heart sinking, Deborah gazed quickly around and found an incongruous bell button. She pushed it and stood there shivering and wet, waiting for someone to buzz her in like she was dropping by a friend's apartment, rather than standing beside the arrow slits and portcullis of a medieval fortress.

Finally, she heard a clanking of metal and a smaller door opened up inside one of the larger ones, like a secret drawer popping open. A man in a navy-blue sweater that looked like a uniform peered at her.

"Yes?" he said.

"I thought the castle was open to visitors," she said.

"It is," he said.

"So...can I come in?"

"Not through 'ere, love," he said. "This is a prison, this is. You don't want to come in here, especially not dressed like that. We'd have a riot on our hands. Castle entrance is round the back.

Just follow the walls round that way till you see the entrance sign."

She thanked him, feeling stupid, and he said, "All right, love," and shut the door.

She walked back into the rain and up between an ancient-looking church and the castle itself, the latter looming with a new solidity and purpose now that she knew it was a prison. It was a dour structure, dark and squat without the elegant whimsy of French or German castles, weathered by centuries and stained with pollution, but still serviceable like a wartime revolver: A building whose past bolstered its present grim purpose.

She found the open door with the entrance sign and the obligatory gift shop. Tours, she was told by the boy at the register—Barry, according to his name tag—went on the hour when everyone had assembled. She looked around. There was no one else there. Dr. Hargreaves, said the boy, slightly defensive, would be along in a moment if she'd care to browse.

She did, partly from curiosity about the building and its history, partly from a museum director's impulse to compare notes. She considered books and pamphlets, plastic soldiers, key chains, and an abundance of toys and publications dealing with witchcraft. She was about to ask the kid at the desk about these when Dr. Hargreaves arrived.

He was a small, stooping, bald man who peered mole-like through gold-rimmed spectacles. He wore gray slacks and a conservative tie and jacket. He was a piece of history himself, she thought, a little slice of the nineteen fifties bustling about as if the world had never changed. Tiredness made her silly, and she grinned at him, so that he looked confused and embarrassed.

"Only one today," said the boy to the professor, nodding significantly at where she loomed in case he might have missed her.

"Right," said Hargreaves. "Well then. That's all right."

It didn't seem entirely all right, Deborah thought. She seemed to unnerve the little man, which—given her safari attire—was hardly surprising. He blinked behind the lenses of his glasses.

"Step this way, please," he said, and she noticed that his gruff, earthy accent belied his meek demeanor. "Now, first off, I've got to say for legal reasons that a lot of the castle is still a working court and a prison, which means no photographs. There are closed-circuit cameras everywhere, so you will be caught if you try it. The penalty for violating that particular law is two years in prison, which you probably wouldn't like very much."

He smiled suddenly, revealing the bleak understatement as a kind of joke, and she smiled back, taken off guard, and liking him for it.

"The earliest surviving parts of the castle are Norman," said Hargreaves as he led her through, "the keep being built around 1150, but there was a Roman fort on this site a thousand year earlier. The gate house at the front of the building—the main prison entrance—did you see it?"

"I did. I rang the bell," said Deborah ruefully.

"Did you, by God?" said Hargreaves, amused. "They won't have liked that. You're lucky you made it round to me. Go in the front door and who knows when you'd have made it out. Anyway, the gatehouse was built in the first decade or so of the fifteenth century by 'enry the Fourth, the first king of England who was also duke of Lancaster as the present queen is today."

Hargreaves, so mousy and nondescript when he was silent, became a character as he spoke, his guttural Lancashire accent with its broad, flat vowels crisply bitten off, stretching his face. She had to listen carefully to catch every word but she liked the sound, which was not remotely like the stereotypical restraint she thought of as English. It made her think of Nick Reese, and she frowned, wondering how she was going to turn the castle tour into something productive.

"Mr. Hargreaves?" she said without preamble as they moved through a great stone arch and down a narrow corridor, "did you write an article about a small gemstone found somewhere close by?"

The color of blood and tears...

The little man, who had been addressing some aspect of the castle's role in the English Civil War, stopped midsentence and turned abruptly to her, his eyes bright with suspicion.

"Seems you have the advantage of me, Miss...?"

"Miller," she said promptly, extending her hand. "Deborah Miller."

He took her hand and shook it, but his eyes held hers.

"Frank 'argreaves," he said. "So you're not just here for the tour," he said, pronouncing the last word *too-er.*

"Not just the tour, no," she conceded. She gave him a wry "got me" smile, knowing but not apologetic. "I'm an archaeologist," she said. "I found a similar stone and wanted to find out as much as I could about yours."

"Where did you find yours?" he demanded.

"Mexico," she said.

"Mexico?" he echoed. His looked baffled and repeated the word. "*Mexico.* What makes you think your stone was related to the one found here?"

"The mineralogical signature," she answered. "They were unusual stones."

"Aye," he said, turning and leading her through a door. "They were that."

"I was wondering if I could see the stone you found so that I might compare it..."

He gave a snort of derisive laughter.

"Nothing to see," he said. "It's gone."

"Gone? Gone where?"

"Not to Mexico," he said, another half joke, "but maybe not so far from there."

"The States?"

"It was bought by a private collector for more than the owners could refuse, though the precise figure was undisclosed."

He said it bitterly, like it still left an aftertaste.

"And that was legal?" she asked.

"There was no reason to suggest any great historical significance, and the gem was—in a manner of speaking—unremarkable."

"In a manner of speaking?"

"It was certainly unusual. Very clear for a colored stone— flawless is the best word. When you held it up to your eye it changed the texture of the whole world. The sky went pale red."

He mimed the action, finger and thumb up to his glasses as if he still had the stone.

"Beautiful thing," he said, snapping back to her. "But without the depth of color prized in rubies, so not especially valuable. *Curious*, the jeweler called it, even unique, but not worth much. The bloke who owned the land nearly gave it to the castle for nothing. Then he gets this offer, from America—or so the rumor went—and that's the last anyone sees of it. The land where it was found has changed hands since then and it seems the gem did too. Whoever bought it first sold it on, quietly, supposedly to some collector."

"Of gems?"

"Of occult objects."

"Occult objects?" Deborah repeated. "Meaning what?"

"Oh, you know," said Hargreaves with a dismissive gesture. "Magic crystals. Bunch of New Age rubbish."

"Why would anyone think it was magic?" she said, almost stumbling on the absurdity of the last word.

He shrugged.

"People with more money than sense," he said. "Who knows what goes on in their heads. And now you've got one. A magic gemstone, I mean. Or have you?"

He fixed her with that look of his again, and she flushed.

"Actually," she said, "it's been stolen."

"Has it indeed?" he said, giving his half-joking smile again. "Isn't that interesting? Now, if you'll step this way, I'll show you the Shire Hall."

For a moment Deborah just stood there, watching the man, but then she saw what was in the next room, and she strode quickly after him, her heart in her mouth.

Chapter Thirty-Five

■ ■ ■ ■ ■

James closed his eyes against the sun, pushed his toes into the sand, and sipped from his piña colada. It was perfect and served exactly how he liked it, the rum and pineapple served in an actual coconut with the top sliced off. The coconut was green, which surprised him, and didn't taste quite as—well, not quite as *coconutty*—as he had figured it would, but it was perfect all the same. The waves were crashing rhythmically on the white beach, and right next to him, wearing this little bikini with perky yellow and green penguins on it, was Alice, pale as the sand and pinking on her back and shoulders. Soon he'd offer to rub some sunscreen on her and she would lazily agree, like it was no big deal—him touching her in that weirdly intimate but public way, massaging the cream into her rose tattoo with the barbed-wire thorns—and he would smile and sip from his drink and wait to see what happened when the sun went down. Considering where they had been a couple of days before, thought James, pushing his glasses up his nose, things had worked out pretty well.

They had taken a bus from Valladolid to Cancun, where they spent one night in a generic hotel, and then hitched a ride down the coast with some Swedes who had been making for the biosphere at Sian Ka'an. With their earnest environmentalism and habit of playing loud, chattering techno music, they proved dour company. When Alice had announced that she wanted to get off in Tulum and go to the beach instead of the bio reserve, James had been delighted.

After the smog and concrete and crowds of Cancun, Tulum was positively Edenic, particularly outside the hotel zone where accommodations were what Alice called "tropical chic": thatched cabanas on the beach with excellent plumbing, patio restaurants serving local fish, and little tourist shops stuffed with masks and beads. There was a Mayan ruin sitting right there on the cliffs, but they hadn't checked that out yet. It was all a bit more pricey than Cancun, but it felt like he imagined Tahiti would: exotic and a little bit exclusive.

James didn't really like the water, so he spent a lot of his time sitting under the palm-thatched shade on the sand while Alice waded and swam in the ocean. It was on one of these water excursions, while Alice was splashing about and chatting to some sun-blackened local fisherman in a dinghy, that James's cell phone first rang. It was the first call he had gotten since arriving in Mexico, and though he kept it charged, he had not even noticed that the resort got a signal.

"James?"

"Professor Bowerdale? I thought you were…"

"In jail?" said Bowerdale. "I am. But the upside of a corrupt police service is that your money always counts, even in prison. That money has also bought a little information about the location of our stolen grave goods."

"How did you—"

"It doesn't matter," said Bowerdale, cutting him off. "Let's just say that for some of our Mayan villagers, blood may be thicker than water, but it amounts to less than the price of a flat-screen TV. James, I don't have a lot of time, so listen carefully. I have a proposition for you."

And James listened, watching Alice plunge in and out of the waves. When Bowerdale was done, James paused and said, "That it?"

"That's it."

"OK," said James. "How much?"

And then they had haggled, and James—knowing he was talking to a man who was used to being in charge but who was now a little desperate and willing to spend some of the money he had in considerable amounts—felt powerful and important. And secret.

Yes, that too.

And, he thought, as Alice came wading out toward him, breasts bouncing, that was what he liked best.

Chapter Thirty-Six
■ ■ ■ ■ ■

Hargreaves moved out of her way and Deborah stared. The Shire Hall was a vast, semicircular chamber, its walls hung with shields of varying sizes—hundreds of them—all adorned with coats of arms. Deborah moved directly toward them and started scanning, picturing the crest from the ring and trying to find a match.

It will be here, she thought, ignoring Hargreaves. *It has to be.*

But the more she looked, the less certain she became. Hargreaves was talking about the room, which was a court of law, and its famous trials, but he was also watching her. She could sense it, but couldn't stop looking at the shields.

"The smallest shields belong to the high sheriffs of the county, as appointed by the monarch," he said blandly. "The medium ones belong to the constables of the castle, again by royal appointment. The largest are the shields of the monarchs. The castle has always had ties to the monarch, but since 1399, it's been one of the king or queen's official properties as seat of the duchy of Lancaster. Is there a particular one you're looking for?"

Deborah was two-thirds of the way round the room and had seen nothing resembling the symbols on the ring.

"A crest," she said. "I had relatives from this area."

"Oh?" said Hargreaves, not believing her. "Miller, right? Isn't that one of those names often adopted by Jewish immigrants in America?"

"That's right," she said, just enough challenge in her voice so that he would know he'd have a fight on his hands if he wasn't careful.

He smiled, and some of the tension in her neck and shoulders eased.

"There *were* Jews in medieval England," he said. "But it wasn't what you'd call a welcoming country. In 1190, the Jews of York were rounded up, locked in the castle, and massacred by Christian zealots, many of whom—surprise, surprise—owed them a lot of money. A hundred years later, Edward the First threw all Jews out of the country on pain of execution. It was four hundred years before they could come back. I'm guessing you won't find your coat of arms here."

Deborah considered him for a long moment, and the great vaulted chamber where countless men and women had been sentenced to imprisonment, deportation, and death was utterly silent.

"It's not my family crest I'm looking for," she admitted, turning back to the shields so he wouldn't see her face. "It's connected to the site I've been working on."

"In Mexico?"

"Yes. It has an arrangement of rings and a checkerboard. But it doesn't matter. It doesn't seem to be here."

"I know all these," said Hargreaves. "Rings and a checker-board? You won't find that design here. Did you expect to?"

"No, not really," she said, turning back to him, despondent. "That massacre in York," she said. "I've never heard of it."

"Not the kind of thing we advertise," said Hargreaves. "The original castle was wood. The round keep that's there now was built later. Thirteenth century, I think. It's called Clifford's Tower because—"

His voice trailed off.

"What?" Deborah asked.

"Come with me," he said.

He marched her from the Shire Hall and along the silent castle galleries until he came to a small library, cluttered and untidy, stuffed with books and papers.

"'Scuse the mess," he said, pushing his way through and pulling a heavy volume down. He thumbed through it quickly till he found a picture of a round stone tower on a conical green hill with a steep flight of steps up the side.

"I take it this isn't usually on the tour," she said.

"Hardly," he answered, but he shot her a broad grin and she guessed he was glad of the change.

"I like playing tour guide, generally," he said, his eyes back on the book, "but sometimes it gets wearisome, and the bits that the visitors get most excited about aren't the parts I like talking about."

"Like what?"

"Oh you know," he said. "The ghoulish stuff. There's a chair in the Drop Room," he said. "With wheels on it."

"The Drop Room?"

"The hanging room," he said. "Where the condemned waited to be executed."

"And what's the chair with wheels?" she asked.

"Like I said," Hargreaves answered. "I don't like talking about it."

He kept his eyes on the book and said no more, and though she was curious to see what seemed to so rattle the man, she said nothing.

Hargreaves turned to a glossy close-up of a tower door with two carvings of coats of arms. He set the book on a precarious pile on the desk, bustled round to the other side, and rooted in a drawer, emerging after a moment brandishing a large magnifying glass. He thrust it at Deborah, and she took it.

"Well?" he said.

She peered through the glass at the crests in the picture and took a sharp breath as the image sharpened. The stone was eroded by time but there was no question.

"This one," she said, putting her finger on the crest. "It's not exactly the same as the one I saw—mine had a kind of oval at the bottom—but the rings and checkerboard are identical."

"Coats of arms varied from generation to generation," said Hargreaves, "modified by marriage and new titles. This is Clifford's Tower in York, site of the Jewish massacre I was telling you about, so called because of either Roger de Clifford, who was hanged there in 1322, or—more likely—because of Henry Clifford, last earl of Cumberland, who garrisoned the town for the royalist cause during the Civil War. The other coat of arms belongs to King Charles the Second. I could be wrong, but I'd say that your missing crest belonged to the Clifford family."

"But York is a long way from here, isn't it?" said Deborah, who was trying to connect the dots.

"Does this have something to do with the gem you were asking about?" said Hargreaves, shrewd and interested. "Well, yes. But the Cliffords had several houses and the ancestral seat was in Skipton, halfway between here and York."

"And the place where you found the gem?"

"Malkin Tower Farm, about twenty miles from here on Pendle Hill."

"How far is that from Skipton?"

"No more than ten miles," said Hargreaves.

Deborah stared at him.

"How do I get there?" she said.

Chapter Thirty-Seven

Nick Reese drummed his fingers on the edge of the old wooden table, then got up and walked the length of the room twice. There was a single leaded window and he stood at it for a moment, looking out over the lawn to the entrance where a gaggle of tourists in pastel anoraks drifted aimlessly. Skipton Castle remained a perennial draw, apparently. He checked his watch then returned to the table, awoke his laptop, and checked his e-mail. Still nothing.

He rose and strode over to the great fireplace, gazing up at the age-darkened oil painting of Lady Anne in her austere finery. She wore a delicate ruff whose stiffened lace covered her neck, though not in the old Tudor fashion that made it look like someone was serving your head on a plate. She had dark, intelligent eyes but a plain, fairly nondescript face, and her dark hair was almost aggressively unadorned, swept roughly back under more lace. Clustered around her, gazing implacably out of the frame but all slightly smaller in scale, were her servants and children, though it wasn't always easy to tell which were adults. There was no sign of an obvious husband, and she was painted larger than the rest: a seventeenth-century snapshot of a domestic but distinctly hierarchical scene. It was not a painting from life so much as a statement of her status, which was hardly surprising, he supposed, given her achievements in life. Without her, the castle in which he now stood probably wouldn't exist at all.

He considered the coat of arms that hovered above her right shoulder: a gold shield and crown divided into quadrants, two showing six rings arranged as an inverted pyramid, the others a checkerboard bisected by a stripe of red. It was, unmistakably, the same crest as had been on the ring found at the Ek Balam tomb, except that it was missing the elliptical shape beneath.

He smiled to himself, momentarily forgetting his impatience, and drew from his pocket the photocopy of a Privy Council record dated 1633 announcing the arrival of a thirteen-year-old page boy by the name of Edward de Clifford "to wait upon his Majesty the King." There seemed to have been some uncertainty about the "de" prefix, because it was heavily scored out. There was no mistaking the carefully etched heraldic crest that stood by Edward's name, however, nor the curious elliptical eye shape that had been added to the Clifford coat of arms.

Nick Reese flicked a glance at the door. What was keeping the man?

He sighed. He was no expert on heraldry but he knew that this whole thing was unusual. Coats of arms were modified when their owners married or attained a new title, so why would a thirteen-year-old boy wear a crest different from that of his parents? The boy had been introduced at court by Lady Anne Clifford's second husband, Lord Herbert, though that man would not have actually been the boy's father. Perhaps Lady Anne's first husband, Richard Sackville, third earl of Dorset, who had died in 1624, was the boy's father. But that didn't make sense either. The official record gave Lady Anne five children but reported that none of her boys made it to adulthood. The curiously modified crest under which Edward had arrived at the court of King Charles I was not used by any of the other children, who were associated only with the standard Clifford symbols. And if the boy did not survive to manhood, why was there no record of his death?

Nick Reese had an instinct for the parts of a story that did not line up, an instinct that had served him well in the past. There was something very curious about this Edward de Clifford, and if he could find out what it was, he might be able to explain how the boy's ring—and perhaps his arm—wound up in an ancient Mayan tomb on the other side of the Atlantic.

His phone rang.

He flipped it open and considered the caller's name on the screen: Chad Rylands. Reese scowled but answered it anyway.

"Tell me you have a date of internment on that finger bone and an age of the victim at the time of death," he said. "Or are you spending all your time in London at the clubs?"

"I told you, I can't do those tests myself," said Rylands, ignoring the jab. "I'm waiting for the lab report on the DNA sample from the small finger bone. The people at the INAH physical anthropology section at the Regional Yucatan Center— the nerve center where all the finds are catalogued—aren't calling me back."

"I don't want to hear what you can't tell me, Chad. I want answers."

"Communication has gotten a little tricky since the murder of the site foreman."

"Figure it out, Chad," said Nick, his voice flashing fire. "Just get me those results."

"OK."

"Good man," said Nick, blithe again. "But if you don't have the results, why are you calling me?"

"She's here," said Rylands.

Nick Reese turned swiftly from the window as if struck.

"Miller?"

"Well, she's here too, but I meant the other one."

"Where?" he said.

"England. She was in London," said Rylands, "but she's moved."

"Where to?"

"How should I know?" said Rylands.

"It's your job to know, Chad," said Nick Reese.

"It's my *job* to study skeletal fragments," Rylands protested. Sometimes he sounded like he was fourteen.

The door opened and a middle-aged man in a pale suit and stained red tie appeared. He was carrying a plastic file and wearing white cotton gloves. He wore a brass lapel plate that said "Mr. Smythe-Jenkins."

"I've got to go," said Nick into the phone. "E-mail me later."

He hung up and turned, smiling, to the man who was setting the file down on the table with exaggerated caution.

"This is everything pertaining to Edward Clifford," said Smythe-Jenkins in a rich, plummy accent that originated nowhere in the vicinity of the castle. "I have to ask you to wear gloves as you handle the contents, and I'll need your signature here, here, and here."

He indicated a form where he had made "x" marks with an ancient fountain pen.

"I can give you one hour with the contents of the folder," the man continued. "Photographing, scanning, or otherwise recording the documents is forbidden, though you may make notes or copies in pencil on your own paper."

Nick nodded and signed, fluently scribbling "Jonathan Sanders" in the spaces provided.

"I will return to check on you," he said, turning on his heel and walking out.

An hour gives me plenty of time, thought Nick.

He waited at the window, listening for the man's clipped footsteps to recede. Down below, moving from the gatehouse with the shell room that served as Skipton Castle's ticket booth, an uncommonly tall woman was striding briskly toward the castle proper.

Deborah Miller.

Nick smiled a short, hard smile. That was fast. Last he heard, she was in Lancaster. He wondered how she had made the connection and how much of a problem it was going to be.

"Quite the little reunion we have going, isn't it?" he said into the silence.

From his pocket he took a folding knife with a sharp, three-inch blade. He pushed a chair up to the fireplace and, with four long cuts, sliced the painted canvas of Lady Anne Clifford out of the frame. He rolled it up tight, then took the plastic document folder, zipped it into his laptop case, and walked through the door, pausing only long enough to make sure his exit was clear.

Chapter Thirty-Eight

■ ■ ■ ■ ■

Deborah had taken the train from Lancaster East to Skipton through red brick towns and those tiny, irregular fields—deeply green but wild looking—that defined the Pennine countryside. The dry stone walls looked wild too, she thought, so old and arbitrary, like they were natural features of the ancient landscape. As Deborah left the train station and made her way through Skipton's narrow streets, she felt keenly out of place, a modern urban flamingo absurdly dressed in shorts and work boots.

She bought a ticket to the castle and began to wander its sparsely furnished chambers, wondering what she had hoped to find. There were several versions of the Clifford coat of arms, most strikingly one over a doorway off the courtyard, flanked by wyverns, but none of them showed the oval shape beneath the now-familiar rings and checkerboard. She sat on a circular stone plinth under a yew tree and consulted the guide sheet. It marked out a forty-stage sequential tour with black–and–white illustrations, each marked with snippets of history.

The yew tree she sat beneath had apparently been planted by Lady Anne Clifford in 1659. This woman refurbished the structure extensively after the English Civil War, during which the castle had been a royalist stronghold, surviving a three-year siege by Cromwell's parliamentary forces. Lady Anne—born here in 1590 and once a young favorite of Queen Elizabeth's—had won the castle and the other elements of the Clifford estate after a lengthy legal battle over her right to inheritance. She had been, it seemed, an iron-willed woman, sure of her own mind, whom even Cromwell had been unable to intimidate. Deborah decided she liked her.

When the first policeman entered the courtyard, she could tell from his manner that something was wrong. At his heels trailed an elderly man with a brass name pin, presumably an employee of the castle. He looked flushed and upset.

"No," he said to the policeman, "stay there. There's only one way out of the castle, through that door. Don't let anyone leave."

He hurried through a door and up a flight of steps, but his face looked desperate. Whatever he was looking for, he clearly thought the search vain.

Deborah looked after him and then turned to the cop who met her eye and nodded.

"Problem?" she said.

"A theft," he said, looking a little bored. "Just a painting and some old papers. Some bloke walked in, asked to see them, then carried them off. Not what you'd call a maximum-security facility."

"Was the painting valuable?" she asked.

He shrugged. "Probably. Old family portrait."

"Who of?"

He shrugged again. "No idea. Whoever took it is probably long gone, unless he's wandering round the castle looking for other stuff to lift. There'll be CCTV of him leaving, probably, but unless they get a car number plate they can forget it."

She thought she might coax some details out of him, although she guessed he'd clam up as soon as the old man returned. He was a young man, and he carried himself a little stiffly. She uncrossed her long, cold legs slowly but stayed seated, so her height wouldn't intimidate him.

"Why would anyone steal old paintings and papers?"

"Not just old paper," he said, smiling knowingly. "Documents. Letters, I think. From, like, the seventeenth century."

"Wow!" she said, playing up her American accent. "That is so cool. Like a movie. In the States, we keep all our seventeenth-century documents in vaults or something, not just lying around where people can walk off with them. But you guys just have so much history here I guess a few papers don't seem like much."

She spoke admiringly, as if the cop was personally responsible for the grandeur of his national heritage.

He nodded. "So where in the States are you from?"

"Atlanta, Georgia," she said, turning on a bit of a twang she didn't know she could do.

"Yeah?" he said, impressed. "Hence the shorts, right? Probably weren't ready for our bloody awful climate."

"Right," she said, grinning inwardly at the idea that she would dress like this in Atlanta.

"And you're just visiting, doing the sites and what have you?"

"That's right," she said, as if he had seen right through her. "So these stolen letters," she went on, "who are they from?"

"The old bloke said they're from someone called Edward Clifford. Letters to his mum." He shrugged and smirked. "Sounds like a lot of fuss about nowt to me," he concluded.

"His *mum*?"

"Her what built this bit of the castle, supposedly," he said.

"Lady Anne?"

He paused, pleasantly surprised. "So you're a history buff, eh?"

"No," she said, trying to be girlish. "Just read it on my guide thingy." She waggled the piece of paper.

"Oh," he said. "Right. So you're staying in town?"

"No," she said, pouting her disappointment. "I've got to be heading out this evening."

"Oh," he said, smiling. "Pity."

"Isn't it?" she said.

The old man returned, bustling out of a different stairwell and into the courtyard.

"Anyone passed this way?" he demanded.

"No, sir," said the policeman. "I suggest we return to the house and start filling out the necessary…"

"Stay here," the other shot back. "Don't let anyone in or out without speaking to me first."

"Sir, may I remind you that since this is a crime scene, the presiding authorities are the local constabulary, as represented by yours truly, so if you…"

"Just stay here till I come back," barked the older man. He stormed across the cobbles, out through the Norman arch, and down the steps.

The policeman flushed, and his lips were pursed.

"Someone doesn't seem to know who's in charge," said Deborah, in a manner she hoped was supportive. "If anyone will catch the thief, it will be the police, right?"

"Precisely," said the cop, straightening up again. "Civilians lose a proper perspective on crime when it involves them. They forget that *we* are the professionals, and they're best leaving things to us."

He had recovered some of his dignity, but he shot a frown back through the arch where the old man had gone.

"So these letters that have been stolen," Deborah ventured. "They are the only copies?"

"No," the policeman scoffed. "That's the thing. They have copies of everything. 'Transcripts' he called 'em, made donkey's years ago in case..."

"Someone walks off with the originals," she completed for him.

"Exactly," he said, laughing.

"And where are they?" she said.

"The copies? I've got one here," he said, reaching into his jacket and withdrawing a sheaf of folded papers. "Old man insisted I had one so I could *compare them to the originals should I find the culprit*," he said, mimicking an aristocratic demeanor. "Like I can search someone without probable cause! If he recognizes the bloke who swiped them, I'll nick him. If he doesn't, I won't be performing cavity searches on anyone who happens to be in the castle, will I?"

He caught himself and shot Deborah a slightly abashed look, as if he might have offended her.

"Can I see them?" she asked.

"As far as I'm concerned, love, you can have them. Souvenir of Skipton Castle."

"Thank you," she said, beaming. "Thank you so much."

Chapter Thirty-Nine
■ ■ ■ ■ ■

Alice was used to being looked at on the beach. She didn't think her body was that great, but it was well proportioned and everything was still where it should be. Besides, you could put a camel in a bikini and men would stare at it. It was a funny thing, but when a woman wore anything remotely provocative—anything that showed a lot of leg or a little cleavage—men seemed to think you were wearing it for them. It didn't matter if you didn't know them or hadn't even met them before: you could see it in their eyes, that pathetic certainty that you were putting on a show just for them.

James was the worst, because for him it wasn't even just about sex. It didn't matter what she did or said, how completely she ignored him or made fun of him; he still got that wistful look whenever she looked him in the face. For James it was about relationships. It was about love. For all she knew he was already there, or thought he was. She rolled her eyes at the thought.

So she sat out in the sun, reading a paperback mystery she had borrowed from the restaurant's little stock, knowing that two-thirds of the men she would see today would be checking her out. She didn't give a damn. Mostly. There was one guy who was watching her who had caught her eye. He wasn't like the rest.

He was pale and athletic, and stayed out of the sun, sitting on the shaded patio with his book and his sunglasses. He was alone—no family, no girlfriend—but he was no beach bum either. He wore long-sleeved shirts and expensive-looking chinos, and always had a laptop with him. His hair was cropped crew-cut short, but he had a moustache and goatee that gave him a rugged look. She'd seen the skull tattoo on the back of his neck walking past his table at breakfast: its eyes seemed to follow her as the man's real ones so carefully did not. She was intrigued by him, and not only because he didn't stare at her tits like the others, but he made her uneasy all the same. He reminded her of a bad guy in a movie, but in a good way. It gave her a little thrill when she saw him out there this morning, because James had announced that he was going up to see the ruins.

James had obviously wanted her to go with him, though he wasn't quite lame enough to beg her, and once he had gone on about how great they were supposed to be, he couldn't abandon his plan just because she wasn't interested. That would be too obvious even for him. So he gave her the puppy dog eyes and showed her pictures from some old guidebook that showed the stone buildings overlooking the ocean—as if she hadn't seen enough damned ruins. Then, when she looked hard at him and told him to shut up about it because she wasn't coming, he slipped away.

A little after ten o'clock the guy with the tattoo came saunter-ing along the sand, walking slowly but with no pretense of going anywhere but to her. Alice turned away to smirk, then returned her blank gaze to the Caribbean as if she hadn't seen him.

To her surprise, he didn't speak, but settled into the deck chair next to her as if they were already together. She turned to him, ready to offer some pretense at outrage, but he spoke first.

"Where's your friend?" he said, not looking at her, staring out to where sky and water met.

"Went to the ruins," she said. "He'll be gone a while. Why?"

She didn't bother to keep the amusement out of her voice. She hadn't decided yet how far she would let this go. She smiled inwardly. She'd get a kick out of this, she could feel it. She'd been so bored and finally, here was something different.

"What's he doing there?" said the man. He had an accent she couldn't place, Eastern European, maybe.

"How should I know?" she shrugged. "Looking at rocks, I guess. What else do you do in ruins?"

"You might dig," he said.

She looked at him then, and found his face hard and unsmil-ing. She shaded her eyes even though she was wearing sunglasses.

"Was there something you wanted?" she asked.

He took off his shades then and his eyes were ice blue. They slid over her body and his smile was cool, a smirk to match hers.

"Everyone wants something," he said.

"I didn't ask about everyone," she came back, playing now. "I asked about you. What do you want?"

"Two things," he said. "The second we can discuss later."

"And the first?"

"Why don't you come with me, and I'll show you."

She snorted with derisive laughter at the line, but she got up and followed him across the sand toward the cabanas nonetheless.

Chapter Forty

■ ■ ■ ■ ■

Deborah read the letter in the back of a taxi while the driver tapped at his navigation system in the hope of pulling up a hotel or bed-and-breakfast close to Malkin Tower Farm. She read it quickly, then again, more slowly, dwelling on its insinuations.

Being the seventh day of June, the year of our lord sixteen hundred and fifty

My honoured mother, for so I ever will think of you. By now you will have learned what I dearly wished to tell you myself: that I have left England at last, as I often said I would. It was a hard thing to go, not least in leaving you, though I pray you will understand. The court was too decorous for such as I. I know the labours you undertook on my behalf came from your desire to see me prosper, from a love for what the world finds unlovable, and you must not think that my leaving is a rejection of you or of your efforts. On the contrary, I take them with me. They sustain me. They give me hope that I may yet find a place where men will not see in me the dark stars which reigned at my nativity.

Thou knowest—no one more than thou—how I have laboured to honour the trust you placed in me, the life and living you gave me when the world was sure to despise me as a thing sent forth marked by sin. If she—you know the she I mean—had never come to London, all might have been well, but God saw fit to bring her back into my life, and from that day forth the world which you and I had built could not endure. The King my sovereign did much to protect me but calumny will out. I am only sorry that my shame—her shame—erased all you had done for me.

In the hurly-burly of the great unrest, the war and its aftermath, I dared to hope that all might be well, but memories in government are long, and I fear my very shape prevents forgetting. Even with the death of the King's cause and the most barbaric treatment of his royal Highness, I had hoped to retain some place in the commonwealth, but now I see that this cannot be. I will not drag the names of those women dearest to me through the mud, though one be dead. For you to remain unscarred I fear I must vacate these climes forever, leaving behind, I hope, the cruelty and ignorance I have borne for the past thirty years. I enter my self-imposed banishment with hope that in leaving, I may improve what years you have left to you, though my future is unknown to me and full of terror. Where I will alight, I cannot say, though I have a mind to explore something of the lands recounted by our infamous countryman, Thomas Gage.

I must aboard now, but I swear that—unless I perish on the journey—you will hear from me, howe'er infrequent, and unmatched to my love. Weep not for me. You have shed tears enough. For my part I—perhaps—am shedding my past like a snake its skin. Only those parts with you will I keep like the jewels I bear with me.

I remain forever a debtor to your love and compassion.

Edward ~~Dev~~ Clifford

The year 1650, thought Deborah. One year after the central event of the English Civil War—the hurly-burly the letter writer alluded to—the trial and execution of Charles I: one of the few dates from British history still lodged in her head. If the thirty years the writer referred to meant his life to date, then he was born in 1620. Somehow the boy had come into contact with the king's court, had perhaps been a servant or junior counselor. He would, like Lady Anne Clifford, have fought for the royalist cause during the Civil War and, on their defeat and the execution of the king, had decided to leave the country forever. It made a kind of sense, though what those words about his shape and the mark of sin meant, she couldn't imagine.

Suddenly the driver spoke up.

"Well there's a turn-up," he said. "I didn't think you'd find anywhere to stay out there, but it turns out that Malkin Tower Farm *is* a hotel. You want to go? It's nearly ten miles."

"Yes," she said. "But let's stop in town first. I'll need to get some warmer clothes. Can you meet me back in an hour?"

"One hour, right here," he said. "I'll wait five minutes."

"Deal," she said, unfolding herself out of the car.

There was a department store called Rackhams on the main street, so Deborah went there first. In the men's department, she grabbed a pair of 501s—always a safely unisex bet—and moved off in search of shirts and sweaters. What she found was on the baggy side, but it would do. She crossed to the women's side and added some underwear to her cart, and checked out. Back outside on the street, she found an outdoor supplies store called David Goldie, where she bought a pair of low-end walking shoes, some thick socks, and a light waterproof jacket.

Pleased with her haul and the efficiency with which she'd managed it, she met the taxi driver as planned. She realized as the cabbie drove out of town that she'd have to start watching her expenses so things didn't get out of hand; Powel hadn't exactly signed off on her little side trip.

The thought raised other questions about what she was trying to achieve, other than not being either in a Mexican jail or within earshot of her mother and her plans to demolish all the memories of Deborah's father.

Come pick through Dad's things…

Identifying what the jewels were, where they had come from, and how they had reached Mexico would not, after all, tell her where they were now, and if they were still in Mexico it could be a long time before she could even return to find them. In a sense it helped that Bowerdale was in prison, since that meant the police might not be looking widely for other suspects, but that was, she instantly knew, a cowardly and disloyal thought. She would be going back soon, she knew. She didn't especially like Martin Bowerdale, but she didn't believe him capable of what had been done to Eustachio, and she had a duty to try and earn his release.

As she waited for things in Mexico to cool down, she would learn what she could about what had been stolen from the tomb. She would spend the evening studying the video footage of the grave goods, but first she would call Steve Powel, her official link back to the site and whatever was going on there. She had never been able to set up the video conference call she had promised him. Maybe doing it now would mollify him a little.

The cabbie pulled up to Malkin Tower Farm holiday cottages, and she was pleasantly surprised to see a series of converted stone farm buildings. In the distance, a dark, steep hill—almost a mountain—dominated the surrounding landscape. As they'd first driven west from Skipton, it had been picturesque, but as they got closer it seemed to loom, and Deborah felt its brooding presence whichever way she looked.

"That's Pendle Hill," said the driver.

He said it darkly, like the name should mean something to her, but offered no further explanation. Deborah was unaccountably relieved to find that when she stepped out of the cab, she couldn't actually see Pendle from Malkin Tower Farm.

She paid the driver and took her belongings to what looked like the main cottage. Deborah took the smallest room, quaintly named "the piggery"—which it almost certainly had once been—because it was cheap, clean, comfortable, and, since it was a separate building from the rest of the cottages, private. The ceiling was low, but not so much that she might actually bang her head. She unpacked quickly. It was getting late, though the light still held, and she realized with a shock just how far north she really was. In the winter it probably got dark not much later than midafternoon, but in summer—albeit a cold and rainy summer—the light would hold till nine or ten.

She called Steve Powel, turning on her laptop's built-in webcam. It was a strategy designed to make it harder for him to yell at her. People felt tougher when they couldn't be seen. He answered quickly, agreed to the video conference with impatience, and then demanded to know where she was and what the hell she was doing. He looked distracted, sitting at his desk with the trophies and the pictures of his daughter on the shelves behind him.

"I can't search for the missing grave goods in Mexico so I'm trying to figure out what they were and how they got there," she said. "Maybe that will help."

"Maybe," he answered, looking skeptical. "Where exactly are you, Deborah? I want an address."

She gave it to him, explaining the link to the pale ruby-like stone that had been found at the farm, but he looked impatient.

"I need you back in Mexico," he said. "I need you looking for the stolen artifacts."

"And as soon as it's safe to go back, I will," she told him. "A few days is all I want, if you can assure me that I'm not going to be thrown into prison the moment I get there."

"I'm working on it," he said. "But if you're right about those grave goods being European, we need to prepare for an extradition battle. If they aren't part of the indigenous culture, all bets are off and I want to be able to bring them back to the States."

"If they're European, there'll be Europeans who want them returned," said Deborah.

"That's a lot grayer legally than taking Mayan goods from Mexico. Try to keep it out of the papers and we'll have time to figure out what we have and how hard to fight for it. Maybe there's a touring exhibit in it."

Deborah told him she would do what she could. "I'm sorry, Steve," she said. "I'll make this work."

"I hope so, Deborah. I really do."

"How are things there?" she said, trying to soften the tone of the conversation.

"Hectic, Deborah. Stressful."

"And Angela?" she persisted, determined to find something that would take the edge out of his voice.

He blinked and seemed to peer at his computer screen.

"She's fine," he said. "No change. Why?"

"Oh, I can see her pictures on the shelves behind you," said Deborah, floundering. "No change?"

"I just mean, yes," he said. "She's fine."

"Beautiful girl," said Deborah, suddenly wishing she hadn't set up the video connection after all. She knew she looked fake. She looked over Powel's shoulder to the largest picture on the wall, a headshot of his daughter wearing the gold necklace she seemed to wear with all her costumes. A lucky charm, perhaps. Rachel's had been pearl earrings their father had given her one Hanukkah before he died.

"I'm sorry, Deborah," said Powel, "but I really have to go. Keep me informed, OK?"

Deborah hung up and sighed. It was too late to go snooping about the site where the crystal had been found, and she was hungry. Dinner, bed, and then an early start: hopefully in twenty-four hours she'd know if there was any reason to stay in Lancashire to investigate further.

Chapter Forty-One

■ ■ ■ ■ ■

Once the idea had occurred to her, it took her ten minutes of eyeing the phone sideways as she bustled about to call her mother. Just as she was about to lose her nerve and disconnect, her mother picked up. "So you're finally calling," said her mother. "Where are you?"

"England," said Deborah.

"England? What do you know from England? I thought you were in Mexico."

"I was," said Deborah, wearying fast, "but something came up."

"Quite the jetsetter these days. Too bad you can't squeeze in a visit to Boston once in a while."

"To visit a house I've never seen before?"

"I haven't sold it yet. Our house, I mean, not Steve's place. I don't see the big deal. It's just a house. It's not like you ever visit."

"It's where I grew up," said Deborah, getting up and starting to pace. "It's where we all lived together."

"With your father, you mean."

"Yes," said Deborah, reproachfully. "It was our place."

"You wanna buy it? Make me an offer."

"Funny."

"I just don't see the big deal."

"I know."

"What's that supposed to mean? You think I'm insensitive because I'm moving forward?"

"No, Ma."

"Your father's dead, Deborah."

"Who could ever think you insensitive?"

"I'm just saying."

Deborah said nothing.

"Steve is a good man," said her mother. "You'd know that if you came by once in a while. He makes me happy."

"I'm sure he does."

"You know, Debs, finding a man might make you happy, too."

"I'm perfectly happy, thanks," said Deborah.

"Yeah? All this charging around, digging up old things and dead people. You're still young. You should be with the living. What do you care about all that dead stuff? I just don't understand it."

"Clearly."

"And now you want to hold on to this huge old house like it's your personal archaeological site, your little window into a past that died with your father."

"Don't try to get inside my head," Deborah cut in, hearing her mother's voice hardening.

"God forbid anyone should do that, right, Debs? God forbid anyone should give you a little perspective, a little insight from someone who's been around the block a few times."

"You've not been around my block," Deborah shot back.

"How could I?" her mother said. "I couldn't get near your intellectual level, could I? I'm not smart enough for you, not like your father. I was never good enough for you."

"*You* were never good enough for *me*?" Deborah said, incredulous. "How about putting it the other way round?"

"I'm sure I don't know what you mean."

"You would have done anything for Rachel. You did!"

"Let's keep your sister out of this. I treat you both the same."

"Oh, please."

"I get to see her more, is all. And sure," she said, conceding the point but defiant in doing so, "I *understand* her. Her life. Her marriage. Her job. It all makes perfect sense to me. What I don't understand is turning into a spinster surrounded by books and bits of old crap you dug out of the ground."

"Ma, I've got to go," she said. "I'm sorry, but I can't do this right now. I'm tired and stressed, and…I'll call you back soon, OK?"

She hung up. She gripped the phone tight in her fist, waiting for it to ring, feeling the strange discomfort of disappointment when it didn't. She nearly called back to apologize, but she knew it wouldn't be that simple, that she wouldn't be permitted to say sorry and leave it at that. Her hanging up had been a reflex, like leaping out of the window of a burning building. She could call back, but the room would still be on fire. She turned the phone off and slipped it into the pocket of her jeans. Why had she thought calling her mother was a good idea? Everything had been so strange lately, so inconclusive. Perhaps she had hoped that if she could resolve something in her personal life then the rest of the stuff she was wrestling with would feel more manageable.

Well, so much for that.

Deborah checked with the landlady and then walked down the narrow farm road and back toward the town, inhaling the cool, damp air with its smell of grass and the tang of manure. As she walked she tried to make sense of the letter from Edward Clifford to his mother—it didn't seem quite right. "My honoured mother, for so I ever will think of you." Did that mean she would always be dear to him, or that he would continue to think of her as his mother even though she wasn't? If she wasn't, how did he come to bear her coat of arms, albeit so curiously modified? The letter gave Deborah the sense that Edward's self-imposed banishment—presumably to Mexico—was done in part to spare his "mother" further hardship. She was most tantalized by the reference to "the jewels I bear with me." Could they be what was found in the Mayan tomb? The dates would fit, and it was not inconceivable that an Englishman could find his way to Mexico, particularly if he went via Spain and came across with colonists or as part of a religious mission.

She arrived at the Cross Gaits Inn and—feeling tired and in need of a little indulgence—ordered a Bombay Sapphire martini at the bar, very dry, two olives.

"A lady who knows her mind," said the barman. "Don't get much call for martinis around here." She watched him pull down the gin. He was a heavyset man, but strong and broad shouldered. His complexion was pinkish and mottled and his shirt was dotted with sweat, but he had a confident, forthright air that

Deborah would have associated with blue-collar New York if he didn't have that tough, teeth-baring Lancashire accent.

Deborah took a menu and chose a table by the window, carefully cradling her drink, smiling as she heard the next customer order two pints of bitter. Cocktails, apparently, weren't the norm in Lancashire pubs. The pub was quiet and only two other tables were occupied. She ordered Chicken Tikka Masala and when the barman returned with her cutlery and condiments he asked her where she was staying. She told him Malkin Tower Farm and he smirked.

"Come to see the witches?" he said.

Deborah just looked baffled.

"Witches?" she said. "What witches?"

The barman paused to consider her.

"You serious?" he said. "The Pendle witches, of course."

"I'm sorry, I'm not familiar with them," she said.

"You didn't know this was witch country?" He turned to the barmaid who had come to wipe off the table and said, "Chantelle, listen to this. She's come all this way...America, right?"

"Right," said Deborah, starting to feel like an exhibit in her own museum.

"All the way from America to Pendle, sightseeing, like, and has never heard of the Lancashire witches!"

Chantelle, a pale, moon-faced girl with streakily-dyed blonde hair, raised her eyebrows.

"Honest to God?" she asked.

"Honest to God," said Deborah, smiling.

"We got witches all right," said the barman, laughing. "Hold on, let me go get my wife."

This was apparently a joke, and Chantelle laughed, as did the party who had ordered the pints of bitter. Deborah was becoming a celebrity.

"The year was 1612," said the barman. "It started right here. Most famous witch trial in English history. Ten people executed in Lancaster for multiple murder by witchcraft, mainly on the testimony of a nine-year-old girl."

"Jennet Device," said the man who had ordered the bitter. He was in his twenties and wore round glasses that made him look bookish.

"Am I telling this story or are you, Neil?" said the barman to him.

"Get on with it, then," said the man, grinning.

The barman took a seat opposite Deborah.

"It all started just down the road," he said, "right where you're staying."

Chapter Forty-Two

■ ■ ■ ■ ■

Nick Reese pressed the phone to his ear and squeezed his eyes shut. He had been dreading the call.

"Why the hell did you take the painting?" said the crisp English voice.

"Deborah Miller was in the building," Nick answered, trying to sound composed. Trying to sound like he really believed that he hadn't buggered the thing up. "She was clearly following a lead. She would have found her way to that room eventually. I thought that if I could prevent her from seeing the painting it would at least buy us some time."

"But in fact," the other interrupted, "it turns out that the theft of obscure old paintings makes them less obscure. It puts them, in fact, in every paper, local news bulletin, and webpage in the area."

"The castle is a mausoleum and their filing system primitive in the extreme. I gambled that they wouldn't have a file image ready to go."

"As gambles go, it didn't work out so well."

"Not as such, no, sir," said Nick, pacing irritably and trying to keep that irritation out of his voice. "But we don't know that she actually saw the picture, and unless she is actively looking for it..."

"Nick, by your own admission, the woman is shrewd and resourceful. If she hasn't seen the picture yet, she will very soon, either because it's staring at her from the window of every TV showroom in the country or because she may just be capable of typing a couple of key words into Google."

Nick took a breath but said nothing.

"Yes?" barked the voice, suddenly.

"Yes, sir," he agreed.

"We have to assume she's seen the painting. So?"

"So she'll realize it is important because of the theft. But I don't see how she can know as much as we do. We're still way ahead."

"Make sure it stays that way and be prepared to take drastic measures if the situation begins to change."

"Absolutely," said Nick, becoming still and straight. His training at the academy had prepared him to take drastic measures, as the person on the other end of the line well knew. Physically, he was still in great shape, as good as nearly a decade ago when he joined the force. But being capable of extreme measures and being comfortable with them were two different things.

"And you're sure about the painting?"

"I'm going to double-check right now, sir," said Nick. "I'll call you back as soon as I know."

He hung up and called Chad Rylands, unfurling the painting as he did so. He spread it out on the tabletop and pushed a book onto each corner to keep it flat. As Chad began to talk, Nick stared at the picture, specifically at one figure beneath Lady Anne, the face half obscured by the dark patina of centuries, and the soot from fireplaces and tallow candles.

"What did you hear from the lab about the finger bones?" he asked as soon as Rylands picked up.

"You were right," said Chad, and there was a hint of wonder in his voice, along with something that might have been fear. "I don't know how you were right, but you were. The bone itself was shorter than you would expect, even for someone born four hundred years ago, but it didn't reveal much more than that. The lab was able to extract DNA evidence, however, and that's where things get interesting."

"Go on."

"There was evidence of autosomal dominant mutation in fibroblast growth factor receptor gene three, almost certainly resulting in achondroplasia."

"So the hand in the tomb," said Nick, still staring at the painting, "was not a child's."

"Not a child's, no."

Reese stared at the portrait for another moment, slotting the evidence into place. He was getting close, but he wasn't the only one, and that meant trouble.

Chapter Forty-Three

■ ■ ■ ■ ■

The taxi driver sat in his black Hackney cab in front of the Skipton railway station where he'd returned after taking the gawky American woman out to Malkin Tower Farm. A large woman had emerged from the station and was now standing by the curb, a phone pressed to her ear, so motionless that he didn't know if she was about to get into the cab or not. He didn't like the look of her.

Not that he could see her, exactly. The woman's face was obscured by the hood of her blue plastic rain slicker. She'd dumped her modest luggage—it looked more like shopping bags—at her feet while she talked on the phone. Except that she didn't talk. What he heard through his rolled-down window gave him the creeps. She made noises low in her throat that said she was attentive and in agreement, but that sounded like the purring of a large cat.

He half hoped she'd just walk away. She probably didn't know where she wanted to go and then would complain about the fare when she got him lost. She probably smelled too. The only bag she hadn't set down looked like a tightly woven basket, and this she had clasped to her chest as if someone might try to rip it from her grasp. He'd wait another few seconds, and if she didn't at least acknowledge his presence, he'd pull away and leave her to whatever poor bugger was next in the rank. It was close to his knocking-off time anyway and he fancied a pint before going home.

"You getting in or what, Missus?" he said.

For a second there was no change, and then she lifted her head slightly and he could see her eyes. Although she was otherwise motionless, they sparkled with a strange energy. Finally, the woman's gaze seemed to focus, like she was noticing him for the first time.

"One second," she said.

It should have been polite, almost apologetic, but it wasn't, and it unnerved him. He also thought she sounded like she might be American.

Two Yanks in one day. Weird.

He met all sorts in this line of work. He'd had his share of drunks spilling out of Rooder's and Strata, and sometimes they were more than drunk, though Skipton wasn't Bradford or Leeds, thank God. But this woman was something else entirely. He couldn't put his finger on it but...

"Malkin Tower Farm," she said, leaning in close so that he flinched slightly.

In other circumstances he might have laughed at the coincidence, but the strangeness of the woman stopped him. They were surely connected, these two American women who had to be taken somewhere he'd never been before, but something in her manner stopped him from remarking on it.

He watched her settle into the spacious back of the hackney in the rearview mirror, pulling her clutter in after her. She had pocketed the phone and now sat like a perching bird.

"You'll want to take the A59 west," she said.

"Yeah," he said. "I know."

He took his foot off the brake and the car rolled forward with its customary chugging rattle, which vanished as he picked up speed.

From that moment on she said nothing and never so much as looked to the side, always staring straight ahead through the windshield like she was driving herself. Only after Gisburn when they were heading south on the A682 did her attention turn to the basket in her lap. He watched her, fascinated, as she lifted the lid of the basket in her lap and peered inside.

As she did so, she purred again, as she had when she had been on the phone, and he said, "What's in the basket?" before really deciding to do so.

Her gaze swung up to the mirror so quickly that he shrank from it, staring hurriedly ahead, but she didn't speak, and after a moment, he risked another look back. She was still staring at him, but there was the shadow of a smile on her face, which broadened when she realized that she had left the lid slightly off the basket. She adjusted it, closing it properly, but not before he—with a thrill of horror—had seen a long reptilian leg reach out from inside. In the same instant, whatever was in the basket emitted a long, tremulous call that raised the hairs on the back of his neck.

Chapter Forty-Four

■ ■ ■ ■ ■

James was sick of Alice's attitude to him, her presumption. But today it had worked in his favor. She thought he'd gone away all disappointed, but in fact he had gotten his stuff together and taken a tourist bus to Coba, where there was a large Mayan city right in the jungle. James had heard there were spider monkeys and that the ruins felt like something out of Indiana Jones.

Should be pretty cool.

But he wasn't going to see the tourist stuff, and that was cooler still, as was the fact that in his backpack, along with the cryptic notes he had scribbled in his journal, was a folding trowel and a hand pick. They made the bag heavy, but he slung it up between his shoulders and walked toward the site entrance, wondering vaguely what he would tell Alice later. He imagined how she would respond: surprise, certainly. Excitement too. And she'd be impressed, and maybe that would be enough. Maybe they would have sex, and maybe after that he'd be able to walk away from her and get on with his life. By then he would have some real money to play with, thanks to Bowerdale.

James knew nothing about Coba and, for once, didn't much care. He bought his ticket, the cost of which included a map. He rented a bike then set off into the ruins, which were spread out and overgrown. He passed the Grupo Coba with its Temple of the Church, whose weather-beaten stepped pyramid was almost conical, like an immense termite mound rising up out of the jungle. He'd read that Coba was used for those shots of the rebel base rising above the rainforest in *Star Wars*. If that was true, it was also, he thought, pretty cool.

He rode east, turning right at a sign that marked an over-grown path toward one of the city's ancient ball courts.

He couldn't take the bike all the way and had to leave it propped against a tree. The vegetation was dense, and after five minutes, he was sure he had lost the path and was wandering aimlessly in the jungle. There were bugs everywhere, and even though he sprayed himself with mosquito repellant, he was getting covered in bites. He hadn't seen a single person since coming this way, and though that had initially excited him, he now began to feel simply lost and frustrated. And then, without warning, he was there.

The ball court was much smaller than the one at Chitchen Itza, more like the one at Ek Balam, which had similarly sloped sides. James scanned the site, checked the instructions he had scribbled down, and walked into the jungle, moving diagonally from one corner of the stone terrace. He took twenty long paces, feeling like a kid playing pirates, and came to a patch of secluded ground under a huge tree: ground that looked dark and uneven as if recently disturbed.

He checked to see that he was still alone, then set to work. The ground was indeed soft and he didn't need to use the pick. The trowel worked just fine, and in less then ten minutes he had removed enough of the dirt to see the edge of a purple canvas bag. He would have preferred to hear the chink of his little spade on the lid of a chest, but this would do very nicely. He uncovered the rest of the bag and hauled it out. He replaced all the dirt, gently tamping it down with his feet when he was done. Only then did he turn his attention to the contents of the bag.

He had seen it all before in the Ek Balam tomb, of course, but couldn't resist just laying it out and gazing at it for a few minutes. Everything was there: intact and beautiful, even the bones. He picked up the highly polished log inset with bright, decorative stones and turned it over in his hands. It was about eighteen inches long and carved with images of a jaguar with quetzal feathers, traditional symbols of power and grace among the ancient Maya. He turned it end over end, studying the carving closely. It was a full two minutes after he had blown off the dust and dirt that he saw the crack that outlined the body of the springing jaguar: there was a visible seam. Excited, James pried at it with a pocket knife, and within moments, the log split easily into two perfectly crafted halves. Inside was a brown folded parchment bound with faded red ribbon. He freed the ribbon gently, working it sideways till the paper slid out, and read the letter to himself, delighting in the fact that he was the first person to see what it contained.

It wasn't easy to decipher. The penmanship was spidery and erratic, the letter shapes and sizes wildly inconsistent, like it had been written by a child. It took him a couple of minutes to make it all out, then he read it again, not sure what he had discovered.

He was sweating from the digging and the humidity of the jungle, but he felt a rising thrill as the contents of the letter registered. The treasure they had found in the Ek Balam tomb was only the beginning.

Chapter Forty-Five
■ ■ ■ ■ ■

"At the beginning of the seventeenth century," said the barman, fixing Deborah with a serious look, "Pendle was a wild and sparsely populated place known as Pendle Forest. There was not much to hold the people scattered across the region together, except for Newchurch. It's an old church about three miles west of here, and the place people had to go for Sunday service or risk being fined by the state."

The barman's name was Ralph. He owned the pub, and Deborah could tell from the slightly amused hush of the others in the pub that this was not the first time he had told his tale to a stray visitor.

"Among the people who made the trek to Newchurch each Sunday—or were supposed to—were two poor families anchored by a pair of old women. One was called Anne Whittle, known locally as Old Chattox, perhaps because she was constantly muttering and chattering to herself. The other was Elizabeth

Southerns, known as Old Demdike, a blind, lame woman who owned no more than a single smock. Both lived by begging and from time to time working as "wise women": curing sick cattle, banishing the evil eye, turning soured beer back the way it should be. Important stuff, if it worked, stuff right at the heart of the community."

"Spoken like a true barman," said Neil, the man with round glasses, laughing. He'd been listening attentively, as if ready to correct the story if necessary.

"Beer is food!" said Ralph, slightly defiant. "Anyway, the two old women knew their stuff, but they feuded with each other. Also, people were afraid of them, thought they had dark powers. And not just the old women themselves, but their children and grandchildren too. There were stories of grudges, stories that went back as far as 1595—almost twenty years before the trials—rumors of people like Christopher Nutter and his son Robert, and Old Demdike's son-in-law John Device, all being bewitched to death by the Chattox woman.

"Legend has it that Old Demdike's granddaughter, Alizon, inherited the dark powers. First, the young girl cursed a local miller who had underpaid her mother for some field work. Soon after, the miller's daughter grew sick and died. Two years later, Alizon Device was begging at a market and asked a peddler for some pins. He refused her roughly. 'Pins?' says he. 'Let's see some money, first. You'll get no pins from me, baggage.' 'No?' says she, 'then I hope your own pins prick you to death.'"

The barman leaned forward, still holding Deborah's eyes.

"And no sooner than she had said it," he continued, "did the peddler fall down, paralyzed and unable to speak. He was taken to a tavern, and though he lived, he was lame from that day forth and could only speak with great difficulty."

"He had a stroke," said the man in the round glasses.

"Quite possibly," said Ralph. "But Alizon thought she had done it. She confessed as much, and told how she had been visited by a black dog who told her how to lame the peddler. She said Old Demdike had trained her in witchcraft and brought the black dog to suck at her breasts when she was just a lass."

"She said this at trial?" asked Deborah.

"Before the trial," said Ralph. "The peddler's son appealed to the local magistrate, who forced Alizon's confession. He got not only the story of her own witchcraft, but other stories of her grandmother Demdike's workings in the dark arts: how she had bewitched John Nutter's cow to death, magically turned milk to butter, and cursed the Baldwin child till she died. Alizon didn't stop with her own family, but went on to implicate Old Chattox, said she'd killed little Anne Nutter for laughing at her and used a clay figure to kill the child of John Moore who had accused her of souring his beer.

"Finally, Demdike, Old Chattox, and the Chattox daughter, Anne Redfearn, were arrested and interrogated. Both old women confessed—and in detail—to long histories of witchcraft. Demdike said the devil first came to her in the form of a small boy and she gave him her soul in exchange for the power to kill. She learned how to make 'pictures in clay'—doll versions of her victims—which she would then torment with pins, or fire, or by slowly crumbling them to dust, creating sickness, pain, and death in the actual person. The devil granted her a familiar who appeared to her as a dog, a cat, or a hare, and which came to her home at Malkin Tower to suck her blood."

"She lived at Malkin Tower?" said Deborah.

"That's right," said Ralph. "The foundations of the cottage where she lived are on the land where you are staying. The present buildings were built from the stone and timber that remained when the tower was demolished."

Deborah said nothing. The pub had grown oddly silent as everyone listened.

"Chattox also confessed to killing cattle and otherwise using evil spirits to serve her ends. Her daughter Anne Redfearn said nothing, but was implicated by the others, and by Alizon, who had already confessed. The laws against witchcraft were stringent. Two days later, all four women were sent to Lancaster Castle to await trial at the assizes. And the matter triggered the only recorded instance of a witches' Sabbat in England. It took place in 1612, on Good Friday "

"A Sabbat?"

"A kind of meal and meeting, but also some kind of ritual event like a black mass," said Ralph. "Simply put, it was a gathering of witches."

"We can only imagine what that meeting was like. It was probably little more than a hurried gathering of friends and family to discuss what was to be done about the incarceration of the four women, but it drew a lot of people. If we can believe the evidence of those in attendance, they met to give a name to Alizon Device's familiar spirit in hopes it would release the imprisoned women by using magic to destroy Lancaster Castle and kill the jailor."

"They thought they could do that?" asked Deborah.

Ralph shrugged and rubbed a broad hand across his sweaty face.

"We'll never know," he said. "The testimony against them came largely from Jennet Device—who, as we said, was nine. It's thought she was manipulated by those in charge. She implicated her mother, Elizabeth Device, plus Demdike's daughter and a dozen others. Among them were women who had no clear connection to those imprisoned, such as Alice Nutter, who was a woman of land and property at Roughlee, a town nearby. The little girl publicly picked each 'witch' out of a lineup, taking each of the supposedly guilty by the hand."

"She may as well have taken them by the throat," said the man in glasses with feeling.

"They didn't convict on the evidence of a child?" said Deborah. Jennet was younger than Adelita.

"They did," said Ralph. "King James's new laws gave greater freedom and urgency to those prosecuting witchcraft."

"Terrorism is the new witchcraft, then," said Deborah, sitting back.

"And in those days witchcraft was also terrorism," the barman agreed.

"Guilty until proven innocent," said Deborah, thinking briefly of Martin Bowerdale languishing in a Mexican prison.

"In effect, yes," said Ralph.

"So what happened?" said Deborah, not sure she wanted to know.

"Over two days, nineteen suspected witches—mainly women— were tried. The suspects were packed into a dungeon below the well tower in Lancaster Castle, shut up in pitch darkness, a room twenty feet by twelve with a seven-foot ceiling, without ventilation or sanitation. Three months they stayed in there, those who were originally arrested anyway. Not surprisingly, Old Demdike didn't survive the imprisonment. Of those that did, ten were found guilty and hanged."

Deborah stared at him as he began to count them off on his fingers.

"Old Chattox, her daughter Anne Redfearn, Elizabeth Device and her children, Alizon..."

"Alice Nutter, Katherine Hewitt, Jane Bulcock, and her son, John," put in the man in round glasses.

"And Isobel Roby," said Ralph. "All hanged less than a mile from Lancaster castle. The only member of her family to survive was the child Jennet, who had been set up on a table so that she could be seen and heard clearly as she denounced those she had grown up with, including her own mother. Hanging was an unpleasant death, a matter of strangulation before the invention of the long drop that broke the neck, but it was at least better than the burning they would have had on the continent."

"What about the little girl?" said Deborah, thinking of Adelita, whom she had promised to see again. "Jennet?"

"Returned to Pendle Forest and carried the weight of what she had done for the rest of her life," said Ralph. "Except that there was a nasty twist. Twenty-one years later, she was accused of witchcraft herself and had to go through it all again, this time from the other side of the dock. Revenge, perhaps. People round here have long memories."

"But she was just a child manipulated by the authorities," said Deborah.

"Even so."

"There's one other thing about the Sabbat I haven't told you," said Ralph.

"What about it?" said Deborah.

"It happened at Malkin Tower," said Ralph. "They found clay images of people and human teeth dug up from graves at Newchurch. About ten yards from where you'll be sleeping tonight. So. Sweet dreams."

As Deborah managed a smile and drained her glass, the silent pub exploded with laughter.

Chapter Forty-Six

■ ■ ■ ■ ■

Nick Reese left the hotel where he was staying at a brisk walk, moving quickly through the dark and damp flagstone streets of Skipton to where he had parked the beige Toyota Corolla in a half-empty pay lot. He was, as usual, alone.

It was odd being up in the north again, close enough to home for it to feel oddly familiar and just as oddly alien. He had lived in London for a decade and traveled around the world. Now, these streets, with their pie shops, curry houses, and chippies, seemed quaint and slightly absurd, like models on a railway layout or reconstructions in a museum.

Scenes from my past, he thought.

Not that he fit in any better in London.

Out of habit, he looked around him as he walked. The shops were closed, and the pubs would have rung for last call. Somewhere he heard a man singing drunkenly, then a cackle of girlish laughter, but the night was otherwise quiet.

There were only three other vehicles in the lot and only one caught his attention: the gray transit van squeezed in next to his car, so close that getting into the driver's side was difficult. He slid in between the two vehicles sideways, muttering curses, and in the process put his left hand on the van's hood. It was warm.

A practically empty lot, but this van had parked in so tight he could barely open his car door.

Which, in turn, meant...

The rear doors of the van kicked open and two men came out of the back, one white, one black, the latter with what looked like a blanket held tight to his chest. Another man slid out of the passenger's side and was coming around the front.

For a moment Nick Reese did nothing but scowl, then he reached for the keys in his jacket pocket. In a moment, the first man was on him, pinning his arms to his side and jerking him around so the black guy could throw the blanket over his head.

"What the hell...?" Nick said, sputtering with indignation and fear.

Then, just as the blanket was high enough to block the man's line of sight, Nick Reese shed the pretense of surprise and panic, and became a different man entirely. He kicked upward hard, connecting with the guy's groin. In the same instant he reached forward with his left hand then snapped his elbow back high, a sharp staccato gesture that caught the second man on the side of his head. The pressure pinning his arms weakened, and he snatched his hand from his pocket, pulled it back, and thrust hard with the heel of his palm into the face of the winded black man. The man's head shot back and he crumpled, but the white guy behind him caught him in a headlock and pulled back hard so that Reese's feet were almost lifted off the ground.

The man was bigger than him, stronger, and smelled of Juicy Fruit gum. Reese tightened his stomach, kicked off with his feet, and flipped backward and over the top, using the other man's momentum against him. Reese would have landed flat on both feet behind him, but there wasn't enough room between the car and the van, and he fell awkwardly on the hood of the Corolla. But the action had at least broken the choke hold and given him a clear view of the third man—the driver—advancing from the hood of the car, another big guy, this time in shades and sporting a crew cut. He was reaching into his jacket for a weapon.

Reese turned, grasped the van's roof rack, and used the grip to stabilize a wild roundhouse kick at the gunman. The height of the van gave him reach the gunman hadn't anticipated, and the kick caught him neatly under the jaw, just as the black automatic came into view. He dropped, and Reese turned and aimed another kick at Juicy Fruit, who, still dazed from Reese's flip, turned obligingly into it.

Reese jumped down, seized the gun hand of the driver, and butted him hard in the face like he was heading an in-swinging corner kick. The man crumpled, clutching his face. With a deft twist, Reese relieved him of his weapon, spinning in the same moment to aim it squarely at Juicy Fruit.

Nick Reese, one. Van-driving amateurs, nil.

The man immediately backed off. Reese opened the car door and slid in, switching the gun to his left hand and keeping it trained on the only attacker who was still upright till he had the key in the ignition. As the engine came to life, he put it in reverse with his right hand while his left still aimed the pistol through the open door. Then he took his foot off the brake and rolled the Toyota back, opening the door wide so he had a broader field of fire. He grabbed the wheel with his right hand, shot the car into a tire-squealing turn, and sent it peeling out of the parking lot, his eyes and weapon locked on the man by the van whose hand was frozen in the air inches from his shoulder holster.

For a second the two men looked at each other, and it was like Death had paused to see what would happen next—then the Toyota was careening out into the streets of Skipton. Reese tossed the gun onto the passenger seat, checked the rearview mirror for signs of the van, then closed the driver's door and reached for his seatbelt.

Well, that was bracing, he thought.

He glanced at the automatic on the seat beside him, a Glock 35. They hadn't been amateurs. They just hadn't expected him to be quite so professional.

Chapter Forty-Seven

■ ■ ■ ▩ ▩

The long northern day was finally over by the time Deborah had begun her walk back to the Malkin Tower Farm. It was funny, she thought, without actually being amusing, how much the name of the place had changed for her in the last couple of hours. Before, it had been quaint and rustic. Now it brooded like the hill that was the heart of the area, a presence marked by the sinister nature of what had once been done there.

There were lights on at the farm cottages, and she experienced an almost unreasonable relief at the sight of the stone building that had once been the piggery. A bottle of spring water had been set at the door with a hand-scribbled note that said simply "Fresh!" taped to the cap. Deborah picked it up, let herself in with her key, and cracked the seal on the bottle.

She kicked off her walking shoes, which had begun to rub just above the heel, and poured herself a cup of the water as she waited for her laptop to awake. The water had a slight aftertaste, a very slight but not unpleasant bitterness that tasted of the earth. She checked the label: Penine Springs. Local.

She took another mouthful and, ready to do some research, typed, "Gold rod dove" into her search engine. What came up was a mixture—everything from wedding motifs to dictionaries of Biblical imagery—but over half of the list on the first page contained the word "scepter." She opened three of them and read about European royal regalia that included scepters adorned with doves as symbols of peace or the Holy Ghost.

Royal regalia? she thought. Maybe she should e-mail Marissa Stroud. She was the expert, after all.

She tried another search: "Skipton painting theft." Instantly she had several local news reports on the theft of the painting "and various papers, some antique" from the castle. The second had an image of the picture itself. She copied it to her hard drive, then opened it and considered it.

It was conventional enough. A portrait of a seventeenth-century lady, pale and formal, against a black background. She looked severe, and her finery was restrained rather than luxuriant. A woman of purpose. At her feet were arranged the people in her life, staff, servants, children, husbands, and fathers. The news story said it was Lady Anne Clifford—the name rang a bell from when Deborah had been reading about her earlier at Skipton Castle. The painting in the coat of arms in the picture matched that on the Mayan ring, except that there was still no ellipse overlaying the lower part of it.

Deborah sighed. She had hoped that the stolen painting would have completed her search for the crest and pointed her onward, but it didn't.

So why steal the painting? she asked herself. *What does it reveal that someone wants to keep secret?*

She considered it again. Maybe it was the material of the picture itself, something written on the back of the canvas, or—if she was going to be really conspiratorial—a shadow painting underneath the surface image. But unless she could lay her hands on the painting itself, she could do no better than scrutinize the image on the screen and hope there was something there.

She went back to the woman's face. It was pale and austere, and the eyes stared back at her with something like hauteur. They were cold, dark eyes, and the mouth was hard, without mirth or compassion. Then, without warning, Lady Anne smiled.

Deborah recoiled, thrusting herself away from the desk but staring at the image on the computer screen.

What the hell...?

The image was still staring back at her, but now her thin lips wore a hard, sinister smile.

It must be some kind of computer animation, she thought. *Someone hacked the site and tinkered with the graphics. Some kind of flash program...*

But Lady Anne shook her head very slightly and her eyes sparkled black as beetle shells. No, she seemed to say, this was no computer glitch.

Deborah had backed all the way to the bed, but she couldn't take her eyes off the grinning woman's face, which seemed even paler than it had before, cadaverous, as if the skin had grown translucent and Deborah was seeing bone beneath it. And then the eyes rolled back till only the whites showed, and Lady Anne's mouth began to open, wider and wider, till it filled the screen, and inside was only darkness, but squirming with living, terrible things, and Deborah shrank back, eyes closed, trying to shut the image from her mind.

She clamped her hands over her eyes, hiding in the dark, but somehow that made it worse, because she was sure that the woman had somehow climbed out of the computer and was now in the room. Deborah had started to sob frantically, eyes still closed, moving farther and farther up the bed, burying her face in the pillow. At the foot of the bed she felt the woman coalesce, skeletally thin and pale in her heavy black dress and lace.

I won't believe it, thought Deborah.

And she opened her eyes.

She stared at the foot of the bed and there was nothing there, just the desk and its chair askew. The laptop open. Deborah had already breathed out with a kind of relief before she realized that the computer screen that had featured the painting now showed just an empty gilt frame, and that the door into the piggery was wide open. Standing there, framed against the blackness of the Pendle countryside beyond, was Lady Anne Clifford.

Chapter Forty-Eight

■ ■ ■ ■ ■

Except that it wasn't her exactly. She was hooded, partially, and the face was...*wrong* somehow, but not in ways Deborah could pinpoint. She seemed older, more hunched.

Demdike?

She didn't know where the idea came from, particularly since she had no idea what the witch would have looked like, but come it did, and forcefully. The old woman stood there still and silent, staring at her, and Deborah felt like the breath had left her body. For a moment the room seemed to surge, and she clung to the bed to steady herself, and in that moment the colors seemed to blur and swirl as if she was going to pass out. She felt cold with dread but could not take her eyes from the figure in the doorway, who stood there, motionless.

Deborah sat bolt upright on her bed, terrified. She could think of nothing to say or do, as if Lady Anne—or Demdike— had drained her of all will, all self-control. It was like being inside a dream. She could sense disaster ahead, but watched herself unable to resist gliding toward it.

The old woman—who was no longer hooded—was beginning to mutter soundlessly, her lower jaw working but the words impossible to hear.

Chattox!

Her eyes were still hard and black, fixed on Deborah, and something was moving under her dress, an animal that laced itself between her feet. Deborah gazed at the ripples in the coarse dress fabric that the movement made, fascinated with horror, and saw the creature's leg stray from the folds, so that she flinched and looked away.

Then she could hear the words Old Chattox was saying, questions about Skipton, and Lady Anne, and Edward de Clifford, and she was sure that if she could answer them all, the witch would leave her, would let her live. So she said everything she could think of, all she had discovered so far and how, not remembering and articulating, but just opening up the knowledge she had as if she was pouring it out like milk from a pail.

She talked, and the time passed, and then she realized that she was alone. The computer screen showed the Lady Anne painting as it had always been—smileless—and the room was cold. Deborah closed and bolted the door, then shut the computer down and crawled into bed in her clothes, staring fixedly at nothing, waiting for sleep or dawn, whichever came first.

Chapter Forty-Nine
■ ■ ■ ■ ■

Alice could still smell him on her hair, a thought she liked even if the scent itself—some overly spicy aftershave that he wore in abundance—didn't particularly please her. She considered showering before James got back, but didn't feel like it. Actually, it was more than that. She kind of wanted James to figure it out. This might buy her some space, or might lead to a fight, which was OK too. Alice enjoyed a good fight from time to time, although it seemed almost pathetic to fight with James. She preferred a burlier adversary.

The guy she'd just slept with—Dimitri, he said his name was, though she didn't believe it—was a better match for her. He'd impressed her by seeming even rougher and colder than her ex, who had once shoved her out of the car at a hospital ER with a broken arm and a black eye he'd delivered after she'd thrown a beer bottle at his head during a fight.

Once she and Dimitri had actually gotten down to it, they had barely spoken, and then—right when he was nearly done—he had began to mutter in some language she didn't understand but that might have been Russian: little staccato words spat out at her, almost certainly insults. His eyes had been hard and sour, his mouth full of contempt, and she guessed what he was calling her. So she called him names right back, thrilled by the animal brutality of it, till they had finished and he had left.

He had worn his gun holster even after he had taken everything off. It may have been for self-defense, she guessed, but she was pretty clear he kept it on because he knew it made her hot. It was a weird-looking gun: small and almost round, a revolver with no hammer. She had nearly stroked it when she was on top of him, but had thought better of it. Not all the steel in his face was about lust, and she had quickly admitted to herself that part of her attraction to him was that he scared her a little.

Maybe more than a little.

How long would it be before things turned unpleasant? She liked his aggression, the fact that once he had decided he wanted her there was no question in his mind, no doubt, no hesitation, no politeness or game-playing, no inquiries into her feelings or her past. But she couldn't deny he had been rough, and though she had enjoyed it, she knew that the more they did it, the more things would escalate, till she was bruised or worse. Maybe she'd wind up with a broken finger or jaw, or get dabbed with cigarette burns. Tough, she liked, but that shit she could do without.

But she didn't think Dimitri could be as bad as her ex. There was something about him under the toughness. For one thing, he had nightmares. He hadn't slept with her for more than half an hour, but his rolling around had woken her. He spoke in his own language and woke up looking badly freaked out, though when she asked him about it he gave her a steely look and said it was nothing.

Fine by her.

But then he had made an entirely different request of her, one that made her rethink the way he had suddenly showed up on the beach. In a way, she was glad to find out that it hadn't been a chance encounter, that he had been looking for her before they ever saw each other. If it took the shine off what she had assumed was just animal attraction, it elicited an altogether different sort of thrill. She was even amused to learn that it would almost certainly involve James.

She looked up as James came in the door three hours later and could instantly tell something was up. He didn't ask her about her day or try to kiss her, but sat on the edge of the bed, sweaty and trembling, fingering the straps of a dusty duffel bag she had not seen before. She ignored him for a while, but he said nothing, and that started to worry her. When James had something on his mind, you couldn't shut the guy up. She had decided to have that shower after all, and did so in the spirit of someone walking out of a fight the other person refuses to have. If she kept ignoring him, she figured, maybe he would get angry and they'd be able to move on.

But when she got out of the shower, still wet and with the too-short towel wrapped loosely around her—which always got his attention—he was still sitting there, staring at that raggedy duffel bag like it might explode.

"What's in the bag?" she asked.

"Nothing," he said.

"Yeah? Looks like something."

"It's not."

Alice frowned, then opted for a different tack.

"How were the ruins?" she asked.

"Didn't go," he said, still not looking at her. "Not the Tulum ruins. I went to Coba."

"Coba?" she said, surprised. "What for?"

"Something I had to do."

She paused then, considering him, and he finally looked at her. He looked weary and sort of spooked. He might even have been crying, which wasn't entirely out of the ordinary for James.

"What did you have to do, James?" she asked, focused now.

He shook his head vaguely. "Nothing. Better you don't know."

"What is it?"

"Nothing, Alice. Leave it."

He wasn't telling her something, but he wanted to. She was sure of it.

"I'm going to head out in the morning," he said. "Just me. I'll pay up the room till the end of the week. After that, you'll have to take care of it."

Alice was genuinely shocked. He had obviously been steeling himself for this, planning the words so he could actually do what was so not in his nature and walk away from her.

"Where are you going?"

"Not sure yet," he answered. "Just…away."

"I could come with you," she said. Her hair was dripping cold down her back.

"No," he said, shaking his head again sadly, distantly.

"What's the rush?" she said, taking a step toward him so that the hem of the towel she was wearing touched his knee.

She paused, watching him, feeling his weakness.

"What's in the bag, James?"

"Nothing," he said. His wide eyes made him look like a startled bird.

"Come on, James," she said, taking another step toward him. "Why don't you show me?"

"No," he said. "I can't."

"Sure you can," she said, sliding into his lap and letting the towel fall away. "I bet there are things I can show you."

And then his face was buried in her neck, his body shuddering with sobs so that he couldn't see her smile, couldn't see in her eyes what she saw in the mirror over his shoulder: that rapid play of exhilaration, contempt, and—just flashing into her eyes for a moment—a deep and anguished self-loathing like a cry so clear, so painfully shrill that she couldn't believe he didn't hear it.

PART 4

Chapter Fifty

■ ■ ■ ■ ■

Porfiro Aguilar slid out of bed as silently as he could and went to the shuttered window. He had been dreaming of Mexico City, sitting in Ligaya—his favorite restaurant in Colonia Condesa— eating tequila-flamed mussels out of the shells, uncomfortably aware that all the waiters looked like Eustachio. His plate was rimmed with blood and he had woken suddenly.

As he cracked the shutter he saw what had woken him. There were two police vans in the street below, no lights or sirens, but several men wearing flack vests over their white shirts and carrying automatic weapons. They were going into the building next door: the lab.

Aguilar checked that his companion was still sleeping, dressed hurriedly in jeans and a white cotton shirt, grabbed his wallet and cell phone, and slipped quietly out of the room.

By the time he got down there, the police were already in, already disconnecting computers and hauling stuff out to the vans.

"What is going on?" he demanded, but the first cop ignored him. "You can't take this stuff!" he exclaimed. "I need this equipment. I'm working..."

"Who are you?" said a stocky captain.

"Porfiro Aguilar," he said, "I'm deputy field director and artifact analyst for the Ek Balam dig. I need those computers."

"You'll get them back," said the captain.

"When? In what condition?"

The cop just shrugged and smiled slightly: not his problem.

"Who is in charge here?" Aguilar demanded.

The cop's eyes flashed to the corner of the room where a white man in a gray suit was surveying the work with a clipboard in hand. Aguilar took one look at him and knew him for a *norteamericano*.

"I don't understand," he said. "This is a local investigation, right? Who's he?"

"The man in charge," shrugged the cop.

"Meaning what?" Aguilar demanded. The cop was annoying him.

"He's the man who tells me what to do," said the cop, and that, said his final shrug, was all he knew and more than he cared about.

Aguilar's anger flared. He sure as hell wasn't going to let his work be tossed into a van without a fight.

"You mind telling me on whose authority you are confiscating this equipment?" he demanded in English as he marched over to the man in gray.

The man peered at him over his clipboard for a moment then went back to what he was doing.

"You're Porfiro Aguilar?" said the man, still not looking at him.

"That's right."

"And you performed the analysis of the gemstone recovered from Ek Balam?"

"Yes," said Aguilar, uncomfortably aware that the man had still not said who he was. "It was only a few preliminary tests, little more than an examination with magnification, why?"

"And what did you determine?" said the man, meeting his gaze at last, and tipping his head back a little so that he seemed to peer down his nose. He was middle-aged and slim, but lithe, strong-looking, and he seemed unusually still and self-possessed.

"Just that it was some sort of crystal formation, perhaps a low-grade ruby," said Porfiro. "Uncommonly pure, but of weak color."

"Anything else?"

"We don't have the facility to get much else," he said. "If we hadn't just dug it out of the ground and were pretty sure it had been there several hundred years at the very least, I'd say it was man-made."

"Because of the purity?"

"Yes."

"Any other reason?"

"No."

"And you came to no other conclusions about what it was, how it came to be there, or what it might be used for?" said the suit.

"No. Nothing. I sent it to another lab for a full chemical analysis."

"Which determined what?"

"That the stone contained ferric iron and chromium."

"Meaning what?"

"I have no idea," said Aguilar. "It's an uncommon combination, I guess, but that's all I know. What is this about?"

"And who did you share this information with?"

"Everyone at the site. It wasn't a secret."

"And where is the gem now?"

"In the safe," said Porfiro, nodding toward one of the storage rooms. "The local lab sent it back to me with the results. I was going to send it to the States for analysis, but I needed Mexican government approval to do that. I wrote to them, but I haven't heard back yet."

"That won't be a problem," said the American. "Could you get it, please."

"All artifacts found at the site are part of the patrimony of Mexico," said Aguilar, concerned for what was about to happen next. "I can show you the stone, but it can't leave the country without the approval of my government, and then only for a short period—for analysis or display—before returning to Mexico. It's part of our cultural heritage."

"Well," said the man, with a tight smile, "that seems to be the question, doesn't it? Can you open the safe, please?"

"I can, but you understand that you can't take the stone to the States, right?"

"You've made your position very clear."

"It's not my position," said Aguilar, his irritation getting the better of him. "It's the law, Mexican and international. You can't take it out of the country."

"Just open the safe, please, sir, or I will have you removed and we will open the safe by force."

"The artifacts in there are extremely fragile and priceless," Aguilar spluttered. "You can't blow the safe open without risking serious damage…"

"Then I suggest you open it," said the other, still showing no emotion.

He looked down. It always felt like this dealing with gringos, like every play had to be a bluff because you just never had the cards. He shrugged and walked to the storeroom. He used his body to shield the dial of the safe as he laid in the combination—a futile gesture of defiance—then reached in and withdrew the single cardboard box inside.

"Open it, please," said the man in gray.

Aguilar did so, setting it down on a workbench and unwrapping the contents gingerly, like he was performing delicate surgery on a small animal. The gem had only been small, but even so, Aguilar knew before he folded back the last flap of fabric, that it wasn't there.

"Oh my God," he muttered.

"Get me a list of everyone who knows the combination to the safe, and a schedule of when you know it was opened after the gem was put in," said the American. He seemed completely unsurprised, neither angry nor upset, not even impatient with such incompetence.

"What's going on?" Aguilar demanded.

"First thing in the morning, please," said the other. "The list."

Again Aguilar shrugged and nodded, defeated, feeling like some damned native outmaneuvered by foreigners with better weapons.

The man with the clipboard had already returned to it, so Aguilar—ignored—walked out, his footsteps getting heavier and faster as his frustration spilled over. He slammed the door, found his way into the street, and then marched up to the dorm, only remembering at the last moment to be quiet when he reached the door of his room.

He eased the door open, stepped inside, and closed it carefully so that the latch made the smallest click, but the bedsheets stirred, and Krista Rayburn sat up.

"Porfiro?" she said.

He sat on the edge of the bed, and in his head he heard the American's question again: "And you came to no other conclusions about what it was, how it came to be there, or what it might be used for?"

Used for? What did the man mean?

"You OK, hon?" Krista asked. "What is it?"

"I don't know," he said. "I really have absolutely no idea."

Chapter Fifty-One

■ ■ ■ ■ ■

Deborah woke late and unrefreshed. Her body felt both weary and jittery, as if she had drunk too much coffee, and her eyes stung. She was exhausted, she told herself, so much so that she had fallen asleep while working at the computer and had a nightmare about Lady Anne and the Pendle witches. That was what had happened. She shrugged the dream off—though it lingered in her head, detailed and hard to the touch like no dream she had ever had—and set about her plans for the day.

She had picked up a map in the pub and now studied it while she munched on the toast she had requested from the kitchen. The memory of the dream was fresh enough that she hesitated as she reached for the laptop. Instead, she called Skipton Castle, announcing herself as a journalist working for the *New York Times*. She wanted to know all she could about what had been taken.

The man she was connected to said he was not at liberty to discuss the matter.

"Who can?" she said.

There was another silence, then he said, "Castle employees are not to express opinion or convey information on the subject."

"Who told you not to talk? The castle owner?"

He seemed to search for the word. "The authorities. Now," he said, as if he had already revealed too much and was keen to be out of the conversation, "if you don't mind..."

Deborah hung up and opened the computer. She quelled a moment of uncertainty and returned to the website where she had found the painting. The story was no longer there, nor was there any image of the painting online. She tried a variety of searches, but though the links to the news stories about the theft were there, none of them worked, and she could find no accessible images of the painting itself anywhere.

Curiouser and curiouser, she thought. Deborah definitely felt like she'd fallen down the rabbit hole.

She picked up the phone again and called Lancaster Castle. "Miss Miller," said Hargreaves, pleased, in his gruff way, to hear from her. "What can I do for you?"

"I'm trying to track down an Edward Clifford or de Clifford," she said. "He was the son of Lady Anne Clifford," she added, involuntarily turning her back on the computer so as not to be reminded of what she had decided to call a dream. "But he might not have been. I'm not sure."

She was gambling that his interest in history would make him want to help. He had, after all, revealed something of his own preoccupations, even anxieties. She remembered his face when he talked about that wheeled chair in the Drop Room, sure that though he had left all the important details out, he had—in his way—confided in her. She wondered again what the wheeled chair meant.

"You think that coat of arms you were looking for belonged to this Clifford character?" said Hargreaves.

"Perhaps," she said.

"Hold on." It sounded like *Ohwed on*, that rich, broad dialect that seemed so at odds with his scholarly persona.

"I've got some books here," he continued.

She waited while he muttered and thumbed through. Then he said simply, "No."

"What do you mean?"

"Lady Anne Clifford had five kids. None of the boys survived and none was called Edward. Maybe it's a different family entirely."

"He called her 'mother' in a letter I have. I think he was born around 1620. There's nothing about him?"

"Not in the genealogical records."

Deborah frowned. What had it said in the letter? Oh yes: "My honoured mother, for so I ever will think of you."

What the hell does that mean? Was she his mother or not?

"Is there a precedent for someone like Lady Anne adopting a boy if her own sons didn't survive?" she asked.

"It's suspected that Lady Anne's father George *effectively* adopted a boy fathered out of wedlock on a local servant girl," said Hargreaves. "'Old on, I've got it here." There was a moment while he flipped pages, muttering "George Clifford" over and over as he scanned the pages. "Got it. An Ellen Smith had a bastard son called John in 1599. Ellen's sister Alice was then a tenant of George Clifford, third earl of Cumberland..." He muffled the receiver as he talked to someone else in the room while Deborah listened. "Barry will sort out your ticket, love. I'll be with you in a sec. Tour will be delayed a minute."

"I should let you go," said Deborah, as he came back on the line.

"Castle's been here a thousand years," he said. "They can wait five minutes. Anyhow, where was I? This says Ellen went on to marry a Henry Hartley, raised the child as that man's son, and lived well on a stipend from George Clifford that bought their silence."

"And this Ellen Smith was based where?"

"Roughlee Old Hall," said Hargreaves.

The name rang a bell—it had been part of that story told by the barkeep. Farther, Deborah had noticed on her map earlier. She snatched it up. "It's little more than a mile from here."

"But that still doesn't help you," said Hargreaves. "It shows a connection between the Cliffords and families in the Pendle Forest, but for one thing it's twenty years too early for your Edward—Old George was long dead by 1620—and for another, the point of paying the family off was so the kid *wouldn't* claim the Clifford name. If this Edward was calling himself Clifford then it's a different situation entirely. He couldn't do that unless he'd been welcomed into the family."

Deborah felt defeated.

"I don't understand it," she said. "This guy seems to have been known to King Charles the First. May even have been some kind of prominent courtier, but I can't find who he was."

"Fear not, lass," said Hargreaves. "I'll poke around."

"Thanks," she said. "Oh, one other thing. You said that the gem found at Malkin Tower was bought by a collector of occult objects."

"Supposedly," he said. "The man who sold it is dead, and if anyone knows exactly where it went, no one's talking."

"Right, but when you first told me that, I didn't actually know about the witch connection to Malkin Tower," she said, feeling a little embarrassed by the admission. "I'm probably the first visitor to Lancaster Castle who didn't know who its most famous inmates were."

"Probably so," he said with a chuckle.

"Anyway, that made me realize: the buyer you spoke of must have assumed the gem had power because of its association with the witches."

"Right," said Hargreaves. "It's rubbish, of course, doubly so since there was no tradition of crystals or stones being used in witchcraft in seventeenth-century England. All that New Age stuff about crystals and Wicca is completely different. The Lancashire witches weren't practitioners of some alternative religion. They were poor, uneducated people who clung to whatever power people assumed they had, and their charms—such as they were—were garbled old Catholic prayers tacked on to folk remedies and curses: old-fashioned sympathetic magic. They weren't Goddess worshippers, they weren't practitioners of some pre-Christian fertility religion, and they didn't use magic stones. Whoever bought the Malkin Tower gem did so based on nothing more than coincidence or what we scholar types call *cultural association*."

Another blind alley, then.

"OK," she said, deflated. She scanned Clifford's letter again and her eye fell on the phrase "Where I will alight, I cannot say, though I have a mind to explore something of the lands recounted by our infamous countryman, Thomas Gage."

"Does the name Thomas Gage mean anything to you?" she asked, conscious that she was clutching at straws.

"Amazingly, yes," he said. "He was an English Catholic who joined the Spanish Franciscans and went to Mexico as a missionary. He then converted to Anglicanism and wrote a rather unpleasant book about his former brothers and their work. It was published in…hold on…" There was a paused while he checked. "Sixteen forty-eight."

Two years before Edward Clifford made a similar journey.

That was something, she supposed. Clifford had intended to go to Mexico, to escape Europe entirely and make a new life for himself. She had guessed as much, but it at least showed she was on the right track.

So why didn't it feel like she was making progress?

"Well, I appreciate your help," she said. "If you stumble upon Edward Clifford's name elsewhere, would you mind giving me a call?"

He said he'd be glad to and took down both her number and her e-mail address, but she hung up with a sense of having run into a wall. Before she shut the laptop down she did a quick search for crystals, experimenting with the key words "ruby," "chrome," "iron," and a host of others. She got nothing that was clearly useful except the oblique remark that a combination of chromium and iron was indeed very rare but might enhance a ruby's *optical properties*, whatever that meant.

She showered to clear her head, laced up her walking shoes, slung her laptop case over her shoulder, and set out heading west. She needed fresh air, and a walk to see to the historic grounds of Newchurch seemed in order. Following her map, she soon reached the hamlet of Roughlee, once the home of Alice Nutter, the lady of property hanged as a witch in Lancaster.

Before long, she spotted the church with the swelling, gloomy mass of Pendle as a backdrop. There was a footpath that climbed up the hill, beginning with ancient stone steps, but Deborah had business in the old church first, and she entered the churchyard through a blue painted metal gate.

The church was like a dozen others she had glimpsed from train windows over the last few days: a rectangular nave with a sloping roof, and a square battlemented tower with a clock at the west end. She was looking it over casually, taking in the setting that had a kind of windswept beauty, when she saw something that made her breath catch. She stared at it, her eyes wide.

There was no doubt.

Halfway up the church tower, set into the stone, was a curious oval shape with a dark center: an elliptical eye exactly like the one that, alongside the Clifford coat of arms, adorned the ring they had found in Ek Balam.

Chapter Fifty-Two

■ ■ ■ ■ ■

Hargreaves hung up the phone and chewed his lower lip thoughtfully.

"Barry," he said. "Fancy leading the tour?"

Barry, seventeen, an aspiring history student due to begin university in the autumn, had looked at him like he'd just divulged the whereabouts of the Holy Grail.

"Seriously?" said Barry, pushing his lank hair out of his eyes.

"Seriously," said Hargreaves. "I want to nip down into the archives for a few minutes. You can handle this lot, right?"

He nodded at the assembled tourists who had clustered around the gift shop: a family with a petulant preteen boy, an elderly parson type, two enthusiastic American backpackers, and a dowdy middle-aged dear in a blue mac.

"Absolutely," said Barry. "Brilliant. I won't let you down, sir."

Hargreaves smiled at the boy's enthusiasm and on his way to the basement stopped into the kitchenette to make a cuppa.

After the water boiled, he put an inch of milk and two sugars in a souvenir mug, poured the boiling water into a pot with two teabags, and left it to steep.

The library was two doors and a short flight of steps down from the kitchenette. It may once have been a storage room that had been pressed into service as a dungeon when the castle got overcrowded. It was stone flagged and windowless, and had been used to store prison records for fifty years or so. Some of the older files were still here—or at least the pompous and partisan jottings that had passed for files in those days—but the twentieth- and twenty-first-century stuff had all been removed. Hargreaves was glad. One of the reasons he liked history was because the grim injustices of the past were just that: past. It was one thing to show the cramped cells to the tourists, or the manacles used to chain the Australia-bound deportees, or even the wheeled hanging chair, which had been used to get the lame Jane Scott to the gallows in 1828, but it was another thing entirely to have to deal with the reality of a modern prison.

The wheeled hanging chair had always haunted him, though. Jane Scott had been a pathetic and guileless creature who had attempted to cajole a man into marrying her by claiming to be a wealthy woman. In order to get that wealth, she had bought arsenic from a druggist in Preston where she lived, claiming it was for the rats. She blended it into a porridge that she fed to her parents. Her father had vomited most of it up, but the doctor had not been able to save her mother. The man she had been interested in, a man who had probably seduced her and then reneged on whatever promises of marriage he had made, was quick to witness against her and she had fallen apart. When the guilty verdict had been read to her, she had broken down, confessing to the poisoning and to the killing of two illegitimate children, one hers, one her sister's. By the time she came to be executed, her health declined so much that she could no longer stand.

Hargreaves had dreams about it. He wasn't sure why. Nothing had stamped itself on his subconscious like that damned chair, squeaking on castors as the pitiful, stupid woman was wheeled out to her death. As he had told Deborah Miller, the tourists loved that chair, and it was only in that room that he was glad of the prison's policy disallowing photographs.

Imagine them mugging for the camera beside that thing.

The castle was full of old horrors. It had, after all, been the site of brandings and beatings, incarcerations in darkness, filth and disease, and, of course, of countless executions—more than two hundred and fifty between the years of 1782 and 1865. But it was Jane Scott and her chair that had gotten under his skin and lodged there.

He shuddered and pushed the idea from his mind.

As Hargreaves turned on his computer—the one without the dodgy mouse—he remembered his tea. He was just stepping out when the phone began to ring. It was a prewar black thing that felt brittle and it seemed to ring out of the past. Hargreaves cursed, then resolved to get his tea anyway. The only person who knew he was there was Barry, and Barry would just have to fend for himself for once. If it was important, he'd call back.

He sipped at the tea as he carried it down the hallway, but it was too hot. He set it down on the stained table where he was working and started thumbing through indexes.

The royal court records were full of Cliffords, most of them connected to Lady Anne, but there was no Edward among King Charles's courtiers. Then he tried searching family records on court servants and pages, and there it was: Edward Clifford, a page attending on His Majesty for four years, starting in 1630. There were details of his conduct and training, so that the boy must have been considered something of a rising star. Hargreaves reached for his tea and sipped it, wondering why the boy seemed to be under the protection of prominent people, and why he needed it. After 1634, Edward was back in Skipton. In the 1640s, he did "honorable service" during the roundhead siege of the castle. He seemed to have had dealings with Cromwell himself in the immediate aftermath of the Civil War in London, but in 1649—the date the king was executed—he disappeared from the record entirely. He opened an e-mail message to Deborah Miller, typed in the pertinent details, and sent it.

He was about to quit when he spotted one last tantalizing reference, also from 1649. The Lord Protector—Cromwell—"on the advice of both George Withers and Sir Henry Mildmay," earnestly sought out Edward Clifford "as a royalist traitor to the State." *Withers and Mildmay*, thought Hargreaves, sipping his tea. *Why are those names familiar?*

He opened a search engine and typed them in, but at the same instant, the phone rang again.

It was Barry, and he sounded rattled.

"What is it boy? I'm working."

"Mr. Hargreaves," he sputtered. "I've lost one of the visitors on the tour. She's vanished. We were moving out of the Shire hall and I realized she wasn't with us anymore. She could be anywhere. It could be part of a prison breakout," he said, sounding hysterical. "I'm going to lose my job, aren't I?"

Hargreaves told him to calm down and call the security office, and said he would be right there. He was smiling as he hung up, but then he heard a sound in the stacks behind him, and his smile stalled. At almost the same instance, the colors on the computer monitor seemed to swirl so that he had to grip the table to keep from falling.

He blinked, listening, and then he heard a faint squeak like turning metal. A sense of foreboding filled him, but he felt rooted to the spot. Two seconds passed, three, then it came again. And again. He felt cold, stricken with dread, and then glimpsed something gliding beyond the stacks, visible only through the gaps above and below the books: a shape like a haggard woman, her head down. She was sitting but somehow kept moving, drifting along the floor like she was on wheels.

Jane Scott.

She had come for him at last.

Chapter Fifty-Three
■ ■ ■ ■ ■

James sat on the end of the bed under the mosquito nets and watched her read. He had known he would eventually show the letter to Alice despite all his protestations to the contrary, but he should have held out longer. They had made love properly at least, but she hadn't bothered to conceal how much that had been an unspoken deal.

You show me yours...

Something like that. It left him feeling weak and dirty, but it had done two good things. It had given him someone he could confide in about his predicament, which made him feel less lonely, and it had taken some of the shine off Alice. He had known, of course, that she was hard and selfish and manipulative, but he hadn't had the power to walk away from her. He was captivated. Now, oddly, in the moment where they were closest through sex and the shared knowledge of their secret, he felt more distant from her. This was, he thought as he watched her read the scrawled sheets of folded parchment, a good thing. He knew he could not trust her.

When he had opened the canvas bag she had whooped with delight and triumph, and her eyes had been full of a wild light that was more than just exhilaration. It was, what? Rapture? A joy beyond anything she had shown when they'd made love, certainly. But it wasn't surprise, and that bothered him, because there was something hidden in her face that made him think she had already known what he would be bringing back from Coba.

But how?

He sat up and read the letter again over her shoulder, peering at the rough and uneven writing.

My honoured mother,

Much has happened since I last wrote and the consequences of my small doings have caught up with me at last. This will be, I fear, my last letter, nor do I think it will ever reach you. The Spanish priest who bore my former correspondence is no longer here, nor are any of his compatriots. The circumstances of their departure is the bulk of my story, but it is also its end, and though leaving this life grieves me little, it pains me that I will not see you again and that my words will lie with my poor remains forever. Or rather, a part of them.

I have, I think, learned impetuousness from thee, though I did not suck it from thy breast, and defiance wherein the cause is just. You schooled me in much but nothing of greater import did I learn at your kind tutelage than that the world can be a most wicked place and that it is right and proper to sometimes stand against it.

I have been here amongst the Indians of that region of New Spain called Mexico some dozen years, and in that time I have seen much not dreamt of in the land of my birth, things of great beauty, and skill, and things which are too terrible to report, even to one such as you who are made of sterner stuff than most. Some of those terrible things were done among the Indians themselves, but many more were visited upon them by our European cousins the Spanish, who have made it their purpose to conquer this land and strip it of its resources. The Yucatan has been spared some of the most appalling aspects of the conquest, because it lacks the precious metals and other minerals which the Spanish seek to send back to their homeland, but they have brought great hardship nonetheless, even in spite of their own priests who have—in my sight—urged patience from the soldiers. But the army, though it has some good, God-fearing men, has many in it which are no more than a disordered rabble of drunkards who are here for profit, and are quick to use the sword and the noose. I have heard of whole villages strung up by ropes from the trees, the very babes lashed by the throat to their desperate mothers' heels. Perchance the forest breeds a wildness in the Indians, but barbarism lives not in what we know or believe, but in our actions, and in this I have seen the Europeans stoop to acts our country's worst villains and hangmen would balk at. The Indians are but poorly armed and of a desperate poverty wherein they live and die by the meager crops they raise, so that a drought produces famine. It has been easier here for the invaders than in places dominated by the so-called Aztecs. Here there is little unity between villages, and the old civilizations which boasted mighty armies have long since passed. The worst years were a century agone, but the Indians still live under a great burden, and sometimes that burden becomes more than usually weighty.

The latest dispute arose when a captain from Valladolid moved his troops through the forest near the village. It was said he had once seen most bloody action, an uprising by Indians far south of here in which they had executed several Spanish and some Indians who worked with them in horrible and unnatural ways. The captain's wife was among the murdered. He took to heart then a most vile hatred for the Indians, and revenged himself with his troops upon a neighboring village, killing many in battle and executing those he captured in ways which—save the removal of the hearts, which the Indians had done as a sacrifice to their gods—was the copy of the brutal acts he was avenging. When word reached Spain of his response he was—it is said—told to desist from future reprisals, but either the order never reached him, or he ignored it. He brought his troops north, raping and destroying all he found, till he came to Ek Balam.

We had word of their coming, and I was able to use what able-bodied men we had to arrange archers on the pyramids in the ancient town where the villagers still live as I once stood upon the walls in Skipton to fire down upon the roundheads. Our numbers were few, some twenty-six men and a few women and children strong enough to fight, but the enemy had expected little resistance, none organized. When they rode into town we met them with several volleys of arrows and though we killed none right away—they being well armored against bows—several were injured or lost their horses and caused great confusion and disorder among the troops. The Spanish fired their harquebuses but hit none of our men, and as they sought cover, were two of their soldiers killed with arrows. As the Spaniards split up, some seeking to regroup and some fleeing outright, we leapt down onto them and tore them from their horses. In the struggle which followed I did meet the enemy captain and cut off his arm with the sword I wore when holding Skipton for the King.

At this the remaining Spaniards fled, though the Captain still breathed, and—under my guidance—did one of the village women tend his wound. For two days I thought he would die, but he began to gain some strength. At first he would not speak, and showed great hatred for myself and the Indians, even those who nursed him back to health, but I visited him every day, and at last we did pray together with some of the

Maya who had been called to Christ by Spanish missionaries, albeit to a version of the old faith marked still by their own superstitious practices. Yet should I not call them superstitions though I countenance them not, as I have grown wary of discounting the Catholic view, though I hold fast to my own. It seems to me now that we see the world from the slim angle of the place where we were born, altered only slightly by our slender experience of others.

The Captain stayed with us a month, but then his troops arrived with a new commander, one Gomez, and emissaries from Valladolid who came with plans to execute all who remained. As you can well believe, they were much surprised to find the Captain still alive, and marvelled more so when he did speak on our behalf. But yet Commander Gomez was implacable: his troops would visit upon the village, he said, the same number and manner of deaths and mutilations that the Captain and his men had suffered. It was to be an eye for an eye and a tooth for a tooth. I spoke then for the village, urging patience, and the Captain too did remind Gomez that the attack upon us had been quite unwarranted. The man shed tears for those who would be killed, though he himself had been poised to kill them but two months earlier.

It took hard debate, but we at last prevailed upon the commander to spare the Indians, yet on one thing he would not be moved. I had assaulted a captain of the Spanish nation, and that could not be excused. It was determined that the blow I struck be returned upon me, and the following day at first light the commander struck off my right hand just below the elbow in imitation of the blow I had given the captain. At my request, he used my own sword because I would not be defeated by an enemy blade.

This is the reason for my poor penmanship for I have had to use my left hand for all things since and I have little skill at it. A further penalty I must endure was to leave the people with whom I had lived, banished to another part of the peninsula never to return. The remains of my right hand will lie here, at their request, in an ancient tomb, but the rest of me, and all I brought with me from England—yea, even that for which I first did flee—will travel west to places where I am known to neither Spaniard nor Indian. One of the Indians (properly called Maya) will go with me, for my health is poor, and I fear that the loss of blood allowed some other infection in and that leaves me weak and sweating. When I first came here I might have survived both hurt and illness, but now I fear they will o'ercome me.

I have spoken to my Mayan friend about my past, what I carry, its great value and significance, and he has agreed to lay a small part of it here in Ek Balam with the hand I gave for the village. The rest will come with me to a great, forgotten place he has named to me called Uxmal where, he says, it is fitting for me live out what time remains to me, and there or thereabouts to die. From what he says I see a tale which smacks of heavenly purposes, for there I may measure out my poor length upon the earth like an old hero returning—though in another land—to his birthplace. It is strange and fitting that my life should come to this almost circle, where that which made me once despised now makes me most admired and binds me once again to kings.

And so farewell, Mother. I fear I will not write to you again, nor do I expect you will ever read these words. The precious stones and metal I once hoped to bring triumphant back to the land of my birth will lie with me here, but that, methinks, is not so bad a thing. Man is man, it seems to me now, despite of race, creed, or nationality. I have lived with those who had all and those who had nothing, indeed, I end where I began. The skin and language of those who will lay me in the earth is different from she who took me first to church, but their poverty is the same. I have found as much good grace, kindness, and dignity in the poor as I have in nobles, princes, and kings. I loved the King for what he did for me and mine, but it no longer seems a treason to imagine a world where none wears a crown. As such it will lie with me in tribute to she who bore me and who lived most despised and dejected even of the poor who knew her. My last letter will be to her though we both know she is long past reading it.

Do not blame me for this, dear Mother. I have a little changed is all, as experience will make a man change. Pray for me still and know that I die.

Your ever-loving and most grateful son,

Edward

Alice turned to him and her eyes were wide with such excitement that James almost forgot his newly discovered wariness.

"James," she exclaimed, "this is amazing! It sounds like we have only part of the treasure!" Her eyes flickered from the duffel bag back to the letter. "See! 'Only a small part' was left in Ek Balam. The rest has to be in Uxmal. It can't have been found during excavation or we'd know about it, so it's still there, waiting to be found!"

"Uxmal is a big place," said James. "And he doesn't even say he'll die there exactly. Look," he said, stabbing a finger at the relevant paragraph. "'There or thereabouts.' Not much to go on, is it?"

"Sure it is," said Alice. "We just have to find which parts of the city haven't been excavated. Maybe we could take a metal detector."

"Dream on," he said. "A metal detector would never have found the small amounts of gold under the massive stone pyramid in Ek Balam," he said. "We need more information."

"Maybe there's something in a Spanish codex or something," she said, refusing to let go of her enthusiasm. "Colonial records of this guy Edward. Maybe the Spanish army knew where he went. Or maybe his death is recorded in a parish registry over there. It may even give his grave site. He was a Christian, right? It sounds like he got kinda eclectic in his religion, so maybe he was buried in a Spanish cemetery in some mission church. It might be as easy as finding a headstone and opening the grave."

She looked thrilled by the idea.

"Man," she said, sitting back on her haunches, still unabashedly naked. "This shit could be worth a fortune."

James frowned and started to put the letter away.

"So when we heading over to Uxmal?" she said.

"I don't know," said James, evasive. "Even if you're right, there's research to be done before we get there."

"Research?" she said, her old scorn returning abruptly. "I'm not going to sit in a pile of books while someone beats us to it, James. Don't be so lame."

"I'm not wandering around Uxmal with a spade in my hand," said James. "It's a waste of time."

"So we'll stop off a few places on the way and you can poke around in your precious *books*," said Alice, "then we'll arrive ready to dig. Sound like a compromise?"

"I guess," said James, feeling again the old impulse to please her.

"Excellent," she said, delighted. She kissed him again, grinning as she did so, thrusting her body at him and laughing so that he wasn't sure if she was making fun of how easily she controlled him, or if she was genuinely happy.

Chapter Fifty-Four

■ ■ ■ ■ ■

Deborah, still staring at the eye on the tower, pressed the phone to her ear.

"When will he be back?" she asked. She knew she sounded impatient, but she needed Hargreaves's expertise now.

"I don't know," said the boy. "Maybe not at all."

"Sorry?" said Deborah. "Is this Barry? I did a tour with Professor Hargreaves yesterday. He was doing some research for me."

"He's in hospital," Barry blurted suddenly. He sounded distraught, close to tears. "He got attacked."

"Attacked? Is he OK?"

"No," said Barry. "It's all my fault. I was leading the tour and this woman went off by herself. The police say it was her who stabbed him."

"Stabbed him?" said Deborah. "Where is he?"

"Hospital," said Barry. "They took him, but they didn't know if he would…"

"Survive?"

"Right."

"Did he say anything about the woman who attacked him?"

"He was crazy!" said Barry, sounding more unnerved than ever. "He was babbling about Jane Scott coming to get him."

"Jane Scott?"

"The murderess who was hanged at the castle in 1828," he said, falling back on his tour patter. "She was too weak to stand so they had to make a chair on wheels to get her to the scaffold…"

The wheeled chair in the Drop Room.

Deborah recoiled from the thought, baffled and horrified.

"A ghost couldn't have attacked him," said Deborah, her voice hushed.

"That's what he thought," said Barry. "The police say he sat there and let this person stab him with the point of a branding iron she took from a case. Right in the chest. There was blood everywhere."

Deborah's head swam. Hargreaves, who had been so kind, so helpful.

Her fault.

She forced herself to calm down.

"Barry, can you tell me what he was doing when he was attacked?"

"He was in the archive room—the library—downstairs," he said. "He had just made himself a cuppa. He was sitting at the desk with his back to the computer."

"Were there books on the desk, or notes?"

"No. Nothing."

"Was the computer on?"

"No," said Barry. "But it was warm. I touched it as I tried to…help him, and I could feel it was warm."

So either he had just turned it off, or his attacker had. If she had, perhaps she was trying to hide something. She could have reshelved books or taken them with her.

"Barry," she said. "I want you to go back down there and turn on the computer."

"I can't," he said. "The police closed the room."

"It's important, Barry," she said, "and if the police are still there, you can have me talk to them."

"What do you want me to do?"

"Open whichever web browser Mr. Hargreaves would have used and see if you can figure out what last appeared in the search window."

"How do I do that?" He sounded steadily more clueless, more childlike.

"Just work through the alphabet, one letter at a time, and see if the window prompts you with a recent search. If it doesn't, move on to the next letter. Write down or copy anything it prompts you with, OK?"

"I don't know," he said again. "The police might not like it."

"I'll deal with the police," she said. "Have them call me. Tell them my name is Deborah Miller."

As she waited for him—or the police—to call back, she tried the church door, her hand unsteady. It was open, so she stepped inside, glad of the silence. The attack on Frank Hargreaves weighed on her like she was shouldering his body. She needed to think.

The church was small and traditional, old wooden pews divided by a central aisle, white walls with arches and columns down the left side surmounted by a wooden gallery, a simple altar—by English standards—backed by a stained-glass window.

A vicar in a black robe emerged from the back of the church and greeted her warmly, nodding in response to her question about looking at the old parish registers.

"What year would you like to start?" he said.

"Sixteen twenty," she said.

"Ah," said the vicar, pausing and turning to her. "Spot of trouble there. We have no original records prior to 1721, but we do have a transcription made by one of my nineteenth-century forbears, Archdeacon Rushton. It goes back to 1574, though there is a gap between 1637 and 1662. Let's see what we can find, shall we?"

They walked through a dark hallway smelling strongly of furniture polish and old flowers, into the vestry and offices beyond the church proper.

"I couldn't help noting that ellipse on the church tower," said Deborah.

"Ah, the All-Seeing Eye or the Eye of God," said the vicar. "The legend is that it's there to ward off evil. The tower is old, maybe seventeenth century, though it has been refurbished a couple of times since then, and there was a church here as early as 1250, so who knows where the eye came from. It could even be pre-Christian. Old stone gets reused as do old ideas and beliefs. This was a Catholic church till the reformation, after all. Maybe its materials came from other faiths too."

He shrugged cheerfully, unconcerned by the suggestion that what seemed so solid and orthodox may have once represented something quite different.

"I know the region is famous for its witches," said Deborah. "Do you think the eye was added after those women were put to trial?"

"To protect the region from old malice, you mean?" he answered. "I suppose. There's no reason to believe it had anything to do with the witches at all, except that this church was the heart of their community. I think the eye was here in some form then and earlier. It could have been part of the church before the present tower was built."

"Have you ever seen it connected to a coat of arms?" she asked on impulse.

He gave her a curious look.

"No," he said. "Have you?"

"I'm looking for an Edward de Clifford," she said, deciding just as impulsively to trust him. "Born about 1620 and raised partly in Skipton."

"Clifford?" he said, raising his eyebrows. "You've probably heard that George Clifford may have had- er...*connections*...among some of the local women. But surely, he was dead by 1620?"

"Yes," she said. "I'm just wondering if his daughter somehow retained connections to the area and formally adopted someone born here. I'm guessing, and without much evidence to go on," she said, suddenly tired and a little desperate. She thought of Frank Hargreaves languishing in a hospital bed and had to push off the rising sense of horror and responsibility.

Hargreaves would want answers. You may have gotten him hurt, even killed. You at least owe him a solution.

The vicar sat her down at a broad wooden table and disappeared for a moment while he recovered a pair of large books, which he lay before her with a thud. One was modern and professionally printed, the other a considerably older binding of yellowing parchment.

"The spelling of names gets a bit erratic in this period, I'm afraid," he said, "so you have to think phonetically. Have you ever looked at Renaissance signatures? Fascinating stuff. Truly amazing how many different spellings a person could come up with: Marlowe, Merlin, and Morley all for the same surname! It can get very confusing. Just try to sound them out and you should manage. Do you have children, Miss Miller?"

Deborah gave him a startled look. "No," she said. "Why?"

"No reason," he said. "I just find that people usually have a reason for getting interested in genealogy. You know, looking forward and backward through time and mortality."

"Oh," she said, inadequately. "Right. Well, it will probably stay quite academic for me. Not sure I'd ever be much of a mother."

The vicar beamed and shook his head.

"I think you'd be a wonderful mother," he said. "I have a good instinct about people."

Deborah felt herself flush and she looked down at the books.

"Anything else I can get for you?" said the vicar.

"I think that's all, thanks."

"The modern copy should contain everything you need," he added, tapping it with one finger, "but if you need to double-check a reference in the original, I'd ask you to be very careful with it. Absolutely no marks on the pages, please."

"Of course."

"I have a few odd jobs to take care of around the church, if you don't mind," he said, "so I'll leave you to it for an hour or so. OK?"

"Fine," said Deborah. "You've been most kind."

I think you'd be a wonderful mother, she thought as he walked away. Well, that makes one of you. And what the hell was that based on anyway? It was absurd. Sweet, perhaps, or at least well-intentioned, but absurd all the same.

She thought of Adelita, her head in a book, grinning up at Deborah, who always gave her space and silence, as her own mother had never done.

There's more to motherhood than staying out of your children's way, she reminded herself. *Planning to play the great white savior bringing liberation and education to the natives? You should be ashamed of yourself.*

And being so, Deborah took out her laptop and turned it on. As it warmed up, she leafed through the book till she found 1620. Each year got about a page, each page contained thirty to forty entries in column form, each marked with the Latin abbreviations *bap*, *nupta*, and *sepult*: baptisms, marriages, and burials. They were mainly just names and dates occasionally augmented with a note.

She opened a new document on her desktop where she could take notes and, seeing that she was getting a strong wireless signal, opened her e-mail. There was a new message from Frank Hargreaves.

It startled her, not so much for what it contained, but because it struck her that this may have been the last thing he did before being attacked. She read it twice, but there was no sign of panic, no delirium, no hint of anxiety about the ghost of some Victorian poisoner. What it did contain was firm evidence of Edward Clifford (not de Clifford) showing up as a page in the court of King Charles I for four years. In that time, Hargreaves said, he seemed to have been well liked by most, looked after by prominent people who looked to his education. The boy must have been bright, may even have been a counselor in training.

Then things changed drastically and for the worse. It wasn't clear why, but Edward fell from grace as dramatically as he had risen, and, at least according to one courtier's diary, it had something to do with his mother. In the space of a month he had gone from being a prominent servant and counselor to being persona non grata. Whatever the cause, Edward vanished from court under a cloud, returning to the north and to Skipton in particular, where he remained till the end of the Civil War. He next returned briefly to London in the year the king was executed, and then left again for good—fleeing, it seemed—with the authorities at his heels.

She reopened the file with the picture of Lady Anne, trying not to remember what had happened when last she looked at it, and she avoided the woman's face, studying instead the figures beneath her. She considered the children, the two boys marked with crosses, their eyes closed in death. Beside them, a little away from the group, was another young man, no taller than the children, but lightly bearded. He wore black and carried what looked like a pen and a book, but there was something strange about the representation of his body. It seemed squat, compressed to the point of distortion, as if the artist hadn't either the skill or the space to draw him properly, though the rest of the painting was expertly done.

She snatched out her phone, then opened a directory on her desktop and dialed. As it began to ring, she checked her watch, calculating the time difference to Mexico. It was too early. The lab wouldn't be open for another couple of hours. She could leave a message though, ask for an e-mail confirmation as soon as they could get her one. She did so, remembering at the last second that she might be considered a fugitive.

Well, they have your cell phone number anyway, and so far they seem happy to have Bowerdale.

She left her number, reread Hargreaves's message one more time, and returned to the entries for 1620 in the records book. Thinking of Bowerdale gave her another pang of guilt. It was too early to call Powel, so she e-mailed him, a long and impassioned plea for Cornerstone to stay on top of the State Department, and for the State Department to stay on top of the Mexican authorities.

She returned to the parish records.

Edward, it seemed, was not a common name in Pendle. Three were born in 1620. One died almost immediately, one went to work on a farm near Clitheroe. The other changed his last name. He was born Edward Davis, on August 4, 1620, to his mother Janet. There was no mention of a father. The scribe, however, had noted in the marginalia that he was "raised at the charge of the Cliffords at Skipton, whose name he took."

"There you are," she said.

So. A poor local woman has an illegitimate child. Lady Anne Clifford of Skipton, who had dealings with the villagers as servants and as half relatives, the result of her father's seeking affection outside her mother's bed, adopted the child, raised it as her own, and sent the boy to school and then to court. Why? And what happened in 1634 that destroyed the boy's hopes for a courtly career? She went back to Hargreaves's message and read the lines about Edward's fall from grace:

"There's a courtier's diary from the summer of 1634," Hargreaves had written. "The bloke sounds like a snake, but you might find something of interest in his venom for Edward Clifford. He wrote, ''Tis one thing to have a beggar, a whore, and a famous fool for a mother, 'tis something quite different for that mother's evil to be made manifest in the shrunken child.'"

Deborah sat back, confused. How could anyone at court know anything about Edward's real mother? But the charge of whoredom and beggary could not possibly be leveled at Lady Anne.

She was mulling all this when the phone rang. She snatched it up.

"Barry?" she said.

But it wasn't Barry. It was Jesus at the INAH physical anthropology section at the Regional Yucatan Center, whom she had only spoken to once before.

"You called?" he said. "I heard your message. Rylands did not give you the information?"

"Rylands?" she said. "What information?"

"The bones from the hand you sent are no more than three hundred and fifty years old. Not Mayan. European. There's a tiny fleck of steel in the bone. The steel is almost certainly Spanish—not Hispanic—Spanish, from Spain. A sword, probably."

"I see," she said.

"Probably the arm was cut off by a sword."

"Anything else?"

"Yes," he said. He had clearly saved the best till last. "We were able to extract DNA from the finger bone. It was not a child. It was a man, an adult."

"But the bones were too small," said Deborah, though even as she said it her eyes flicked back to the image of the tiny, bearded man standing below the portrait of Lady Anne.

The mother's evil made manifest in the shrunken child...

"He had achondroplasia," said Jesus.

Deborah stared at the figure in the painting and something in her mind slid into place.

"He was a dwarf," she said.

"*Exactamente.*"

Chapter Fifty-Five

■ ■ ■ ■ ■

Deborah sat on a bench against the wall of the church with her laptop case beside her, waiting for the boy at Lancaster castle—Barry—to call. The vicar had put the books away, walked with her out to the churchyard, and advised her not to look for witches' graves. "Don't believe what tourists say," he said. "No convicted witch would have been buried in this consecrated ground, even so-called gentry like Alice Nutter."

"So what happened to their bodies if they're not in buried here?"

"Dumped in a communal pit," said the vicar, "their graves unmarked. People were scared of witches even after they were dead."

And with this grim pronouncement he left her, and she sat looking down over the sloping graveyard with its varied head-stones—some slick, upright, and new, others ancient, lurching, and weather-beaten like dead teeth.

She thought of Edward Clifford, who had been born with dwarfism into a poor rural community in the early seventeenth century. She couldn't begin to imagine what life would have had in store for someone in those circumstances, had not the austere and defiant hand of Lady Anne Clifford not scooped him up. Could she have believed that her careful nurture would have compensated for what an ignorant and superstitious age might see as marks of evil on his body? What had the letter said?

The court was too decorous for such as I. I know the labours you undertook on my behalf and know that they came from the best of intentions, from love for that the world finds unlovable...

Too decorous indeed for a poor Lancashire boy marked by dwarfism. Yet, for a time, at least, he seemed to have been successful, and perhaps Lady Anne had thought he would continue to rise. Robert Cecil had risen to be Queen Elizabeth's most powerful counselor, she recalled, despite being unusually small and hunchbacked. Perhaps Lady Anne saw Cecil—whom she would have known as a child at court herself—as a model for the boy she had rescued from poverty.

So what had happened? Edward Clifford had four good years at court, then nothing. Clearly he retained—along with his adoptive mother—his royalist sympathies or he would not have been defending Skipton Castle against Cromwell's Parliamentarians during the Civil War, but it seemed unlikely that it was politics that lost him his position. The war, after all, didn't begin till 1642, by which time Edward had already been gone from court for eight years. Why? Something must have pushed him from court in 1634, something that did not tarnish his respect for King Charles.

Deborah fished in her bag and drew out the water bottle from the cottage, unscrewed the top, and took a sip. She knew whom the arm in the tomb belonged to and where he had come from, but that seemed to make little difference to the larger question of what had been buried with him and where those things were now.

It was cold and damp in the churchyard. Deborah sipped from her water again and noticed that the light had shifted. What had been rustically picturesque before seemed darker now, lonely and isolated. The wind had picked up and cloud had covered the pale sun. She gazed down through the monuments and headstones—all much larger than those common in the States—and was aware of a shape at the far end of the cemetery that she hadn't noticed before. Someone, she thought, was kneeling on the ground. Beside the figure was a black dog, which seemed to be turned toward Deborah as if watching her.

Deborah rose, picked up the laptop case by its strap, and, without a clear sense of what she was doing, began to walk slowly down the path through the graves. Getting up made her light-headed, and she clutched a great stone cross till the dizziness passed. Then she drank again from her bottle and continued to walk. She stumbled, the ground swimming up to meet her, and a wave of apprehension broke out like sweat over her body, so that she felt like she was in a dream in which she couldn't stop moving toward something she did not want to see. And then the path turned and there was the huddled figure, a woman, her back to Deborah, but her old, clawed hands visible as they dug out the grave dirt in handfuls. She was wearing a silver ring with a rough turquoise stone. Beside her was the dog, looking at her, its body quite still. Arranged on the edge of the flat-topped stone were five human teeth and a clay figure with a tangle of hair attached.

Deborah turned to flee, but she was unsteady on her feet, and as the dog shot out in front of her she fell hard against a raised gravestone. She stood, clutching her shoulder, and began to weave up the path toward the church. She breathed in the cool air and thought it cleared her head a little, but when she looked up she saw a man standing by the church tower, a black man in a long trench coat. There was no sign of the dog.

She hesitated. The man was coming down toward her and his strides were long and purposeful. Without thinking further, she cut off the path to the right, moving in among the graves and dropping to a crouch. She paused behind one large headstone, then scuttled quickly past two more, then cut up toward the church.

Her head seemed to be clearing, but the sense of alarm would not leave her. She glanced back but could see no sign of the old woman who had been digging teeth from the earth, and suddenly Deborah was sure there had been no such woman. It had been some kind of waking dream like the one she had had at the cottage the previous evening. There was no demonic black dog running through the cemetery either, and she considered standing up and walking calmly back up to the church. She could find the vicar and ask him to call a doctor. Something was wrong, but she had recovered enough of her old rational self to think it had little to do with witches and demons.

But when she did start to move, she saw the man, his trench coat flapping in the wind. She crouched again to get out of sight. He was walking through the graves, searching. He was no devil, but he was also not the vicar. Below the coat, he wore a crisp white shirt with a tie. She thought she had seen him before, on a train perhaps.

Yes. On the train from London to Lancaster.

He was tall and young and athletic, dangerous looking in a precise, military kind of way. He was also—she felt sure—looking for her, and she was just as sure that she did not want him to find her.

Chapter Fifty-Six

■ ■ ■ ■ ■

Though the headstones were huge, there just wasn't that much cover in the graveyard and no clear way out. Down one side was a high brick wall, overshadowed by yew and sycamore trees. Deborah risked a look around the great brownish headstone behind which she was hiding and saw the man turning and looking about. He had lost her for a moment. He was standing no more than thirty yards away, his back to her, and she watched as he shrugged out of his trench coat and tossed it over an adjacent grave. As he moved, she saw that he was wearing a pistol holster with a large automatic on his left side.

She ducked back behind the stone and tried not to panic. Calling the police was no good. They'd take too long to arrive and wouldn't arrive ready for a firefight. She had to get to where the vegetation was densest, then work her way back up toward the church and beyond. The graves were random in their arrangement but were still in linear ranks, which meant that hiding among them was like being among oversized dominoes: if the man in the trench coat took a step or two, changed his line of sight by only a few degrees, he would see her. She looked back to where she had been: still no woman digging in the dirt, and now—her head clearing still further—even the idea that she had seen such a woman seemed preposterous. Beyond that spot the top of a brick wall ran up to the road in scalloped terracing that matched the steep drop of the churchyard. At its lowest point, the wall was only four feet high. If she could get there without being seen—crossing the open center of the cemetery and its path in the process—she could get over the wall and follow it up to the street.

Easier said than done.

She slipped her head through the strap of her laptop case so that it wouldn't swing, gripped the edge of the headstone in front of her, and peered round. The man in the trench coat hadn't moved, but as she looked she caught another blur of movement from up close to the church: the black dog was back. It was snuffling through the graves toward her.

It's just a dog, she told herself. *Not a devil or a familiar.*

But if it came sniffing around her, it might be trouble enough. The man with the gun had seen it too, and now he turned toward it, watching where it went. Deborah chose quickly. She ducked back down the hill, keeping low but moving as fast and quiet as she could in the long, damp grass. One row of graves, two, then stop. She flung herself down, no idea if he had seen her or not. She was breathing hard and her heart was racing.

She had put some distance between herself and her pursuer, but she still needed to get across the path. Overhead a wood pigeon cooed, owlish. The sky was getting darker and she felt the first drops of rain.

Good, she thought. *Might make me harder to see.*

She got as low as she could, her face in the wet grass, and angled her head around the gravestone. Nothing but crosses and headstones. Had he moved? Slowly, her muscles aching with the effort, she got to her hands and knees. In front of her was one more grave marker with a great stone angel, greenish and blotched with lichen, then the path and no cover for thirty feet. She didn't know where either the gunman or the dog were, and trying to find out would probably get her spotted. She crouched, her legs tightening like a sprinter in the blocks.

She bolted out from behind the grave clutching the laptop to her chest, didn't pause behind the green angel, and sprinted hard toward the brick wall, dropping and rolling as softly as she could as soon as she was among the gravestones. Even as she ran she held her breath, waiting for the shot or the bark, but nothing came. She skittered a little in the dirt as she launched herself into the heavy ferns that had overgrown the corner of the cemetery, but didn't know if she had been seen or heard. The wall—now more clearly stone, not brick—was only a few yards away. Old broken headstones had been propped up against it, and there were heavy trees and shrubs growing alongside it. The pattering of the rain was nearly loud enough to drown out the thumping of her heart. She took another breath and ran.

She almost made it.

Chapter Fifty-Seven

■ ■ ■ ▨ ▨

Some of the graves, she had noted, had low ornamental iron railings, no more than a few inches high, their corner posts capped with little rusting fleurs-de-lis. Deborah was nearly at the wall when some matted ferns she stepped on turned out to be hiding one of them. Her foot snagged on the rail, and she fell heavily on her hands. She didn't cry out, but the fall had been loud enough.

She heard the dog bark and knew it was coming. By the time she was up and running, vaulting the wall as well as her stinging hands would let her, she could hear the gunman coming too.

But she was committed now, and if there had been any doubt about the man's interest in her, his pounding pursuit wiped that out. She had no choice but to run. She landed clumsily on the other side of the wall and found herself on steep, uneven turf. She barely broke stride, pounding up the hill toward the road as quickly as she could, knowing he couldn't yet see her, knowing too that he was wearing street shoes to go with his suit, and that she—in walking boots—had an advantage on the slick turf. Her grazed palms shrilled with pain, but she put her head down and ran, hard as she could, thighs pumping steadily up the hill.

It took her a second to realize that she was in a kind of backyard and that there was what looked like a house between her and the street. There were no lights on, no sign of life, so she ran past it, bursting out onto the road and hooking right past the church, still at a full run. Then, on her left, before the houses began, she saw a narrow flight of steps, almost a passage, leading steeply up between stone walls and heavy shrubbery. She had no idea where it led, but it provided a cover that the empty street did not. She bolted up the stone stairs.

The steps turned, and Deborah found herself emerging in the open at a fence with a gated stile. She pushed through the little sprung gate, closing it silently behind her, and ran on. The steps were gone now, and she was on a dirt path across a swelling pasture. Behind her, the village of Newchurch fell away. Ahead, she could see nothing till she cleared the brow of the hill and found herself confronted with the brooding purple gray of Pendle itself. There were cows all around, and a hundred yards or so ahead an abandoned piece of farm machinery with a great iron roller—perhaps ten feet long—browning with rust. She ran to it, round it, then flung herself down in the long grass behind it, biting back her sobs of panic and exhaustion.

She might, she supposed, be lucky. If she had gotten up the stairs before he had seen her, he might never find her. But if he *had* seen, she was now alone and there would be no witnesses to whatever happened next.

Should have gone to a house, she thought.

But there hadn't been time. If he'd wanted her dead, she would have been before anyone answered the door, though *why* anyone wanted her dead, she had no idea.

She lay facedown, feeling the cool rain on the back of her neck, her hands flat against the metal of the roller, which was colder still and numbed the cuts on her palms. It stood about three feet high: more than enough to hide her from anyone coming up the path, but also obvious. She rolled carefully onto her back, listening, and for a moment she saw the rain-darkened sky and felt the looming presence of Pendle behind her head.

A hell of a place to die. And for what? Why does the man in the trench coat want me dead?

She was trying to banish that thought when the phone in her laptop bag trilled. She reached desperately to silence it, her fingers fumbling wildly inside, and heard the unmistakable sound of movement just on the other side of the iron roller.

She stopped breathing, lay there motionless on her back, gazing straight up into the gray sky, her eyes filling with raindrops like tears, but unblinking, so she would see him when he leaned over, pistol in hand. The phone rang on, piping its silly, electronic notes, and for a moment, nothing happened. Then she heard his weight shift, felt it almost through the ground, and heard something like a breath. He sounded big, imposing like the hill itself, so that an unreasoning part of her wanted to cry out at the unfairness of it all. Then he moved again, and the gray sky was filled with his massive head and blank, uncurious eyes.

For a second Deborah just stared, then her breath came and she laughed, a loud boisterous guffaw and rolled over. The huge bull, his muzzle black and wet, lowered his head to the turf where she had been lying, and began to chew the wet grass as if he hadn't even seen her.

Deborah snatched the phone from her bag and caught it on the last ring. It was Barry in Lancaster.

"OK," he said. "I have news."

Chapter Fifty-Eight

■ ■ ■ ■ ■

While James figured out how they were going to get to Uxmal, Alice announced she was going for a last swim and to take a look at the Tulum ruins. James had given her a questioning look, but he didn't seem suspicious so much as a little wounded that she wanted to be alone, and she was used to that.

Tulum was built much later than Ek Balam or Uxmal, thirteenth century or so, and had thrived as a port as the rest of the Mayan world disintegrated. It was a very different place from the other ruins she'd visited. The city inside the walls consisted mainly of platform buildings with fortified temples, rather than the pyramid structures she had grown accustomed to. There were some cool relief carvings of the local diving god shown upside down on the lintels above stout colonnades, but what really made the site impressive was its location, perched up there on the cliffs.

The tourists, who were arriving in greater numbers as the day progressed, seemed lost, unsure what they were looking at and what it all meant. Alice amused herself listening in on an elderly couple who didn't know the difference between Maya, Olmec, and Aztec, and who then remembered the Incas and got still more confused. The old lady looked quite upset when it became clear she had no idea who had built what they had traveled so far to see. Alice, wanting to help, started explaining about the limits and time frame of the Mayan world, its separateness from the Incas of Peru and the later Aztecs of the regions north of Yucatan.

"So who are the Olmecs?" said the old woman, who was already smiling with relief.

"Earlier," said Alice. "Like maybe fourteen hundred BCE to about four hundred BCE. Later civilizations like the Maya and the Aztecs grew out of them. They had things that show up in those later cultures like bloodletting sacrifice and a ritual ball game."

"Aren't you sweet, dear," said the old lady. "And so clever. Thank you."

"You're welcome," said Alice, who felt suddenly embarrassed. She turned, and there, up on one of the high cliff structures, was Dimitri, watching her.

Finally.

She excused herself and walked away from the couple, climbing up toward him and wishing for trees and shadows so that he couldn't watch her all the way up. He was wearing a white button-down shirt with jeans and sunglasses, and looked sweaty but quite calm. As she got close to him she smelled his aftershave again and felt a rush of confused emotions. There was no one else around, no one to see what they might do together, or what he might do to her.

"You're early," she said.

He ignored her and sipped from a bottle of blue Powerade.

"We'll be leaving after lunch," she said.

"Travelling how?"

"Not sure yet," she said. "James is working on it."

"You have the letter?"

She drew it carefully out of her pocket and began to unfold it, but he snatched it from her and unfolded it himself, a bead of the Powerade dropping onto the parchment.

"Careful," she said, but he shot her a hard, unreadable look, and she glanced away.

"I can't read this shit," he pronounced after a moment, his accent thicker than usual. "What is this? English? What does it mean?"

"It means he buried the rest of the stuff in Uxmal."

"Stuff?"

"Treasure," she said. "Gold, jewels, precious stones."

She said it quickly, looking out over the sun-bleached site. She had thought about the shiny yellow metal and the pale, glowing red stone all morning and had decided that she wasn't simply going to hand them over to Dimitri.

"Where in Uxmal?" he said.

"I don't know."

He shot her that look again, this time whipping off his sunglasses so she could see the ice in his eyes.

"I don't know," she said again. "If James knows, he didn't tell me, OK?"

"Find out," he said, biting off the words, his gaze returning to the parchment. "Type up a copy of this," he said, thrusting the letter back into her hand. "Properly, so I can read it. E-mail it to me."

"It's English," she said, slightly petulant. "A bit old-fashioned and the writing is weird 'cause the guy was using his left hand, but it's English. You can read English, right?"

She had gone too far. She started to apologize, but he grabbed her face with one hand, fingers and thumb on either side of her mouth, and squeezed till she felt her cheeks bleed against her teeth. Tears started in her eyes.

"Just get me the copy," he said, thrusting her head back as he released her, "and make sure I know where you are all the time."

"I'm sorry," she whispered. "I just meant..."

"You hear what I said?"

"Yes, I'll tell you where we are, I'll get you the copy."

"And don't tell this James anything," he said, standing up to leave. "Tell him, and I kill you. Both of you. And if you find the treasure and it's not in my hands one hour later, I'll kill you. You understand me?"

She nodded. Had he just said the word "kill"? She tried to absorb it. She looked at his face again, appalled at how dramatically she had underestimated this man. How could she have trusted someone she knew so little about?

He stared at her aggressively. "What? I can't hear you."

"Yes, I understand," she said, pushing her tears away and setting her face in the flinty look she'd learned to wear when the going got tough. "I understand."

"E-mail it to me at that Gmail address I gave you. You have a laptop, right?"

"Yes, I do. I will."

"Good." He reached for her and she flinched, but he just smiled and traced his finger around the rose tattoo on her shoulder, then up her neck and along the line of her cheek. It was a thoughtful, even tender gesture. "Then—when all this is done—maybe we go away together," said Dimitri.

"Yes," she said, a tiny, hopeful smile flashing into her eyes and lips. "I'd like that."

Chapter Fifty-Nine

■ ■ ■ ■ ■

Deborah phoned a taxi from her hiding place on the hill and didn't leave that spot till the driver called to say he was parked at the foot of the stairs in the village. She had him drive her to Skipton, and en route she phoned the Malkin Tower cottages and paid her bill by credit card. She would not be picking up her belongings, she said. The landlady said that was fine, that she could send them on if necessary, and Deborah thought she sounded careful but very slightly relieved, as if someone had already inquired after her.

Or was sitting there now, waiting for her to come back.

"You didn't leave a bottle of spring water for me outside the cottage door last night, did you?" she asked the landlady.

"No, love," said the woman. "Were you short?"

"No," said Deborah. "It's fine. I've had a lovely stay."

As they sat in traffic outside the railway station in Skipton, Deborah took out the spring water bottle. It still had a few mouthfuls left. It looked clear enough, but on careful inspection she could see that the bottle had a pinprick hole just below where the cap sealed. She had been drugged, and had repeated the process by drinking from the bottle again in the churchyard. It had made her hallucinate, making real the troubling images that had been festering in her subconscious over the last two days, just as poor Professor Hargreaves had hallucinated a nineteenth-century poisoner in her wheeled chair going to execution.

Barry had said he had "just made himself a cuppa": tea. Someone—presumably the woman who had gone missing from the tour—had spiked it to disorient him before her attack.

Whatever Deborah had been given, it had made her paranoid as well as delusional. Yet she was sure she had given information to someone very real who had come to the piggery to find out what she knew. It was almost funny how that same paranoia may just have saved her life in the churchyard. The gunman, after all, was real enough. If she hadn't been so terrified when he first appeared, she might have let her guard down for a crucial moment...

Was it possible that the gunman was part of the hallucination? She thought not. The more she considered what had happened the previous night, the more she thought that the altered state into which the drug had pushed her had come on and passed quickly. It had been all over in perhaps twenty minutes, and that was after drinking half the bottle. This afternoon she had taken only a few sips, and her head had been clearing before the man in the suit arrived. The dog, she figured, had been real. Perhaps it was seeing that that had given her hallucinations shape, led to the image of the crone digging teeth from the ground—just as the dog had been in the barman's story of the witches. She wrapped the bottle in a plastic bag and put it away. At some point, she would want its contents tested.

Barry had told her that Hargreaves had been searching for anything to do with Edward Clifford, but among the items he had looked for were two unfamiliar names—George Withers and Sir Henry Mildmay. Deborah repeated his searches and turned up another bitter testimony from an unhappy seventeenth-century courtier. He referred to Mildmay, who seemed to have been a prominent official under Cromwell, as the "Knave of Diamonds." A strange name. She wondered about coats of arms and gemstones.

And then she stumbled on something so bizarre that her breath caught.

Surely not?

It couldn't be. She had to see Hargreaves.

She took the train to Lancaster and a cab to the Royal Infirmary.

There was a policeman guarding Hargreaves's door who demanded to see some form of ID. She showed him her passport and signed in while he scanned a notepad and—more discreetly—checked what looked to be a grainy black-and-white photograph. CCTV images, she guessed. The castle was a prison, after all. Cameras everywhere.

The policeman—a young man in a black uniform sweater, tall and prematurely balding—followed her into the room and stood behind her at the door.

"Just pretend I'm not here," he said.

Deborah nodded and took a seat by the bed.

Hargreaves was unconscious. He looked old. His face was pale and waxy, and his eyes were sunken, though some of that was probably because she was unused to him not wearing his glasses. His chest and left shoulder were heavily strapped, and he was hooked up to drips and monitors that beeped periodically. On impulse she took his hand, which was large and strong but whose skin felt silky, paperish.

"I'm sorry," she said. "This is my fault. I should never have asked you to help."

She glanced over her shoulder to the cop, but he was pointedly looking away as if trying to afford her some privacy. Deborah scribbled her cell phone number on a pad on the nightstand, added her name and a sincere but inevitably inadequate apology, then got up to leave. At the door she hesitated, looked at Hargreaves one more time, then stepped out into the hallway, the policeman at her heels.

"Known him long, have you?" asked the cop.

"No," she said. "We just met."

"Good of you to visit," he said.

Deborah wasn't sure if he was probing, but it seemed as good an opportunity as ever.

"Do you have an ID on the attacker?" she said.

He seemed taken aback, and his manner seemed to shift. He stood a little straighter and his voice stiffened as if he was reading a teleprompter.

"No official identification of a suspect has been completed at this time," he said. "Investigations are ongoing."

"Could I see those pictures?" she asked.

"Pictures?"

"The CCTV images that you used to see if I was a match for the possible attacker," she said evenly.

"Oh. Those," he said. "Well, those are official..."

"I think I might be able to identify one of the people in them."

"Actually, we have identities for most of them," he replied, slightly affronted. "Most are castle employees, and most of the visitors on the tour paid their entrance fee by credit card, so we already have their names."

"Most," said Deborah. "But not all. Not your prime suspect. The woman."

He raised his eyebrows, but his expression relented.

"I spoke to the boy who works in the gift shop," she said. "Can I see?"

He hesitated, debating with himself, then impulsively dragged the glossy pictures out and passed them to her. They were grey and grainy, full of bright spots and deep shadows where you could see nothing useful, but just clear enough to make out the details of the faces on the huddle of people in the castle hallway: Barry, a family with a boy, a couple of teenagers, and a man in a dark, old-fashioned suit. At the back of the group was a middle-aged woman in a voluminous raincoat and a plastic headscarf. Her face was long, heavy, and unmistakable.

Marissa Stroud.

"Anyone look familiar?" said the policeman.

Deborah thought quickly. If she told him what she knew now, she'd never get out of town today.

"Afraid not," she said. "But could I take down a contact number in case something occurs to me?"

The policeman fished a business card from his pocket, and she thanked him, apologizing for not being more helpful. She traced her way back to the front door and took a cab to the station. Twenty minutes later she was on the train to London, but she waited ten more minutes before calling the policeman back and giving him Marissa Stroud's name, hanging up as soon as she was sure he had it down right.

She slept a little on the train, waking briefly in Crewe, and then again at Watford, where she watched a businessman using a laptop and realized he was getting a wireless signal provided by the railway. From there on she used her laptop to download everything she could find on George Withers and Henry Mildmay. The former, it turned out, was a poet, and the latter—the Knave of Diamonds—a public servant of sorts. Their lives were quite separate but intersected over a single extraordinary incident. Deborah's mind raced.

Once in London, she took a series of tube trains and emerged into the rain, umbrella-less and weary. She walked down to the river close to Tower Bridge in sight of the *HMS Belfast*. It was the city as she might have imagined it, sprouting antique church steeples and postmodern glass towers, impressive, straddling time, so that even though it made her feel like a tourist, she didn't mind so much. She bought her ticket a stone's throw from where the infamous gallows had once stood and walked down to the sprawling urban fortress that was the Tower of London.

Chapter Sixty

■ ■ ■ ■ ■

Gloria Pickins was hungry. She reached into her desk drawer and found the packet of devil's food cakes. They were low-fat, and the chocolate tasted waxy, but they were still an indulgence, and she ate them furtively, like a squirrel nibbling acorns before some stronger rival stole them. As she munched, she brushed the crumbs off the manila folder in front of her. Mr. Powel had been gone most of the morning but she expected him back in the office within the hour.

She liked Mr. Powel. He was a good boss who respected her professionalism and made no unreasonable demands on her. He paid her absurdly well and gave her seasonal bonuses, though it wasn't always clear to her what the season was that prompted the gift. Christmas, certainly, but others were scattered throughout the year, appearing without clear regularity or warning and identified with obscure names she had had to look up: Lamastide was one. Whitsun and Michaelmas. They were old English names that he borrowed whimsically, but the money was real enough. He would call her into his office and ceremonially present her with an envelope of anything from two to five thousand dollars.

"Excellent work, Mrs. Pickins," he would announce. "Here is your Whitsun bonus."

He smiled that open, avuncular smile of his, so that she was never sure if he was quite serious. He always did it when they were alone, and he always concluded the meeting with the same words: "And remember, Mrs. Pickins. This is just between us."

Sometimes he winked, sometimes he just turned back to his computer and began tapping away, picking at the keys like a bird eating seed.

And she did keep it to herself. She didn't even tell Albert where the extra money came from, not that he would notice. Mr. Powel paid her minimal attention, which was fine by her. Gloria liked her privacy too, so it was an even exchange. It was part of why they got along so well.

So it felt like a small violation entering his office by herself, and she knocked cautiously to make sure he hadn't snuck in without her seeing. But he had trusted her with a key, so it was acceptable. He would understand.

Still, she turned the knob cautiously and opened the door only partway so she had to step around it to get in, as if that made it less of a crime. She had the manila folder tucked under her arm. She was used to the office, of course, but rarely saw it without him behind the desk, and it felt different. The photographs, for one. There were so many of them.

Angela. Smiling, skating in tournaments with her gold pendant necklace, or heading out onto the ice in practice sweats.

She was a lovely girl, but the number of photographs struck Gloria as a little overwhelming, and it made Powel's office feel like a shrine. Maybe because of that, it felt almost like she was barging into a sacred place when she reached for the mahogany cabinet, took a breath, and opened both double doors wide. A light came on inside so that the contents on the glass shelves seemed to flash then glow with an unearthly brilliance that made the pupils of her eyes contract. For a moment she just looked.

There were books, old books, stained and spattered, their titles etched in obscure languages into the cracked leather binding. There were parchments in glass frames, marked with strange symbols, some abstract, some stylized images of heavenly bodies and animal heads. Some looked like ancient seals or stamps. There was a pair of glass chalices into which had been set heavy candles the color of old blood, and ancient amulets and figurines cast roughly in metal or chipped from stone. There were animal horns wound with cord and carved with obscure runic letters, and there were large mounted crystals of various colors. In the center was one more photograph of Angela, this time simply sitting beneath a tree with yellowing leaves. Beneath the photograph sat a human skull, brownish and mottled, and in goblets on either side were smaller bones soaking in some black, viscous fluid. Beside the skull was the thing she was looking for: a finely made wooden box lined with black velvet on which nestled a strange knife. Its blade was made of what looked like dark, greenish glass, the edges irregular and flaked but lethal-looking. She picked it up gingerly and considered it.

"Mrs. Pickins," said a voice behind her.

Gloria spun to find her employer standing right at her elbow. In her surprise the knife slipped through her fingers and fell, but

Powel stooped fast, catching it by the handle before it hit the floor.

"I'm sorry, Mr. Powel," she said. "I didn't hear you come in."

"No harm done," he said, "though we were lucky there. I could have got a nasty cut or—worse—the blade could have hit the floor. Obsidian is very fragile."

He returned the knife to its box, closed it, and set it on the desk. Then he closed the door behind him. He had his attaché case with him and he set this down, opening it without looking at her, then reached inside.

"What if I had been someone else?" he said.

"You are the only one with a key to the suite," she said, unoffended. "I certainly wouldn't have taken the risk if I thought anyone else could walk in. I just wanted to make sure everything was ready."

He nodded.

"Naturally," he said. "Do you have the envelope?"

Mrs. Pickins opened the folder she had set on the desk and removed a large padded FedEx envelope.

"Excellent," he said.

He lifted a Ziploc bag from the attaché case and handed it to her. It contained a lock of blond hair, bound at one end by a rubber band.

"You have the address?" he said, as she slipped the bag into the envelope along with the box containing the obsidian knife and sealed it up.

"Of course," she said, slightly affronted.

"Of course," he echoed. "Track it, please. I want to know when it gets there."

"Absolutely," said Gloria Pickins. She took a step away from the cabinet and then caught herself. "Shall I close this up for you, Mr. Powel?"

"No," he said, his eyes moving slowly over the contents. "Leave it open."

Chapter Sixty-One
■ ■ ■ ▪ ▪

The Tower was, perhaps, the greatest of England's storied historical landmarks. The present buildings spread out from William the Conqueror's eleventh-century keep, or White Tower, which stood in the middle, a square stone block broken with windows and ornamented with corner turrets and crenellated battlements. Around it the famous ravens circled. Legend had it that if they left, the Tower and—by extension—the nation itself would crumble. To be on the safe side, the present ravens, Deborah read in her guidebook, had select flight feathers clipped.

It was another overcast day promising rain, so the crowds at the Tower, Deborah thought, were to be expected. Still, she hadn't anticipated the lines for the special exhibits, some of which extended out and around the inner walls in a long queue. Deborah checked her watch irritably.

She was there because of George Withers and Henry Mildmay, though she was far from sure what she believed yet.

Both men had been republicans working under Cromwell during the English Civil War and its aftermath—Withers, the poet, and Mildmay, the keeper of the jewel house where sat the royal regalia.

The fortified museum where the crown jewels were kept.

Even now the idea worked on her system like adrenaline.

Cromwell's puritanical revolutionaries despised kingship and its trappings as superstitious iconography. It made sense that when they executed the king, they would also do their best to denigrate and devalue those items that had once been symbols of his power. Enter Withers and Mildmay. Politically these men were at the very opposite extreme to the royalist Edward Clifford, and history had documented a particular anecdote that nicely illustrated their politics and their contempt for the monarchy. For a joke, Withers had been crowned king in Westminster Abbey using the actual crown that had been taken from the Tower with Mildmay's consent. Mildmay, who was later blasted by the Earl of Pembroke as the Knave of Diamonds, and whose job it had been to protect the contents of the jewel house, had allowed every item to be removed. Withers and his pals had taken the vestments, scepters, crowns, and all the royal regalia in an iron chest to the ancient church where English kings had been crowned for centuries. There they had mockingly "crowned" Withers, and the poet had proceeded first to march out about in a stately fashion, and then "with a thousand ridiculous and apish actions, expose the sacred ornaments to contempt and laughter." The crown had once been sacred, so Cromwell and his men had done their best to make it absurd and contemptible, if only to strip it of the aura of authority that had once kept the nation in awe.

All this had been in the article that had so captivated Deborah on the train ride to London, and she replayed it in her head now as she entered the inner courtyard. She was getting close to the Bloody Tower, where Walter Raleigh had been imprisoned by King James for thirteen years and where—according to popular tradition—the sons of Edward IV were quietly murdered. Most people believed Shakespeare's version of events, that they were killed by Richard III, a man whose villainy was somehow made manifest by his hunched back and withered arm. Deborah thought of the dwarf Edward Clifford—or Davis, as he was born—and wondered how he had negotiated a culture that saw deformity as a sign of sin.

She passed the green where Lady Jane Grey and Anne Boleyn had been beheaded and, seeing that the lines had not yet shrunk, headed into the White Tower, past a group clustered around a yeoman warder, resplendent in navy blue trimmed with scarlet. The White Tower contained pillars decorated with flintlock pistols, wall displays of muskets and swords, life-sized models of horses barded for battle, and Henry VIII's armor. The air was filled with camera flashes that bounced off glass and polished steel till she felt she was going to get a headache. It got worse in the room with the headsman's axe and block, where the tourist excitement—as Frank Hargreaves had said of Jane Scott's hanging chair—bordered on the ghoulish. She kept moving on and up to the top floor where there were racks for gunpowder barrels. Somehow most of the crowds from the floor below had dispersed, and for a moment Deborah found that she was actually alone in the ancient stone chambers at the top. She browsed for a minute or two, wondering if the lines outside would have gone down, and then she turned and realized she was alone no longer.

A familiar black man in a trench coat, the man who had pursued her through the graves of Newchurch, was standing a few yards away, looking at her.

Deborah drew in her breath sharply and immediately checked the only way out: a stone spiral staircase that descended all the way down to the castle basement, a route he was now blocking. There would be security cameras everywhere, but no one would get to her fast enough if the man had come to kill her. Somewhere outside, a bell started ringing, high and persistent like a fire alarm.

"Deborah Miller?" said the man, flashing a wallet card emblazoned with the letters *CIA*, "I'm agent Kenneth Jones. We need to talk."

Deborah had been poised to sprint past him for the stairs, but now she hesitated.

CIA?

"What about?" she said.

"Come with me, please," he replied.

"I don't think so, Jones," said Deborah. "If that's actually your name. I could run off a CIA badge on my home computer in ten minutes, so let's talk here."

People would be arriving any moment, she thought. They were bound to. That would give her witnesses and, perhaps, an opportunity to escape. She was not about to be led down that spiral staircase by an armed man.

"I'm afraid that won't work," said Jones.

He was an American, or had the accent down, but it was a polished professional tone untouched by regional dialect. The bell was still ringing, and though the man had said nothing, she sensed that he was aware of it. He was tense and urgent.

"We'll talk here," she said again, her eyes flashing round the chamber for signs of other people coming in, but there was no sound or movement anywhere on the top floor.

Where was everyone? Was it a fire alarm?

"This is a sensitive matter," said Jones, and now he reached inside his jacket. "I'm afraid I must insist."

She knew his hand would emerge with that heavy-looking automatic she had seen in the cemetery. She launched herself toward the stairs, and the movement caught him by surprise. Instead of drawing the gun, he spread his arms to catch her, and as she tried to barrel past he flung himself on her, clamping her arms to her side and slamming her into the wall so her face scraped painfully against the stone.

He was powerfully built, and with a surge of fear she knew she could not hope to wrestle free. Instead she stamped her hiking boot heavily onto the toe of his shoe, and when he gasped and his grip relaxed a fraction, she dug her left elbow hard into his stomach. It was a lucky blow and he was momentarily winded. She burst out of his grip, running full tilt for the stairs. By the time she had begun her descent, he was up and after her again, no more than two or three seconds behind.

Deborah clattered down the spiral staircase, her feet echoing on the wooden steps, grasping at the iron handrail as she half ran, half jumped down, two, sometimes three steps at a time. It was like descending into a well. She passed locked iron gates but still saw no one. The man behind her was coming at least as fast. She could hear his breathing in the stone tube as he pounded down behind her. He was gaining.

She kept going, barely able to breathe, her eyes wide with panic.

Please God, let there be someone at the bottom, she thought. *People. Anybody.*

A few more seconds and he would catch her. She fought back a sob and then, when it wouldn't completely go away, turned it into a shout for help. She screamed as she ran, trying to get her voice above the endless bell, and her cry sounded deafening in the stairwell, but it bounced off walls that had heard many such cries for mercy over the centuries.

She pushed the thought away and tried to pick up her pace. She must almost be at the bottom. Just one more effort. She leapt farther than ever—too far—and missed her footing on the edge of the stair. Her ankle buckled and she fell hard down the rest of the steps, sprawling onto her back as she rolled out onto the stone flags of the basement chamber, a room of vaulted brick arches stuffed with artillery pieces.

The man in the trench coat loomed over her, pistol in hand, but it was only when someone spoke that she realized that they weren't alone. The people she had been hoping to find were here after all, but it was instantly clear that they were not who she had expected, and when she started to sit up, she heard the unmistakable sound of weapons cocking: she froze, finding herself staring down the bayoneted barrels of half a dozen automatic rifles.

Chapter Sixty-Two

■ ■ ■ ■ ■

Deborah doubled up on the ground, her head squeezed into her chest, her eyes squeezed shut and her hands over her ears, trying to shut out the deafening volley of sound that would surely come next.

Nothing happened. Then the alarm bell stopped.

She could almost smell the tension, stiff in the air like electricity. The silence was total and as heavy as the cannonballs in the racks beside her. She opened her eyes and, very slowly, adjusted her position so that she could see what was happening.

The man in the trench coat was standing in the stairwell, arms raised above his head, his gun dangling by the trigger guard from one finger. As she watched he lowered it carefully, bending at the waist but keeping his eyes fixed on the other men. He set the gun down, kicked it gently sideways, then straightened up and put both hands on his head.

There were five men, two kneeling, all in navy-blue uniforms with a red stripe down the trouser, white belts, and berets with a red and white plume. But if their uniforms looked ceremonial and old-fashioned, their guns were absolutely contemporary: automatic rifles with knife-bayonets. Deborah opened her hands to show she had no weapon, and started, very slowly, to sit up.

Only then did she see the man who was not in uniform. He was wearing jeans and an open-necked shirt under a black leather jacket, and he was training an automatic pistol on the man in the stairwell. It was Nick Reese.

Deborah stared at him, openmouthed.

"You should have talked to me while you had the chance," muttered the man who had said he was Kenneth Jones of the CIA.

"She'll be perfectly safe with us," said Nick.

"Of course she will," said Jones. "Why wouldn't she trust an archaeological photographer."

"Step away from the gun," said Nick.

"You're going to be in serious trouble," said the American.

"As are you," said Nick. "You know how many laws you've broken in the last week, Kenneth? You're meddling in things that aren't any concern of you or your government."

"Wait," said Deborah. "So he *is* CIA?"

Nick said nothing. The black man gave her a smile and a nod.

"Like I said," he remarked to Deborah. "Serious trouble."

"This is British soil," said Nick. "Nowhere more so. Escort him to a safe room."

The CIA man stepped away, but though the riflemen kept him in their sights, pivoting and adjusting with mechanical precision, he never took his gaze from Nick until they had directed him up a wooden staircase and out.

"Come on, Deborah," said Nick, holstering his weapon and offering his hand to help her up. "It's time we talked."

For a moment Deborah just stared up at him, then, very slowly, she took his hand and rose awkwardly, testing her weight on her aching leg. Her mind was racing, and she couldn't quite banish the thought that she should still be running. Since when did Nick Reese order soldiers around? Who did he work for?

He led her out of the White Tower and through the deserted gift shop.

I should get something for Adelita, she thought wildly.

But then they were out in the open and crossing the equally deserted inner ward to the Waterloo barracks. The crowds were gone; in fact it looked like the entire castle had been evacuated. Only the yeoman warders and the soldiers were visible, and the empty fortress felt uncanny, like she was on a movie set or inside a dream. She hesitated at the doorway he had led her to, and he turned.

"What?" he said. "This is what you came to see, isn't it?"

She nodded, still mute.

"So let's do it," he said. "I won't quiz you, or insult you by pretending not to know why you are here. I'll tell you what you came for, and we'll take it from there. OK?"

She nodded.

"After you," he said, stepping aside so that she could stroll in—no waiting for busloads of tourists to shuffle through in front of her—to the Tower's most famous exhibit: the crown jewels.

Chapter Sixty-Three
■ ■ ■ ■ ■

"I was sorry to hear about Professor Hargreaves," said Nick. "Doubtless you already figured out who did it."

"Stroud," she said.

"Is that a guess or did you know?"

"I knew as soon as I saw her face caught by the security cameras."

"Any idea why?"

"She has two specialties," said Deborah. "One of them is Mayan epigraphy, the other is royal regalia. Sometimes the two overlap, but she was hired for her work on Mayan writing. It was only later that I started to wonder about the jewels and their link to crowns, scepters, and other things European."

As they talked, they wound their way through the rope swag that usually channeled hundreds of visitors at a time from room to room. The difference was that now, it was just the two of them.

"I spoke to the boy who worked in the gift shop," said Nick.

"Barry," she added reflexively. She still felt numb with confusion.

"Barry, right," said Nick. "He told me the names of the two gentlemen Hargreaves had been researching for you—George Withers and Sir Henry Mildmay—and I knew you'd come here. You didn't need to, of course, but that's you, isn't it, Deborah: impetuous but thorough. It wouldn't have been enough for you to leaf through a book or two. You had to actually come."

"What did you threaten Barry with?" she countered. "To get him to talk to you, I mean."

"Barry was keen to assist Her Majesty's government with their inquiries."

"Meaning what?" she demanded. "You're not police."

"No," said Nick, "I'm not."

He reached into his jacket and pulled out a wallet not unlike the one the CIA man had flashed. The badge showed a stylized lion surrounded by a series of gates and stars with a crown at the top. It read "Security Service," and below the motif it read "*Regnum Defende*," but in smaller print was the name she knew: MI5.

"You're an agent?" said Deborah.

"An officer," said Nick. "Yes."

For a long moment, Deborah just stared at him. She knew instantly that he wasn't lying. He clearly had the authority to evacuate the Tower of London and order around its guards, and he was more convincing in this role than he ever had been as an affable photographer.

"MI5," she repeated. "And you were going to tell me about this when?"

"I wasn't," he said. "Sorry if you feel misled, but that's the nature of the work."

"I don't *feel* misled," she said. "I *was* misled."

"Like I said," Nick answered. "The nature of…"

"The work, yes," Deborah concluded. "I get it."

"When we were in Mexico…"

"Forget it," she said quickly, not wanting the further humili-ation of hearing him defend his flirtation with her in the name of queen and country.

"I don't want you to think that I was only pretending to have a good time with you. I liked you. Like you. You're interesting. Different."

She gave him a sharp look.

"In a good way," he said. "And beautiful, though you do your best to hide it."

She stared at him until he looked away.

"Great," she said, adding, "I guess. And this CIA guy, Jones, you knew him?"

Reese laughed ruefully.

"Let's just say we've met," he said.

"Which means what?"

"He and some of his mates arranged a little party for me in a Skipton parking lot," he said. "I suppose he wanted to ask me a few questions about your adventures in Mexico. We didn't get off on the best foot."

Deborah felt annoyed. Reese seemed to have all the pieces of the puzzle but only wanted to dole them out to her bit by bit.

"I'd like to look at what I came here to see," she said, her tone cool.

Reese's voice became cautious, professional. "Yes, you should take a proper look at the cases. You're getting a private tour, after all. We even shut off the conveyor belts, so you can have rather more than the allocated twenty-eight seconds visitors usually get. Take as long as you like. When you're done, I'll be sitting by the exit and we can talk."

"Fine," said Deborah. "Oh, and you might want to examine this," she added, handing him the spring water bottle from her bag. "I'm sure you military intelligence types have the very best labs."

"What is it?"

"You tell me," she said.

Deborah walked through the deserted Jewel House exhibition in a daze. Here she was, alone, surrounded by the most dazzling display of opulence and power in the world.

There were gold ceremonial staffs and maces—massive two-handed things—and the gold ampula shaped like an eagle, which contained the coronation oil. Of course there was the coronation spoon. There were robes and stoles, spurs and swords. There were orbs and scepters, also gold but set with pearls and precious stones and topped with crosses and doves. One looked almost exactly like the one she had glimpsed in the Mayan tomb. Another scepter was set with a massive teardrop-shaped diamond weighing, according to the display, over five hundred carats. Other cases contained gold chalices and plate, candlesticks, flagons, Christening fonts, ornate salt cellars, cisterns, ladles, and other meticulously crafted golden objects.

Then there were the crowns: St. Edward's crown, which was used in the coronation of the present monarch, and the crowns of the Queen Mother and Queen Mary, both trimmed with ermine and set with thousands of diamonds, many of them huge and flawless. There was the imperial crown of India and countless others, including Queen Victoria's dainty confection of almost twelve hundred diamonds. It was overwhelming.

What it was worth, Deborah couldn't begin to guess. One of the minor crowns alone would be worth millions. And yes, the official story was that it was all real, that the display contained no copies, only the genuine article. The doors she had passed through were huge steel affairs so that it felt like you were stepping into a massive safe.

She went back through the exhibit to be sure and then sat beside Nick Reese, saying nothing.

"I'm sorry I didn't tell you who I was," he said.

"You had your reasons," she answered, not looking at him.

"And my orders."

"So now what?" said Deborah. "You want to know what I know?"

"Yes. What you don't know, I'll tell you. Fair enough?"

"Sure. And Nick? How about nothing but the truth from you from now on."

Nick nodded and even smiled.

"Edward Clifford was born to a poor woman in Pendle called Janet Davis," she said. "He was a dwarf, and very clever. He was adopted by Lady Anne Clifford of Skipton, through whom he got a good education and was trained as a court scribe and counselor. As a boy he served King Charles the First as a page and seemed to have been on the fast track to power, but something went wrong in 1634, and he fell from favor. I don't know why."

"Me neither," said Nick.

"Anyway," Deborah continued, "Edward remained loyal to the king, and when Cromwell and the Parliamentarians took over, Edward fought for the royalist cause against them. He garrisoned Skipton Castle and held out despite a long Roundhead siege.

"But the Royalists lost," she went on. "King Charles was imprisoned, tried, and finally executed in 1649. Cromwell was a Puritanical iconoclast who despised the pomp and ceremony of kingship. He sent a poet called George Withers to the Jewel House at the Tower of London and, with the permission of the Parliamentarian keeper of the Jewel House—Sir Henry Mildmay—had all the crown jewels impounded. They played with them, trivialized them, dressed up in them, like boys playing with a dead snake. Mildmay and his associates then broke the crowns up and sold the entire royal regalia off cheap, deliberately, I suspect, to show how little they thought of them; no wonder Mildmay's enemies called him the Knave of Diamonds. Anyway, while a few pieces were later recovered during the Restoration of the Monarchy ten years later, the ancient crown jewels of England effectively ceased to exist."

She paused, but when Nick didn't respond, she continued.

"The present crown jewels of Britain date from the Restoration, when King Charles the Second was crowned in 1658. By then Cromwell had been dead two years and his son had been unable to keep the Protectorate alive. Parliament opted to revert to a constitutional monarchy, and the body of Cromwell was dug up, tried for treason, and "executed": his body hung in chains and his head displayed on a pike outside Westminster Abbey. Efforts were made to recover the lost crown jewels, but apart from a twelfth-century coronation spoon—currently on display back there—no major pieces were found, and the royal regalia had to be rebuilt based on what they could remember. In terms of ancient history, everything in there," she said, nodding back to the glittering exhibits, "is new.

"I'm going to go out on a limb and say that the original crown jewels, items going back to before the Norman Conquest, regalia associated with Alfred the Great, Edward the Confessor, and all the medieval kings and queens of England, from Henry the Second in the twelfth century through to the Tudors, weren't totally destroyed. I think most of their crowns, scepters, orbs, and diadems of all kinds were bought up or otherwise collected by Edward Clifford, a royalist from Pendle, and smuggled out of the country."

She sat there, thinking about it, feeling at last the weight of all that history, and then added, half to herself, "Somehow he wound up in Mexico, and that is about all I can tell you, except that at some point he must have sent one stone back to England, or perhaps he took it up to Lancashire himself before he left the country, and buried it at Malkin Tower Farm. Why, I couldn't say, but it's too much of a coincidence to say it got back to the parish where he was born by chance."

"A tiny portion of this huge trove of jewels was in the tomb we unearthed at Ek Balam. I'm not sure how it got there, but I think—and I'm pretty sure I'm not the only one who believes this—that the gems and bits of metal we found were part of the regalia of England's ancient monarchs. How you could begin to put a price on what such a find would be worth, I don't know."

"And it is the position of the British government," said Nick, inserting himself into her monologue at last, "that they must not find their way onto the open market, that they should be returned to England to be kept as a national treasure of boundless cultural significance."

Deborah felt the weight of her knowledge like a tangible force pushing her into her seat.

"As you can imagine," Nick said, still professional, "I am empowered to take extraordinary action to ensure that that happens."

"How nice for you," she said.

"This isn't the way I wanted things to go, Deborah," he responded, frowning.

"Hey," she said with a shrug. "It's your country."

"Mother Britain?" he said, gesturing toward the exhibit of riches she had just left. "Hardly."

"Because you're just a working-class lad from Lancashire?" she said, unsure why she was being so caustic but unable to play nice. "Or was that a lie too?"

"Not a lie," he said. "And yes, I have to protect the interests of Her Majesty's government, including its cultural property. That's my job. But no, kings and nobles and power isn't the world I came from either."

"So why are you telling me all this?"

"Because you want to know what's going on."

"No," she said. "You're telling me because you think I can still be useful."

He looked away for a moment, then nodded.

"You may have relevant information," he said.

Now it was her turn to look away. He added hastily, "And because I value your perspective, Deborah."

"Fine," said Deborah. "Whatever."

He looked like he was about to respond irritably, then took a breath and redirected the conversation.

"Why do you think Marissa Stroud came to England?" he said.

Deborah sighed.

"She is obviously looking for the crown jewels," she said, "and knows that the stones we found in Ek Balam were part of a larger trove that is, presumably, still in Mexico somewhere. But she didn't know where. She came to the UK because she thought that uncovering their past would somehow point to their present location. Whether she found what she was looking for, I have no idea, but I think I told her some things that may have helped."

"Like what?"

"I don't know," she said, studying her hands. "I was drugged. I told her what I knew about Edward Clifford, I think. I don't think she had all that information before."

"I see," said Nick.

Deborah colored and clenched her fists.

"Where is she now?" she asked.

"Stroud? She boarded a flight outbound from Manchester a few hours before she was correctly identified as a person of interest in the Lancaster Castle assault."

"Heading where?"

"Already touched down in Cancun, Mexico," said Nick. "And you know what that means, right?"

"Time to pack my bathing suit?"

"Consider it work for an Anglo-American accord."

PART 5

Chapter Sixty-Four

■ ■ ■ ■ ■

It took James and Alice six hours by bus to get from Tulum to Merida, and another two to go from Merida to Uxmal. There had been no police checkpoints, no problems of any kind, but James was restless. He had read what he could find but was no nearer to determining where in Uxmal they should look for Edward's bones and the treasure that lay with them. That was Alice's word: *treasure*. The first few times she had said it she had seemed embarrassed by it—as she should be—but thrilled at the same time. Now there was something else going on with her that he couldn't put his finger on, a note of panic and urgency. She had been jumpy when they got on the bus, always looking around as if expecting someone to arrest her. James had told her she was going to draw attention to them, and she had become oddly compliant. She hadn't been sleeping well, he knew. It was just odd that the treasure hunt she had found so exciting now seemed to scare her.

James had found no records of this Edward character in any Spanish account of the conquest, nor much sign that the Spanish had even known Uxmal existed. When the Spanish got there, and certainly by the time of this mystery Edward from England, Uxmal had already been abandoned for hundreds of years. With no Spanish town close by, it remained a jungle-shrouded ruin until Waldeck, Stephens, and Catherwood got there in the 1830s and 1840s.

James and Alice booked a room they couldn't afford at the hacienda by the ruins. Soon enough, he hoped, he'd get paid by Bowerdale and money would be less of a concern. It was a beautiful, grand old hotel that had been built for the archaeological staff working on the ruins, all tiled floors, potted palms, and old-world ceiling fans, and there was a guitar trio playing folk songs. There was a pool and a garden with towering palms, and their bathroom had a whirlpool tub and a stained-glass window of toucans and egrets. For James, who had never stayed anywhere so decadent in his life, it was glorious, a secret pleasure that made him want to dress up and drink rum cocktails served from silver shakers by waiters in white tuxedos.

In his heart, James knew they couldn't hope to find the treasure, and he didn't really care. He was tired of running around, tired of feeling stupid, and tired of being everyone's whipping boy. Yes, he had to finish what he started for Bowerdale, so he would go through the motions, but he felt beyond caring about history or artifacts. All he wanted now was to stay in this wonderful place and relish what he'd originally hoped archeology would offer: a glimpse of the ancient and the exotic, something he would look back on all his life.

The following day they hid the canvas bag under the extra pillows and blankets in the wardrobe, then went to the ruins proper. They were all James had hoped for and more. Chichen Itza was more impressive in scale, sure, but it was packed with tourists and souvenir sellers, and there was much that you couldn't get close to because the structures were roped off. He had liked the observatory with its dome-like tower and the dense ornamentation of the Nunnery and Church, but Uxmal was a different experience entirely. For one thing, it felt virtually deserted, even when the tourist buses arrived, and the fact that it received a fraction of the visitors meant that those who came were free to wander and climb where they wanted. When he scaled the great pyramid, inching up the high steep steps on all fours, he could sit up there on the top looking down on the site, and be almost completely undisturbed. The place still belonged to the jungle and its creatures.

The Pyramid of the Magician was unlike any other Mayan structure: a great three-story structure whose base was oval, so that the massive platforms had curved edges. It had monumental staircases up to temples on the top and loomed over a vast quadrangle of stone buildings whose intricate friezes were set with carved stone latticework, figurines, and masks of Chaak. James was used to the image of the rain god with its fearsome, bulbous eyes, wide, square leer full of teeth, and its huge, hooked nose. The images were reproduced all over the Yucatan, often in the same composite form, each portion of the face carved from a different square block so that the whole looked oddly linear, almost robotic, like a pixilated computer image, but nowhere had he seen them in such obsessive profusion. This was a city that lived or died by rain. It was hardly surprising they worshipped Chaak so earnestly. James wondered vaguely how much human blood had been poured out, how many living hearts cut from their bodies with obsidian knives, to appease the god and bring a little rain.

He walked round to the Palace of the Governor, climbed another monumental staircase, and sauntered along the great long building, gazing up at the fretted and sculptured frieze adorned with the obligatory masks of Chaak, then stepped into a recess with the typical triangular Mayan arch. There was no one around. He could have just stumbled out of the jungle and discovered the site, the first white man to see it since that Edward guy came here to die three hundred and fifty years ago. Down below him on a platform surrounded by the close-cropped turf where the iguanas sprawled was a stone throne shaped like a saddle, each end carved into the head of a crouching jaguar. It was weathered and stained yellow with lichen, but it was the seat of a king or a high priest: a throne of power.

With sudden clarity James saw what he had to do. He would waste no more time skulking around the ruins looking vaguely— blindly—for somewhere to dig. He would get the canvas bag from the hotel room, tell Alice what he planned to do with or without her, and then he would return to the States. There he would be greeted as a cultural hero, a scientist. He would reveal his find to the world, shake off Bowerdale entirely, and return with a legitimate excavation to Uxmal where, one day, he would make a discovery still greater than what he had dug up for Bowerdale in Coba.

James stood tall, sure of his actions for the first time in weeks, maybe years, and that was when he noticed that Alice was now in the space below him. She sat on the jaguar throne, staring up at him. He faltered, even at this distance feeling her skepticism chipping off some of his confidence. She wouldn't like it, this new conviction of his. She had been getting steadily more and more jumpy all day. She constantly sidled up to him and said "Well?" as if he was supposed to just point at the ground and say, "Here. Get the spade."

James made his way back to the staircase smiling to himself and walked down to where Alice sat, wearing her usual mixture of watchfulness and studied apathy. On the hulking throne, she looked small and childlike. She saw him coming and looked back over her shoulder, as if afraid someone might see them together, and James felt a rush of anger and hurt, which solidified his resolve.

No, he thought again, with something like triumph, *She isn't going to like this at all. And that's just too bad.*

Chapter Sixty-Five

■ ■ ■ ■ ■

After England, Deborah found Mexico hotter than ever. She had sat apart from Nick on the plane—an accident of getting last-minute seats that she was glad of—and they had barely spoken except for a few minutes at Gatwick when she had set her jaw and demanded that he answer her one question.

"What?" he said.

"Why are the CIA involved?" she said. "The original crime was the murder of a Mexican citizen, and the root cause seems to be about the recovery of British cultural property, so why are the CIA there at all?"

He smiled mirthlessly and looked away, as if trying to decide how much he could say, but when he looked back at her and shrugged, he seemed to be telling the truth.

"I don't know," he said. "The guy we caught in the Tower—Jones—didn't talk, and we were quickly pressured to release him. It could be that the imprisonment of Bowerdale and the involvement of Stroud, both of whom are Americans, raised their interest, but I see nothing in the case so far that would draw Intelligence interest unless, for some reason, they already had their eye on one or both of them."

"The CIA monitoring a couple of aging archaeologists?" Deborah scoffed. "Why would they?"

"Why would the CIA try to kidnap a British officer on UK soil?" Nick replied. "I have no idea, but I have the bruises to say they did."

"Maybe they see the jewels as some kind of bargaining chip with the British government?"

He shrugged again.

"Deborah, you're just going to have to trust me on this: I really don't know why they are involved. It makes no sense to me."

"Trust you?"

"Yes," said Nick, his face softening a little. "I said I was sorry I couldn't explain before but—"

"I'll see you in Mexico, Nick," said Deborah. She had turned and walked briskly in the direction of the duty-free store.

Now, cooped up in a hot rental car speeding along the turnpike road toward Valladolid, they said nothing. Nick had asked her if she had slept on the plane, and when she responded that she had but that it had not been enough, he suggested that she put her seat back and nap while he drove. She had muttered a thank-you that was barely polite, then cranked up the AC and lain back, closing her eyes.

She didn't sleep. It was impossible for her to get comfortable in the cramped vehicle, and Nick took several phone calls as he drove. She couldn't help but listen in, and what she heard kept her mind turning. The American embassy, it seemed, had kept up pressure on the Mexican police, and they were poised to release Martin Bowerdale unless harder evidence linking him to the crime emerged very soon. The sudden interest of British Intelligence seemed to have been a factor too.

"I hope you're right about him," said Nick.

"I never really liked him. But I just can't believe he's guilty. And anyway, we'll need him if we are to search other sites for the jewels," said Deborah, not opening her eyes. "No one knows the Mayan world better. If evidence against him does emerge, they can rearrest him. Innocent until proven guilty."

"Not here," said Nick. "And let's just be sure he is innocent before we let him leave the country."

"He was arrested because he stayed and the police needed to arrest someone," said Deborah. "If I'd stayed, they would have arrested me. Bowerdale is a pompous blowhard, but he's not a killer."

Nick didn't answer.

They reached Valladolid by two in the afternoon and the sky was bright and hot. Moments before, Nick had received another phone call confirming Bowerdale's release.

"Yes," said Nick, "I'll vouch for him. We'll be over to pick him up in..." He checked his watch. "Twenty minutes."

The jail was only a few blocks from the archaeological institute, and they found it without difficulty. It was stuffy inside and smelled of cigarette smoke and body odor. Nick flashed his badge at the desk officer and introduced himself in competent but clumsily accented Spanish.

"I'm Nick Reese, British Intelligence. I'm here to collect Martin Bowerdale."

"*Signor?*"

"Martin Bowerdale," Nick repeated. "The American."

"We are all Americans, *signor*," said the officer, smiling. "Yes, the archaeologist. He is not here."

"What?"

"He was released."

"When?" asked Deborah.

The cop shrugged. "Ten minutes ago, maybe fifteen."

"Where did he go?" Nick demanded. "Did no one tell him we were coming to collect him?"

"He said it was not necessary," the cop answered. "He did not say where he was going, but we still have his passport, so he cannot leave the country until the case is closed."

"Did someone else pick him up?" asked Deborah.

"No," said the cop, still quite cheery. "He walked. That way." He pointed.

"He must have gone to the institute," said Deborah. She felt confused and irritated. *What the hell was he playing at?* They had things to discuss. It was so like Bowerdale to pull this high-handed crap. The man had just spent a week in a Mexican jail and he sauntered off like he'd been at the Club Med.

She loped back to the car with Nick at her heels, the Englishman hanging back because his phone had rung again. She turned expectant, but all Nick said was, "Interesting, thanks," then hung up.

"Bowerdale?" she asked.

"No. Your water bottle."

"What about it?"

"You were right," said Nick, snatching the car keys from his pocket. "It was laced with a flavorless cocktail of tropical plant extracts and Bufotenin."

"What?" asked Deborah, folding herself into the front seat.

"Bufo is the Latin word for toad," said Nick, starting the engine.

"Toad?"

"Bufotenin is a secretion from a gland on the back of a large species of marine toad found throughout the Yucatan. It's poisonous but also…"

"A hallucinogen," Deborah inserted. "Of course. The toxin was ingested by Mayan priests during rituals. It supposedly gave them a sense of crossing into a spirit world."

"It's a tryptamine," said Nick, "related to the neurotransmitter serotonin. Exactly what it does is disputed, but tests have shown subjects experiencing a range of hallucinations from LSD-type visual distortions—swirling colors and such—to seeing things that aren't there, and feeling a paranoiac sense of impending death."

"Sounds about right."

"The other ingredients seem to be mushrooms and water lilies—all Mexican—but exactly what they do or how they react with the bufotenin, we're not sure yet."

"Was Hargreaves poisoned with it too?"

"Still waiting for lab results on his tea, but I expect we'll find he was, yes."

The car eased through the narrow streets, pausing at every speed bump and intersection, so that they could have walked there just as quickly. Inside the institute they found Porfiro Aguilar, who was clearly surprised to see them.

"Is Martin here?" Deborah asked.

"Bowerdale?" said Aguilar looking quizzical. "He's in jail."

"No, he's not," said Deborah. "You're sure he's not here?"

"You can look in the lab, but I haven't seen anyone up there all day except Krista."

"Krista Rayburn is still here?" said Deborah.

"She left for a while," said Aguilar, "but then she came back. Quietly."

Deborah considered him. He looked cautious, even evasive, but before she had time to say anything, Krista Rayburn herself, still perkily pretty, strode in. She came in addressing Aguilar.

"It's not there," she said. "I thought you left it..." She saw Nick and Deborah. "Oh," she said. "You're back. Hi."

"What were you asking him about?" said Deborah, ignoring the impulse to exchange pleasantries.

"What?" she said. "Oh. The van. I was going to drive up to the site, but it's not parked out in the street."

Aguilar frowned. "Hold on," he said, turning to a board of hooks with keys in the corner of the office. He scanned them and his confusion deepened. "The keys are gone."

"Well, now he has transport," said Nick.

"Who?" said Porfiro.

"Martin Bowerdale. I guess he didn't want an archaeologists' reunion."

Out in the lobby a door banged, followed by hurried, purposeful footsteps. The office door swung open and a black man in a dark suit stepped in, his face hard with anger.

The CIA man, Deborah thought. *Jones.*

"You let him go?" he said.

"Excuse me?" said Nick, indignant.

"Don't play that with me," said the CIA man, rounding on him. "You let Bowerdale go."

"He was released by the Mexican police," said Deborah.

"At your insistence," said Jones, pointing from Nick to Deborah.

"He can help us," said Deborah, feeling defensive and angry. "And why shouldn't we advocate for his release when he was imprisoned without any evidence against him?"

"Why shouldn't you get him released?" he repeated, suddenly and unnervingly calm. "Let me get this straight. Why shouldn't a civilian and the agent of a foreign government interfere in the Mexican trial of a US citizen and a matter of national security?"

"National security?" said Deborah. "Whose?"

"Ours!" yelled Jones, suddenly losing his measured tone. "You still have no idea what you are dealing with, do you, lady? Yes, a matter of US national security that now involves various foreign agents bent on all manner of malfeasance against the United States."

"This is crazy," said Deborah. "I don't believe it."

"Yeah?" Jones shouted back. "So what's he doing here?"

Again he stabbed a finger at Nick.

"My reasons for being here have nothing to do with US national security," said Nick.

"Oh, OK," said the CIA man. "Then I guess everything's fine. Who wants to get ice cream?" He turned to go, then paused. "I'm gonna go do my job now," he said. "Don't get in my way."

Chapter Sixty-Six

After James found her at the throne, Alice had started a fight with him. How could she not? He was so stupid. He'd said he wanted to take a few more photographs around the site for memory's sake.

"We'll be coming back here day after day until we turn up the treasure," Alice had said, though she'd felt like she was pointing out the obvious. "We'll probably have this place memorized before the search is over."

"I'm done with that," James had said. "I'm not going to spoil my experience of this site by hunting for something we'll never find."

Spoil his experience?

Alice was aghast. It was absurd. *He* was absurd, and she had told him as much. He had shrugged and started walking away, smiling this condescending Buddha-grin like he'd just attained enlightenment or some fucking thing, so she had gone after him and told him to his face that if he wasn't going to try to find the treasure she was leaving for good. He could forget it. All of it.

"All what?" he said, seeming genuinely unsure.

"Everything, James," she yelled back. "Me. I'll leave and you'll never see me again. You got that? I'm serious."

For a moment there he had just stood there, looking at her, and his smile had turned some, saddened so that she was sure she had him, but then he had just said, "OK, Alice. Good-bye," and turned away.

"I'm not kidding, James," she said, startled by the fact that it was him who was being so quiet and serene while her voice was breaking. "I'll go and I won't come back."

"You have to do what you think is right, Alice," he said. "I'm sorry."

She couldn't believe he knew she was bluffing. Backed into a corner by her own rhetoric, she'd had no choice but to turn on her heel and march away, heading back toward the Pyramid of the Magician and on to the hotel. It was a long walk, but most of it was open so she couldn't even slow down in case he was watching.

As she left the site and walked over to the hacienda, she shook off some of her distress and channeled her anger into something colder and more familiar. If that was the way James wanted it, she would show him. She would begin by checking out of the hotel, and if he thought that fucking canvas bag would still be in the wardrobe when he got back, he was sadly mistaken.

She marched through the lobby and up the elegant stairs to the gallery where their room was. Room service had left new bottles of spring water at the door and she snatched them up gratefully. It was a hot day—they were all hot days here, she thought, irritably, but she was flustered from shouting at James and the exertion of her hurried return—so she broke the seal quickly and drained half the first bottle in one long swallow. She wouldn't be saving any for James.

Alice began throwing her clothes into her backpack. She took out the purple canvas bag and looked around the room to see if she had missed anything. The movement—twisting around as she scanned each corner—seemed to unsettle her, and for a moment the chamber seemed to swim, the colors blurring. She closed her eyes for a moment to steady herself, but when she opened them she was aware that something was wrong. She didn't feel well, but there was more to it than a little too much sun or dehydration. Something was wrong with the room.

She turned more slowly, surveying everything, trying to home in on the source of her unease, and her gaze fell on the bag that sat on the bed. But it didn't seem simply like a bag anymore. It was something else that merely *looked* like a bag. She was amazed she had not noticed it before. It wasn't a bag; it was *disguised* as one. She stared at it, stricken with fear, and then, as she looked at it, it began to open by itself, the zipper easing slowly back. Inside in the darkness, something was moving.

Alice took a wobbly step backward, her hands over her mouth. She was cold and sweating heavily. The zipper continued to part and inside she glimpsed the bones of the severed hand. They had been mere pieces bundled together, but now they were fully knit again, an entire arm that began to crawl out on spider-leg fingers.

It couldn't be, she thought, staring as it pulled itself free, reaching and walking at the same time.

She tried to scream, and now the hand was out of the bag and dragging after it was something bigger, something worse. Because the hand was not unattached anymore. Somehow it had reconnected with the corpse, and that too—all of it—was climbing out. The body was not skeletal like the arm, but covered in black and ravaged flesh that hung in tatters and dripped with something dark and thick. It wanted her. It wanted her like all men wanted her and she had to get out.

The corpse was almost out now, and she could smell the stench of decay. And then she saw that the thing's other arm was scored with something dark in the blackened flesh: the image of a rose with drops of blood falling from barbed wire.

No.

She didn't dare to turn her back on the thing that was crawling out of the bag, so she moved cautiously, upending a lamp as she felt behind her for the door handle, but when she got there it was already open and there was someone there, a woman in a shawl that covered her head like a veil. The woman seemed to hover there in the doorway, and then she came in and walked to the bed, and to the bag, so that for a moment Alice couldn't see what she was doing as she bent over it, and then she had it and was walking out, taking it with her. Alice shrank back, sobbing, telling her yes, please take it, get it away from her, don't let it touch her…And then the woman was gone and Alice was alone again.

She curled up on the cool tiles and squeezed her eyes shut so that she wouldn't see the way the room seemed to shift and spiral. She lay like that for half an hour, though she had no sense of the passage of time until she started to feel calm and stable again. She sat cautiously up, wondering vaguely why the canvas bag from the wardrobe was not on the bed, remembering slowly that someone had been there. She got up, eyes widening, and a new dread building in her chest, but then the door opened again and someone came in.

It was Dimitri. She recognized him, though it was like seeing him through frosted glass and his words echoed oddly when he demanded what she was doing. She said something about the bag, and he grasped her by the shoulders and began to shake her. What was she talking about? The bag from Coba? Where was it? Who took it?

She told him she wasn't sure of anything, that there had been something terrible inside the bag and that she had to get rid of it. Some lady had been there and she had taken it, she said, but her explanations just made him angrier, and he slapped her hard across the face with the back of his hand.

She fell badly, and the pain somehow cleared her head a little more so that she knew what had happened, and she started to say how sorry she was, but he just hit her again, harder this time. His face was red with fury and his eyes hard. When she fell this time, she stayed down for a moment, waiting for her vision to stabilize, trying to compose herself enough to get up. He came for her again and she put up her hands to block his punch, but then James came in. She saw his face shift suddenly as he took in the scene, and then he was running at Dimitri, throwing himself onto him.

Alice scuttled back out of the way, jamming herself into the corner as the two men fought. Except that it wasn't really a fight. Dimitri shrugged James off and knocked him down so that he lost his glasses. It might have been OK, but James got up again, groggy but determined, and that was when it happened.

Dimitri was wearing a light jacket in spite of the heat, and Alice suddenly realized why. His hand flashed inside and came out with a gun, not the odd little round thing he wore lashed to his chest, but something bigger, with a heavy barrel almost a foot long that she knew was a silencer. She shouted something, but James came at him, his eyes flashing anger and defiance.

The gun coughed twice, and James seemed to pause, frozen, before crumpling to the floor. For a moment, Alice could only stare, and then, as the tears started to her staring eyes, she began to scream.

Chapter Sixty-Seven
■ ■ ■ ■ ■

Deborah spent the whole of the next day in the lab with Aguilar. Krista had found reasons to go up to the site at Ek Balam, but Deborah thought she was being cagey, and Aguilar got tense every time Krista showed up. Something was going on, but whether it was important, or just some *relationship* thing, Deborah couldn't say. Immediately, she heard her mother's voice in her head: "How like you to assume that relationships aren't important."

Not now, Ma, she thought.

Aguilar was a good-looking man, and Krista was conventionally pretty, and both were smart and shared the same professional interests, so she shouldn't be surprised. So why was she? Why was she always surprised when people connected, even briefly? And why, she wondered—Nick Reese's image flashing through her head irritatingly—didn't she?

"I'm too busy," she said aloud.

"What?" said Porfiro, looking up from his microscope. "Too busy for what?"

"Oh," said Deborah, flustered. "Just—you know—too much to do. This site…" She gestured vaguely with her hands, and Aguilar nodded solemnly, as if she was making sense.

"I just wish we had more material to work with," he said. "If only we knew where the rest of the grave goods were. Do you think Bowerdale knows?" he asked.

"If I knew that…" Deborah trailed off.

"Let's face it," Aguilar said bitterly. "The only reason Bowerdale would be heading away from us was if he was going toward the missing artifacts. We both know him well enough to know that."

"Maybe," said Deborah, not wanting to think about it. She changed the topic. "Aguilar, why did Krista come back to Mexico?"

"What?" said Porfiro, looking defensive. "Oh, you know. Workaholic, I guess. Aren't we all?"

Deborah held his eyes for a moment, and finally he shrugged and smiled apologetically. It was a confession of sorts. Deborah nodded, and he breathed out, smiling again, broader this time, before returning to his microscope.

Deborah checked her watch. She was hoping to get up to the village to see Adelita before the day was out. She had brought her a stuffed bear dressed up, ridiculously, like a yeoman warder of the Tower, and a book on English royal history. If she could make sure everything here was all right, she could take the remaining van.

She opened her laptop. She wanted to see if Hargreaves was up and about. She had called the hospital twice but he had been resting and they wouldn't patch her through. If he was getting his e-mail they might schedule a time to talk.

But when she opened her e-mail there were two messages, one from an unfamiliar address—probably spam—the other from her mother.

Perfect, she thought. *Dropping me a line to tell me what she thinks my childhood home will fetch, no doubt.*

That wasn't fair.

They were just so different, Deborah and her mother, always had been. Deborah had been her father's daughter, and once he had gone, her mother had seemed like the enemy, the wicked stepmother, the...

Witch.

Deborah frowned, not liking the way the word had come to mind. She opened the e-mail reluctantly, expecting to find it spiteful and petty in ways that might justify Deborah's sense of herself as the aggrieved party. It was, however, more careful than usual, and though it wasn't what you would call tender, there was a note of feeling in it that she couldn't imagine her mother actually saying.

Hence the e-mail. She knew she'd never get it out if she called.

She had received an offer on the house. She would delay the sale if Deborah would come. She wanted to see her, wanted to talk face-to-face, didn't want any more angry phone calls, didn't want to sell without Deborah coming home first. *That*, the letter said, *would be terrible. It would put us back.* Deborah wasn't sure what that meant. Put who back? Her mother and Steve, delaying their plans? Or did it mean Deborah and her mother? She ended, "I love you, Debs. I know you don't always think so, but I do."

The words she never said.

She was considering how to respond to this when she opened the other note, but it all went out of her head when she read the new message. It said simply: *I'm sorry. Really sorry. His name is Dimitri, I think. I think he's Russian. Not sure. I'm sorry. —Alice.*

Attached to the message was a document. It began:

My honoured mother,
Much has happened since I last wrote and the consequences of my small doings have caught up with me at last...

Deborah sat bolt upright, her eyes wide. She checked the name at the end of the letter and then reached, fumbling for her phone.

This is it, she thought. *It's what we needed. Evidence of Edward Clifford's final resting place. He went to Uxmal!*

And then the phone in her hand rang before she had had chance to dial, and she answered it, flushed with excitement, her eyes scanning the letter on the screen.

"Nick!" she exclaimed. "I was just about to call you..."

"Deborah..."

"You're not going to believe this," she said. "Edward Clifford wrote another letter..."

"Deborah, listen," he said, and his voice was leaden. "Something has happened."

"What?" she said, still staring at the computer, but now only absorbing Alice's string of apologies.

"It's about James," said Nick. "Bowerdale's graduate student. His body was found in a hotel in Uxmal this morning. He had been shot at close range...Deborah? Are you still there?"

But Deborah could only stare blankly across the lab, through the side shafts of sunlight from the windows, saying nothing as her eyes filled with tears.

Chapter Sixty-Eight
■ ■ ■ ■ ▪

Deborah and Nick drove west toward Merida and south to Uxmal, barely speaking. Deborah drove because it gave her something to concentrate on, though the toll road had almost no traffic and it was all too easy for her mind to wander as they sped through miles of scrub jungle broken by occasional fields of corn and agave.

She had replied to Alice's e-mail, but she doubted she would hear back. She had forwarded the message to an account Nick had given her but so far nothing useful had returned from whatever searches and tests he had initiated. Not that she expected any. She didn't know who this Dimitri was, didn't really believe in him. She had called Powel to give him the news and he had sounded shaken, though the line was unusually bad. She had told him they were going to Uxmal, that she was still looking, but she couldn't bring herself to talk for more than a minute about something that seemed so irrelevant next to James's death.

It was your dig, she told herself. *If nothing else, it was your dig. And these were your people.*

James was just a kid. He thought of himself as an archaeologist, but he was little more than a child, wide-eyed and full of excitement and potential.

Deborah lowered her foot involuntarily and the car sped forward.

"You want to talk about it?" said Nick, sitting up.

"There's nothing to talk about," she said, eyes on the road.

"Seems like there is."

"No," she clarified. "I don't want to talk about it."

So they didn't talk about it—or anything else—and the miles slid by. In the back of the car, still stuffed into a red plastic bag, were the souvenirs she had brought back for Adelita. She had never made it up to the village, and that too felt like a failure.

Two hours later Nick started making phone calls, and by the time they reached Uxmal, Kenneth Jones, the CIA operative, was there to meet them.

"Now maybe we'll get that Anglo American accord," Nick remarked.

It took a while for the American agents to show any sign of that accord. There were two of them, Jones and another man called Freykes, a quiet, middle-aged white man in a gray suit whose professionalism couldn't mask what she took to be resentment. He didn't want to work with the English agent. Neither did Jones. They were acting on orders from higher up. There were some muttered apologies for previous encounters, but there was a posturing stiffness to the way the men interacted that she found tiresome.

Deborah was relieved to find the crime scene already tidied up, the body long gone. Jones was working closely with the local police, he said, and other agents were en route from the States. His manner was businesslike, formal, pointedly not blaming anyone. Deborah had been bracing herself for his rebuke, his allegations of amateurism and reckless incompetence, and maybe if she had come in cocky and unaffected by the news he would have unleashed them all, but he took one look at her and just gave her a nod of greeting. He even offered his condolences, but Deborah couldn't even find the words to thank him, and there was a long, awkward pause till Nick, still professional, took him aside to talk, *secret agent to secret agent*, thought Deborah bleakly. *As if I needed further evidence of why I shouldn't be here.*

But if she expected to be ignored, left to go her own way from then on, she was wrong. She heard them muttering in the hallway outside, but no more than five minutes later, they were back and, without explanation, continued to include her in the conversation. Nick had shown Jones the e-mail from Alice—or, as he said, "allegedly" from Alice—and asked him if the name Dimitri meant anything to him. Jones shook his head without meeting their eyes and Nick pressed him.

"You want our help on this, you need to be honest with us," said Nick.

"*Our* help?" said Deborah. "I'm not on your side."

"Fine," said Nick. "We need your archaeological expertise, right, Agent Jones?"

This was obviously what they had been discussing outside. Jones seemed to hesitate, not liking it, then nodded.

"I'm not crazy about having civilians in a hot zone," he said, "but under the circumstances I don't think we have a choice.

Besides, I know a bit about you. You've worked with the FBI on two occasions, productively. We could use your expertise."

"I'm not an expert," said Deborah, seemingly for the hundredth time. She shot Nick a glance, but he showed no response to this news of her past, which, she suspected, meant he already knew about it. Unaccountably, the fact that he had never said so annoyed her. "I'm especially *not* an expert on Uxmal," she added. "I've never even been here before."

"That's how you pronounce it?" said Jones. "Well you're more of an expert on *Oosh-mahl*," Jones said, mimicking her pronunciation of the word, "than we are. You're the best we have till the others get here. That could take a couple of days, maybe longer. So let's walk."

They moved briskly from the hotel to the archaeological remains, passing through the ticket and orientation area with a flash of Jones's badge, through the quadrangle of souvenir stores and facilities, and then up a long path that stepped gradually up to the site itself. It was hot outside after the shade of the hotel, and the air was alive with the steady rasping buzz of insects.

At the perimeter fence were low-slung derelict buildings. They moved along a narrow paved way flanked by trees, probably the original *sacbe* route. To one side was a shallow circular reservoir, and up ahead was a massive, looming pyramid with curved sides and a broad ceremonial staircase up the side facing them.

Deborah couldn't help but smile. She had hoped she would get to see this during her visit, and it was, if anything, more impressive than the pictures she had studied. She had known it was here, but it was still a surprise and a privilege to see it, like glimpsing a jaguar. From down here the pyramid looked almost impossibly sheer, the stairway close to vertical and the rounded sides pointing up like the entire mountainous structure had pushed up from the world below. The stonework was immaculate, and the combination of the proportional elegance of the thing—its balance and regularity—coupled with the extraordinary engineering required to raise it in a world without modern machinery, electricity, or even metal tools took Deborah's breath away.

"That's the Pyramid of the Magician," said Deborah, unable to keep a note of awe out of her voice.

The CIA man paused and gazed at it for a moment and something of his professional demeanor slipped away as he shaded his eyes.

"Cool," he said, meaning it. "And that's like a thousand years old?"

"Give or take," said Deborah.

"Huh," he said, admiring.

"Any word on Bowerdale?" said Nick. Deborah thought he sounded impatient.

"No," said Jones, turning to him.

Nick seemed to give him a searching glance and Jones opened his hands.

"Look," he said. "You say you want me to trust you and I've said I will, but that means you have to trust me too. So when I say I don't know where Bowerdale is, that's because I don't know where Bowerdale is. OK? He can't have gotten from Valladolid to Uxmal in time to kill James, so he's not a suspect anyway. We'll catch up with him later."

"And this Dimitri character," said Nick, pressing. "Is he real or did Alice make him up?"

Jones gave Deborah a swift look.

"You realize you are helping your government in a very delicate situation," he said, "and that while your assistance is appreciated, were you to reveal hereafter anything of a delicate or sensitive nature, it might be considered grounds for charges of treason?"

"I'm aware," she said. "So?"

"He's real," said Jones.

Deborah stared.

"You know him?" said Nick.

"In a manner of speaking," said Jones. "Dimitri is not his real name. He's a Serbian freelancer."

"Freelancer?" said Deborah. "Which means what?"

"Hit man and gun runner," said Jones. "Linked to Bosnian atrocities in the midnineties."

"Gun runner?" said Nick, emphatically persistent. "As in, an arms dealer?"

"That's classified," said Jones.

"Didn't we just have this conversation?" said Nick.

"There are some things I am not at liberty to reveal," said Jones.

"Bollocks," said Nick, pausing under a shady tree where a pale iguana with dark vertical stripes lounged. "You might be able to demand her help," he said, nodding at Deborah, "but if you want the assistance of Her Majesty's government, you're going to have to be a bit more forthcoming, mate."

"Why are you pursuing the stones?" demanded Jones.

"They are of ancient cultural significance to the Crown," said Nick.

"OK," said Jones.

"So this Dimitri," Nick pressed. "He's dealing in what, antiquities?"

"That's right," said Jones.

"You're lying," said Nick.

Deborah thought Nick was right. Jones had looked hurriedly back to the pyramid. But then Nick wasn't telling the truth either, or not all of it. So she did.

"The Brits think that the stones and other objects buried here might be the lost English crown jewels that were supposedly melted down and sold off by Oliver Cromwell between 1649 and 1658 when the monarchy was restored."

Both men stared at her, both aghast, if for different reasons.

"You want him to come clean," she said to Nick, "then so should you."

"That wasn't your call," he said.

"No," she said. "Nothing is, but here I am. Now it's your turn," she said, turning to Jones.

"Wait," he said, wrapping his brain round the idea. "You think we're looking for a lost crown?"

"Several," she said. "There wasn't one English crown. There were lots. Some had special authority in terms of coronation, but each king or queen added wealth to the royal regalia—usually riches and gifts they received from other monarchs or items they commissioned themselves. So yes, that's what he's looking for. Now, what about you?"

"Well," he said. "Gold and precious stones are worth a lot of money. Money drives war and terrorism. If this Dimitri gets a major cash haul, it's guaranteed most of the money will go into guns that ultimately will be bought by terrorists."

"This can't just be about money and guns or you wouldn't be here," she said. "There's more to it than that. What is it?"

"I don't know what you mean," he said.

"You're lying," said Nick again. He turned on Deborah. "Thanks," he snapped. "So you blew my interest without getting anything in return. Brilliant."

Jones said nothing, but he couldn't contain the shadow of a smile.

Terrorism?

She let her thoughts swirl, looking from the pyramid, and suddenly it struck her.

"It's not just the monetary value of the stones," she said.

"You said it was a matter of national security," Deborah said. "You keep talking about terrorism, and you have only ever referred to the grave goods as gems. You haven't mentioned the metal, the bones, or any of the other things we're looking for: only the stones. Now our analysis said the gems weren't that valuable, so it can't be about their intrinsic value as precious stones. But we're talking about naturally occurring crystals, right? And there are lots of uses for crystals. In industry, for instance."

"And in weapons technology," added Nick.

"Bowerdale worked for the military," said Deborah. "He did topographical survey work on the White Sands missile range in New Mexico."

"That's it, isn't it?" said Nick, looking at Jones.

"Missiles?" said the CIA man. "I don't see the connection."

"It's not just missiles they test at White Sands," said Nick. "They work with military lasers there, some of which are built around crystals. The US Army has been working on the development of solid state military lasers for years."

Kenneth Jones said nothing and was very still.

"Lasers, yes," said Deborah. "I read something about how the rare combination of chrome and iron in a ruby might enhance a laser's optical properties..."

"But the crystals used in lasers are manufactured, surely?" said Nick. "They aren't naturally occurring, and there's no way a primitive culture—Mayan or English—could artificially manufacture crystals of any kind."

Jones looked away again.

"I have the original specs for the crystal scanned by Aguilar," said Deborah, "and those for the Malkin Tower stone. I'm sure British intelligence could figure out why Dimitri wants them based on that information."

"Transfer that information to a foreign power and you'll spend the rest of your life in prison," said Jones, stern but clearly on the defensive.

"Aguilar sent it out the day we found it," said Deborah. "He contacted people all over the world trying to match the signature because the stone was so unusual. Anyone who wants to know already does. They just don't have the stones themselves, and you're going to need me to find them."

Jones held her eyes for a long moment, then nodded.

"OK," he said. "You want to know everything? Fine. But this stays between us on pain of serious charges leveled..."

"Yes," said Deborah, "we know. Get on with it."

Jones took a long breath, then said, "Lasers stir up specific kinds of atoms and light comes out. If you reflect those photons back into the excited atoms, still more light is generated, but this time the light comes out only in one direction. All the light has the same wavelength and color—depending on the gain medium, which determines the types of atoms used. Direct all that light and it will incinerate whatever you target. Not surprisingly, the military has been chasing lasers for decades, but they couldn't generate the power required to do what we wanted them for."

"Knocking missiles out of the sky," inserted Nick.

"Among other things, yes," said Jones, "although our goals are pretty modest right now. We've tried chemical lasers fuelled with ethylene and nitrogen trifluoride, but they're too bulky and the chemicals have to be constantly replaced. If these things are going to be successful, they need to generate at the very least a hitting power of about a hundred kilowatts: enough to detonate an incoming mortar round. The chemical lasers didn't come close, nor did the free electron lasers that were supposed to arm Reagan's Star Wars program in the eighties. So we went back to the solid state lasers that we were working on back in the sixties using slabs of artificially created corundum: specifically ruby. We've made big strides, but the power output is still low, and the crystals heat up too much, so you need a minute or more of cool-down time between each burst, which is no use in a battlefield situation."

"And you think," said Nick, "that the gemstones we found in Ek Balam, of which there are more somewhere in Uxmal, are better."

"That's what it amounts to," said Jones. "We don't know exactly what they are because we haven't seen more than those low-level tests you performed, but the chemical composition is extremely unusual, and yes, the combination of iron and chrome might well enhance the optical properties in ways significantly improving the capability of the laser. But it's the crystalline structure that's getting the attention, because it looks like it might lead to considerably less phonon scattering, slower heating, and faster cooling cycles. That means more power ready for rapid use and reuse. Personally, I'm skeptical, but there is no question that they are very fine, very rare stones without flaws, and it is possible—*possible*—that they may be considerably more efficient than those we have been working with. If they are, we can use them and, more importantly, learn to replicate them. But, like I said, I'm skeptical."

"It hardly matters how they work at this point," said Deborah. "It's about what this dealer—Dimitri—thinks and what he is prepared to do to get hold of them."

"It's also about who he might sell them to," added Nick.

"He might sell them to us," said Jones. "But only if we offer him the most. More likely, they'll end up in the hands of military scientists in rogue nations or undesirable organizations. We have intel to suggest he's talking to practically everybody; and you can imagine what top brass thinks of rogue nations or terrorists building portable military lasers faster and more powerful than ours."

"If they could bring down a shell or missile," said Nick, thinking aloud, "they could bring down aircraft."

Jones nodded.

"With a single burst," he agreed. "With a rapidly cycling laser you could knock down an entire squadron in seconds while covering your ass from anything incoming. You can do a lot of things with a powerful, rapid-fire laser. If someone—a terrorist organization, for instance, could get hold of a weapon like this, particularly if it's relatively small and mobile—well, it would be a game changer. We can't let that happen. If there are more gems buried around here, we need to find them before Dimitri does."

Blood and tears, thought Deborah.

"So where do we look?" asked Nick.

Jones looked at Deborah. "I was kind of hoping you could tell me," he said. "Deborah?"

How the hell should she know? She wasn't an expert on Uxmal, wasn't even an expert on the Maya. Hell, she wasn't even really an archaeologist! She was a museum director. She knew less about this place than all of the people who worked for her. What did she know that could possibly help them now?

Edward Clifford.

She knew more than any of the others about him, and suddenly, as she stepped out into the sun and gazed up at the pyramid whose base they were skirting, she thought that that might be enough.

Maybe. Just maybe.

She shielded her eyes and stared. The pyramid had stepped levels, and in the center was an opening in the tapering shape of the typical Mayan arch, above it what looked like chambers and structures on the top.

"We start there," she said.

"The Pyramid of the Magician?" said Nick. "There are dozens of structures on this site. Why there?"

"Because the Pyramid of the Magician is only one of its names," she said. "The first archaeologists to come here were told a legend about how the pyramid was built in a day by a man who came from the nearby village of Kabah. He was unusually small, something the Maya, for some reason, associated with mystical power. The other name for the structure is the Pyramid of the Dwarf."

Chapter Sixty-Nine
■ ■ ■ ■ ■

The pyramid was roped off—the only part of the site that was—but a flash of Jones's badge got them access with no problem. Getting permission to do any kind of excavation, on the other hand, was another matter entirely. There was no sign of anything useful in the stone rooms on the top or in the hollows cut into the pyramid body, neither the one facing the entrance nor the one on the west side that overlooked the Quadrangle of the Nuns. There could, of course, be secret chambers inside or beneath the pyramid itself, but they had no way of knowing and wouldn't know where to begin digging even if they were sure there was something to be found. From the top they had been able to look out over the whole site, particularly the Quadrangle, above which chairs had been set up in readiness for the evening's light show. It was supposedly an impressive event, complete with booming soundtrack that echoed across the pyramids, inaugurated in the 1970s during a visit by England's Queen Elizabeth.

More royalty, Deborah thought.

She sat with Nick Reese and Kenneth Jones under a tree at the pyramid's base and drank water in silence.

"I could get a fleet of bulldozers and we could level the damned thing," said Jones, after an hour of pacing in the hot sun.

"That had better be a joke," said Deborah.

"Not sure my government would think the preservation of a Mexican ruin was worth letting weapons technology onto the open market," he said.

"Maybe that's the problem with governments," said Deborah.

"Hold it," said Nick, heading off the spat before it could flare up. "Just explain to me why you think the legend of the pyramid being built by a dwarf is relevant. Because Edward de Clifford was a dwarf? That's it?"

"There's also the witch connection," she sighed, "though frankly I don't know what to do with that."

"Right," said Nick. "It's not like Lady Anne Clifford was a witch!"

And there it was. Deborah sat up.

"That's it," she said.

"Lady Anne *was* a witch?"

"No," said Deborah. "But she also wasn't Edward's mother. Edward's name wasn't de Clifford. It was Davis. His mother's name was Janet. But...oh my God..."

"What?" said Nick.

But Deborah just leapt to her feet and snatched out her cell phone, looked at it.

No signal.

She glanced up at the pyramid, which was about a hundred feet high, then scanned the horizon. There were no phone towers, but the Great Pyramid over at the south end rose considerably higher than anything else in the site, including the Pyramid of the Dwarf.

She began to run.

She crossed the grass in long, powerful strides, running like a giraffe through the ball court, past the house of the turtles and the western side of the governor's palace, along a roughly marked dirt path through thin, scrubby trees. At the foot of the Great Pyramid, she paused for breath, then started to climb. The steps were high and narrow with clean, sharp edges, sheer as a ladder, and she did not look down until she reached the top, sweating heavily with the exertion, but all focus on the signal display on her phone. Two bars, which was good enough.

She tried the hospital first, but Hargreaves had been discharged. She tried Lancaster castle and was told that he was resting at home and no, she could not have his home number. She asked for Barry in the gift shop and had Hargreaves's number thirty seconds later.

The professor answered on the second ring.

"I was wondering when I'd hear from you," he remarked.

Deborah began to say some conciliatory things about his injury but he cut her off.

"We can catch up later, lass," he said. "What's on your mind?"

"I thought the *de* in de Clifford was some old French form, but in the letter he sent to Lady Anne he crossed out "dev" not just "de." He had started to write his birth name and replaced it with his adopted name: Clifford. I think he was writing Davis, his birth biological mother's name: Janet Davis. But the vicar at Newchurch warned me about spelling variants, and I'm wondering now if he wasn't writing Davis, but Device."

"Bloody hell," said Hargreaves. "Then Janet Davis could be..."

"Jennet Device," said Deborah. "The nine-year-old girl on whose evidence her mother and the others were convicted of witchcraft and executed in 1612."

Hargreaves blew out a low whistle.

"But that wasn't the end of her story, was it?" said Deborah. "In 1612, she was a witness for the prosecution, but in 1633, she was a defendant, right?"

"Right," said Hargreaves. "She would have been about thirty then, and this time the star witness was an eleven-year-old boy called Edmund Robinson who had axes to grind against a lot of local people and was looking to make some money as a witch finder. Seventeen people were convicted and sent to Lancaster Castle, one of them being Jennet Device—Janet Davis—but the case attracted attention. Several of the women were taken to London to be examined by jurists and medical men for signs of witch marks on their bodies. William Harvey, the king's physician, who was always close by—the king had had childhood rickets so he kept a good doctor at hand—examined the women for unnatural markings in July, 1634. The king himself interviewed them."

Deborah turned to face the stone carved macaws on the temple frieze and said, "Say that again?"

"The accused were interviewed by King Charles the First himself," said Hargreaves. "He was curious about witchcraft, as his father James had been, and he was particularly intrigued by this case."

"Because he knew the son of one of the accused," said Deborah. "What happened?"

"It's not clear," said Hargreaves. "The king pardoned them all. The Robinson boy's story collapsed under cross-examination and the women were sent back to Lancaster, though some of them were still in prison a year or so later, presumably because they had debts to pay off. We don't know what happened to Jennet. She vanishes from the prison records probably because she died, though she may have been quietly released."

Deborah thanked him and promised she would call again soon. She owed him, she said. Again.

After she had hung up, she sat where she was feeling the hot sun burning her pale arms, gazing out over the site as bees buzzed around her head. The temple at the top was so high that the jungle looked like carpet, level and unbroken by anything except the soft yellow stone of the structures, and when she gazed off to the horizon she could see the curvature of the earth itself as if she was looking out over the ocean.

So now you know, she said to herself.

Edward's fortunes at court rose on his intellect, and perhaps because the king, having suffered rickets as a child, was less quick to see the dwarf's physical limitations as a sign of evil and corruption. But Edward's fortunes fell when his biological mother was dragged once more into whatever passed for headlines in the 1630s.

She thought of the lines from the courtier's diary that Hargreaves had e-mailed her before his attack: *'Tis one thing to have a beggar, a whore, and a famous fool for a mother, 'tis something quite different for that mother's evil to be made manifest in the shrunken child.*

So. Edward's mother was charged and brought to London to be gawked at as a witch from the wilds of Lancashire, already famous because of the 1612 trials. How people had found out, she couldn't guess, but someone had put two and two together and it had all come out, Edward's humble origins and his mother's tortured and infamous history. Edward tried to protect her, and the court started whispering and pointing.

Witch child. Freak.

The king had protected him as best he could, even protected Jennet, throwing out the trumped-up charges against her—actions that would make Edward a confirmed royalist throughout the Civil War, even if his faith in monarchy fell away thereafter—but he couldn't protect Edward's reputation at court. He was damned by association.

Guilty until proven innocent.

Since he'd been unable to change what he looked like and who his mother was, Deborah saw now why he had taken one of the crown jewels to Malkin Tower where his mother had lived. Perhaps it was where he'd had also been born, and she suspected that the stone had been buried as a memorial to Jennet Device. She must have been dead by the time Edward came to Mexico. The jewel he had buried there was indeed a kingly gift, a fragment of the crown worn by one who had saved her from execution, though he had not been able to save himself. The king was executed in 1649 and Edward fled the country immediately after.

Edward had never forgotten either of his mothers, the one who birthed him and the one who raised him, and in different ways—she thought—he loved them both. But Lady Anne was prominent, powerful, and very much alive when Edward met his end. Jennet was none of those things, and it was, she thought, to Jennet that Edward would have consecrated the remaining jewels. Some would lie with the arm he sacrificed for the Mayans he lived with, but the others would lie in his final resting place, and that, she felt sure, would not be somewhere bound to him so much as it was bound to her.

Nick reached the summit of the pyramid first.

"You're fast," he said breathelessly

Jones was right behind him, but he clearly didn't like heights.

"Next time you need to make a call," he said, tearing his gaze from the long drop down the side of the structure, "just ask to borrow my satellite phone, OK?"

"The legend says that the Pyramid of the Magician was built by a dwarf born out of an egg by a witch from Kabah," said Deborah again, the elements of the story chiming in her mind as she made the connection. "Since the Maya associated dwarves with power and magic, Edward's height actually helped him for the first time in his life when he came here. He knew he was dying, and he had decided that England might be better off without kings after all, though he had loved one for the favor he had bestowed upon his family. He decided to bury the stones in the earth, in a shrine to his poor, wretched birth mother."

"Where?" said Nick, glancing from a pocket map up and over the site spread out below them.

Deborah reached over, took the map, and flipped it over. On the other side was a set of inset archaeological plans to other smaller sites in the Uxmal region: Sayil, Labnah, and Kabah. In the last of these, in a scattered site split by Highway 261, was a remote building.

"There," she said.

It was labeled simply "The Witch's House."

Chapter Seventy

■ ■ ■ ▩ ▩

Marissa Stroud had almost reached Merida when the phone rang. She had been driving nonstop for two hours, and the rental car's air-conditioning was loud and ineffectual, so she almost didn't hear it. She snatched it up and said simply, "Yes?"

"They are making for Kabah," said the voice.

"Not Uxmal?"

"They think the grave is in Kabah, a monument to his mother."

"His birth mother was one of *them*?" she said, awed.

"One of the witnesses in the first trial, and one of the accused in the second."

"Jennet," said Marissa, and she almost sighed with pleasure. *Of course.*

That was the link she had not been able to make. But any frustrations at being beaten to the punch by Miller were utterly overshadowed by Marissa's joyful wonder at the perfection of the thing: Clifford was the son of a witch and had borne those hallowed gems to a land where magic still ran deep.

It made sense, and not simply in terms of plausibility. There was a symmetry to it, and that was all to the good. Symmetry was good. Balance. The universe required equilibrium. The anthropologists called it sympathetic magic, when you enacted something in ritual to make it happen in reality—sticking pins in a clay image to make someone lame—but there was more to it than that, and it had much to do with equilibrium. The Maya scattered blood so that Chaak would bring rain. Sacrifice was about gifts to the gods, but it was also about balance.

"Where in Kabah?" she asked.

"A place called the Witch's House."

Again, Marissa smiled at the symmetry of the thing. She wondered if Edward Clifford had come to Uxmal and heard the tale of the dwarf magician hatched from an egg in Kabah, or if his being here had somehow shaped the legend itself. The story was reported to John Lloyd Stephens in 1840, and it was considered an ancient tale, but how ancient? Eight hundred years, or only two hundred?

"Who will be there?" she asked.

"Miller has recalled the original team," said the voice. "Except for you and Bowerdale. You should expect the rest to be there: Porfiro Aguilar, Krista Rayburn, Chad Rylands, Reese the British agent, and at least two from the CIA."

"The CIA?" she said, surprised for the first time. "Why?"

"Not sure. Something to do with the jewels as weapons. The man who killed the boy, James, and kidnapped Alice, the man who shot at Miller the night Eustachio died, is some kind of arms dealer."

Marissa frowned, staring at the road ahead. So this arms dealer was the one complicating things. She recalled the surprise she'd felt at the sudden burst of gunfire from above that night she'd been in the tomb. How she'd doused her lamp and waited quietly while the shooter hunted Miller in the *cenote*. How she'd waited to make sure the gunfire was over before returning aboveground, leaving behind the body of the Mayan in the tomb and the copper tang of his blood in the air.

"Perhaps…," said the voice on the phone.

"What?"

"Maybe it's too risky. There are too many people involved. Perhaps we should just…"

"No," she said. "I will call when I get there." She moved her thumb to the power button, but then stopped and asked one more question. "How is she?"

"No change."

Marissa nodded, and for a moment her eyes prickled with tears so that the road swam. Then she hung up and checked the rearview mirror and considered the long, irregular bundle that filled the entire back seat. It was draped with a wide knit blanket in bright colors and was quite still.

No change.

Well, there would be. There was power here. She patted the canvas bag on the seat next to her, as if the bag and its contents—its polished wooden log inlaid with gems, its twisted metal fragments, and the gold ring nestled among old bones— was a favorite pet. She knew what these artifacts were worth, now more than ever. Had the king himself worn them when he interrogated the witches? Had he worn them when he laid his hands on the people to cure them of scrofula? The hands of the king had healing powers, said Charles and his father, who had revived the old ritual of laying hands on the sick to show the rightness of his claim to the throne.

The king was the right hand of God, and in him lay power beyond that of mere parliaments and counselors, politicians and jurists. And the sign of kingship was the crown and royal regalia. What power the king wielded was bound to them, seared into the stones themselves. But it could be accessed. She was sure of that. There was a way to draw the power forth, and since they had lain in the Mexican earth so long, she thought that the way to that power was as likely to be through the Maya as it was through the English. The gems were of the earth and they knew no nation. They were as at home in the new world as in the old, more so, perhaps, because the old world had smashed its rituals, sacked its chambers of magic and ancient power, struck the heads from saints and kings. The world as the Maya knew it was still a place of magic and mystery, a place of sacrifice, of power. The Maya understood what the English had forgotten, that there were superhuman forces that could be tapped through ritual and that sought to echo the essential symmetries of the world.

And Mayan magic required Mayan blood.

Marissa Stroud glanced from her watch to the rearview mirror as she pulled over and stopped. She climbed out of the car and opened the rear door on the driver's side. On the floor under the driver's seat was a zippered pouch, which she opened and from which she withdrew a syringe with a long needle whose cap she removed. Then she pulled back the colorful blanket and considered the girl.

Adelita Lucia del Carmen Lacantun lay half turned toward the rear window, her hands and feet bound, her eyes closed. She looked smaller than when she was awake, thinner, more frail. What was she, twelve? Thirteen? Something like that. Stroud had barely spoken to her before she had returned to the village to pick her up and knew little about her. She had known the girl was bright and would recognize her, but that only made it easier. She had mentioned Deborah Miller's name and offered her hand and the girl had taken it guilelessly, as kids in the States would never do. She was an innocent, and that, as the ancient Maya had known, was all to the good. Marissa considered the sleeping child, stroked her cheek, and picked a fragment of clay from her tangled black hair. She felt her pulse and checked her breathing, then turned the girl's left forearm until she could find the vein.

The child had already told her more than Miller could possibly know: stories entrusted to her by her dead grandfather, whose life Marissa had taken when he wouldn't tell her where the stolen grave goods were. She didn't regret it. His death had been a respectful sacrifice to the magic that protected Mayan tombs. He, of all people, should have known that.

Adelita had told her all about their family's ancient promise to Edward Clifford. His dying wish had been to lie undisturbed with the treasures he had brought with him, that they should not adorn any new king. More important was Marissa's certainty that once on site the child would be able to guide her to the bones and the rest of the jewels. That would be half of the girl's purpose fulfilled. One more act of symmetry and all would be well.

Chapter Seventy-One

■ ■ ■ ■ ■

"They could use your help, you know," said Chad Rylands.

Deborah looked up from her laptop, remembering where she was and what she was supposed to be doing.

"I'll be right there," she said, scowling. Rylands, Nick Reese had revealed, had been paid to send him information while Deborah had been in England.

They had erected a makeshift shelter with a tarp on the ground with nylon tent fabric pulled tight over poles, and Deborah was sitting under it. It kept the sun off little besides the computer screens, but she kept coming back here while the others did the real work of surveying and clearing the ground. In a way, she was hiding. She didn't like feeling responsible for the success or failure of their search now, didn't like the eyes of the agents on her, watchful, expectant. But she wasn't just hiding. Something was bothering her. The picture still felt incomplete.

She had borrowed Jones's satellite phone to call Hargreaves again and pump him for all he knew about the sale of the Malkin Tower stone, but he had nothing beyond what he had already told her. At the time, it had been an insignificant little gem with some kitschy appeal because of its link to the 1612 witch trials. Those who fancied themselves latter-day witches—redrawn in largely benevolent Wiccan tradition—valued crystals and precious stones, so one with possible links to famous witches of yore had immediate appeal. It had changed hands twice but there was no record of who owned it now.

She had called Powel in Chicago to update him on their situation—he was, after all, paying their bills—but he had been out. Deborah had spoken to his hawkish secretary, Mrs. Pickins, and left a message as to where they were and what they were doing.

"He'll be back within the hour," the secretary had said.

"Gone to see his daughter?" asked Deborah.

Mrs. Pickins coughed, then said in a formal tone that reprimanded Deborah for the inquiry, "I really couldn't say."

She hung up and was about to leave the shelter when something occurred to her, a possibility, albeit a strange one, an unreasonable one. It came into her mind as the memory of an ornately framed photograph, a photograph of a beautiful blonde girl...

Surely not.

She turned back to the laptop that Jones had wired through his satellite transmitter. She opened a search engine and typed in "Angela Powel," then, as an afterthought, added "skater." Almost half of what came up was clearly irrelevant, but several seemed to point directly to her benefactor's daughter. Two of them were on competition sites where she was listed as senior champion, but a third was a *Chicago Tribune* piece from six months earlier. Deborah stared at it and her heart sank.

"No," she said aloud. She closed her eyes, willing the story to change: "Local Skater Hospitalized in Accident." Beneath the headline was a picture of Angela Stroud in her sparkling gold necklace with the garnet-colored pendant.

Her lucky charm…

The article told of a collision on the ice during practice, just the kind Rachel had always dreaded. A young man was executing a double axel jump as Angela, skating backward, was launching into a double lutz. They hit each other in midair, and the man was badly gashed by Angela's skate. He landed on her. She had no time to brace herself for the fall, and hit her head on the ice. She convulsed and was rushed to hospital for emergency brain surgery.

The girl, said the article, was the daughter of local philanthropist Steven Powel, who had raised her alone since separating from his wife shortly after Angela's birth. The story ran out of steam and was filled out with accounts of other skating accidents.

She scanned the rest of the search results and found another story, this one only a month old, which revisited the story of the talented local girl and Olympic hopeful who still lay in a coma at one of the University of Chicago hospitals. "Her father rarely leaves her bedside," one of the nurses said. "At this point, I guess we're hoping for a miracle."

Chapter Seventy-Two
■ ■ ■ ■ ■

It was like they had gone back to the beginning, Aguilar thought. All this laying out of tools and equipment, the hurried surveying of the site and sectioning off of the areas to be cleared. Except that this was not Ek Balam, this was Kabah. There was no swaggering Bowerdale to oversee everything, because Bowerdale—Aguilar could still not quite believe it—hadn't turned up yet, though why he was on the run, no one seemed sure. The work proceeded in an anxious hush while the *norteamericano* agents watched. Miller stalked about looking concerned and urgent. Last night she had briefed them on what had happened, or part of it, and he was still wrestling with the idea that their poking around in the dirt could actually be bound up with all this other stuff: international espionage, intrigue, and murder. Aguilar thought of Eustachio often these days, but now he also thought of the graduate student, James. He wanted to know what was going on, and that was why he had come when Miller called, but he also wanted it over, closed and done, so that he could go back home.

With Krista?

Perhaps. He wasn't sure yet. Wasn't sure she would come if he asked her.

Kabah was a Puuc Maya site in the Chenes style, and its grand feature was the palace of the masks, adorned with countless regular faces of the hook-nosed rain god. The palace contained alcove chambers where swallows nested, and the air was full of the swooping birds, chittering and calling, but the place was otherwise almost completely deserted. Of the few tourists who came to Kabah, none made it across the highway where a great Mayan arch marked the *sacbe* route to Uxmal ten miles away. There was a pyramid, but it was unrestored and overgrown, its edges rounded off by time and weather, and the so-called Witch's House where they were now was set back along a dirt track that wound through dense woods.

Work had been done on the structure before, as was clear from the numbered blocks that sharpened the corners of one building, but the reconstruction had never been completed and the site was turning back into jungle. Aguilar had done all he could to get detailed excavation reports, but they were moving too fast. Again. He had said as much to Miller but she had barely acknowledged his concern, and he had seen in her face that this was not really archaeology anymore. Perhaps it never had been.

He shouldn't be surprised then, he supposed, to find metal detectors among the site equipment. That was a first, looking for metal in a Mayan dig. Miller said they were looking for a grave, one that had not been disturbed by previous excavations but that would be marked by filler earth that was only about three hundred and fifty years old. Unless it was a very shallow grave, the metal detectors would be useless, so he had suggested they begin by probing the ground for signs of less compacted earth. It still felt like they were looking for a needle in a haystack, and Aguilar was surprised to find he wished they had Bowerdale with them.

Even in daylight the Witch's House gave him the creeps, and the sun would be down within the hour. In Ek Balam the site had been largely open with only isolated trees breaking up the grassy expanses between structures, but Kabah on this side of the highways was a dense forest of thin, stunted trees, with vines and brambles encroaching from all sides. Aguilar hated the jungle: the humidity, the flies, the constant fear of finding a fer-de-lance poised to strike each time you moved a log or a stone. Aguilar had a morbid fear of snakes, and knew the place was alive with more than the big lumbering iguanas. One of the locals said there really were jaguar in the woods: rare, but out there. As if they needed something else to worry about.

The Witch's House itself was little more than a stone chamber on an unexcavated mound a little farther up the path. They had swept the sides of the mound, trimming back the undergrowth with machetes so that they could see what they were dealing with, but it was hot, slow work, and their lack of progress was starting to annoy them. It hadn't been reasonable to expect that they would make the find on the first day, but he had been hoping for it anyway, and now the light was starting to fade.

He drank from the cooler constantly, but they couldn't keep the water cold for more than a few hours, and it was evening, so the "coolers" had been warm since lunchtime. If this had been a real dig they might have had a generator, but the only power they had came from the van batteries, and they couldn't squander that on refrigeration. So he drank the warm water and scowled, and was about to pour himself another cup when Krista shouted, and suddenly everyone was running.

Chapter Seventy-Three

Dimitri paced while Bowerdale stared at the map for the thousandth time. Alice was curled up on the back seat, as she had been for at least two hours. It seemed like days since Dimitri had been asleep, and even his naps had been scarred by the dream. "Well?" he said.

Bowerdale shrugged, putting one hand to the bruise that stretched from his jaw up to his blackened right eye, and smiled in what was supposed to be a reassuring way. But Dimitri knew he was scared. So he should be. They wouldn't be in this situation if Bowerdale hadn't involved that idiot James, packing him off to Coba to dig up the bag. Dimitri knew Bowerdale had been trying to cut him out of the deal, trying to partner with some kid who would do as he was told. Well, the kid was dead, though Bowerdale hadn't known that till he wandered into Uxmal looking to find his little errand boy. Finding Dimitri instead had freaked the archaeologist out, and Dimitri had given him a beating for emphasis.

"I'm not sure," Bowerdale said. "It would help if I knew why they had gone to Kabah."

"How should I know?" spat Dimitri. "You think they call and tell me? I just follow them, but now they have CIA with them. We have to know where they are going and we have to take it before they get it. That or we let them get it, then take it from them."

Bowerdale flinched, nervous in his rumpled seersucker suit. Dimitri hated that suit and Bowerdale's dandified airs. He couldn't imagine why any man would dress like that, especially out here where there was no one to impress.

"Take it?" said Bowerdale, his eyes flashing about. "How?"

Dimitri drew the gun, the CZ 75B, a decent Czech 9mm, with the ten-inch silencer, and considered it significantly. He didn't like using the silencer. It felt wrong when the gun fired and it increased the chance of jamming. Most of all, though he couldn't explain why, he missed the sound of an unmuffled weapon, the crack of it, the flash from the muzzle. The silencer made the gun absurd, apologetic, with its polite cough. He missed the authority, the command of the thing.

"You can't," stuttered Bowerdale, staring at the gun. "There are too many of them."

"Then you'll have to figure out where the stones are before they do," said Dimitri.

It had been like this in Bosnia, he thought. When things had gotten bad—really bad—when there were only those who would do what was necessary and those who would not. Lots of them had balked. He had not. You put your mind to it and did it, and any fear or anxiety was squeezed to nothing so that it only bubbled up in dreams.

The bulletproof women and children hemming him in against the back of the truck, their eyes locked on his so he couldn't see to shoot...

He had grown what they called a thicker skin, though the skin was around his brain, enclosing his mind so that he felt nothing except the desire to get it done and move on. He sensed this would be like that. The girl was falling apart, and the man, though he pretended to still care about the stones, had already given up, unwilling to do what was necessary and only there at all because he was terrified of what Dimitri would do to him if he tried to run. As he should be.

Earlier, the three of them had climbed one of the palaces in Kabah and he had scanned the area with binoculars, but Miller and the others were nowhere to be seen, and the deep gold light was fading. The map showed other ruins on the west side of the highway, but the only one you could see from here was that rough, moldering pyramid, and there was no one there. If they were at one of the more remote sites, it might be impossible to get close without being seen, and whatever he said to Bowerdale, Dimitri didn't want a firefight with the CIA. He needed a diversion, or darkness, which was why they were now waiting in the car for the last rays of light to go.

He was thinking about this when he saw another car pull into the lot. He trained his binoculars on it and watched as a familiar woman got out.

Chapter Seventy-Four

■ ■ ■ ■ ■

Krista Rayburn just knelt where she was and stared, the cry still on her lips.

It was a slab of limestone about halfway up the mound and covered with about six inches of soil. She had been probing the earth as they cleared the weedy undergrowth, and her rod had struck something hard. She tried it twice more, mapping the size of the stone. She scrabbled at the dirt first with a trowel and then with her hands, pulling up the grass and vine so that the covering mat of vegetation tore free like a rug, green on one side, a thick tangle of roots on the other. Once she had started to pull, it had come up almost in one piece, revealing a stone the size of a small door.

Carved into the surface was a crude relief of a man, short and barrel-chested, but without the hawkish profile of the locals or their flattened skulls. The light was low enough that she got as much from her fingertips as from her eyes, and she swept them over the slab hungrily. The carved figure wore the feathery wings of the Ek Balam kings, and he brandished a sword in his one good hand. The other was missing from the elbow. And on either side of the figure was a letter, not a Mayan glyph, but an English letter: an *E* and a *C*.

Edward Clifford.

They were all around her by then. No one spoke, but their shadows made it even harder to see, so someone trained a flashlight on the stone. Then they used mattocks and picks to prize the stone free, working them into the crack around the edge and then leaning all their weight on the handles. The stone was heavy, but they worked silently, sweating, adjusting, until a finger of dark space appeared down the left edge. Then they moved to the right side and repositioned their tools. Krista caught Porfiro's eye as he wiped the perspiration from his unreadable face.

Everyone pitched in. Even the CIA men used crowbars and logs as levers to work the slab free. Aguilar began repeating a Spanish word she didn't know, and it became a rhythm they worked to, straining in unison, pausing, then pulling again, until—with a low, rasping, groan, the stone began to move. They slid it to the side rather than flipping it over, so that they were less likely to break it, and then stood there in silence, panting, hands on knees, staring.

Chapter Seventy-Five

■ ■ ■ ■ ■

It was hard to see past the grave goods to the human remains, but Aguilar would have a fit if he started moving things out of the way, so Chad Rylands shifted his position and guided the beam of his flashlight as carefully as he could. The right arm of the skeleton was severed just below the elbow. Even from here, and surrounded by all this gaping and gasping, it was clear that the bones of the thighs and upper arms were severely shortened, and the skull was disproportionately large with a prominent forehead. Below the knee and elbow the shortening was less profound, but the feet seemed undersized. He would need proper analysis to see if they displayed the separation between the third and fourth digits characteristic of achondroplasia, but he was as sure as he could be: this was the skeleton of the dwarf whose hand lay under the great pyramid in Ek Balam. The discoloration of the bones fit Miller's guess as to the date of internment—about three hundred and fifty years ago—but confirmation would take analysis of a kind he couldn't do squatting by a hole in the ground of some Mexican forest. If only he could get all that other stuff out of the grave, and get rid of his gawking colleagues, he could get some real work done.

Chapter Seventy-Six

■ ■ ■ ■ ■

Nick Reese had not removed the camera's viewfinder from his eye since the grave had been opened. He zoomed and fired the shutter, aware of little beyond the tiny electronic pop of the flash followed by its faint recharging whine. As he recomposed and shot, parts of the ancient Jewel House inventory he had read a thousand times in documents from the interregnum ran through his head. He carried a copy of the 1652 transcription made by Cromwell's agents folded inside his camera case, and though he couldn't have recited it perfectly, the items chimed in his memory as his eyes raked the contents of the grave.

One large blue sapphire, ten large diamonds, and as many rubies. 232 pearls. Four rubies in a fleur-de-lis, seven diamond crosses. 20 sapphires, 83 pearls. A small crown found in an iron chest, formerly in the custody of Lord Cottington, weighing 2 1b. 10 oz., whereof three ounces are allowed for the weight of the stones. The globe, weighing 1 lb. 5 oz. Two coronation bracelets, weighing 7 oz.: Three rubies balases, set in each of the bracelets. Twelve large pearls. Two scepters, weighing 16 oz. A long rod of silver gilt, weighing 11.5 oz. One gold cup set with two sapphires and two rubies balases, weighing 15 oz. Diverse pieces of broken gold enameled, put together in a bag, weighing 5 lb.

Queen Edith's crown, enriched with garnet, pearl, sapphire, and some stones, weighing 50 oz.

King Alfred's crown of gold wire-work, set with precious stones and two little bells, weighing 79 oz.

A dove of gold, set with stones and pearl, set with studs of silver gilt. A large gold staff with a dove at the top. One small staff, with a fleur-de-lis on the top. Two scepters—one set with pearls and stones, the upper end gold, the lower end silver.

The queen's crown of gold and precious stones, weighing 3 1b. 10 oz.

The imperial crown of massy gold, weighing 7 1b. 6 oz., enriched with precious stones…

He couldn't be sure, was too excited to judge, but he thought most of it was here. Maybe all of it. Centuries of history and culture—all long since deemed irretrievably lost—lying heaped among bones in the Mexican dirt. Nick zoomed and snapped and recomposed in a kind of frenzy, willing the flash to charge faster.

Chapter Seventy-Seven

■ ■ ■ ■ ■

Deborah saw the gleam of bright metal in the flashlight, and the sparkle of gems, but her eyes stayed on the skeleton beneath. The bones were dark and stained, but she felt no revulsion, only a warm sense of recognition and closure that blended equal parts joy and sadness. The figure was twisted slightly to one side and the skeleton had collapsed, but her eyes moved to the skull, and for a moment it was like looking at someone she had known long ago. The body seemed small so that she was forcefully reminded that they had first assumed the bones had come from a child. As the flashlights played over the grave, and Nick Reese's camera flash began to fire, Deborah sank to her haunches and put her hands to her face, thinking of the child born misshapen and despised to an outcast mother on the slopes of Pendle Hill, and all he had gone through before being laid to rest so very far away.

Beside the body lay a rusty sword with a basket hilt.

Edward's sword, she thought. The sword that had hacked away his arm at the elbow as part of an honor debt aimed to protect the people who had taken him in, people among whom he did not belong.

And around him the jewels he had kept to commemorate a man who had spared his miserable and embattled mother, the jewels that had once meant everything to the old world order and its version of power, now returned to the earth in a land that would abandon monarchy entirely.

The skeleton wasn't much more than half her size, and Deborah knew why she empathized so much with this forgotten outcast, the man whose size and shape, combined with his intellect and stubbornness had made him a perpetual outsider. She knew that feeling. She sensed it in people's eyes as they flashed up her six-foot, two-inch frame, when they asked what her husband did, how old her children were, or when she'd last taken a vacation, and then gave her that confused look, their lips always holding back the questions she heard in her mother's voice:

Why can't you be normal?

Or the franker notes of contempt and hostility.

Weirdo. Loser. Freak.

As she sat gazing into the tomb, she suddenly realized that the body had been buried with more than the treasure he had brought with him. There were jade beads and decorated ceramics, sea urchin spines and a wooden jaguar mask with inlaid shell eyes: Mayan grave goods fit for a king.

So Edward had found a way to fit in after all.

Ken Jones's satellite phone beeped. Deborah didn't take her eyes off the grave, and it was at least a minute before Jones appeared next to her in the dim light.

"Miss Miller," he said. "Are you familiar with Adelita Lacantun, Eustachio's granddaughter?"

The name brought Deborah round sharply, but there was an odd sense of whiplash, almost like vertigo.

"Yes, of course. She helped out at the Ek Balam site some. Why?"

"She seems to have gone missing."

"Missing?" Deborah echoed, stricken with dread. "What do you mean?"

"She was last seen in the company of an American woman identified by the people in the pueblo as someone who worked on the site before it was closed. We think it was Marissa Stroud."

Chapter Seventy-Eight

■ ■ ■ ▪ ▪

It was a logistical nightmare, not unlike the original tomb find. Aguilar straightened his aching back, leaning and arching against the strain, and began planning. The daylight was gone and they would need work lights to do any real detailed study, but they couldn't leave the artifacts in the ground exposed to the elements. A stiff breeze had been building and there was a good chance they would get rain—maybe a lot of it.

They had plastic storage bins in the van. They would have to move everything there, slowly and as carefully as possible, videotaping everything as they did so. Reese, the Englishman, could do that. The rest would do the loading. Maybe the CIA guys—the black guy and the gray-suited one who had led the raid on the lab—would help. If they didn't they'd be here till morning, and it had already been a long, stressful, and exhausting day. Aguilar would do the artifact retrieval and any immediate conservation that seemed necessary, but all they could do was label everything, pad it, and box it up.

Aguilar blew out a long breath. He was still sweating from moving the stone, and the prospect of the recovery effort, an effort that should properly take days, seemed impossibly wearisome.

Madre de Dios, he thought. *Why can nothing go smoothly on this godforsaken project?*

There was a tarp in the van that they might be able to set up on logs and wires as a shelter over the grave like the makeshift tent they had put up to cover the laptops. That would buy them some time if there was a sudden downpour.

Yes, he thought. *That should be their first priority.*

Second, actually. First he needed a drink. He had a bottle of tequila under the van's driver's seat, which he had intended to share with Krista back at the hotel, but that would have to wait. He couldn't afford to be even slightly out of it while they worked, and besides, he felt a headache building just behind his eyes. He was dehydrated.

"Water break, everyone," he said. "Then we erect a shelter over the site and start moving everything into storage. OK, Deborah?"

She was still perched on the edge of the grave, looking at the body. She could have been miles away, and when she heard her name she looked up, her face blank, then nodded silently. She was giving him control of what happened next, which was probably smart. She had been out of it since they had gotten word that Eustachio's granddaughter had been kidnapped. Aguilar felt ashamed that he seemed to feel less for the girl than Miller did, but he had a job to do, and one of them needed to stay focused. He took a long draft from the water cooler, which wasn't as warm as it had been earlier, thank God, and then he handed it off to Krista, watching her pale throat as she swallowed.

"Let's conserve those flashlights," he said. "We're going to be here for a while and we don't have backup power beyond the spare batteries."

The cooler had made the rounds, and when it came back to him he lifted it high and turned on the tap so it poured straight down his throat till he couldn't swallow anymore. He offered it to Krista again and then considered the ground. They were going to need to get the van as close as possible without damaging anything on site. He took a few steps and shone the flashlight onto the weedy grass scanning for stones. The last thing he wanted was to damage the underside of the van.

Back there in the dark he heard someone laugh. Rylands, perhaps. Aguilar didn't think he'd ever heard Rylands laugh before, but it wasn't surprising that it should come now. There was an exuberant mood around the camp. Even the CIA agents felt it: a bubbling of excitement and satisfaction. They didn't know what they had found yet, but however dubious they might be of Deborah's tales of crown jewels, they knew they had something important, even if it wasn't Mayan. They were about to write their way into archaeological history. Already had in fact.

He didn't like moving too far from the others and into the darkness of the woods where the vehicle was parked. There was something primal about the forest that made you feel like the trees were watching, whispering to each other as the wind stirred them. The van looked out of place there, unwelcome, and despite the heat that continued to hang in the dark air, Aguilar shivered. He returned his light to the ground and kicked at a rock, planning which way he would drive through the site. The stone rolled, but not far enough, so he stooped, picked it up, and flipped it a few yards into the trees. He reached for another and was still bent over when he saw the snake.

It was a heavy-bodied thing with a triangular head, a fer-de-lance, he thought, and quite lethal, but there was something odd about it. It was too big, for one thing, and seemed to coil into the underbrush yards away. As Aguilar watched, it seemed to flicker with a greenish light that pulsed down its length. He took an unsteady step backward, only to find another one, curling through his legs. He cried out and jumped sideways, almost dropping his flashlight, but as he moved the beam over the ground he saw more of them. A nest? No, it was worse than that. They were coming up out of the ground, and as the soil broke apart he could see bodies under the earth, some skeletal, but others still holding the remains of flesh and fiber. One of them, he was suddenly sure, was Eustachio, though how he could be here, Aguilar could not begin to guess.

The ground in front of him split open like a husk, and another corpse was pushed up to the surface, a long, sickly orange serpent spewing from its mouth. Aguilar turned to run, but the ground was alive with snakes, boiling up out of the earth, slithering out of the eye sockets and rib cages that lay inches below the surface. Dimly, like someone in a dream, he became aware of screaming back where the others were, though he could not take his eyes from the ground to look.

Chapter Seventy-Nine
■ ■ ■ ▨ ▨

Deborah knew what had happened the moment the beam of her flashlight seemed to swirl, its particles slowing and drifting in a haze that scattered color. She had drunk last, and only once, but she felt the force of the drug in a rising terror that was amplified by the scenes around her. Someone was screaming. Krista, she thought. Rylands had sprinted off into the darkness like he was being chased, and one of the CIA agents was lying on the ground, his eyelids fluttering and a ribbon of blood running down his head. She fought to make sense of it all.

She had been talking to Jones about something important, though she couldn't remember what, and then he had stopped talking. She wasn't sure what had happened next, but a moment later he was on the ground. It looked like he was having some kind of seizure.

It's not real, she thought, mouthing the words, whispering to herself. It was the water. While we were moving the stone, someone got to the water…Chattox. Or Old Demdike.

But she knew it wasn't them, knew it was someone else, someone she knew, though she couldn't find the name. She turned and shone her flashlight back to the grave, and there was someone there, crouched over, scrabbling at the dirt. A woman. And in the grave laid out, pale in death, was Adelita.

The woman turned toward Deborah, but she had no eyes, and the mouth hung open as if the jaw were disconnected. It was black inside and wide enough to fall into.

Ma?

The word ran up her throat from her belly, tearing as it came, so that she felt her insides wrenching and buckling.

No, she countered. *Not real.*

Deborah tried to take a step toward her, but it was like pushing against something with substance, yielding, black and viscous as if the night itself had coalesced and begun to harden. It came from the woman's mouth. The darkness seemed to spew from her gaping jaws. It surrounded her, a deep, oily blackness that grew more solid by the moment. Deborah pushed against it but could not take the step, and then something hit her and she fell.

It was Nick Reese. He had run into her full pelt, not seeing her at all, so there was no bracing for impact, no slowing before the collision, and she went down hard, holding her head. He fell half beside her, half on top of her, and his breathing was fast and uneven, his eyes mad.

"Get me out of here!" he gasped, still not really seeing her. "I shouldn't be here."

Deborah clutched the spot above her eye where he had hit her with his head, and rolled, the darkness seeming to brighten with the pain of the impact, but her head cleared a little, and she seized him by the wrist as he rose and tried to run.

"It's not real," she managed. "It's the water. That woman…" She turned but was disoriented. "How much did you drink?"

"What?" He looked at her as if he had never seen her before, his eyes moving uneasily from her face to the darkness behind her. "I don't belong here."

"How much did you drink?" she said again. She felt clearer already, as if telling him what had happened had somehow convinced her own senses. But somewhere back there the eyeless woman still clawed in the dirt. Deborah could sense her. She was coming now, with those hollows where her eyes should be and that terrible, gaping cave of a mouth.

Not real!

"How much did you drink?" she repeated, focusing on Nick.

"I don't know," he said. "A cup?"

She sat up and swept her flashlight over the clearing. It was chaos. The others were doubled up, shouting, pointing at nothing, running. Two of them—including one of the CIA men—were lying down, motionless. Jones was on his hands and knees, his arms over his head. Either the others had drunk more than she had, or Stroud had used a considerably greater dose of her toxic cocktail this time.

Stroud! That was her name.

It had just come to her. Deborah seized this and stood up. The ground seemed to roll around her and she had to steady herself, but she was vertical and alert.

Stroud.

And there was something else elbowing into her memory.

Adelita.

Deborah checked the grave, but even from here she could see the child was not there. Another hallucination. But Stroud *had* taken Adelita. That was true. Why?

Deborah ran, stumbling, to the dark rectangle in the earth of the Witch's House, forcing herself to slow before she fell, but the woman was gone. She had been there though. That had not been a hallucination. Deborah knew because the bones had been disturbed and most of what had been in there with them was gone.

Chapter Eighty

■ ■ ■ ■ ■

Marissa Stroud carried the duffel bag over her shoulder and walked quickly along the track through the forest without a lamp. There was just enough light to see by, and she felt lit from within by a sense of purpose. There was a rightness to it all, a symmetry. The ease with which she had doctored the water coolers while they stared at the grave proved it.

The universe aligns for those who know its rules.

Then there was a light coming along the path toward her. It was erratic, flashing about, like whoever was carrying it was running and didn't know where he was going.

Without pausing for thought she moved right, stepped off the path and into the trees: four long strides and then she dropped into a crouch, the bag and its sacred contents shrouded by her skirt, her head down so that her hair fell over her face. Then she became still and silent.

She could hear them coming toward her but she did not look up. She already knew who it was. The student—Alice—and the thug with the guns. And Bowerdale. As they got closer she closed her eyes to focus her hearing, and she could tell which was which, the girl sobbing and whining, the thug's rough curses, and Bowerdale's labored breathing as he struggled to keep up. She listened, half seeing the flash of the light, red through her eyelids, but they did not pause, and in another second, they had gone on ahead to the site. She counted to ten slowly, then returned to the path, thanking her gods once more without surprise. It would happen as it was meant to. She could almost sense their hunger for the sacrifice to come.

Chapter Eighty-One

■ ■ ■ ■ ■

It had all gone wrong. Bowerdale wasn't sure when it had started: probably when Dimitri first arrived. He had, he supposed, been warned during that first phone call when his usual artifact buyer had backed off like there was a gun to his head. But hindsight was no consolation whatsoever, especially now that he could no longer see how he might get free of the situation. He was—or had been—a respected archaeologist, a top man in his field. Now he was being pushed around by this European Neanderthal, forced to keep hold of the girl who had flouted his advances and had become a whining wreck. He didn't know why Dimitri wanted to keep her around, but he was pretty sure that if he let go of her arm, she wouldn't run.

He would.

He had known long before he heard what the Serb had done to James. He had been stupid to think he could just walk away from a man like Dimitri, that he wouldn't still be waiting when he got out of jail. Involving James had been a mistake too. He saw that now and regretted it bitterly. If he could wipe out everything that had happened in the last weeks, Bowerdale thought fervently, he would, but that wasn't possible. All he could do now was try to make sure he got out of it alive.

Right now Dimitri thought he was useful, and that would stay true as long as they were picking around Mayan ruins. The moment they stopped, or the moment Dimitri realized that Bowerdale's specialist knowledge meant precisely damn all, then he would become both unnecessary and inconvenient. Bowerdale was under no delusions about how someone like Dimitri dealt with people he thought were in his way.

So as the big Serb strode down the forest track with that over-long pistol in his hand, Bowerdale held Alice close as he had been told but took the opportunity to mutter into her ear.

"We have to get out of here," he said. "We have to stop him."

She had been sobbing, but she stopped suddenly and gave him a wild look, her face inches from his so that he could tell she wasn't breathing. Then her eyes flashed guiltily to Dimitri, and when she turned back to Bowerdale, she shook her head, fast and small like a terrified child.

"Keep up," roared Dimitri.

And suddenly it struck him that it hadn't been Dimitri's arrival that had made everything go wrong, hadn't even been his own boneheaded pursuit of the stones and his clumsy inquiries about their possible applications. It had not even begun when they had found the tomb. It had begun years ago, perhaps decades, at some point when he had forgotten why he had gone into archaeology in the first place, some moment when career and salary and status had drowned out the raw wonder he had once felt when confronted with the remnants of the past. Somewhere out there in the night were places where people had once lived and worshipped, places that would once have filled him with awe and reverence, sensations he had not felt for decades. Now he was a ghost, a shadow of the man he had been, drifting purposeless in the footsteps of his former self, a mere echo...

"I said, keep up," Dimitri spat.

As they scuffled along after him, Bowerdale felt the woods open up, and around them to their right were stone structures. Up ahead, he could hear strange noises: shrieking and laughing, he thought, but also howling and crying.

What the hell was going on there?

Dimitri reached into his shirt and drew another pistol, this one smaller and with a barrel so short you could hardly see it, and walked toward the Witch's House with his arms cocked, a gun on each side at shoulder height.

Then someone was coming toward them, sprinting hard down the dark path, panting and sobbing as they ran from the ruins. Dimitri hesitated fractionally then he raised the larger pistol in front of him and fired. In the darkness you could see the flash of the gun, but there was almost no sound beyond the sort of noise you might make by hitting a potato with a pin hammer. There was smoke after that, more than he would have expected, so that for a moment the woods smelled like the Fourth of July, and only after he had processed that did he realize that the man who had been running toward them was gone.

Dimitri kept walking, barely glancing down to where Chad Rylands lay crumpled half in the woods, his legs sticking out onto the trail. Bowerdale stooped to him, releasing Alice, who went immobile again, but Dimitri barked at him without turning, "Keep up," as if nothing had happened.

It was too dark to see much of the Witch's House itself, but a light had been left by the grave site. There were people scattered around, some of them lying on the ground, some of them running about. It was chaos. They were whimpering and shouting. Krista Rayburn was screaming from the top of the mound as if she was being assaulted from all sides. Alice's knees gave way and Bowerdale let her fall.

Dimitri stood staring at the grave. He stirred the bones with his foot, then turned, his face dark with fury.

"They're gone," he bellowed. "They're fucking gone. Who has them? Where are they?"

He turned, pistols raised, shouting at the first person he saw. It was Aguilar, who was standing with his feet close together on a stone, his body twisting as he stared at the ground around him.

"Where are they?" Dimitri demanded, and he put the muzzle of the silenced pistol to Aguilar's temple.

"He doesn't know," shouted Bowerdale. "Look at him! He doesn't even know you're there."

"Where are they?" Dimitri repeated.

Aguilar continued to scan the ground as if it was alive with something terrible, and Bowerdale, seeing the flash of fury in Dimitri's face, knew he had less than a second to decide.

It was easy to blame Dimitri for all that had gone wrong, but Martin Bowerdale knew that that was a dodge. Dimitri would be nowhere without Bowerdale's hunch that Eustachio had ridden the motorbike to Coba to bury the gems. Bowerdale wished he'd never returned the call after Dimitri had first contacted him. That seemed like a long time ago now. That was when Bowerdale thought he was calling the shots, that Dimitri was reasonable, that they could split the find and the money that came from it. Back then, Dimitri had made it sound like that was the way it would work. But it was more than obvious now that Dimitri was not capable of sharing.

It was only after the gems had disappeared that Eustachio had been murdered in that gruesome fashion. And who had done it? Not him or Dimitri—even though the thug *was* responsible for chasing Miller into the *cenote* and nearly killing her. No, Bowerdale still didn't know who'd murdered Eustachio or why. But one thing was certain: he'd opened the door for Dimitri. If he hadn't, James and Chad Rylands might still be alive.

He might still be able to atone for it.

He ran at the Serb, head lowered, arms spread, and launched himself. He made contact just as the pistol coughed and spat its smoke and flame and the shot went high into the jungle night.

Bowerdale was a big man, but his fighting days were long over. The weight and surprise of his attack sent Dimitri sprawling, but the Serb was up on his feet before Bowerdale could get to his knees. He didn't see the kick coming till it connected with his cheek, and the shock of the pain blindsided him utterly. He thought something snapped, but his hands went not to his face but to the ground for something—a rock, a pick, something he could wield as a weapon—though his fingers found only grass and dirt and air.

Then Dimitri was looming over him and Martin Bowerdale found himself looking into the black eye of the pistol.

For a moment nothing happened, but the screaming confusion of the site seemed to fall away, and Bowerdale, catching the scent of the jungle in his flaring nostrils, suddenly saw in his mind the Mayan city of Palenque as he had seen it as a boy visiting with his parents. He must have been no more than eight. He had not thought of that moment for years and had never thought of it as important, but he remembered now standing at the foot of the Temple of the Inscriptions, gazing up the monumental staircase to where his mother, wearing a blousy white shirt, was gazing out, eyes shaded with one hand. He saw his little boy's hands as they thumbed the film advance on his tiny Kodak Instamatic, and he remembered the awe and the sudden, surprising thought that people made a living by exploring such places.

And just then, between the tightening of the trigger and the flash of the muzzle, Martin Bowerdale smiled.

Chapter Eighty-Two

■ ■ ■ ■ ■

Deborah had seen them march into the site—Alice and Bowerdale and the big, pale man who must be Dimitri—and she had thrown herself down in the grass and vines, dragging Nick down with her. He had struggled against her, still delirious with panic, and for a second that had attracted the beam of Dimitri's flashlight. She held her breath, but then the light went back to scanning the site till he found the grave. He had only stayed there a few moments, and then he was shouting.

What happened next took only seconds, but it seemed agonizingly slow, and she almost thought she could get up and run over to them before the inevitable shot came. That was, of course, nonsense. She would have covered maybe half the ground before Bowerdale died, and then the Serb would have shot her too.

So she lay, facedown in the dirt, Nick babbling beside her, and she waited for them to go, wishing there was something she could do, hating the feeling of weakness and ineptitude that threatened to drown her like the cool waters of the river beneath Ek Balam.

When Dimitri left, still shouting at a sobbing, broken Alice, she had got up slowly, first checking to see that Aguilar had not been shot. He hadn't, but he was completely incoherent. Nick reacted badly to the Mexican's terror, drawing his weapon and waving it unsteadily.

"Give it to me, Nick," she said, firmly, getting right in his face. "It's me. Deborah. Give me the gun."

He seemed bemused but had not resisted as she gently reached up for the pistol and pried his fingers from the grip.

Bowerdale was dead. She had known that before she checked the body, but the fact of it calmed her somehow, steeled her resolve. There was no sign of Rylands. She tried to get some sense out of the CIA men, but, like Aguilar, they were too far gone. Krista Rayburn was still standing on top of the mound, shrieking like a banshee.

Which leaves you.

"Give me your phone," she ordered Nick. "I have to go."

He stared at her, blank.

"Nick," she said. "Listen to me. I have to go."

"Where?" he managed.

She thought. This was no longer about the gems. It was about the life of a little girl that was to be taken, sacrificed, to save another.

"She'll go to a ritual space," said Deborah, thinking aloud. "Not in Kabah. There are too many agents around here and likely to be more as soon as you get word to the police or whatever government agencies can get here first. But she's in a hurry, so she won't go far."

She paused, then, knowing she was gambling, said, "Uxmal. It has to be. And she'll make either for the Pyramid of the Magician— the dwarf—or for the Great Pyramid. I'm going. Now."

"Wait," he said drowsily. "I'll come with you."

"No, Nick. Try to look after the others till the police arrive."

"Right," he said, still vague.

"Where am I going, Nick?"

"What?"

"Where am I going? Come on! Keep it together."

He seemed to search her face for the answer.

"Kabah!" he said. "You're going to Kabah."

"No!" she shouted back, stung with frustration. "I'm going to Uxmal."

"Right," he said. "Uxmal. OK."

"Right. I'm going now."

"Deborah," he said, catching her by the shirt and pulling her face toward his.

"What?"

"Be careful."

And he leaned in to kiss her.

"Look after the others, Nick," she said again, pulling back. "And remember: It's not real. Anything you think you see, it's just the drug."

As she walked away she dialed the phone and summarized what had happened, first in clunky Spanish, then in fast, insistent English to the police dispatcher. Then she hung up, knowing it would take too long for them to reach her, knowing that it was all on her now.

And then she ran down the forest path, thrusting the pistol into her waistband, running hard past the ruins to the side, through the trees to the great arch that marked the *sacbe* to Uxmal and the van that sat alone in the parking lot. She had a set of keys in her pocket and snatched them out as soon as she saw it squatting there, toad-like, in the dark. Her thinking was almost completely clear, but she still felt unsteady and anxious. What had Nick said about the bufotenin: it instilled "a paranoiac sense of impending death." Considering she was chasing a gunman and a woman bent on human sacrifice through darkness and jungle, that seemed only appropriate.

Deborah turned the engine over and snapped on the headlights.

She drove fast, barely touching the brake except at junctions, putting her foot down hard the rest of the time so that the engine raced and complained. Beside her on the passenger seat was the heavy black pistol, and her right hand kept straying to it, fearful of the thing, far from sure how to use it, and desperate that it would not come to that. Nick would send word. She was only five minutes from Uxmal now, but the place would be crawling with cops and US agents when she got there.

At first, she thought her wish had come true. Cars and buses crowded the parking lot, though the site had closed hours ago. But none of them were official vehicles, and the truth hit her as she ran into the site, shouting at an attendant to call the police and ignoring his attempts to stamp her ticket.

The famous Uxmal sound and light show was tonight. That was why people were still filing in to the seats overlooking the Quadrangle of the Nuns beside the Pyramid of the Dwarf Magician. And it meant that either Stroud would have gone somewhere else—in which case all was lost—or that she would make for the Great Pyramid.

So Deborah ran away from the carefully lit path, as she had when she had needed to phone Hargreaves, pounding her way toward the ball court, the house of the turtles, and the governor's palace, behind which sat the Great Pyramid itself. She was halfway there before she heard the booming sounds of the PA behind her, the Spanish voices relaying high points of Uxmal's ancient history while the buildings around her lit up red and yellow and green, the banks of lamps below them belting out enough power to saturate the massive structures with color.

The great pyramid itself was in darkness. Deborah pushed the gun she had been carrying back into her waistband and then cautiously began to climb the steep, ladderlike steps up to the temple at the top on all fours. She seemed to have been doing the same thing ever since she came to the Yucatan.

Back in the Quadrangle of the Nuns there was a crash of symphonic music, the lights shifted, and the pyramid she was climbing was suddenly bathed in cool, blue light. Deborah looked up and saw at the top, against the backdrop of the frieze wall with its recessed alcoves and masques of Chaak, a human figure half in silhouette, half splashed with the turquoise glow.

The shape was wrong, the head somehow distorted.

A mask? With some kind of headdress.

Deborah thought the figure was speaking, but then the PA from the sound and light show cut out all other sound as a chorus of voices spoke in unison, a long slow and echoing chant of the rain god's name:

Chaak!

Deborah hesitated, unnerved by the sound and the silence that followed it. She felt for the gun at her back, and then started up the stairs again, too late realizing that her touch had dislodged the pistol. She felt it sliding out as she took the next step, reached hurriedly round to catch it, but the motion threw her off balance. She flung herself against the steps to keep from falling, and knew the gun was gone before she heard it clattering off the steps below her.

Chaak! called the voices echoing from the speakers behind her.

She paused in the silence and looked down but couldn't see where the gun had gone. She climbed again, faster now, recklessly, clambering apelike up the monumental staircase.

She was too close now to see what was happening above her, and there was no cover from which she could watch or time her appearance. Her best weapon was surprise. She took only a half pause at the very top, stiffened her muscles, and sprang over the final step not knowing what she would find there. In the same instant, with a final cry of *Chaak!*, the pyramid and its macaw-stamped temple at the top turned a deep crimson.

Adelita lay bound and gagged on the stone platform, her skin daubed with a blue paste, the Mayan color of sacrifice. The child's eyes were wide and glassy: her abductor must have made her walk up the pyramid, only binding her legs when they reached the top. Beside her lay a clay figurine with what looked like a lock of silver-blonde hair fastened to it, and around her in a rough circle were items from the Witch's House tomb: pouches of jewels, scepters, and ceremonial rods, an assortment of silver and gold objects studded with gems.

Standing over the girl was Marissa Stroud, wearing a dark cape of jaguar skin and holding a long knife of flaked obsidian that sparkled like shards of glass in the red glow. On her head she wore a mask that left only her mouth uncovered, the mask itself bearing the features of the jaguar, the fangs of the upper jaw bared as if the woman's face was emerging from the animal's throat. Around her neck was a roughly fashioned cord onto which jewels from the hoard had been randomly threaded, and above the mask sat a twisted crown inlaid with stones that flashed darkly.

Rubies.

Stroud stood facing forward to the rest of the site, with the great alcoved frieze wall behind her, but she did not react to Deborah's appearance. She was chanting to herself, whispering, *"Teche a caah a uilah u yich a yumil can,"* then moving from Spanish to English and back to ancient Mayan so that Deborah caught only "symmetry" and "daughter," standing with her head tipped back and arms spread like some strange crucifix. As if to complete that image, Deborah saw that Stroud was bleeding heavily from her hands and mouth.

A blood sacrifice.

She thought the big woman's eyes might be closed.

So Deborah ran at her, leaping over the prone child and snatching at the woman's arms just as the knife blade began its downward sweep. Stroud fell backward, momentarily stunned by the attack, but she held onto the knife, and as she swung it wildly Deborah shrank from it. The conquistadors had learned long ago what obsidian could do to human flesh.

Chaak! roared the unseen crowd again, and the light went out.

Chapter Eighty-Three

■ ■ ■ ■ ■

The darkness lasted only a few seconds, but it was, briefly, total. Deborah sensed Stroud moving but could see nothing. She was also terrified of stepping backward off the platform. Even if she only fell down the stairs she doubted she'd survive, and in parts the drop was vertical. So she held her ground, dropping to a half crouch and spreading her arms, fingers splayed, to catch the other woman. She didn't realize how close Stroud was till she heard the faintest rush of air and felt the scalpel-clean slice of the obsidian against her left palm and forearm.

For a moment there was no pain at all, only shock, and she took a step backward with no clue if there would be stone or a hundred-foot fall through empty air behind her. Then her skin and the muscle beneath it began to sing with the terrible ecstasy of the gash and she clamped her other hand to the wound to gauge how deep it was. Her arm from elbow to fingers was slick with blood. She bit back the panic and moved her other hand along its length.

No spurting. Please God, no spurting.

There wasn't. She clutched the wounded arm to her chest, feeling a shrill of pain, then stood up and kicked wildly into the night to ward Stroud off. Deborah's first kick found nothing and threatened to upend her with the effort, but the second caught the other woman in the midriff, and as Deborah weaved away from where she thought the lip of the platform was, she sensed Stroud doubling up.

Then with another choric bellow of *Chaak!*, the light came back, blue again, and there was Marissa Stroud, holding her stomach with one hand as the other held the shimmering stone blade in front of her. She had torn the mask from her face, and her eyes were dark with a deep, lethal-looking rage. The crown had fallen but she still wore the necklace of beads and precious stones and it swung with her movement as she whirled and straightened for another attack. Adelita, gagged and bound, lay before her, watching, her eyes wild.

Deborah kicked at Stroud again, precisely this time, connecting with the woman's wrist so that her arm jerked and the massive knife flew up and out of her grasp, flashing in the blue light. Stroud cried out, more with anguish than pain, and for a moment time seemed to slow as she scrabbled at the night to catch it. It scythed through the air and then fell. Stroud tore her hand back from where it had cut her, and the ceremonial knife shattered against the platform, exploding into a million sparkling shards like rain.

"No!" she screamed, then pointed an accusatory finger at Deborah. She was wearing the ring from Edward's grave. "You," she spat. "I knew it would be you."

"We don't have to do this, Marissa," said Deborah, forcing herself to focus.

"We?" the other shot back. "*We* don't have to do anything. I have to do this."

And as she said it, she stooped and snatched up something small and silvery: a syringe with a long needle. She came up with the hypodermic clutched like a knife, her eyes locked on Deborah's.

"I don't need the knife to kill the girl," she whispered. "The ancient Maya knew all manner of ways to sacrifice children."

"But why?" she managed. "Why the girl?"

"Balance." She said it dismissively, taking a step toward Adelita. "Her grandfather was the beginning. With the girl, I end it."

"You can't believe that," said Deborah, trying to shove down the horror that it was Stroud who had killed Eustachio, and had tried to kill Hargreaves. She had to stay in the moment. She had to save the girl. She paused, feeling the heat in her wounded hand, as she circled up toward the masked woman. "How can killing Adelita help Angela?"

That stopped her. For a moment Stroud's mouth opened and no sound came out, but her eyes were full of alarm, while behind and below the ancient Mayan city shifted into golden light and the music and voices began again.

"I know about Angela Powel," said Deborah, looking for the woman's resolve to crumble. "I know about the accident. I know she is your daughter."

The music continued to crash, but there was a strange sense of stillness on the pyramid. Stroud seemed stricken, whether by the memory of her daughter lying motionless in a Chicago hospital or by the surprise that Deborah knew about it, Deborah wasn't sure. For a long moment she seemed to hang there, immobile, caught in some terrible indecision, and Deborah wondered if she was crying.

Deborah spoke, her voice lower, gentler.

"You know it won't help, Marissa. How could it?"

The woman seemed to wilt a little, and the syringe she held above her head seemed to lower fractionally.

"How could it help?" Stroud repeated, her voice small, as if she was talking to herself. "Because it *has* to."

And she straightened, her grip on the hypodermic shifted, and she was coming again, resolute and powerful, all emotion wiped from her face save a cold and murderous determination.

And then, quite suddenly, she wasn't. There was a noise like a distant cough, then she faltered and stopped, all purpose slipping from her. The needle lowered, but it did so absently, and then one leg seemed to buckle and she sank to her knees at the very head of the great staircase. Only then did Deborah notice that there was a fresh pattering of blood dripping from her robe onto the stone.

"All you people do is talk," said Dimitri, stepping out into the light from one of the alcoves at the east end of the frieze wall with a silenced pistol. "It's very American. Very annoying."

Deborah shrank back but he wasn't coming any closer. Slinking out of the alcove behind him was Alice, looking childlike and defeated, red, swollen eyes downcast as if too ashamed to look at her.

"The stones aren't what you think they are," said Deborah.

"I see," he said. "And what do I think they are?"

"You think they might be part of a military laser," she said.

For the second time in the last few minutes she saw the astonishment her words had produced, saw it land in his face, but she suspected it would do no more good than brandishing Angela's name had done against Stroud. In fact, Dimitri's eyes quickly hardened and Deborah thought she might have made a mistake.

"I'll decide about that," he said.

He was a powerful man, with a military-style crew cut and precise moustache and goatee. His eyes looked so cold and dead he could have been one of the skulls carved on the walls of Chitchen Itza. In his gaze she saw no possibility of mercy, no spark of empathy or hesitation.

"Take the jewels from her," he said.

Marissa Stroud was still kneeling at Deborah's feet, bleeding, dying for sure, but still just upright, the syringe loosely cradled in her left hand. Deborah looked to the ruby-studded crown where it had fallen then to the roughly constructed necklace that Marissa must have prepared herself, a double looped cord that had been threaded through armlets, diadems, little crowns, and other pieces of the royal regalia. Cautiously, watching Dimitri and the half-casual way he followed her movements with the overlong pistol, she stooped to Marissa Stroud and lifted the makeshift necklace over her head.

"I'm sorry," she whispered to Marissa, sure now that the woman, who had crumpled onto the backs of her legs, her head lolling forward, was dead.

The necklace was heavy and irregular, and it was too dark to see if the stones that matched the Malkin Tower gem were there.

"Alice," he said. "Bring them to me."

Alice seemed to shrink back toward the alcove, and Deborah thought she heard a sob, but when Dimitri spat her name again, she came forward, skulking sideways like a whipped dog.

"Alice," said Deborah as she came close, "you don't have to..."

"Shut up," said Dimitri, the gun leveling at her face.

Deborah thought wildly about hurling the necklace of gems and artifacts off the pyramid into the jungle, but she knew that would only delay him and get her killed.

He's going to kill you no matter what.

She wanted to argue the point with herself, but she could see it in his eyes and there was no debate. She remembered Bowerdale. James. And suddenly she realized it must have been this man who pursued her into the *cenote*, shooting at her as if for sport.

Alice shuffled up to her, head down, and Deborah held out the necklace. Alice took it, then looked up suddenly and snarled.

"You dropped one, you clumsy bitch."

Alice dropped to a squat, picked something up off the stone, and stood up again.

"You always thought you were so smart," Alice said, staring at Deborah. "So much better than me. Ordering me about like you were the queen of the fucking world. Now look at you."

Deborah blinked, amazed, and then flinched as Alice reached back and slapped her hard across her face.

"A cat fight," said Dimitri, amused. "Nice."

Deborah tasted blood, but she didn't let go of her wounded arm, which was throbbing. In fact, she was almost as stung by what Alice had said as by the blow. She hung her head, suddenly exhausted and defeated, and it was only then that she realized that the hypodermic that had hung limply from Marissa Stroud's dead fingers, was gone.

She forced herself not to look up, not to stare at Alice, not right away. When she did raise her eyes, Alice had already reached Dimitri, was handing him the cord of threaded treasures and coronets with her left hand. Her right hand was lost in shadow, but as Dimitri took a step so that the great lamps that splashed the temple with rich blue light played over the gems in his hands, that hand flashed toward his back.

He flinched as if stung, his back arching, and then he was turning toward her and the gun was coming up.

"What did you do, you little whore?" he demanded, his free hand reaching for the syringe that was sticking out of his back, its plunger fully depressed. "What...?"

Alice took a step backward, but there was a look of triumph in her face that had burned off the skulking terror.

"What the hell...?" he began again, aiming the gun at her. Then something stopped him. He seemed to stagger, as if losing his balance, and then he turned slowly and his eyes were wide. For a moment he was quite still, but then he began to sputter in words Deborah didn't know—his own language, she guessed—and there was horror in them. He wheeled and fired the gun, two, three times, shooting blindly so that the stones of the frieze sparked and fragments of lead and stone flicked across the temple platform.

Deborah ducked instinctively, trying to cover Adelita, but he wasn't shooting at them. He wasn't even clearly shooting at Alice, though there was a fair chance he would hit her. He seemed to be shooting at things only he could see, and as his panicked guttural cries grew faster, more desperate, Deborah found herself amazed by what could strike a man like him so full of terror. It was like he was fighting something he knew he couldn't kill, emptying his pistol at people who just wouldn't die.

Then there was only the clicking of his empty gun. He seemed aware of this, dropped it, and reached inside his shirt, tearing it open as he started to pull another gun free. Alice seemed to anticipate it, as if she knew it was there, and she rushed him before he had it ready. It went off as she made contact, and after the silenced pistol this one seemed to boom like a canon that tore a hole in the night and shot a foot of flame out of the barrel. He brought his knee up hard, and Alice collapsed in a heap. Her attack had given him focus, and now he aimed the gun squarely at her head.

Deborah sprang, coming at him low and fast, covering the yards between them in two strides, blindsiding him as the gun went off in a flash and a wall of sound so intense, so close, that for a moment after it there was only whiteness and silence.

Dimitri cannoned sideways, struggled to regain his balance, and took one final step into a place where there was no stone, only air. For the briefest of moments he seemed to hover, trying to grasp what had happened, and then he was falling through the night and the darkness and the recorded chorus calling *Chaak!* to the stone floor a hundred feet below.

Then there was silence.

Deborah moved back to Adelita, not wanting to look, but Alice had moved to the lip of the platform and was gazing down to where he fell. As Deborah fought to release the child's bonds with her good hand, she heard Alice's voice, distant and dreamy, as if she was talking to herself, say, "I wonder what he saw."

"Saw?" said Deborah.

"The hallucinations," said Alice, not looking round. "They come from inside you, from the things that scare you. He used to have bad dreams." She said it almost tenderly. "I wonder what he saw."

She remembered Nick Reese running frantically through the Kabah site muttering, "Get me out of here. I don't belong here."

None of them did.

"I'm sorry about the slap," said Alice, still absently, gazing out over the site whose structures shifted from gold to green again as the music and voices returned. "I was just trying to…"

"I know," said Deborah.

But then Adelita was sitting up and sucking in air through her mouth, and her wet eyes were wide, and Deborah was folding her into her arms and holding her tight to her chest so that all thought went away.

"It's OK," she whispered. "It's over."

"Whoa," said Alice, suddenly.

Deborah looked up and followed the other woman's gaze, stricken with panic.

He's not dead. He's coming back…

But she was not looking down but across to the governor's palace where, silhouetted against the moonlit sky, was the shape of a large cat. It was standing quite still, and with a breathless rush of feeling that brought tears to her eyes, Deborah realized that it was looking directly at them. For a moment that felt like eons they looked at each other, the women, the girl, and the jaguar, and Deborah felt the distinction between herself and the cat collapsing so that for a moment she seemed to be looking through its eyes, seeing her here with Alice and Adelita, feeling only the animal's instinctive caution and isolation. And then it was over. The jaguar took two loping bounds down the other side of the palace, its coat shining blackly in the moonlight, and was gone.

PART 6

Chapter Eighty-Four

■ ■ ■ ■ ■

The police helicopter took the site team to Merida for hospital observation, but as soon as it was clear that the CIA agents would be flying on to Chicago, Deborah insisted that they first return Adelita home.

No one felt like arguing.

It was a little after dawn when they reached the village of Ek Balam. Word had reached the Maya that they were coming, that they were bringing the girl with them, and the whole pueblo turned out for their arrival. Adelita had been quiet but was regaining something of her old poise, and the reception by her friends and family completed the transformation. She sprinted gleefully into her mother's arms, and the family turned in on themselves, weeping and laughing, forgetting everyone and everything else. Deborah watched, but when she felt her eyes prickling, she turned to Nick Reese and said, "Time to go."

"You sure?"

"I'm sure."

Adelita spotted her and ran after her, hugging her, but it was like she was tied to her parents again, enclosed in a kind of bubble, and Deborah was outside it.

That's OK, she told herself. *Better this way.*

"You saved my life," said Adelita.

Deborah remembered saying the same thing to the girl after that fateful storm so long ago, and recalled the girl's response. She waved the remark away and shrugged.

"Thank you," said the girl's mother, in English.

Deborah just nodded, then raised a hand in farewell.

The chopper had them at the airport in under an hour. Deborah had said little on the flight to Merida but looked down at the jungle trying to spot pyramids and other remains as they flew. She sensed the men watching her, and when, just before they boarded the plane, they approached her, she brushed them off.

"I'm fine," she said.

"That's a nasty cut," said Kenneth Jones, eying the palm-to-elbow bandage.

"They've cleaned and dressed it," she said. "There's nothing else they can do and I need to get back to the States. There's work I have to take care of."

"Given what you've gone through, I'm not sure travel is wise."

"You know, Kenneth," said Deborah, taking a step closer to him, "last night you didn't know what day it was, so I don't think you're in any position to say what is and isn't going to be too taxing for me."

The black man looked away, his brows knit, and for a second she thought he was angry, that he thought she was rubbing his nose in what she had done while he had been out of it, but then he grinned.

"And would I be right in thinking that this work of yours would take you to Chicago rather than Atlanta?" he said.

"You need me," she said. "One last time."

"She's right," said Nick Reese. "She's the only one who holds all the pieces of the puzzle."

Jones looked at the floor for a moment, then began to walk. "Why don't you tell me about them once we're airborne," he said.

As well as Eustachio and James, Dimitri, Bowerdale, and Stroud were all dead. The doctors thought Chad Rylands would make a full recovery. The bullet had gone through his stomach, and he was in surgery now but was, they said, out of the woods. Porfiro Aguilar and Krista Rayburn, like the CIA men, seemed no worse for the drugs they had ingested, though the hospital staff weren't ruling out occasional relapses as was possible with hallucinogens like LSD. They just didn't know enough about the mixture Stroud had used, though their labs had plenty of sample to analyze from the cooler at the site. Nick had not drunk as much, and Deborah still less. Alice was under suicide watch at the hospital. She would never be the same, Deborah figured, but maybe that was true for all of them.

There were a lot of questions to be answered, and it wasn't yet clear who would ask them and whose government they would work for. Nor was it clear if there would be charges against the survivors. There had been protocol violations, minor law infractions, and lots of bad judgment, but the only one who might face arrest was Alice, and Deborah doubted it would come to that. For Steve Powel, director of Cornerstone, the man who had sent her to Mexico in the first place, and then sat in his Chicago office, surrounded by pictures of his skater daughter, things would not go so easily. He had, it seemed, been in contact with Stroud throughout, had been the one to get her name in front of Deborah as soon as it was clear they needed new people on their team. Powel and Stroud might have been separated, but Deborah suspected they had always been bound by their daughter, and the accident had brought them back together, however quietly.

Deborah talked it all through on the plane, and even the professional agents, who she figured had heard it all, gaped and squinted in disbelief.

"And you think," said Jones, "that Powel promoted the entire excavation to recover these jewels with a view to using them in some kind of black magic ritual designed to revive his daughter?"

"I don't think he knew Edward Clifford had gone to Ek Balam, no," said Deborah, "and I don't think they saw it as *black magic*, but I do think Powel suspected what the Malkin Tower stone was after he bought it. He had to have known there was a link between the Pendle farm and the crown jewels through the Cliffords, so I'm pretty sure he knew Edward had gone to the Yucatan. Cornerstone had been involved in digs all over the Mayan world, and though I doubt he was actively searching for the missing crown jewels, they were clearly on his radar. Though they had been separated for sixteen years, he had been married to Marissa Stroud, who was one of the world's authorities on royal regalia. She had been poking around in those records for years. I don't know where it came from, but they both became fascinated by the occult, and when their daughter was hurt and left in a coma, they turned to legend and superstition. Desperation, I suppose. Nothing else had worked."

"Crazy," said Jones.

Deborah nodded, but sadly. "I guess when people lose a child, or think they will..."

The sentence was left hanging in the air, fading into the steady background noise of the aircraft.

Is that how Ma feels, she wondered suddenly, *that she has lost me, that I've slipped away from her over the years and she doesn't know how to get me back? That without Dad, our bond is dissolving completely?* The idea surprised and unsettled her even as she tried to dismiss it. *Ma? Is it possible?* Or was she just projecting, wanting to believe that her mother still needed to know they were connected, bound by invisible filaments of personal history, or fused at the level of the blood and bone of their so dissimilar bodies.

She thought of Lady Anne Clifford and the faceless, demonized pariah, Jennet Device.

Janet Davis, she corrected herself, the alternate name bringing the woman almost into the present so that Deborah felt that she could almost see her.

"So we know the gems aren't magic," said Nick Reese, breaking the silence. "No great surprise there. But what are they?"

"If you're asking whether they are the solution to decades of research into solid state military lasers," said Jones, "I'm betting they're not, but we won't know till they have been carefully analyzed. Bowerdale knew a little about the crystals used in laser technology, and he recognized some signatures in the initial chemical and physical analysis of the stones that piqued some people's interest, but I don't think they'll turn out to have the value he or Dimitri thought they did."

The irony sickened Deborah. *All those lives lost.*

"Like I said, we'll see when the analysis is complete," said Jones, seeming to read her look.

"So long as they aren't damaged in the process," said Reese, "and so long as Her Majesty's government gets full access to all results."

"I don't think you get to set the terms of what happens next," said Jones.

"I think I do," Reese countered.

"And why would that be?"

"Because the gems concerned are property of the English Crown," said Reese. "Literally, in this case."

Jones gave Deborah a look. "You buy that?"

"The evidence is circumstantial right now," she said, thoughtfully, "but it's pretty compelling."

"So you think we've found the lost crown jewels of England?" he said, daring her to say *yes*.

"Yes," she said. "I think so. They may be incomplete, they may be damaged, and they may not be as impressive as the ones on display in the Tower, not as intrinsically valuable, but yes: the crown jewels of medieval and renaissance England going back to Alfred the Great and Edward the Confessor, which makes them about as old as the pyramids of Uxmal and Ek Balam."

"Which also makes them a British Natural Treasure," said Nick Reese, "so no, you can't chop 'em up to see if they make your lasers better."

"I said it before and I'll say it again," said Jones. "If there's a choice between foreign cultural history and domestic national security, which way do you think the US government will go?"

It was a rhetorical question, and Deborah, depressed by it, looked out of the aircraft window to where the runways of O'Hare International Airport were just coming into view.

Chapter Eighty-Five

■ ■ ■ ■ ■

Steve Powel had been taken into custody before dawn and long before Deborah's plane touched down in Chicago. He had gone quietly, she was told, and though he had not yet been charged he was making no demands for lawyers or release. His secretary, Mrs. Gloria Pickins, had also been taken in for questioning, but it might be weeks before a clear sense of what had happened emerged and the case could proceed to trial. Various occult objects had been found in Powel's home and office, including some human bones, but it was believed they had been acquired from grave robbers and their agents, and there would be no serious charges against him that did not involve what had happened in Mexico and the UK. There was no sign of the Malkin Tower stone in any of his collections.

As they drove into the city, Deborah began to adjust her left arm and shift in her seat.

"You OK?" asked Nick.

"I think it may have reopened," she said. "Maybe I should get it looked at again."

"We have people on staff in the office," said Jones.

"That's OK," she said. "Just drop me off and I'll swing by the hospital. Excuse me," she called to the driver. How close are we to East Fifty-Fifth Street?"

"Right now?" he said. "Not very. But I can get you there."

"That would be great," she said. "Corner of Ellis, please."

"I didn't know you knew the city so well," said Nick, watching her carefully.

"I had to spend time here with Cornerstone," she said, looking out the window. "What happens to Cornerstone now?" said Nick.

"I have no idea," she answered.

They dropped her at the junction she requested, and she said she'd call within the hour.

"Don't leave town," said Jones, half-seriously. "There's still a lot we don't know."

She agreed and walked briskly away down to the hospital entrance, but once the car had pulled away, she paused, then moved away from the emergency room. She found an information desk, asked her questions, and five minutes later was standing outside a private room telling a nurse she was a family friend.

Angela Powel lay still, wired to monitors, IV drips running bags of fluid into her system. Her head was unbandaged and her pale gold hair spilled out onto the pillow. For a long moment, Deborah just looked at her, trying to imagine how it would be different if this had been her own daughter, but she couldn't do it. She thought of Adelita and her parents and, feeling something real for the girl who had been her friend in Ek Balam, wondered what her loss would have been like.

Terrible, she thought. *An absurd injustice that proved the arbitrariness of the universe.*

Which was, she suspected, how Steve Powel and his estranged wife had felt about the ridiculous accident that had left their beautiful and accomplished daughter lying here. No wonder Marissa Stroud had wanted to believe in symmetry, in an order to the cosmos that she could somehow manipulate with the old surrogacy of Mayan ritual and sympathetic magic: the torturing of one human as a sacrifice to the gods, the offering of one child to save another. It was, she thought, a kind of love: selfish, desperate, and irrational, no doubt, but love just the same. w

It's what any good father would do, Powel had said, when she asked him about the work and expense involved in his daughter's skating. The phrase seemed loaded now, and Deborah wondered again, were all parents like this, ready to do anything, no matter how destructive, to protect their own?

You'll never know, the voice in her head said.

The thought came fully formed, born entire in the moment, and she recoiled from its certainty with defiance that beat back the thrill of despair. She stared at the girl lying in this endless sleep, and wondered why the idea bothered her so much. She wasn't even sure she wanted children, was certain she didn't want any now. So why should the thought that she never would feel so upsetting?

"You about done?" said the nurse, reentering the room.

"I think so," said Deborah.

"You can stay longer if you like."

"I don't think so. I have…things to do."

"Well, it's nice to have someone other than her father here," said the nurse, checking the chart at the foot of the bed and monitoring the levels in the IV drips. "I don't think she really gets to hear any voices other than mine, ain't that right, girl?"

Deborah, realizing the nurse was talking to the patient, shifted uncomfortably.

"You think she can hear you?" she said.

"Maybe," said the nurse. "Guess we won't know till she wakes up. Stay awhile and chat if you like. Read her a magazine or something. Or not."

She grinned and stepped out.

We won't know till she wakes up.

If she wakes up.

Deborah sat down and put her head in her hands. She took a deep breath and then sat up.

"OK," she said aloud. "You don't know me, Angela, but I thought I'd stop by. I'm Deborah." She hesitated, embarrassed, then pressed on. "I'm going to tell you a story about a dwarf magician and his witch mother..."

She talked for about twenty minutes, meandering, doubling back, trying to make sense of the tangled narrative, and each time she did so she apologized for her ineptitude as a storyteller. When she was done, she sat in silence for five more minutes, then she stood up and was about to take a step toward the door when she paused and, on impulse, moved back to the bed. With her right hand she brushed back the girl's hair, then very gently touched the girl's sparkling necklace with its single garnet-colored stone pendant.

The Malkin Tower gem. Like the others, it was the color of blood diluted with tears. Her lucky charm.

Deborah touched it with one finger, then reset the pillow and left the room, letting the door thud shut behind her as she walked through the hospital corridor.

Nick Reese was waiting for her outside.

"Is it there?" he said.

She nodded.

"Still?" he asked.

She nodded again, and they walked in silence. The air outside was hot and humid, touched with the scent of the traffic, but she didn't mind it.

"You have any kids, Nick?" she asked suddenly.

"No, why?" he asked.

"I'm just...No reason," she said. "Listen, can you give me a minute. I have to call my mother. You know. Family stuff."

"Sure. I'll wait over there. Listen," he added, earnest. "Back in Kabah by the Witch's House, when I..."

"Tried to kiss me?"

"Right," he said, looking abashed. "That was the drug. You know that, right?"

"I thought the drug made people paranoid," she said, arch. "Made them see terrible, terrifying things."

"Maybe it does different things to different people," he ventured.

"That's what we're going with?" she asked, smirking now.

"For the moment," he said, smiling back.

"I've got to make this call."

"Right," he said, taking a step away. "Then maybe we can get that drink?"

She considered him seriously for a moment, then nodded.

"That would be nice," she said.

He smiled, hesitated, then took a couple of steps backward, turning into his stride still smiling. She watched him go, then took out her phone, took a breath, and still not sure what she was going to say, began to dial. As the phone rang at the other end, Deborah remembered that moment in Uxmal in the darkness of the ruins when the jaguar had gazed across at her and, for a moment, time and distance had fallen away and it was like she was seeing herself. In some ways, they were all alone, all strange and out of place, through the centuries: Edward Clifford. Janet Device. Stroud, certainly. Eustachio with his secret. Maybe even Dimitri.

And you, of course, always prowling the ruins of other people's lives, peering in and slipping away when they got too close, never quite belonging, always alien as the jaguar or the gemstones you found in the Ek Balam tomb.

She hesitated, unsure what to think of that, but then she heard her mother's voice saying "Hello?" and the great cat slipped back into the ruins as she became herself again.

THE END

Thanks, Acknowledgments, and Some Details of the Hazy Line Between Fact and Fiction

As readers who are familiar with my work know, I rely on historical fact in my novels; though the story itself is strictly fictional, it seems reasonable to try to sketch where reality ends and my own flight of fancy begins. My core characters are, of course, invented, though some figures from the novel's back story are real enough. The Lancashire witches were as I have described them, as was Lady Anne Clifford, though she had no adopted son Edward, who is my own creation. I was born and raised only a few miles from Pendle Hill and though I was far enough from it to be out of its literal shadow, I grew up surrounded by tales of the witches. Much of what I've set down here is derived from Thomas Potts's (in)famous contemporary account, augmented by more recent scholarly takes on his version of events, but I owe a huge debt of gratitude to local historian John Clayton, who has endured all my questions and whose answers have helped shape the story. The Eye of God on the tower of Newchurch is real, as are the other details of the landscape, including the Malkin Tower cottages, from which visitors can visit Pendle and environs. I am grateful to the staff at Lancaster Castle for fielding questions.

George Withers and Henry Mildmay were real, as was the breaking up and selling off of the medieval and renaissance crown jewels. With the exception of the coronation spoon that Deborah notes, the present-day collection at the Tower, spectacular and storied though it is, dates from the 1660s and later. Though some pieces were recovered by the state during the Restoration, the ancient crown jewels of England remain lost.

Though the story evolved away from it, my first impulse was to make Thomas Gage a part of the novel. Gage was an Englishman who journeyed to Mexico as a Franciscan friar with Spanish missionaries in the 1620s and 1630s. In England in 1648 he published a problematic but informative book on his travels, immediately before my fictional Edward Clifford set out on a similar course. My primary consultant on Mayan archaeology has been the extraordinarily helpful and patient George Bey, one of Ek Balam's foremost archaeologists. Without him, and his willingness to share his insight into Mayan culture and fieldwork, this book could not have been written. I'm also grateful to Sarah Werner and Pascale Aebischer; Kathy Reichs for details on bone analysis; Jim Born for firearm tips; Sarah Brew on skating; and to my colleagues at UNC Charlotte, particularly Jen Munroe on Lady Anne, to Carlos M. Coria-Sánchez and Michael Doyle for clarifying points of Mexican law and language, and to Deborah A. Strumsky, Scott Hippensteel, John Bender, and Lee Casperson for insight on crystals and their use in laser technology.

In all things, I take full responsibility for any errors made here. I will post images associated with all the places in the book on my website, www.ajhartley.net, where I can also be reached if you have comments.

Lastly, special thanks to my agent, Stacey Glick, and to my wife, always my first reader, and to those others who have given me feedback on the manuscript, particularly Edward Hurst, Ruth Morse, Bob Croghan, and Mark Pizzato, and to my editor Kate Chynoweth, whose insight and patience helped turn my sprawling drafts into an actual book.

As ever, thanks for reading, and best wishes.

A.J. Hartley

About the Author
■ ■ ■ ■ ■

Photograph © Bill DeLoach, 2005

A.J. Hartley is a native of Lancashire, England, and was born near the town where the witch trials featured in *Tears of the Jaguar* occurred four hundred years ago. He lived in Japan for several years and traveled extensively throughout southern and eastern Asia before moving to the United States for graduate school. After earning his PhD from Boston University, he taught college-level Shakespeare in Georgia and North Carolina. Today he works as a dramaturge, director, theater historian, and theorist in Renaissance drama at UNC-Charlotte, where he holds the Robinson Chair of Shakespeare Studies. He has written fiction for twenty years and is the author of *Macbeth, a Novel* with David Hewson, *Darwen Arkwright and the Peregrine Pact, Act of Will, Will Power, The Mask of Atreus, On the Fifth Day,* and *What Time Devours.*